THE
PHILOSOPHER'S
STONE

A Novel by Colin Wilson

Wingbow Press

PREFATORY NOTE

Bernard Shaw concluded his preface to *Back to Methuselah* with the hope that 'a hundred apter and more elegant parables by younger hands will soon leave mine ... far behind'. Perhaps the thought of trying to leave Shaw far behind has scared off would-be competitors. Or perhaps – what is altogether more probable – the younger hands are simply not interested in writing parables of longevity, or any other kind of parable. Most of my contemporaries seem to feel pretty strongly that the activities of thinking and novel-writing are incompatible, and that to be interested in ideas reveals a deficiency in the creative faculties. And since the critics also like to foster this idea – perhaps out of a kind of defensive trade-unionism – it seems to have achieved the status of a law of contemporary literature.

Now no one has a profounder respect for the critics than I, or strives more constantly to sound like a paid-up member of the literary establishment. But I enjoy ideas. And this seems to give me a rather odd perspective on modern literature. I suspect that H. G. Wells is probably the greatest novelist of the twentieth century, and that his most intersting novels – if not necessarily the best – are the later ones. I am completely unable to be objective about Shaw; he seems to me simply to be the greatest European writer since Dante. And I completely lack sympathy for the emotional and personal problems that seem to be the necessary subject of a contemporary play or novel. Mr Osborne once said his aim was to make people feel. I think they feel too much. I'd like to make them stop feeling and start thinking.

Fortunately for me, I am neither original nor creative,* so I can afford to ignore the contemporary rules. And there is another factor in my favour. Since Shaw wrote *Back to Methu-*

---

* 'But [Colin Wilson's] talent is not creative. His talent is in books like *The Outsider*; and not because *The Outsider* contains any original thought'. John Braine, *The Modern Novelist*, address to the Royal Society of Arts, 7 February 1968.

selah, science fiction has become an established *genre*, and it has even become quite respectable. And in recent years, I have stumbled accidentally into the writing of a few modest works of science fiction.

I must explain how this came about. In 1961, I wrote a book called *The Strength to Dream*, a study of the creative imagination, particularly in writers of fantasy and horror stories. A large part of the book was inevitably devoted to the work of H. P. Lovecraft, the recluse of Providence, Rhode Island, who died of malnutrition and a cancer of the intestine in 1937. I pointed out that although Lovecraft possesses a gloomy imaginative power that compares with Poe, he is basically an atrocious writer – most of his work was written for *Weird Tales*, a pulp magazine – and his work is finally interesting as case history rather than as literature.

In due course, a copy of my book fell into the hands of Lovecraft's old friend – and publisher – August Derleth. And Derleth wrote to me, protesting that my judgement on Lovecraft was too harsh, and asking me why, if I was all that good, I didn't try writing a 'Lovecraft' novel myself. And the answer to this question is that I never write purely for the fun of it. I write as a mathematician uses a sheet of paper for doing calculations: because I think better that way. And Lovecraft's novels are not about ideas, but about an emotion – an emotion of violent and total rejection of our civilization, which I, being rather cheerful by temperament, do not happen to share.

But a couple of years later, an analogy thrown out in my *Introduction to the New Existentialism* became the seed of a science fiction parable about 'original sin' – man's strange inability to get the best out of his consciousness. I cast it in the Lovecraft tradition, and it became *The Mind Parasites*, which was published in due course by August Derleth. Its reception by English critics was unexpectedly good; I suspect this is because I didn't sound as if I was serious.

And so when, two years ago, I became interested in questions of brain physiology – as a by-product of a novel about sensory deprivation – it seemed natural to develop some of these ideas in another 'Lovecraft' novel. Besides, ever since reading Wells's *Time Machine* at the age of eleven, it has always been a daydream of mine to write the definitive novel about time travel. Time travel is a perpetually alluring idea, but it always sounds so preposterous. Even when my friend Van Vogt – the contemporary SF writer I enjoy most – uses it, he makes it sound a joke. The question of how to make it sound plausible is quite a challenge.

It sounds a vertiginous mixture – Shaw, Lovecraft and Wells – but it's the kind of thing I enjoy doing. In fact, I got quite carried away until this novel became twice as long as originally intended. Even so, I had to write part of it as a separate short novel, which August Derleth has published.

A final word. It is part of the game in a Lovecraft novel to stick as far as possible to actual sources, and never to invent a fact when you can dig one out of some obscure work of scholarship. I would modestly claim to have surpassed Lovecraft in this particular department. Nearly all the 'sources' quoted are genuine, the major exception being the Vatican Codex; even so, there is a fair amount of archaeological authority for the hypothetical contents of this codex. The Voynich manuscript does, of course, exist, and is still untranslated.

Seattle-Cornwall November 1967–July 1968

PART ONE

THE QUEST OF THE ABSOLUTE

I was reading a book on music by Ralph Vaughan Williams the other day, while listening to a gramophone record of his remarkable Fifth Symphony, when I came across the following remark: 'I have struggled all my life to conquer amateurish technique, and now that perhaps I have mastered it, it seems too late to make any use of it.' I found myself moved almost to tears by the poignancy of those words of a great musician. Admittedly, he was eighty-six when he died, but for practical purposes – the value of the music he wrote in his last years – it might well have been twenty years earlier. And I found myself thinking: Supposing by some fluke, Vaughan Williams had lived another twenty-five years . . . or supposing he had been born a quarter of a century later. Could I have passed on to him what I now know, so that he might still be alive and writing great music? The case of Shaw is even more to the point, for he came close to the great discovery in *Back to Methusaleh*, and in his early nineties, he remarked jokingly that he was a proof of his own theory that men could live to be three hundred. Yet this is the man who said two years later, as he lay in a hospital bed with a broken leg: 'I want to die, and I can't, I can't.' He came so close, but he was alone; and a man standing alone lacks that final ounce of conviction. Would Columbus have had the courage to reach San Salvador Island if he had been alone on the *Santa Maria*?

It was this train of thought that decided me to tell the story of my discovery exactly as it happened. In doing so, I break my own vow of secrecy; but I shall see that the account is withheld from those whom it might harm – that is to say, from most of the human race. It should exist, even if it never leaves a bank vault. The carbon copy of memory grows thinner year by year.

I was born in the Nottinghamshire village of Hucknall Torkard in 1942. My father was a maintenance engineer in the colliery' of Birkin Brothers. Those who have read D. H. Lawrence will recognize the name; in fact, Lawrence was born fairly close by, at Eastwood. Byron is buried in the family vault at Hucknall, and in my day, Newstead Abbey – his home – was still approached through a typical coal mining village of grimy cottages. The setting sounds romantic; but dirt and boredom are not romantic; and most of the memories of the first ten years of my life are of dirt and boredom. I think of falling rain, and the smell of fish and chips on autumn nights, and queues outside the local cinema on Saturday evenings. I was back there a few weeks ago, and found the place unrecognizable. It is now a suburb of Nottingham, with an airport, an underground railway for commuters, and helicopter stations on the top of most blocks of flats. Yet I cannot say I regret the change; I only have to read a few pages of *The Rainbow* to remember how much I hated the place.

The great conflict of my childhood was between my love of science and my love of music. I was always a good mathematician. My father gave me my first slide rule for Christmas when I was six. And, like most mathematicians, I was almost dangerously susceptible to music. I can remember pausing outside the church one evening, clutching an armful of library books, and listening to the sound of the choir. They were obviously rehearsing – probably some abomination by Wesley or Stainer – for they repeated the same passage of half a dozen notes over and over again. The effect was almost incantatory, and in the cold night air the voices sounded distant and mysterious, as if mourning for man's loneliness. Suddenly I found myself crying, and before I could stop it, the feeling rushed over me like a burst dam. I hurried into the churchyard and flung myself on the grass, where I could stifle my sobs, and allowed the feeling to convulse me until I felt as though I were being shaken by the shoulders. It was a disturbing experience. When I walked home – feeling relaxed and light-headed – I found it impossible to understand what had happened to me.

Because I loved mathematics, and could do complicated sums in my head, my father decided that I should be an engineer. The idea struck me as reasonable enough, although I found something oddly boring about machinery. I felt the same when my father took me to visit the colliery, and showed me the mechanisms that it was his duty to maintain. It struck me as futile to spend one's life keeping a mass of dead metal up to a certain level of efficiency. What did it matter? But I could think of no good reason to object to my father's plans. I spent most of my spare time playing the airs of Dowland and Campion on a recorder, and learning to pick out tunes from *The Messiah* on the electric organ that belonged to a neighbour. Certainly, there was nothing in music that seemed to offer a real alterative to engineering; I would never be more than a mediocre executant.

I can remember clearly the time when the problem of death first struck me. I had borrowed a book on early music from the library. That cold, modal music of the Middle Ages continued to exert its strange attraction over me. In the chapter on ancient Greek music, I discovered the Skolion of Seikilos, with its words :

> May life's sun upon thee smile
> Far from pain and sorrow.
> Life is far too short, alas.
> Death the kraken waits to drown you
> In the sea of earth.

I knew about the kraken, the legendary giant octopus; so, apparently, did Homer. (I presume Scylla is supposed to be an octopus.) The lines made me feel cold. All the same, I went up to our attic and tried out the skolion on our old piano, picking out the Phrygian scale, then playing it through until I understood the shape of the melody. Again, the coldness settled on me, and I murmured the words aloud as I played, feeling the same immense sadness, the sensation of infinite distances, that I had experienced in the churchyard. Suddenly, my mind said : What are you doing, you fool? This is *real*, not a literary metaphor. There is not a person alive in the world today who will still be alive in a hundred years from now ... And I grasped the reality, the truth of my own death. The horror almost choked me. I felt too weak to keep my hands on the keyboard, too weak to sit on the piano stool without support. Then, for the first time, I understood why the idea of engineering struck me as pointless. It was wasting *time*. Time. It was disconnected from reality. Like opening and closing your mouth without speaking. Irrelevant. The watch on my wrist ticked like a time bomb, presenting life's ultimatum. And what was I doing? I was learning to maintain the machinery at Birkin's colliery. I knew that I could never be an engineer. But what could I be instead? What would *not* be irrelevant?

The strange thing is that the experience was not all horror. Somewhere deep inside me there was a spark of happiness. To see the emptiness of things brings its own exultancy. Perhaps because to grasp futility is to recognize that its opposite is implied. I had no idea of the meaning of this 'opposite'. I only knew that the skolion of Seikilos was somehow preferable to mathematics, because it recognized a problem that could not be formulated mathematically. The effect was to weaken my interest in science and to deepen my love of music and poetry. But the conflict remained hidden, and within a day or so, I had forgotten it.

I owe the profoundest debt of my life to Sir Alastair Lyell – of whom I have written at length elsewhere.* I met him in the December of 1955, when I was thirteen; from that time, until his death twelve years later, he was closer to me than any other human being, including my father and mother.

In the autumn of 1955, I became a temporary member of the St Thomas's church choir. It was a Church of England choir, and my family, insofar as they possessed any religion at all, were Methodists; but I had been asked to sing by the choirmaster, McEwan Franklin, who was well known in Nottingham musical circles. At this time I possessed a clear soprano voice (that remained unbroken until I was sixteen), and I belonged to a group of half a dozen boys who often sang in the school chapel. Franklin heard us at an end of term concert in July of that year, and we were all asked whether we would be willing to join the St Thomas's choir for its winter concert season. Franklin had scheduled an ambitious season that included *Judas Maccabaeus*, motets of Lassus, madrigals by Gesualdo, and some Britten pieces. The motets and madrigals were to be performed in a concert that would be broadcast by the BBC Third Programme. Four of the boys were not interested but two of us joined. I sang a leading part in Lassus's *Missa vinum bonum*, and in Britten's *A Boy Is Born*. After the concert, in the chang-

* Introduction to *Sir Alastair Lyell, A Life in Science*, by Leslie M. Baynton, Lord & Fisher, London 1972. This long essay is also reprinted in my *Recreations of a Biologist*, Marsden Cole, 1975.

ing room, I was introduced to a tall, clean shaven man with a face that reminded me of a picture of Thomas Carlyle that hung in our school classroom. I was too excited to pay much attention to him or even to catch his name; but at Franklin's house afterwards – where we had coffee and cakes – he came and sat beside me on the settee, and began to question me about my interest in music. We soon discovered important common ground; he thought Handel the greatest composer in the world, and so did I. Then the talk shifted, I forget how, to the mathematics of infinite sets, and I was delighted to discover that he understood the problems that Bertrand Russell discusses in the *Principles of Mathematics*. (I could never understand how there could be any problem about the *foundations* of mathematics.)

It was one of those occasions that happen once in a lifetime: two minds with immediate and total sympathy. He was forty-five, I was thirteen; but it was as if there was no age difference between us, as if we had been close friends for twenty years. This is perhaps not as strange as it sounds. In my small-town environment I had never met anyone who shared both my loves: science and music. Lyell already knew about me; Franklin had talked about me at dinner a week before. Franklin was always intrigued by the various books that I took to rehearsals – on mathematics, physics, chemistry, biology. Lyell was intrigued by Franklin's description, so he came to the concert that night with the intention of talking to me.

Lyell left early, after inviting me to call and see him at Sneinton – a nearby village. When he had gone, I asked Franklin: 'What did you say his name was?' He told me it was Sir Alastair Lyell, a descendent of the Sir Charles Lyell whose *Principles of Geology* I had been reading only a week ago. I must admit that I felt startled and shaken. I had never, in my whole life, actually talked to anyone with a title; in fact, I don't think I'd ever *seen* anyone with a title. I knew Sneinton; I'd assumed Lyell lived in one of the houses in the main street. When I learned that he lived in a sort of 'manor' surrounded by a park, I was overawed. It was lucky that I had not caught the name when Franklin introduced him; I would have stammered and blushed, or simply been tongue-tied. As it was, I lay awake half the night, trying to grasp the fact that I had been talking to a 'Sir', with no more respect or embarrassment than if he had been the greengrocer.

Two days later, tense and shy, I cycled over to Sneinton. I found the place easily enough, a mile outside the village, and it increased my misgivings: the high stone wall, the man in the gate lodge who rang the house and then told me to go ahead up the drive. The house itself was less grand than I had expected, but still too grand for me. And then Lyell himself came to answer the door, and the shyness vanished. The curious sympathy, that remained unchanged to the end, was immediately there between us. I was introduced to his wife – his first wife, Lady Sarah, who even at this time looked pale and ill – and then we went immediately to his 'museum' on the top floor.

The Lyell museum – now transferred into Nottingham – is too well known to need a description. At the time I first saw it, it was less than half the size it later became; even so, it was enormous. Its chief exhibit, then as now, was the skeleton of the *Elasmotherium sibericum*, the extinct ancestor of the rhinoceros, whose horn grew in the middle of his forehead – undoubtedly the seed of the racial memory that became the legendary unicorn. There was the mammoth tusk, and the skull of the sabre toothed tiger, and the fragments of the plesiosaurus skeleton, which Lyell introduced to me as the Loch Ness monster. Sir Charles Lyell's rock collection was complete – and this was what fascinated me most on that first afternoon. Lyell was, of course, the man who caused the *first* great intellectual revolution of the Victorian era, before Darwin and Wallace and Tyndall and Huxley. Before Lyell, the old Biblical theory of creation had held the field, qualified by Cuvier's theory of violent catastrophes – periodic upheavals that destroyed all life and made it necessary for God to re-populate the world with living creatures. According to Cuvier, there were no less than four creations – which enabled him to explain the fossils of extinct creatures without contradicting the Bible and Archbishop Usher. It was Sir Charles Lyell (1797–1875) who took the incredible step of contradicting the Bible, and showing that living forms are continuous, and that the time needed for their development amounts to millions of years. The uproar was enormous – to be exceeded later only by the Darwinian controversy itself. I had read the story with excitement only a week or so before I now saw the Lyell collection – the very fossils that had led him to his conclusions. Looking around at this enormous room, with its skeletons and bones and rock specimens, I grasped for the first time the *reality* of history. I

14

can clearly remember this moment, as if it had happened ten minutes ago. There was a touch of the feeling I had experienced playing the skolion: recognition that human life is small and self-centred and totally divorced from reality, and that death is our final reckoning, the universe's dismissal of our trivialities. And again, there was that curious core of happiness, the mind's delight in truth at all costs, even if the truth is destructive. And I somehow grasped instinctively that there is no contradiction between these two feelings, that the exultation is not some paradoxical acceptance of our own destruction; that *reality is synonymous with power.*

That afternoon, I understoood why Lyell and myself spoke as equals. I understood that our human time is an illusion, and that the mind is capable of seeing through it. In that museum there was a 'point of intersection of the timeless with time', a moment outside time. And as I look back on it, I can see that I possessed a total intuitive certainty that afternoon – a certainty that my life had reached a new phase, a turning point.

In my dissatisfaction at the prospect of becoming an engineer, I had often daydreamed of the kind of life I would prefer. I had no definite ideas, no clear alternatives; I only knew that I wanted to be allowed to think and study as I liked. My favourite book was Peacock's *Gryll Grange* because I was fascinated by the character of Mr Falconer, who is rich enough to live in a tower, surrounded by servant girls, and to devote his life to browsing through a vast collection of books. (I was also charmed by the whole way of life in Gryll Grange – leisurely conversations about ideas over enormous meals or during country walks.) But even in my most epicurean daydreams I could not have anticipated a life as perfect as the one that I led for the next five years. Lyell ate, drank and lived ideas. As I came to know him better, I understood why I was as important to him as he was to me. He had never met anyone so totally committed to ideas as he was. Even his fellow members of the Royal Society struck him as too blasé, too worldly, too comfortable in the futilities of everyday existence. They had allowed the world to dilute the intensity, the original purity. His own teens had been lonely, for his father's chief interest had been in hunting and fishing, while a younger brother had a practical turn that later led to his becoming a millionaire property dealer. Now he imagined the satisfaction of meeting someone like his own younger self, someone through whom he could rediscover the excitement of science and music, who had not outgrown his hunger for ideas. So he was as happy to discover me as I to discover him; happier, perhaps, since he had formed a mental picture of what he wanted, while I only experienced a formless dissatisfaction. He had never had children – his first wife was sterile. All this meant that I came to a place that had been prepared for me.

Although there was no formal adoption, I became, for practical purposes, his adopted son. My parents had no objection; from a very early stage – long before the thought entered my head – they entertained the idea that he might make me his heir. This was, of course, pure wishful thinking and inexperience, not shrewdness or intuition; still, they proved to be right, in the main.

At first, I spent part of the weekends there. During Easter, 1956, I travelled to America with him to examine the Arizona meteor crater, near Winslow, and to collect specimens. (Five years later we were to visit the scene of the Podkamennaya Tunguska explosion in Siberia, which, we established to our own satisfaction, was an atomic explosion, probably of some space craft from another galaxy.) When we returned from America, I transferred most of my books and other belongings from Hucknall to Sneinton Hall, and thereafter spent more time there than at home. I continued at school to GCE level, after which he offered to pay for my university training. He made no attempt to influence me, but I knew his own views – that a university education is a waste of time, and that few of the first rate minds of the past hundred years have owed anything to the university. (He was a Cambridge man, but had left, at his own request, in his second year, to pursue his own studies at home.) So I refused his offer. Besides, I knew that he could teach me more than a dozen tutors. I never regretted this.

Perhaps it is not entirely relevant to my story, but I cannot resist trying to give a picture of my life at Sneinton in those early years. It was a warm, comfortable house, and the servants' quarters were so enormous that I often lost my way in them during the first months. I particularly liked the windows of the two front rooms, which stretched from floor to ceiling. There was a hill opposite, with trees along the skyline; its sunsets could be magnificent. Lady Sarah loved to sit in the writing room in the afternoons, and make toast at an open fireplace – I think she liked the smell – and drink as many as ten cups of tea. Lyell and I usually came down from the laboratory to join her. (I refer to him here as Lyell although, like his wife, I always called him Alec; to the rest of his family he was Alastair. An amusing touch – the gardener-chauffeur called him Jamie. He was one of the most naturally democratic persons I have ever known.) After dinner, we usually moved into the music room to play gramophone records, or sometimes, to make music for ourselves. (He played the clarinet and oboe, as well as the piano; I was also a passable clarinettist.) His collection of records – mostly 78s – was enormous, and occupied a whole wall, stretching from floor to ceiling. Sir Compton Mackenzie, who once spent a weekend in the house when I was there, said that Lyell probably owned the largest record library in the country after *The Gramophone*. I should mention here one of Lyell's amusing idiosyncrasies; he seemed to enjoy very long works for their own sake. I think he simply enjoyed the intellectual discipline of concentrating for hours at a time. If a work was long, it automatically recommended itself to him. So we have spent whole evenings listening to the complete *Contest Between Harmony and Invention* of Vivaldi, the complete *Well Tempered Clavier*, whole operas of Wagner, the last five quartets of Beethoven, symphonies of Bruckner and Mahler, the first fourteen Haydn symphonies . . . He even had a strange preference for a sprawling, meandering symphony by Furtwängler, simply because it ran on for two hours or so.

My own enthusiasm and interest was obviously important to him. If I became tired or indifferent, I could immediately sense his disappointment. When his wife once protested at the number of hours he kept me working or listening to music, he said: 'Nonsense. Man is naturally a creature of the mind. The idea that brain-work tires people is an old wives' tale. Man should no more get tired of using his brain – if he is using it properly – than a fish should get tired of water.'

Lyell was, of course, an eclectic. He loved to quote a sentence that Yeats attributes to Pater – when Pater was explaining the presence of volumes of political economy on his bookshelves: 'Everything that has occupied man for any length of time is worthy of our study.' He was passionately opposed to the idea of the specialist in any field – certainly in science or mathematics. When I first knew him, his chief reputation was as a micro-biologist. He was the first man to cultivate *rickettsiae* – intracellular parasites of microscopic size – apart from a living host. His essay on mastigophora – a unicellular animal – is a classic that has been reprinted in many anthologies of scientific literature, and his paper on yeast infections, although less deliberately 'literary', is also a classic of its kind. But he refused to be 'typed' as a scientist, and I once heard Sir Julian Huxley refer jokingly to Sneinton Hall as 'the laboratory of a mediaeval alchemist'. After 1952 he was fascinated – one might almost say obsessed – by the problem of the expansion of the universe and quasi-stellar radio sources, and his observatory was one of the best-equipped private observatories in the country, perhaps in Europe. (Its 80-inch reflecting telescope is now in my own observatory near Mentone.) In 1957, his interest moved decisively to the field of molecular biology and problems of genetics. He also experienced a revival of an early interest in number theory – this was a matter in which I exerted an influence – and in the question of how far electronic calculating machines could solve previously insoluble problems.

It may seem incredible to most readers that a man with such a variety of interests should also have time for music – as well as for literature, painting and philosophy. Such a view misses the point. Lyell felt that most men – even brilliant men – waste their intellectual resources. He liked to point out that Sir William Rowan Hamilton could speak a dozen languages – including Persian – at the age of nine, and that John Stuart Mill had read all the Dialogues of Plato – in Greek – when he was seven. 'Both these men were intellectual failures if we judge their mature achievement by their earlier standards,' he wrote in a letter to me. He believed that our limitations are due mainly to laziness, ignorance and timidity.

Only one aspect of my new life saddened me – the alienation from my family. From the first, my two brothers were openly envious. I was sad about this. I had never liked my elder brother, Arnold, much, but I was fond of Tom, who was a year my junior. Both of them began to treat me as a stranger whenever I returned home, and made sneering comments about the 'life of luxury' they must be missing. After a while, their attitude seemed to affect my father, who also became distant and definitely hostile. Only my mother was always pleased to see me. She understood that it was not for the 'life of luxury' that I preferred Sneinton to my own home. Even so, I took care not to say too much to her about my doings there. She would have thought so much mental activity abnormal and unhealthy – as, in fact, have several friends to whom I have described life at Sneinton. The truth is that the life was ideal for me. At thirteen, my mind was hungry; I could feel myself changing almost daily. Without Lyell, it would have been a period of frustration – of increasing desire to live a life of 'sensations and ideas', and hatred of the everyday world that prevented this. The conflict had already started before I met Lyell; I was already beginning to see my life at home and school as completely futile. What Lyell offered me was not abnormal intellectual activity, but a life of discovery and purpose. Thirteen is the age of what Shaw calls 'the birth of the moral passion' – that is, the period when ideas are not abstractions but realities, when they are food and drink. The changes of puberty have altered one's old conception of oneself. Identity vanishes; one's inner being becomes formless, chaos waiting for the act of creation. There is a brooding feeling of anticipation; the clouds lie there, fragmentary, slate grey, waiting for the wind. And a book, a symphony, a poem, is not merely another 'experience' but a mystery, a wind blowing from the future. The problem of death is still far away; but the problem of life seems quite as tremendous. The mind contemplates vistas of time, the emptiness of space, and knows that the 'ordinariness' of everyday life is an illusion. And as the everyday becomes less real, so ideas are seen to be the only reality, and the mind that shapes them the only true power in this world of blind natural forces.

Lyell made no attempt to influence the direction of my studies, except to recommend books to me. He wanted me to make my own discoveries. When I first went to Sneinton, I read Irvine's fine book on the Darwinian controversy, and became fascinated by the period. I read everything I could find about Huxley, Darwin, Lyell, Tyndal and Herbert Spencer, and spent my days in the laboratory, dissecting specimens and examining them under the microscope. I came completely under the influence of Sir Julian Huxley, to whom Lyell introduced me in London. Huxley's belief that man has become the managing director of evolution in the universe seemed to me self-evident. I was fascinated by Wendell Stanley's experiments in which he transformed a virus into a non-living crystal, and showed that it could still cause disease, for they obviously opened up the question of the dividing line between living and non-living matter. Lyell kept me up to date on the researches of Watson and Crick into DNA. And both of us became excited about Stanley L. Miller's demonstration that organic compounds can form spontaneously under conditions that parallel those of the earth of eighteen thousand million years ago. For they raised the supreme question: Is 'life' something that permeates the universe like some kind of electric current, but has to wait for 'conductors' to form before it can enter matter? Or can it play some part in forming the conductor? Neither of us could entertain for a moment Oparin's hypothesis that life arose 'spontaneously' through the accidental build-up of organic compounds.

It was during this period that I stumbled on the trail of the 'great secret' that later became my life work. I was reading an article by Lyell on enzymes – those strange catalysts that act within living cells, and upon which all life depends – when I came across his reference to the autolytic enzymes. I asked him what these were, and he explained that they were enzymes of *dissolution*, that lay dormant in the cell until death, when they take over their task of breaking down the proteins in the protoplasm. 'But if they're *always* in the cell, why don't they cause it to break down while it's alive?' 'No one knows.' He picked up a book, searched for a place, and read aloud: 'The harpies of death sleep in every unit of our living bodies, but as long as life is there, their wings are bound and their devouring mouths are closed.' For once, he seemed puzzled by my intense interest in the subject. He explained that there is nothing very mysterious about enzymes. If you leave meat to hang, it becomes more tender because the enzymes begin their work of breaking down the cells. I persisted: 'But why don't these enzymes attack the *living* cell?' He smiled and shrugged. 'My dear boy, no one knows. But there must be an explanation. We don't really know, for example, why the enzymes in our digestive juices don't destroy the glands that produce them, or the inside of your stomach. Perhaps they're somehow inactive, like a bomb without its detonator, until they're needed. Have a look at Haldane's book on the subject.'

I looked at Haldane's book, but it was too technical for me. The problem continued to nag me for several days. Some time later, I came across this passage in T. E. Lawrence's *Seven Pillars of Wisdom*: 'During our revolt we often saw men push themselves or be driven to a cruel extreme of endurance, yet never was there an intimation of physical break. Collapse arose always from moral weakness eating into the body, which of itself, without traitors from within, had no power over the Will.' I could hardly wait to get to Sneinton to read it to Lyell. But again, he was unexcited. 'Of course the body has resources that become available under crisis . . .' 'But don't you think there might be some connection here with the business of the enzymes?' He looked baffled, and I tried to explain. 'It's the same thing, isn't it? Something about the will that prevents the autolytic enzymes from destroying the flesh while it's alive. And the same thing allowed the Arabs to push themselves to extremes of endurance. Without the will, everything breaks down.' To my surprise, my words seemed to worry him. He shook his head violently. 'My dear Howard, you really can't reason like that. It's not scientific. How do you know Lawrence was right? It might have been wishful thinking. As to the enzymes, there's probably some chemical explanation. You're not reasoning scientifically. Can you devise an experiment to test your theory?' I had to admit that I couldn't. This was one of those occasions when I felt disappointed in Lyell. He seemed to take pleasure in this 'tough minded' attitude. I felt that basically I was right and he was wrong, but I couldn't think of any way to convince him. So I pigeon-holed the question of the enzymes, promising myself to return to it later. Then, in the excitement of other questions, I forgot it.

The first Lady Lyell died in 1960. She had been confined to her bed for a year before the end, so it was not entirely unexpected. She was a strange person, curiously unemotional and detached. I had seen a great deal of her, and grown to like her; but I never grew fond of her. In fact, I occasionally felt an odd kind of hostility. Even when her face was expressionless, her eyes often had a faintly amused expression, as if she found all our talk of ideas an absurd folly to which she was superior. I used to try to draw her into conversation, to find out whether her detached amusement concealed depths of wisdom. She would talk about her childhood, or her travels with Lyell, but she never said anything to indicate profound intelligence. I finally came to feel that her amusement was merely feminine conceit, the device of a fool to justify her shallowness in her own eyes.

A year later, Lyell married again; his second wife was the

daughter of the biochemist, J. M. Knowles. She was a fair-haired, healthy girl, thirty years his junior, who loved riding, hunting and swimming. Lyell was obviously very much in love, and I was now old enough – nineteen – to be amused by it and feel superior. The new Lady Lyell spent a great deal of time on the farm, and insisted on his buying horses. He even agreed to go riding with her every morning. I felt – illogically – that he was betraying science by becoming so completely involved. Her French maid, Juliette, became interested in me, and found excuses for coming up to the laboratory or the observatory several times a day. But I was determined to set an example of the detachment of a scientific man, and I took pleasure in treating her with polite aloofness. I blush now to think of the priggish way I behaved; she was a delightful girl, and I realized that I missed her after she left.

Lyell's death in 1967 came as the greatest shock I had ever experienced. He had gone to China with a group from the Anglo-Chinese Friendship Society. In a small village on the Yangtse, he developed a mild fever that kept him in bed for a few days. He returned to Peking tired, but apparently fully recovered. A Chinese doctor insisted that he should have an injection in case the illness returned. Some kind of mistake was made – I have never discovered exactly what happened. Small blisters formed inside his mouth, and then a large swelling appeared on the back of his neck. Within forty-eight hours, he was dead. Decomposition set in so quickly that the body was flown back to England, and the interment – in the family vault near Inverness – followed twenty-four hours later. I flew to Scotland with Lady Lyell to be present. It was a cold, rainy day, and there were only half a dozen other mourners – it had all happened too suddenly for all his relatives and colleagues to be notified. I should have felt closer than ever to Lady Lyell, since the two of us were the chief mourners. Instead, I felt completely detached. I could see that she was miserable about the loss of a husband and a lover; but she could accept the blow as the kind of misfortune that happens to human beings. And she had consolations. She was still under forty, and more beautiful than ever; she was rich, and she still enjoyed sport and social occasions.

For me, there was something insanely unreasonable about Lyell's death. I find this difficult to explain. Hazlitt says that no young person really believes in his own death, no doubt this was still true for me, at twenty-five. But in a sense, Lyell had become so close to me – or rather, he was always so close, from our first meeting – that he was somehow included in my disbelief in death. The simplest way of explaining my feeling is to say that I felt he was a twin brother. From the beginning, there had been some odd psychic bond between us – the kind of deep and total sympathy that I have occasionally seen between exceptionally happy married couples. It was more than merely personal; it transcended the personal in our mutual love of science and philosophy. As I stood there in the snow, and watched the coffin carried into the stone vault, I experienced the hallucinatory belief that I was being buried alive. In the *reallest* sense, there was a part of me in the coffin. This was why I could feel no sympathy as Jane Lyell burst into tears and clung to my arm. Her grief was real, but it was not deep; I had seen her cry like this when her favourite hunter broke his leg and had to be shot.

The next day, I moved to the cottage in Essex where he and I had worked together on *Principles of Microbiology*. She re-married a year later, but I never met her again. When I discovered how generously I had been treated in Lyell's will, I half-expected her to contest it. But to do her justice, she had little of the mean or petty about her.

Re-reading what I have written, I am aware that I have failed to explain why his death affected me so violently. But in order to make it clear, I would have to write a detailed account of my twelve years at Sneinton – during the last seven of which I was his assistant and secretary. And that, in turn, would require a book as long as Baynton's *Life*. He taught me everything I knew : not only in science, but in philosophy, music, literature, history – even in mathematics, for before I met Lyell, my maths was of the log-and-slide-rule variety.

Most teenagers suffer all kinds of emotional upsets and frustrations; my own teens were completely free of such problems. It would give a false impression to say that I was 'happy'. I was totally absorbed in work. I was an engine working to the limit of its capacity; happiness would have been a pointless irrelevancy. And since I never had the feeling that 'the times are out of joint', I somehow took it for granted that Lyell would live to be a centenarian and that I would attend his funeral in

Westminster Abbey. (I had even chosen the spot, close to Darwin's grave.) His death at fifty-seven seemed so murderously stupid that my sense of 'rightness' was shaken. I felt a cold suspicion that I had been living an illusion for the past twelve years.

Perhaps I should not have gone off on my own; the loneliness made it worse. Lyell had many friends who could have helped me, with whom I could have spent the next six weeks, and talked about the conflict produced in me by his death. Instead, I went to a lonely cottage, a mile from the nearest village. There were heavy wooden shutters up at all the windows, and when I took them down, I could look out on the sea, with its endless, meaningless movement. I tried to work, but it was hopeless. I sat for hours in the window seat, staring at the sea. I had had no experience in self expression or introspection. And since I felt no desire to read or listen to the radio or watch the television, my feelings coagulated, catalysed by boredom.

I think I became a little insane. There was some obscure force struggling inside me, but I felt no desire to do anything. One night, I took a walk on the beach, and looked up at the sky, and wondered how I could ever have taken any interest in the stars. They were dead worlds; and even if they weren't dead, what meaning could they have for me, or for any other human being? What was the point of science, the study of the indifference of the universe? One could understand why men should study to make their lives more comfortable – but why study mere facts for their own sake? What had they to do with us? I began to *suspect* that all science is an absurd misunderstanding.

Lyell's solicitor contacted me. I had to go to London on business connected with the will. Up to this point, I had never expected that he intended to leave me so much money; I knew he meant to leave me something – I assumed it would be a small income or settlement of some kind. The truth surprised me – but even so, I felt almost nothing. It seemed irrelevant. By this time, the very fact that I was alive seemed irrelevant.

His solicitor – John Foster Howard – was a kind old man. He invited me home for dinner, and I accepted out of indifference. In the same spirit of indifference, I accepted several whiskies before dinner, and then drank a great deal of wine with the meal. I had often drunk wine at Sneinton – Lyell was a great connoisseur – but never took any interest in the subject. I felt about wine as I felt about sex – that it was an irrelevancy, of no concern to the scientist. Now I found, for the first time in two weeks, that I was feeling human again. I ended by getting drunk, and talking to Howard at length about Lyell; at two in the morning, they made up a bed for me, and I slept heavily until late the next morning.

I left Howard's after breakfast, and wandered around Hyde Park for an hour – he lived off the Edgware Road. Then I did something that I had never done before; I went into a pub in Soho and ordered a double whisky. When the barman asked me what kind, I looked at him blankly, then said: 'Scotch.' I drank several of these, sitting in a corner of the bar, then ate a sandwich and got into conversation with an old man who said he was a pedlar of jewellery. Two women friends joined him; I bought them all drinks. Suddenly, they seemed the friendliest and pleasantest people I had ever met. I went on drinking until closing time, and then realized that I could hardly walk. I hailed a taxi and told the driver to take me to Liverpool Street Station. My case was still in my hotel room, and I hadn't paid the bill, but I suddenly wanted to be back in the cottage. I slept on the journey and woke up with a headache and a thirst. At Rochford, I went into the nearest hotel and ordered sandwiches and beer. After my third beer, the headache went away. I fell into conversation with a boy of about twenty. He told me he was a farm labourer who worked for twelve pounds a week, and that he intended to get married soon because his girlfriend was pregnant. Suddenly, I felt a great interest in him, a desire for insight into his life. I got him to talk about himself at length, while I bought him drinks – we were soon both drinking whisky. (He went on to mix his drinks in a manner that even I knew must be disastrous.) He told me about his family, his brothers and sisters and cousins, and I remember listening to every word with deep attention. Finally, he remembered that he was supposed to meet his girl-friend, and that he was an hour late. He went off, saying that he would bring her back, because I had to meet her. He left, and I sat alone, staring at the coal fire and sipping whisky. I was surprisingly clear headed considering how much I'd drunk – perhaps because I was unused to it. And as I sat there, thinking about the life that Frank – the farm labourer – had been describing to me, a thought suddenly came into my head: 'I am rich, and free to do whatever I like.' I looked around at the bar – the working men playing darts and drinking pints – and it suddenly seemed clear that I had been ignoring what life was really about. These people wanted to live fuller lives, but they were trapped in an economic machine. I had been lucky. I would be stupid not to seize my luck with both hands. Life was to be lived; science was a fraud. I suddenly remembered authors I had read without much sympathy at the time – Pater, Oscar Wilde, Maupassant. I remembered Jane's French maid Juliette, remembered her shapely legs in black stockings, and wished that she was here with me – or, better still, waiting back at the cottage. When I thought about Lyell, I experienced no pangs of conscience about my present state of mind; after all, he was dead. He had been taken in by the fraud too, and now he was dead. But at least I could try to do some of his living for him. I remembered his happiness in those early days with Lady Jane. Of course . . . he *must* have known the secret. Why didn't he tell me? Why did we go on, living in our absurd, dehydrated, sterlized world of ideas and aesthetic emotions?

By ten o'clock, Frank still hadn't returned. I rang for a taxi, and got home towards midnight. I ate cold meat and gherkins from the refrigerator, then slept on the settee downstairs, where I could see the moonlight on the sea. Again, I slept heavily and late.

I woke up with a headache and a hangover of conscience. But still I felt in no mood for scientific work. I spent a thoroughly wretched day, bored, self-divided, irritable. In the afternoon, I forced myself to take a bathe in the sea, but it was so cold that I was completely numb after a few minutes. I went indoors and dried myself, then wandered aimlessly around the house, glancing at bookshelves, leafing my way through magazines. The Lyells had often spent weekends here, so there were a great many books and magazines belonging to Lady Lyell – books on horses and dogs and sailing, copies of *Vogue* and *The Tatler* and *Country Life*. An hour of browsing through these made me feel suicidal – that most human beings are little better than apes. Then I came across Lyell's books on wine. Some of these had fine colour plates, showing vineyards of the Rhine, Burgundy and so on, and I stared at them with the pleasure that comes from the impersonality of hills. Then I remembered that Lyell kept some wine in the cellar – it was a matter in which I had never taken any interest. I went down to look. It was a good collection for such a small cellar – some hundred or so cases arranged in racks. Another dozen cases were piled near the door, waiting to be opened. I looked into one, and found that it contained claret – Château Brane-Cantenac, one of Lyell's favourite wines. I was overcome by a kind of sentimental nostalgia. I took a bottle upstairs, opened it, carefully decanted it, and drank down a large glass full. It was too cold. I stood the decanter in the hearth, by the wood fire, got out the cheese board, and sat down in the armchair with one of André Simon's wine books on my knee. Soon, to my surprise, I found the decanter empty, and once again, I felt myself steeped in my own past, seeing my life from a distance. It struck me then that the main problem of human life is easy to define. We live too close to the present, like a gramophone needle travelling over a record. We never appreciate the music as a whole because we only hear a series of individual notes.

I felt the impulse to get this down on paper. I found a clean notebook in the study and started to write. At one point, I fetched up another bottle of claret, but forgot to drink it. I was writing about my own life, about experiences that I remembered well, about sudden insights like the one I had just had. I realized that all science has simply been man's attempt to get his nose off the gramophone record, to see things from a distance, to escape this perpetual tyranny of the present. He invented language and then writing to try to escape his worm's eye view of his own existence. Later still he invented art – painting, music, literature, to try to store the stuff of his living experience. It came to me with a shock that art is really an extension of science, not its opposite; science tries to store and correlate dead facts; art and literature try to store and correlate living facts.

And then, the clearest insight of all: science is not man's attempt to reach 'truth'. He doesn't want 'truth' – in the sense of mere 'facts'. He wants wider consciousness, freedom from this strange trap that holds our noses against the gramophone record. This is why he has always loved wine and music . . .

I have summarized my conclusions in two paragraphs; but they took me several hours of writing and several thousands of words. When I had finished, I realized that I had reached a turning point in my life. Admittedly, I had always known this – instinctively. Now I knew it consciously, and the next question was clear: is there any straight-forward *method*, apart from the pursuit of ideas and symbols, for achieving this wider consciousness, for obtaining those 'breathing spaces' when you feel like a bird, contemplating your existence from above, instead of from the gutter?

I was sleepy, and I was drunk again. But it wasn't important. I went to bed, full of a sense of new discovery, of knowing something that would change my life. I expected it still to be there when I woke up, and it was. I knew then how Newton must have felt when he finished writing the *Principia*. It seemed to me that I had made a discovery of great scientific importance – a discovery of what science really aimed at. The next question was: what could I do with it? How could I follow it up?

During the next few days, I did a great deal of thinking and writing, and I came to some important conclusions. The most important of them was this: that although science may not have understood its real aim, religion and poetry had always understood *theirs*. The mystics, like the poets, knew all about this 'bird's eye consciousness' that suddenly replaces our usual worm's eye view.

I went into the Rochford Public Library and found Cuthbert Butler's book on Western Mysticism and a volume by Evelyn Underhill. More important, I found a gramophone record of Finzi's *Dies Natalis*, a setting from Traherne's *Centuries of Meditation*. The books on mysticism rather repelled me – my scientific training was too deep rooted to swallow them easily – but Traherne's words were immediately moving. They made it clear that I had to get to grips directly with the mystics.

It was then that I remembered about Lyell's uncle. Canon Lyell, a cousin of the famous Sir Charles, never achieved the rank of a Victorian celebrity. But his *History of the Eastern Churches* was apparently considered the standard work on its subject – less readable than Dean Stanley's book on the same subject, but more encyclopedic and reliable. I also seemed to remember that he was the author of a book on the English mystics, and had possessed one of the largest libraries of religious and theological works in the country.

For some absurd reason – after all, I could have found all the books I needed in the London Library – I wrote to Alec's brother George, who lived in Scotland, and asked him if he knew what had happened to Canon Lyell's library. A week later, a reply came, saying that he had no idea, but that perhaps another member of the family, Aubrey Lyell, could tell me. He enclosed Aubrey Lyell's address. It was in Alexandria. I decided to make do with the London Library and the British Museum.

That weekend, the phone rang: it was Aubrey Lyell, calling from London. George Lyell had passed on my message. He said he would like to come over and see me, and I said he would be welcome. He arrived early on Saturday evening. He was younger than I expected – a few years older than I was – with black hair and an olive complexion. He was tall and thin, and his figure looked oddly disjointed. He spoke in a faint, breathless voice, as if too bored to raise it. But he seemed to be a cultivated, intelligent man, and after the initial awkwardness of total strangers sizing one another up, we began talking as openly as if we were old friends. At his suggestion we drove into Rochford for a meal. It was one of those evenings when everything seems fated to go perfectly. The food was good; the carafe wine very drinkable; and each of us was thoroughly interested in the other's personality. I talked about Lyell, my home background, and my life since Alec's death; he talked of poetry and mysticism, and told me about a friend of his, a poet called Constantine Cafavey, who had died not long before.

Presently he said casually: 'I'd love you to come back to Alexandria.'

I asked with mild incredulity: 'Are you sure?'

'*Quite* sure.'

'Alright. Thank you. I'd love to.' It had been decided within the space of a few seconds, and I felt a tremendous exhilaration.

As we watched the approaching coastline of Egypt, Aubrey told me that a new chapter of my life was opening. He was right, but not in the way he meant.

His house was a mile outside the city. I was impressed. It was far larger than I had expected, and stood in a great garden with palms and lemon flowers. The grass of the lawn was watered all the time by sprays. The rooms were big and cool, furnished in the European manner. I had spent two days in Cairo with the Lyells and had been unimpressed; this struck me as calm and beautiful, giving me a sensation of inner space. I had once tried to read Durrell, but given up, finding him too full of defeat and masochism; now I understood him. Alexandria is a city to which one must surrender on its own terms, or ignore completely. Admittedly, it made a difference to be staying in a house that overlooked the bay, away from the dust

and beggars and the noise of trams. The city was overcrowded
– this was the year of the Arab-Israeli war – and government
organizations tried to persuade refugees to leave the fly-infested
slums and move to D.P. camps – apparently with no success.
For Aubrey, the war was merely a nuisance; it meant that it was
more difficult to get to his favourite eating places; besides, an
Englishman was likely to be spat at.

I found Aubrey more likeable in his own surroundings; he
relaxed, became more serious, took on the confidence of a
householder and a good host. At supper, we drank an Egyptian
wine of a burgundy type, which I had to admit was excellent,
and he expounded his ideas to me at length. I was struck
because they corresponded roughly to what I had been thinking a few months before, after Lyell's death. He argued his case
well. Ideas were abstract and finally unsatisfying, unless related
to our human needs. They might give an impression of satisfying, as hot tea temporarily removes hunger, but it is an
illusion. Man is 'human', that is to say, he is social by nature.
His social and sexual urges are his deepest; they are as important
to his humanity as breathing is to his body.

His words might once have struck me as true. I now saw
clearly that his preference for emotions, his conviction of the
unimportance of ideas, was merely a symptom of his inability
to think logically or seriously. But he was intelligent, self
critical and sympathetic. When he sensed my basic lack of
inclination for his way of life, he remained an excellent and
courteous host, who had invited me to his house, and who
intended to treat me well until I felt like leaving. I remembered
some of my own feelings of impatience during the days he
spent with me, and felt ashamed. I also found his honesty
impressive. On one occasion, when I had spent half an hour
trying to express my sense of our basic difference as politely as
possible, he said: 'You mean I'm not clever enough to think
any idea through to the end?' I had to laugh when I realized
that my polite circumlocutions had been wasted.

I saw little of Alexandria; I found his library far too interesting.
Canon Lyell had died before he had finished the second volume
of mysticism – it was to deal with the German school from
Eckhart to Boehme. But his manuscript pages had been sewed
together and bound. Most of it had been dictated to a secretary,
whose handwriting was neat and readable. Perhaps it was this

personal touch that made the book so real to me. Most of the works referred to in the MS were also in Aubrey's library – the beautiful four volume edition of Boehme, translated in part by Law (about whom the canon had written in the published volume), rare editions of Eckhart and Suso, Ruysbroek and Saint John of the Cross, and several of Blake's own hand printed books. The canon had written down most of his ideas in the margins and flyleaves, so it was possible to study the development of his thought, as if in an intimate journal. He had even studied alchemy in an attempt to grasp the meaning of Boehme's symbolism. I also began to study the alchemists, and was astonished at how much light they shed on pages of Boehme's text that at first reading I had dismissed as muddle headed and chaotic.

For the first few days, I must admit to finding the mystics baffling and involved. The lack of scientific precision irritated me. Then, at exactly the right moment, I came across the key to them – in Aubrey's record library. He had a great admiration for Furtwängler, and had almost everything Furtwängler had ever recorded, including the Bruckner symphonies. Lyell had often played me Bruckner in my early days at Sneinton, but I had not been impressed. I found him melodious but hopelessly long winded and repetitive. It seemed clear to me that most of his symphonies need to be cut by a half, sometimes more. His church music satisfied me more, but I preferred Handel. Finally, I had stopped listening to Bruckner, and Lyell also lost interest.

Now I came across Furtwängler's remark that Bruckner was a descendant of the great German mystics, and that the aim of his symphonies had been to 'make the supernatural real'. I knew he had begun by composing church music; surely then, it followed that he came to the symphony because he wanted to go further in expressing 'the supernatural'? I put on Furt-wängler's recording of the Seventh Symphony, and immediately understood that this was true. This music was slow, deliberate, because it was an attempt to escape the nature of music – which, after all, is dramatic; that is to say, it has the nature of a story. You listen to its development as you would listen to the development of a story. Bruckner, according to Furtwängler, wanted to suspend the mind's normal expectation of development, to say something that could only be expressed if the mind fell into a slower rhythm. So interpretations that treat them *as* symphonies – like Klemperer's – or as romantic poems – like Walter's – miss the whole point. This music is not descriptive of nature; it attempts to *approximate to* nature.

When I understood this, Furtwängler's interpretations were revelatory. I put them on when the house was quiet, and I calmed my mind, as if I were lying on the seashore, listening to the sound of the sea and absorbing the sun. Then the music induced utter calm, and even the orchestral climaxes seemed as impersonal as the crash of waves. I now made the interesting discovery that instead of seeming too long, the symphonies seemed far too short. They ended just as I had entered fully into their mood. I ended by piling half a dozen long-playing records on the turntable, and listening to assorted movements of the Fourth, the Seventh, the Eighth, without bothering about which symphony they belonged to. With Bruckner, this makes surprisingly little difference, since for him, a symphony was always an incantation to induce the same state of mind, the sense of detachment from our humanity, of entering into the eternal life of mountains and atoms.

The days passed in an enormous sense of peace. The weather was ideal, still cool enough to be enjoyed. Aubrey took me on occasional excursions, but otherwise ceased to bother with me. I found a morning sitting in a café, talking with the Alexandrian literati, so painful that even he could see that I hated it. After that, he would introduce me to visitors with the remark: 'He's studying to be a monk,' and I would slip off to the library as soon as they ceased to notice me.

The month I spent in Aubrey's house catalysed an enormous mental change in me. I found that I even ceased to regret Lyell's death. I would have preferred him to be alive; but my present discovery would have been impossible without his death. I would have continued absorbed in science, and suppressed any other impulses.

Two days before I left Alexandria, I came upon the book that caused my second great change of direction, and introduced me to my life's work. I found it in the bookcase in Aubrey's room one day when I was looking for a biography of Furtwängler that he had mentioned. It had the unspectacular title *Human Ageing, A Biological and Behavioural Study*. I wondered idly what such a book was doing on his bookshelves. Then I remembered several remarks he had made about the business of getting old – about how the past five years had passed like six months, and he expected the next decade to pass even quicker. He said: 'Time's a confidence trick. It's like a crooked guardian who keeps dipping his hands into your bank account. You think you've still got a fortune left, and then realize that you're on the edge of bankruptcy.' He also mentioned some statistic, to the effect that by the end of the century, the average life-expectancy would be eighty-one instead of seventy-four.

I took the book back to my room, and read the first article. And then I recalled my discussion with Lyell about the autolytic enzymes. I turned to an examination of the blood chemistry in healthy aged men, and discovered that there is a striking similarity between that of these men and of 'normal' younger men, although there *is* a marked decrease of serum albumin. I remembered an odd sentence that I had read somewhere: that rats fed on a diet of ecstasy live longer. I recalled Aubrey's remarks about the acceleration of time, and my own observation that Bruckner's symphonies became too short when I was in a mood of total serenity. Somewhere, I knew instinctively, there was a connection between these apparently unrelated facts. And with some other idea of mine that eluded me . . .

It came back that evening, after supper. Aubrey and I had dined alone – I had told him I intended to leave. He wanted to know how I reconciled my love of science with this interest in mysticism. I soon discovered that he had a theory of his own which seemed to fit the facts. He thought of scientists as men afraid to accept the implications of their humanity – perhaps people 'deeply wounded in their sexuality', as Durrell said of his Alexandrians. They were also afraid of death. He, Aubrey said, was not afraid of death; he accepted it as the necessary corollary to his belief that man is intended to be human, to live humanly and sensually. The scientist is unwilling to face death, and so he sacrifices his humanity and tries to identify himself with the abstract and the eternal. And the religious man has the same motive, except that he may believe in an after life for which he has to prepare.

I pointed out that I had been interested in science and mathematics from the age of nine or ten – far too young to take death seriously or think of evading it. Then I explained my own view of the scientific urge – that it is the attempt to achieve the 'bird's eye view', broader consciousness. And as I said it, the connection suddenly came to me, and I stopped speaking.

Aubrey asked me to go on; but I wanted to think this out alone. So I ended lamely, and let him go on talking. And when he found me dull, and went to make a telephone call to a night club, I went out into the garden and sat on a low wall. It was a clear night, and the stars seemed closer than I have ever seen them in England. And now I followed the implications of my idea. By life we mean being alive, being *conscious* – not just 'head consciousness', but the obscure forces of Lawrence's 'solar plexus'. But if life is consciousness, then the problem of prolonging life should be the problem of increasing consciousness – the aim of science as well as art. Ecstasy is increase of consciousness – and rats fed on a diet of ecstasy live longer. It follows that great artists, scientists and mathematicians should live longer than other men. And where mathematicians are concerned, I knew this to be true. Newton – eighty-five. Sylvester – eighty-three. Dedekind – eighty-five. Galileo – seventy-eight. Gauss – seventy-eight. Euclid – ninety. Sylow – eighty-six. Whitehead – eighty-six. Russell – ninety-five (and still alive at that time). Weierstrass – eighty-two. E. T. Bell once remarked that mathematicians either die very young – by disease or accident – or live to be very old. Mostly, they live on. I decided to check the figure – how many mathematicians out of a test batch lived to be more than seventy-five. (I later discovered that it was nearly 50 per cent – as compared to less than 15 per cent in the general population.) I began to try to remember how many artists, philosophers, musicians, have achieved old age. I knew less about these groups than about mathematicians, but even so, I could think of a cross section of such men that seemed significant. Bruckner, admittedly, only reached seventy-two – but he was in many ways a frustrated and unhappy little man. But Sibelius, whose music is equally serene and majestic, lived to ninety-one. Strauss reached eighty-five. Haydn reached seventy-seven in an age when fifty was average life expectancy. Vaughan Williams – another one of the mystical school – reached eighty-six. By this time, I was so interested in my game that I went to the library and took down a biographical dictionary, then began to look up names at random. Plato – eighty-one. Kant – eighty. Santayana – eighty-nine. Tolstoy – eighty-two. Bernard Shaw – ninety-three. H. G. Wells – eighty-one. G. E. Moore – eighty-five. Newman – eighty-nine (although he thought of himself as a permanent invalid!). Carlyle – eighty-six (another valetudinarian). Bergson – eighty-two.

Aubrey came into the study to tell me he was going out, and found me writing down lists of figures. He said: 'Back at mathematics again, eh? Had enough of religion?' I said: 'You say you want to live to an old age?' 'I suppose so, why?' 'Then your best chance is to become a mathematician or a philosopher. In fact, a thinker of any kind. They last longer.'

I showed him my figures. By this time, I had taken down a dictionary of the arts and sciences, and was simply making lists of ages under various headings. Philosophers and mathematicians came out best, with nearly 50 per cent living to be over seventy-five. The average for musicians, artists and writers was lower – but then, a much higher percentage of artists tend to be emotionally unstable or unhappy. The figures showed that the stable ones tended to live as long as philosophers.

Aubrey looked dazed. Then he said: 'Well, you've made your point. But I still intend to go out and drink champagne, and spend the evening with a neurotic young model. What do you think that proves?' I smiled at him as he went out. 'You know as well as I do.'

I sailed from Egypt in early May. I preferred the sea route; I wanted time to think: about practical problems as well as ideas. I wondered where to go next. I was determined that my life should regain the sense of order and direction I had lost since Lyell's death. I liked Aubrey, but the purposelessness of his life horrified me. The thought that most people lived like this almost made me despair of being human. I decided not to return to the Essex cottage; I would go back to Hucknall until I could decide what to do.

On the boat I had a brief attack of dysentery; but even this turned out to be enlightening. I woke up in the night feeling sick, and lay awake, trying to fight it off. The smallness of the cabin, the warmth, the sound of the man in the next cabin tossing in his bunk – all these intensified the sickness. Then I heard the sound of steps outside my door – a sailor or officer on duty, since he was wearing shoes. A few minutes later, I heard low voices that sounded as if they were arguing. My door was opposite a flight of stairs; they stopped under the stairs and continued the argument. One of them kept saying: 'Don't raise your voice,' and the other said: 'I don't see why not. It's none of your bloody business anyway . . .' I gathered that one of them had been in the cabin of a female passenger, and the other had caught him coming out. After a few minutes, they went upstairs, still arguing in low voices. Then I noticed that my interest in their quarrel had made the sickness subside. I had stopped thinking about myself – and the sickness had vanished . . . I recalled a line of Shaw's: 'Minding your own business is like minding your own body – it's the quickest way to make yourself sick.' Why should it be? *Why should thinking about yourself increase the sickness, and thinking about something else diminish it?*

For the next twenty-four hours I was convulsed with retching and diarrhoea; but in between times, I thought about my insight. And the following day, when I was again able to eat a little, I saw the solution clearly. Human beings are unlike any other animal on the surface of the earth in one important respect: they are capable of focusing their minds on matters that have no immediate personal significance for them. The consciousness of an animal is bound to be concerned with its needs and desires; man has this capacity for taking an interest in other things, quite apart from his personal needs. 'Other' things – that was the vital phrase. The human capacity for 'other-ness'. A certain odour or fragment of music could remind me vividly of some other place or other time, and make the present moment vanish for an instant. But this ability to leap away from my own body was not confined to events in my own past life. I could read the biography of a long-dead scientist, and make the same 'leap'. I could make it listening to a symphony of Bruckner, or doing a mathematical problem. The 'other-ness' permits us to draw on reserves of strength that are normally not available to us.

I recalled an incident of my teens. I had heard about the discovery of a fossil coelocanth at Matlock in Derbyshire, and rode over there one Sunday afternoon to see it. There was a strong wind against me; I arrived exhausted. I was tempted to find a café and rest for half an hour over tea and sandwiches, but I was late. So I sought out the man who had found the fossil, and asked to see it. He was an old boatman whose interest in such things was purely amateurish. But his enthusiasm was intense, and he insisted that I go with him to the cave, so he could show me the spot where he found it. We climbed a steep hill, borrowed a lantern from an obliging guide, and then went down a low, steep corridor that plunged into the hill. For over an hour we scrambled around over great slabs of rock, through narrow openings, along moist corridors, while he showed me other fossils embedded in the stone. And when we came out into the sunlight again, I realized that I felt completely refreshed – more refreshed than if I had spent the hour sleeping in the sun. My mind had focused with interest on the matter of the fossils; walking through the caves, I had become aware of the enormous age of the earth, and the brevity of all human history. And with my mind focused on 'other-ness', strength had returned: I had made contact with the inner reserve of power that is inaccessible to ordinary 'personal' consciousness.

This, I realized, was the completion of my argument with Aubrey Lyell. Science is not a meaningless abstraction, unrelated to human life. Like art, literature, music, religion, it is the pursuit of an 'other-ness' that connects us to some obscure source of power inside ourselves.

It was all fascinating – but what did it *prove*? Even though I was convinced that I had stumbled on a fundamental truth, it meant nothing unless I could relate it to definite facts. For example, man is one of the most long-lived animals on earth. A dog or a horse, even a tiger, is old at fifteen. But then, turtles and elephants live longer than men. Were these merely exceptions to a rule – or is there no relation between man's longevity and his capacity for thought? Again, man now lives far longer than in the past. In the time of Shakespeare, a man was old at fifty. A few centuries earlier, and thirty-five was the average expectation of life. Is this increased longevity related to our increased capacity to use the mind, to universal education? Or is it merely due to improved sanitary conditions, shorter hours of work, and so on? Unless one could answer these questions with a definite yes or no, it all remained a fairy tale, a slightly insane theory.

But how could I set about testing it? I racked my brains, but could think of no answer. In the ship's library, I discovered a book that made me feel as though I were being mocked by some obscure demon of science. It upheld the theory that the earth has had several moons, each one of which has crashed on the earth, giving rise to the great myths of floods and universal destruction. According to this book, men were smaller in the Middle Ages (as they undoubtedly were) because the present moon was then further from the earth. In the mean-time, it has come closer, neutralizing the earth's gravity to some extent, and allowing us to grow taller ... and, at the same time, to live longer, since reduced gravity means less wear-and-tear on our bodies!

I remember feeling a kind of superstitious shiver as I read the book. It was as if the fates were warning me that I was drifting dangerously close to becoming a crank. My immediate reaction was a determination to discover the facts about longevity, no matter how long it took. I read the book on *Human Ageing* from cover to cover, hoping to find a point of departure, and finding none. Theories about the Middle Ages were obviously useless; there was no way of testing them. And theories about human consciousness were equally meaningless unless I could devise a way of investigating them in the labora-tory. So where could I begin? Obviously, with the human body and its capabilities. But this was one subject about which I knew very little; it had simply never interested me. In that case, I had to begin with learning about the body.

It would serve no purpose to describe the next eighteen months in detail. I lived in lodgings off Goodge Street, attended lectures in anatomy and pathology at University College, and spent a great deal of time in the British Museum Reading Room. I made almost no acquaintances – I was too absorbed in work for socializing. My chief relaxations were exploring the second hand bookshops in the Charing Cross Road, and wandering around the city. (My favourite time for this was Saturday afternoons and Sundays.) Sneinton was empty for much of the time; Howard – Lady Lyell's solicitor – told me that she spent a great deal of time staying with friends and hunting. So I spent many weekends there – it was only a two hour drive up the M.1. I also spent more time with my parents, now both my brothers were married.

One day, driving back from Nottingham, I switched on the car radio, and heard a voice saying: 'Man's evolution has been the steady growth of his independence from the body and the physical world. His mind seems intent on defying the processes of time. In this respect, art and science have the same aim. A lover of Dickens feels as much at home in nineteenth-century London as in the London of his own day. A historian may know ancient Rome or Athens as well as Oxford or Cambridge.

And a scientist might find the Pleistocene era more interesting than the twentieth century. The human mind objects to being confined in the present. Man's history is the history of a search for wider horizons. And now arises the fundamental question. What is the purpose of all this contemplation? Is it to make us aware of our own unimportance, of the fact that our life is so brief as to be practically meaningless? If so, then science defeats its own purpose. We'd better remain confined by the perpetual horizon of the present, as the fish is confined by its horizon of water. But is this true? Is the final end of human knowledge to teach man his own unimportance? Or are we right to trust that curiously optimistic impulse that drives us to transcend our imprisonment in times?' *

A moment later, the announcer's voice said: 'That was Sir Henry Littleway, delivering the seventh and last of the Leath lectures, under the title *Man the Measure*.'

I experienced a tingling in the nerve ends, a sensation of physical lightness; the feeling that I had arrived at the beginning of a new stage of my journey. I am certain that I am not imagining this feeling in retrospect. It was a flash of second-sight, of definite knowledge of the future. I had never heard of Sir Henry Littleway, but his name suddenly seemed as familiar to me as my own. As soon as I arrived back home, I looked him up in *Who's Who*. Born in Great Glen, Leicestershire, in 1919, educated at Leeds, earned a DSO in Normandy, holder of the McDougal chair of psychology at McGill University 1949–1956, then at the Massachusetts Institute of Technology until 1965. The *Who's Who* I consulted was out of date, but it gave his address: Langton Place, Great Glen. I immediately wrote him a letter, sketching my own background, and explaining my present interest in gerontology. Before I sealed it, I had a moment of misgiving. After all, I had only heard a few sentences at the end of a course of lectures; his views might be diametrically opposed to my own. If he had been at M.I.T., he might be a follower of Skinner and the behaviourists. Still, I had nothing to lose. I walked up to the post office at Mornington Crescent to catch the earliest post next day.

I heard nothing from him for a month. Then, one day, a small airmail parcel arrived with an American postmark. It con-

* I am quoting the version of the lecture that was printed in *The Listener* (8 February 1969), not the version that finally appeared in *Man the Measure* (Gollancz, 1970).

tained a paperback book, *Ageing and the Value Experience* by Aaron Marks, and a letter from Littleway. He apologized for the delay – he had come to America to attend the conference of the American Psychological Association. He had known Lyell slightly and liked him. He expected to be back in London at the end of March, when he would hope to see me; in the meantime, the enclosed book would give me some idea of the work that was being done. He also mentioned some other books on related subjects.

I read Marks's book through in one morning. Then I went to the British Museum, and looked up his other publications, as well as the other books recommended by Littleway: Husserl, Scheler, Cantril, Merleau Ponty, Leicester. I was used to reading and absorbing quickly, but by the end of that first day, I felt as though my brain was fermenting under my skull. It was amazing that there could be so much important work that I was totally unaware of. This was partly due to the fact that it was in a field that had never interested me, the no-man's land between psychology and philosophy. For two years, I had suspected that I was a solitary pioneer in a field that might arouse more ridicule than interest. Now I realized that ideas I had thought daring were commonplace to Marks and Littleway.

I soon discovered that Marks had created a battery of terms that made some of my own neologisms superfluous. His most basic idea was that of the 'value experience'. 'For most of his time,' he wrote, 'man is confined by a narrow perceptual horizon. He is limited in three respects: with regard to space, with regard to time, and with regard to meaning. He accepts life as it comes, and insofar as he experiences values, they are the animal values of hunger, thirst, tiredness, the need for self-assertion and territory. These are so basic that he is not even aware of them as values; they are simply impulses. But then there are certain moments of detachment, moments when he becomes aware of meanings and patterns beyond his present horizon. He sees the wood instead of half a dozen trees. These moments of seeing the wood instead of the trees I call "value experiences" – V.E.'s for short.' *

In other words, Marks's 'value experience' was my 'bird's

* Students of psychology can skip the next few pages. I am summarizing Mark's ideas, which are now as well known as Freud's, because I want to show their part in my own development.

eye moment'. But his definitions were much more precise than mine. The V.E. or meaning-experience can take several forms. For example, the sexual orgasm usually brings this sense of horizons of meaning beyond everyday consciousness, so one might be tempted to say that all value experiences approximate to the orgasm. This would be untrue, because there is another type of V.E. that brings a deep sense of calm. For example, if we read Wordsworth's sonnet on Westminster Bridge :

> Ne'er saw I, never felt a calm so deep.
> The river glideth at his own sweet will.
> Dear God, the very houses seem asleep . . .

it is clear that he was experiencing the *opposite* of the orgasm, something closer to the Buddhist's ideas of nirvana, rapt contemplation. Marks distinguishes these value experiences as moments of 'contemplative objectivity'.

As everyone now knows, Marks was the first to recognize the idea that about 5 per cent of human beings – or of any animal group – belong to a dominant minority, the 'evolutionary spearhead'. The majority of neurotics belong to this dominant minority, for the obvious reason that, having a stronger sense of purpose, they are more easily frustrated. Marks performed a series of famous experiments in which he deliberately induced nervous breakdowns in dogs, rats and hamsters by subjecting them to various forms of frustration. The dominant minority – exactly 5 per cent – had breakdowns in about half the time it took to induce them in the remaining 95 per cent. With these experiments, Marks had taken the decisive step beyond Freud. The dominant 5 per cent is driven by an urge for self-development and maturity. Sexual frustration is an important element in neurosis because sexual development is a vital part of the maturing process. But it is not the most important or basic cause of neurosis.

In general, the dominant minority among human beings behaves and responds very like the dominant minority among other animals. But there is an important difference. A very small percentage of the human 5 per cent – Marks determined it to be about ·5 of the 5 per cent, or ·00025 per cent of the human race – needs to express its dominance by another kind of self expression – the evolution of the mind. Most of the 5 per cent expresses itself through social dominance – it needs to dominate or outshine *other people*. The ·00025 per cent is basically obsessed by the value experience; this is its highest form of self-expression. For these people, all other forms of achievement and dominance seem barren.

But now came the part that really excited me. Marks had performed two series of experiments that placed all this on a solid basis of observation. The first was the cure of 'incurable' alcoholics by inducing V.E.s; the second, the increase of the life-span of old people in a home for the destitute.

The alcoholic experiment was based on the supposition that a large number of alcoholics belong to the ·00025 per cent (whom Marks calls the 'creative minority', borrowing Toynbee's term). Very few really creative people achieve complete self-expression, because the transition from social-orientation – the desire to dominate other people – to genuine creativity – the desire for value-experiences above everything else – is so difficult. The reason for this is simple : it is hard to achieve V.E.s *at will* unless you have outgrown the desire to dominate other people. This means there is a period when a man is 'between two stools'. He has started to lose interest in other people, but has still not reached the point of being able to replace the old domination experience with the value experience. In this stage, the creative minority are likely to look elsewhere for some satisfaction – to alcohol, drugs or sexual excess. The strain may also produce illness – particularly tuberculosis. This explains why so many of the romantic poets and artists died tragically, or became drug addicts, like Coleridge and De Quincey.

Marks used various means to induce V.E.s in his alcoholics – hypnosis, the electronic stroboscope, noise-analysis machines, psychedelic drugs – and cured about 82 per cent of them. (About 23 per cent later regressed to alcoholism, and of these, 9 per cent were cured permanently by a repetition of the treatment.)

The experiment with the old people proceeded along the same lines. In this case, Marks was inclined to wonder whether very old people who have ceased to care about art, poetry or music could be revitalized, or whether something inside might have atrophied. This time he took a cross section of old people, but took care to include several who had once been fond of poetry or music. Once again V.E.s were induced by various means, and then all the subjects were exposed to various forms of aesthetic experience. Since a large number of the subjects had no interest in poetry, music or painting, he also showed several exceptionally fine travelogues of Scandinavia and American National Parks, with three-dimensional technicolour and – significantly enough – music by Sibelius and Bruckner. Here, the results were incredible. All subjects, without exception, displayed an increase in vitality, the total vanishing of apathy. In several of them, this took the form of religious conversion, with revivalistic meetings. The experiments took place in early spring, and all the subjects began to take daily walks, and arranged bus tours of the area (Norfolk, Virginia). And seven out of the fifty subjects, including the four Marks had selected especially, experienced a complete intellectual and aesthetic awakening, and formed a music and poetry society, as well as a reading and discussion group. In all cases, the general level of health rose.

The fifty chosen were all over seventy-five, so that there seemed a reasonable statistical certainty that some of them would die during the next year. (The expectation was 17 per cent.) In fact, all but three were still alive two years later. Eleven more had relapsed to their former state of indifference, but remained healthy.

These two experiments fascinated me – particularly the latter. For it was immediately clear that the successes among the old people were much higher than there was any reason to expect. The alcoholics were already a selected group, because of Marks's assumption that the creative minority produce a larger percentage of alcoholics. So the 82 per cent success was perhaps to be expected. The fifty old people were a typical group; even the selection of four 'creative' ones made less difference than might be expected, because there were less than a hundred people over seventy-five in the home. So comparatively speaking, the success rate was out of all proportion to what might have been expected.

Yet this seems at first unexplainable. Old people have lost their expectation for the future. A cured alcoholic might expect to salvage a great deal of his future, perhaps even to achieve great success. Most of the old people in the experiment knew that they would never be likely to leave the home (which was, admittedly, an exceptionally good one). So why should their relapse rate be so much lower than among alcoholics?

Marks made no attempt to explain it. But the explanation that occurred to me was perhaps the most exciting thing about the whole investigation. We know that people gradually lose the will to live as they get older because the future holds less in store by way of excitement or love or discovery. We also tend to assume that they fail to develop in any other way. 'Do not talk to me of the wisdom of old age,' says T. S. Eliot. But supposing this assumption is mistaken? Supposing, in fact, that the simple process of getting older involves an almost automatic process of maturing – a process of which we remain unaware in most cases because it is counteracted by the running-down process?

Perhaps this is a case where the ancients knew better than we do. They had a tendency to regard the old as naturally wise. Today the opposite is true – age is synonymous with senility. But in early societies, there would be far more to stimulate the aged. Life would be harder; they would have a more active part to play in tribal life, and so on. The running-down process would be slower. (Is this also why so many old documents mention very old men – Noah, Methuselah, etc.?) The natural 'wisdom' would not be counteracted by the running-down process.

And again, *if* this is true (I had to admit that it is a big 'if'), the next step of the argument is even clearer. Man must be closer than he supposes to achieving some of the superhuman attributes. For we have a deeply ingrained idea that old age is *merely* a running down, as it appears to be in most animals. A turtle doesn't get wiser for being two hundred years old. If it can be definitely shown that there is a process in man working against the running-down of old age, then we have proved that there is a basic difference between man and the other animals. The mechanistic view of man falls down. He is not simply a machine that wears out. On another level, he continues to evolve. But his evolution is frustrated by physical decay, *which in turn is the outcome of the collapse of the will*. Marks's experiments make this latter consequence very clear. The alcoholic is an oversensitive person who is exhausted by the complexity of the modern world. Being exhausted, he ceases to have V.E.s. So he drinks to induce V.E.s. He becomes dependent on liquor, ceases to exercise any will-power, and so needs still more liquor to induce V.E.s. He remains pathetically unaware that it is precisely his abnegation of the will that is preventing him having V.E.s. Marks then induces V.E.s by a far more powerful and effective method than alcohol; the result is a lightning flash of insight into the nature of the V.E. – that it depends on vitality, health and will-power. The alcoholic sees that when he thought he was pursuing the V.E. he was actually running in the opposite direction. So he does an about-face – and ceases to be an alcoholic.

On the evening I received Littleway's letter, I wrote him a ten page reply, setting out these suggestions. From then on, I ceased to bother about medical school, and trying to devise experiments to explain the workings of the autolytic enzymes.

A week later, Littleway's reply arrived, together with copies of his *Listener* talks. And again, I had the sensation of the carpet being pulled from under me. Littleway had already advanced a hypothesis very like my own to account for the result of Marks's experiments. It was in the fourth of his Leath lectures, in which he speaks of the history of vitalism, from Lamarck to Driesch and Bergson – with digressions on Eucken, Edouard von Hartmann and Whitehead – and ends by asserting that it will be necessary for twentieth century biology to return to some form of the vitalist hypothesis. Littleway ends by writing: 'The conclusion seems clear. Man is distinguished from the other animals by the intensity of the evolutionary urge that he embodies. He is an evolutionary animal, capable of greater good and greater evil than any other creature – since evil is the outcome of the frustrated evolutionary drive.' And at the beginning of the sixth lecture, he writes: 'The vital force is quantitatively different in man; it strives to become qualitatively different. If he could achieve a more-or-less permanent state of objectivity [he was here referring to Marks's term 'contemplative objectivity'] the evolutionary impulse would become self-sustaining, self-amplifying.'

My first reaction was disappointment. Like Alfred Russell Wallace, I had been repeating the work that someone had already done more efficiently. But when I thought about it, the disappointment changed into a feeling of confidence and optimism. Wallace had reason to be disappointed. The theory of natural selection is an abstract truth that was not going to directly benefit anyone but its discoverer. But if Marks and Littleway were right, the consequences might be practical and immediate; it could be the single greatest discovery in the history of the planet. So I returned with renewed vitality to my books on old age, and waited impatiently for Littleway's arrival.

Anyone who has been reading this with sympathy must have realized that my feelings about the 'secret' swung from one extreme to the other. There were times when I felt so excited that all the world seemed transformed. I would look at the people I passed in the street, and think 'If only they *knew* . . .' And there were other times when it seemed that I might be pursuing a dream. For two million years, man has been more-or-less the same kind of creature. His evolution has been social rather than biological. Is modern man really so different from *Australopithecus*? If you or I were somehow transported back to the Stone Age, would we be so much better off than the Stone Age men? Would we know where to look for iron ore, and how to smelt it to make knives? Would we even succeed in starting a fire in the steaming forests? But if the answer to these questions is no, then how can we hope to completely change human nature overnight? When I reasoned like this, I accused myself of becoming a crank, an unscientific visionary, and I would read a few chapters of Popper's *Logic of Scientific Discovery* as a kind of mental astringent. And then another flash of insight would make it clear that I *was* on to something important, whether I could 'feel' it or not. And then there were the 'in between' moods when I studied my books on gerontology – I had pretty well everything published in English – and felt a kind of qualified optimism, and a determination not to let myself get carried away by enthusiasm.

Early in April, I received a telegram from Littleway, asking me if I could meet him for lunch at his club, the Athenaeum. I spent the morning in the Reading Room, then walked down to Lower Regent Street. It was a bright, clear morning, and I was in my optimistic phase. For the more I thought about Marks's experiments, the more I saw that I had been incredibly lucky. Throughout my teens I had lived a life of ideas, driven by inner purpose. The usual conflict between body and mind had been reduced to a minimum in my case. So with luck, I might become the living proof of my own theory . . .

As to Littleway, I was not sure what I had expected. I had read almost every word he had ever published; on the whole, I was disappointed. Much of it was on the philosophy of science, and this was also his approach in the Leath lectures. So while individual paragraphs seemed to me immensely exciting, it was

46

difficult to see where he was driving. His mind struck me as curiously abstract. I formed a picture of him as a tall, bird-like man with penetrating eyes, a cross between Sherlock Holmes and Wittgenstein.

He proved to be short, powerfully built, with the healthy complexion of a farmer. He recognized me immediately. 'Ah, so you're Lester. Nice to meet you. Like a beer?' There was something energetic, almost boisterous, about him. His voice gave the impression that he would be perfectly happy shouting above the noise of a tractor or combine harvester; his walk had a sort of swing, as if he was setting out for a twenty mile tramp. I am tall and thin, and relatively shy, unless carried away by ideas. I said: 'That's kind of you, sir.' 'Better call me Henry. Everybody does. I'll call you Howard,* if you don't mind. Pint of draught?' We sat in the corner of the bar, and broke the ice by talking about Lyell. By the time we went in for lunch, I felt sufficiently at ease to start talking.

'As I see it, the problem is to try to carry on Marks's experiments. We need some way of measuring the metabolic rate of ageing, so as to be able to check how far it can be slowed down.'

He sliced his way through a huge slab of roast beef.

'You're rather more interested in this ageing aspect than I am. I don't see it as the immediate problem.'

'Then what *is*?'

'The biological problem. Have you read Hardy's *Living Stream*? His suggestion that the genes might be affected by some form of telepathy? That's the sort of thing I'd like to investigate. You see why? Marks's theories about value experiences are all very well – they might be true for psychology – but do they have any meaning for biologists? If they do, it's a shake-up for Darwinism.'

'How would you go about it?'

'Study the gene code. Since Kornberg synthesized DNA at Stanford, there are all kinds of possibilities. If you can duplicate genetic material, it ought to be possible to produce identical specimens to experiment on. You can see the advantage of that? Suppose I experiment with an albino rat, to determine how it reacts to frustration, or something of the kind. When my experiment's over, I've learned a certain amount, but I might wish that I'd tried a completely different line of experiment. I'd like to start at the beginning again, with the same rat.

* This later became Harry.

47

But I can't – because it isn't the same rat any more – it's changed. And if I use a different rat, I don't know how far its differences are affecting my results. Now I can start all over again with the same rat – or with a fairly exact duplicate. At least, that's what I'm hoping . . .'

I was interested, yet already I was beginning to feel disappointed. Somehow, it wasn't what I had been hoping. He went on :

'The same thing with experiments about dominance. What would happen if you put several identical rats together in a cage? Which of them would become dominant, and why? That's one of the things I'd like to discover. Then there's another interesting thing. A few years ago, my daughter had a couple of white mice, and a pet hamster. One of the mice was a bold little devil, full of curiosity. The other was one of those mousey mice – shy and nervous. One day, the hamster got into their cage and bit the nearest one – turned it upside down and bit its stomach. It died almost immediately. And of course, it was the nervous mouse. I was certain of that before I even looked into the cage. But why should I have been so certain? After all, if the other mouse had been nearest, surely it would have died instead? Then I got to brooding about it. Was the shy mouse shy because it got used to being dominated by the other one? Supposing you could have put the shy mouse in a cage with an even shyer mouse? Would it develop dominant qualities? There was no way of finding out, because it was dead. But if both mice could be duplicated, you could try all kinds of combinations . . .'

He saw my expression of doubt.

'I suppose you're wondering whether you could really duplicate mice so they were identical?'

I said : 'No. That wasn't what I was thinking at all . . .'

We broke off while the waiter brought us apple pie and cream, and I arranged my thoughts in order. Then I tried to explain what was bothering me. I told him about Lyell's death, and my increasing interest in this problem of death; of my excitement over the last lines of his Leath lectures – that man has reached a turning point in his evolution; about my even greater excitement about Marks's experiments with old people . . . And now I wanted to attack the problem directly, not in this roundabout way, with experiments on mice and albino rats.

48

Littleway ate his pie and listened without saying anything. When I had finished, he said slowly:

'I agree with all you've said. But we've got to make a start somewhere. I think you're letting your impatience carry you away. I'm twenty years your senior, and I know things can't be done as easily as that.'

'But how about Marks's experiments? Surely *they're* a beginning?'

'In a sense. But Marks doesn't see them in the same way that you do.'

'No? Then how does he see them?'

'Don't misunderstand me. Of course he's interested in this problem of the "evolutionary leap". But at the moment, that's not his major interest. He's interested in the kind of values men need to achieve self-expression, and the kind of society that could give maximum self-realization to everybody. It's a question of social engineering, if you see what I mean.'

As we left the club, twenty minutes later, he was still trying to explain.

'Look, don't misunderstand me. I sympathize with your interests. But I can't see any practical way of testing whether your ideas are correct. It seems to me that all you can do at the moment is speculate. And that's all very interesting, but it's only a beginning . . .'

By this time, I was feeling too depressed to object. I could see that his mind was, in many ways, more acute than mine. He had a fine eye-to-business approach that reminded me of Lyell. So perhaps he was right, and I *was* being idealistic. I had to agree that I couldn't think of any way to test my ideas.

We parted at the corner of Piccadilly outside Swan and Edgars, I to return to the Museum, he to go to Hampstead, where he was staying with friends. As he was about to climb into the taxi, he said: 'Look, I've got things to do in London for the next week. Why don't you come up to Leicester with me when I go there, and spend a few days talking it over?'

I agreed immediately, and walked back to the Reading Room feeling more cheerful. If he was willing to allow me into his home, it meant that he couldn't have dismissed me completely as a crank and a time waster. So it was now up to me to answer his objections, to think out a way of turning my theories into experiments. But how . . . ?

The more I thought about it, the clearer it seemed to me

that Littleway was basically right. Unless I could discover some way of measuring the process of ageing with extreme precision, there would be no point in repeating Marks's experiments with old people. He had demonstrated that longevity depends on a sense of purpose. But surely that was obvious enough anyway? Frankl had made the same observation in a concentration camp during the war: that the prisoners with a sense of purpose lived longest. That left the major question: *what* purpose?

By the time I reached the museum, I was miserable and fatigued again. I had expected so much of my meeting with Littleway – and it seemed to be a dead end. I had been reading an article about certain old men in the Caucasus who often lived to be a hundred and fifty, and who attributed their longevity to goat's milk. Now it all seemed such nonsense that I couldn't finish it. I took Shaw's Collected Plays off the shelf, and re-read parts of *Back to Methuselah*. This deepened my depression. I could see why the politicians in the second play are so disappointed by the Gospel of the Brothers Barnabas. They wanted to be told how they could live to be three hundred. And all Franklin Barnabas can say is 'It *will* happen'. What is the good of believing it will happen, if you've no idea of how to make it happen?

By five o'clock I felt exhausted and bored. Instead of going straight back to my room, I walked down Charing Cross Road to the river, then wandered along the embankment to Black-friars Bridge. This got rid of the headache, but I developed a healthy thirst. So I stopped at a pub in Fleet Street, behind the Daily Express building, and drank a pint of mixed, and ate a sausage roll. The world began to seem more cheerful. I ordered another pint, and sat in my corner, watching the journalists coming in and out, feeling pleasantly detached. Then I started to brood on my problem again, and realized that it no longer seemed so insoluble. My present state gave me the clue. It was not merely that I was slightly drunk. The two pints of beer had only helped dissipate the heaviness left by my lunch. What was important was that my mind was glowing. I had a sense of hovering above the world – the bird's eye view. The beer had relaxed my body, so that it was no longer a nuisance, and my mind had gently detached itself, and was floating loose. The sense of urgency had vanished, for I no longer felt identified with my body. I felt identified with my mind – with ideas, with science, with poetry.

And then I saw the next great step in my argument. My sense of detachment made me think of Keats and the Ode to the Nightingale. I began to repeat the poem mentally, with a delicious sense of sadness and relaxation:

> My heart aches, and a drowsy numbness pains
> My sense, as though of hemlock I had drunk . . .

Thinking about the poem made me realize what Keats had done when he wrote it. He had been tired and depressed, then had started to think about the nightingale . . . and had ended with the sense of detachment, of floating above his personal problems, that I had also induced by drinking two glasses of beer. Now I saw that this is the essence of all poetry – particularly of the romantic poetry of the nineteenth century. Detachment . . . floating . . . freedom from one's personal little problems . . . the sense of wider horizons.

And suddenly, like a thunderbolt, the realization fell into my mind, so that I felt the roots of my hair stir with it. *Of course!* That was the whole meaning of the nineteenth century, of Wordsworth and Keats and Hoffmann and Wagner and Bruckner. Certain people are born evolutionary throw-backs, victims of an atavism, less than fully human. And certain people are the *opposite*. What could one call them? Evolutionary 'throws-forward'? Typically, our language contains no word to describe it. But the fact is as clear as daylight. *The romantics represented the next stage in man's evolution,* or at least, possessed one of its central characteristics – the ability to launch into these strange states of detachment.

Could anything be more obvious, once one had seen it? The previous century had been an age of solid, earth-bound men – Dryden, Swift, Pope, Johnson, Bach, Haydn – even Mozart. And then suddenly, for no apparent reason, you have an age of visionaries, beginning with Blake. But why? Why did Goethe and Coleridge and Wordsworth and Novalis and Berlioz and Schubert and Beethoven have these moments of pure exaltation, when man feels god-like? A 'development of sensibility'? How could it be called a development, as if the change had been gradual? No, it was a *leap* of sensibility, as if there had been a high wall between the eighteenth and nineteenth centuries . . .

So what caused it? Could there be some simple cause – perhaps even chemical? A comet composed of psychedelic drugs, breaking up in the earth's atmosphere and affecting the water supplies? Hardly likely. In any case, whatever the cause, there could surely be no doubt that the romantics and visionaries were presages of the future, heralds blowing trumpets to announce a new stage in human evolution – a new *power* in human beings – this power of detachment, of the 'god's eye view' instead of the 'worm's eye view'. At this point, I emptied my glass and went to the counter for another. And as the girl pulled it, I found myself wondering if my great 'insight' was not merely the result of good beer. But how could it be? Johnson and Boswell and Pope and the rest drank as much as we do – more, perhaps. So did Shakespeare and Ben Jonson. So why did we have to wait until the nineteenth century before men started having these clear glimpses of a *god-like state of detachment?* Why is there nothing of it even in Shakespeare, as great as he is? Or in Milton, with his noble idealism?

By the time I finished my third glass, I was distinctly drunk. But it made no difference. I knew that what I had seen was not the result of alcohol. It was as clear and obvious as any mathematical intuition. It would still be there in the morning.

I strolled back through Soho, and decided to stop for a meal. I ate lobster thermidor at Wheelers, with a glass of lager, then took a taxi back to my room. I kept bringing my mind back to my insight, and examining it again; each time, I felt the deep satisfaction of seeing that it was solid and real, no will-o'-the-wisp. The proof was that I could think about it clearly in spite of a state of exalted alcoholism. Then I found myself asking: What about Littleway? What would I say to him? And the answer was perfectly clear. I would explain my insight. If he understood it, well and good. If not, it hardly mattered. Let him grub away in his laboratory trying to produce identical twin rats. I had better things to do. If necessary, I could work alone. There were worse things in the world than being alone.

I woke in the morning with a slight headache, but without the feeling of guilt that usually accompanies my hangovers. And the insight *was* still there; if anything, it had deepened. I ate a hasty breakfast and hurried to the Museum – I kept a portable typewriter in the typing room. There I made my first attempt to get my ideas on to paper. I wrote in a state of intense excitement, so much so that I worked from ten in the morning until closing time – four forty-five – without a break for food. And all the time, I kept asking myself: 'What would Alec Lyell feel if he could read this over my shoulder?' I *suspected* he would find it unscientific; yet he would not be entirely unsympathetic. It was he who had introduced me to Poincaré's essay on Mathematical Creation, and to Hadamard's *Psychology of Invention in the Mathematical Field*. He was particularly fond of using the anecdote of Kekulé's dream of snakes biting their own tails that revealed to him the ring structure of organic molecules. He understood the importance of allowing the intuitions free rein . . . And so I wrote on for three days, producing about twenty-five pages a day.

There would be no point in summarizing this paper – it is available in several editions – but I must mention a few of its basic points. I began by quoting Littleway's words from the end of the Leath lectures. Then I spoke of Elgar and Delius, two composers of whom Lyell had been particularly fond. This was one of his few tastes that I found difficult to share during his lifetime; I found both composers feeble and sentimental. But after his death, they began to evoke a certain nostalgia, and I finally became an enthusiast. Then it struck me that they are both the perfect symbolic expression of romanticism. Both are suffused with the consciousness of beauty – and the sadness that goes with it. And how obvious this now seemed to me, how inevitable! Man is normally trapped in the trivialities of his everyday life, scarcely able to see beyond the end of his nose. But in certain moments of beauty, he relaxes; his soul expands; he sees distant horizons – of time as well as space. His mind overflows with beauty – for what is beauty but this sudden expansion of consciousness into other times, other places – the delightful relaxation of tension, accompanied by the realization *that man is not really himself unless he is contemplating immense vistas*? But at the same time, he becomes aware of the amount of tragedy and suffering that has gone into producing the world's great music and poetry. And the sense of tragedy is not due only to the thought of the men of genius who died too soon – Mozart, Schubert, Keats and so on. It is just as strong when we think of those who achieved complete self-expression – Leonardo, Haydn, Beethoven, Einstein. For it is the tragedy of man's smallness, his inadequacy, when compared to the greatness he can achieve in creativity.

Every day, as I wrote, new discoveries came to me. For

example, one of my most important insights came in the thoroughly prosaic setting of the men's lavatory outside the Reading Room. I find that when I am mentally tired, it becomes difficult to urinate if someone is standing close to me; their presence causes a tension that prevents the necessary relaxation. One day after this had occurred, it suddenly came to me : What is the mechanism that governs these physical functions? If I wish to open and close my hand, it seems to happen spontaneously, with no effort of will; in the case of our excretory functions, we are aware of a certain *time lapse* between 'giving the order' and the body's response to it. Then it struck me that this prosaic activity of ridding ourselves of waste matter is as mysterious as the sudden inspirations of the poet or the visions of mystics. Sometimes it happens easily and spontaneously, sometimes not. And then, with a flash of insight that made my hair tingle, I realized that the two processes are identical. The reason I find it difficult to urinate with someone beside me is simple; their presence *reminds me of my own existence*. I need to *forget myself* if my body is to function properly. It is obviously the same mechanism I had observed on the boat when I felt sick : power comes from 'other-ness'. Other-ness plays the same part in urinating as in producing poetry.

But the corollary was the most exciting part. *If* this is true, then could we not learn to produce great poetry as easily as to urinate? We would count a man seriously ill if he was unable to excrete or urinate. Why do we not count him ill when his mind is dull and uninspired? Mystical vision should be as natural to men as excreting. Then why is it not? Is this what the Christian church meant by its legend of original sin?

I wrote in a fever, for now I had glimpsed this possibility, it all seemed obvious. *Why* do men die? Death is not 'natural'. There was a time in the history of the earth when death did not exist – the time of primitive worms and amoebas. Instead of dying, the amoeba simply divides into two. It does not die, but its life is one of total stagnation. Death brought individuality into the world, and the struggle for existence. And this struggle brought evolution. If you place a gun against a man's head, he suddenly knows very clearly that he wants to live. Death is the gun placed against the head of all living creatures, the goad of evolution.

And then the solution came to me. If a bank robber points his gun at the clerk, he does not use it so long as the clerk does what he wants . . .

At this point in my writing, I could not go on; I was too excited. I needed to speak to somebody, or simply to walk. Since there was no one to talk to, I pulled on my coat and walked. It was a windy day with a chill in the air, and I wandered around Russell Square, my hands deep in my overcoat pockets, muttering to myself. Precisely . . . Death comes to those who ignore the gun, who have ceased to struggle. But how can this be true? So many people who love life die in agony . . . No, to say that death only comes to those who cease to struggle is untrue. The nature and direction of the struggle is all important. Chicago gangsters struggled violently enough and died violently. But they were only struggling for money and power.

The consequences of this thought seemed so revolutionary that I stopped and stared blankly in front of me. Scientists have always declared that morals and religion are the business of non-scientists; nature is immoral and irreligious, and science knows nothing about right and wrong. But if I was correct, then nature is as interested in right and wrong as the saints or moralists were. While man climbs the evolutionary stairway, he is immune from death. I remembered Bartok's *Miraculous Mandarin* ballet, in which the mandarin cannot be killed while his desire for the courtesan is still unsatisfied – although he has been stabbed repeatedly. I remembered the dogs that used to hang around Sneinton when Lady Jane's dog was in heat, apparently indifferent to wind and snow and the need for food, lying on the lawn for days on end. Why? Because sex is the most primitive form of the evolutionary appetite.

What is it, then, that destroys the evolutionary urge in man? The same thing, for example, that weakens a man's sexual urge after he is married – habit. Repetition and triviality. His horizons narrow. He descends from the mountain top into the valley. But *the will feeds on enormous vistas*; deprived of them, it collapses.

In that case, the first man to develop this evolutionary *faculty* for 'other-ness', for that superb contemplative detachment that I had experienced in the pub, would also be the first immortal: or at least, the first man with a real power to resist the erosion of death.

In that case, the problem was clear. Experiments on rats and all the rest might be useful and interesting; but they were not really relevant. What we needed to do was not to experiment on rats but on poets and philosophers. In fact, *on ourselves.*

A few days later, I met Littleway by appointment in the bar at St Pancras Station, and we took a train for Leicester. He looked tired, and I watched him drink three large Scotches quickly before we boarded the train. He admitted that he hated London – that meeting people and keeping appointments exhausted him. He sat staring out of the window as the train pulled out of St Pancras – we had a first class carriage to ourselves – and said gloomily: 'I suppose that's why people become scientists – they can't stand the chaos of the ordinary world.' I produced my manuscript and handed it to him; he started to push it into his briefcase, then changed his mind – obviously feeling that I would be disappointed unless he at least glanced at it. So he opened it, and read a few pages, looking as if he were sucking a lemon. I could imagine what he was feeling: 'What on earth's this speculative rubbish . . .' But he read on, and suddenly I noticed the signs of interest. He looked up at me, nodded briefly, then went on reading, this time more slowly. After a while, he put the manuscript on his knee, and stared out of the window again.

'It's an interesting idea . . .Worth saying. I've been thinking along similar lines myself, although . . .'

After another five minutes of brooding:

'You see, what you are suggesting is that these "value experiences" can actually *reverse* the direction of human metabolism.' I don't see how we could verify that or otherwise, but it sounds unlikely offhand. I mean . . . human metabolism is like entropy – it runs down. It's against all the laws of nature to think of it running in the opposite direction . . .'

'What about the rats and the diet of ecstasy?'

'Yes, but that's quite straightforward . . . I mean, everybody knows that your morale affects your health. But even if you learned to induce ecstasy at will, there'd be no way of actually measuring whether human beings cease to age so quickly.'

He looked at my essay again.

'And this list of mathematicians and philosophers who've lived to be eighty or so . . . I could cite you dozens who only reached the average age, or died young. How about Eddington – he died at sixty-two? And Jeans – he didn't reach seventy. I knew them both. Even Einstein only reached about seventy-five. Now if anyone ought to prove the truth of your theory, it should be Einstein . . .'

'I don't deny that. All the same, you can't ignore the statistics. It's statistically true that mathematicians live longer than other men.'

He read on for the next hour, and finished the essay. When he laid it down, he said:

'Yes, you've got something. You've got something. But I'm damned if I can think of any way to verify it. I can't think up a single experiment that would prove or disprove all you've said here. Now my experiments with mice . . .'

He described an experiment that a colleague had performed to discover whether dominance among mice was dependent on physical size. It wasn't. Several mice were put together in a cage, and the usual struggle for dominance began – tail biting and so on – until one of them emerged as the leader. He was not physically stronger than the others. This was verified after were then fed on a vitamin deficient diet until they starved to death. The dominant mouse lived the longest – although it was not physically stronger than the others. This was verified after repeated experiments. On the other hand, if the dominant mouse was removed from the others, and starved in a separate cage, it tended to die sooner. (The experiment seemed to me unnecessarily cruel, but I knew enough of the way a scientist's mind works not to say so to Littleway.) Obviously, the leader-mouse's 'morale' was raised by being among other mice that he dominated. Left alone in a cage, his morale sank.

I could see Littleway's point. The question of giving a man – or a mouse – purpose, is such a delicate one. It depends on so many different factors. You can't give him courage in the way you can give him chicken pox – by injecting him with the virus. It depends so much on his own will.

'All the same,' Littleway said, 'you've got something here. I'll get this copied and send it to Marks. He'll be fascinated. And perhaps he can think up some way of testing it.'

A car met us at Leicester station. As we drove out to Great Glen – seven miles away – he said:

'I should explain to you. My brother Roger also lives in the house – admittedly, in his own part. He's . . . er . . . quite unlike me. You'll find him rather odd. He's alright though . . .' He asked the man who drove us – who turned out to be the gar-dener-chauffeur: 'How is Mr Roger, Fred?'

'Oh, the same as ever. He don't alter much.' I sensed heavy irony in the comment.

Langton Place, Littleway's home, was half a mile beyond the village, an attractive place in red brick that had obviously been a vicarage. The lawns and flower beds were beautifully kept. It was smaller than Sneinton, although surprisingly roomy inside. Littleway pointed at a wing that had been built on to the south side of the house. 'My brother lives in there.'

The man who strolled across the lawn to meet us was at first sight unprepossessing – tall, with sandy hair and a freckled face that had no interesting features except a large nose. He wore dirty tennis flannels and sandals with a broken strap. He said, 'Hello, my dear fellow', and scarcely acknowledged his introduction to me. Then, without asking Littleway anything about his work or travels, he immediately launched into an account of some disagreement with a local farmer about a tree he wanted to cut down.

There was a cold supper waiting for us inside. Over the meal, I found myself thoroughly disliking Roger Littleway. He had a drawling, disconnected way of talking, with sudden silences that made it sound as if he couldn't be bothered to waste any more breath. The questions he asked his brother were about American manners and habits. 'Are the Americans really getting more materialistic and corrupt under Johnson?' Littleway said he had no idea – he didn't pay any attention to such matters – but he doubted it. Roger shrugged in a tired way, then said to me: 'Typical Henry. He never notices anything – just generalizes. If you asked him if it was snowing outside, he'd take out his slide rule and say "I doubt it".' Littleway smiled good naturedly, and said: 'That's not true, y'know.' He smiled in the same way when Roger said: 'I heard your Leath lectures, or, at least, two of them. Lot of old rubbish.' When Roger asked what I intended to do at Langton Place, I expected Littleway to put him off with some vaguery, but that was not his way. He began to explain my ideas in a careful, painstaking way, and I sat and writhed as I watched Roger's expression of boredom and amusement. And when Littleway had finished, Roger turned to me and said: 'It's complete nonsense of course. If ecstasy prolongs human life, the romantics ought to have lived longer than anybody. Do you know the music of Scriabin?' I said I did, and he looked surprised – in fact, made it insultingly obvious that he doubted

58

my word. 'Anyway, there's a case in point. The music's all ecstasy – he even called his third symphony *Poème d'Extase*.' 'It wasn't his third. It was his fourth,' I said. He looked startled, and for the first time, looked at me with a kind of respect. 'Of course, how stupid of me. Anyway, he died quite young. So did Delius – another composer who's all ecstasy. So did Wagner for that matter. No, your idea just doesn't hold water.' I disliked his superior manner so much that I decided not to argue; I only said that I thought there were special reasons that explained the life-failure in these composers. Roger said, yawning : 'Oh yes, I expect you can find special reasons to explain everybody who doesn't fit your theory.' In some ways, he reminded me of Aubrey Lyell, but without Aubrey's charm; instead, he was aggressive and boorish.

After supper, Littleway took me to see his laboratory at the bottom of the garden – a large concrete building. It was here that he had done the work on the brain that made his reputation after the war. I was fascinated by his electro-encephalograph, and by his own apparatus for measuring 'brain waves'. His work on inducing epileptic fits by means of the electronic stroboscope is now in general use in treating epileptics. His work on perception in dogs with brain injuries has also achieved classic status (although, again, I have to admit to feeling squeamish about some of his experimental methods). He demonstrated the encephalograph to me, and also showed me various visual illusions that he had been using in his more recent work in transactional psychology. At ten o'clock, we went back to the house, and Littleway said he was tired and intended to go to bed. I said I would probably do the same. But at this point, Roger reappeared and asked me if I would like to see his stereophonic equipment. It seemed hardly polite to refuse. Littleway said : 'Don't keep him too late – he's tired,' and went off to bed. I followed Roger Littleway through a green baize door into his own wing of the house.

The furniture was modern and expensive, as well as pleasant to look at. The paintings on the walls showed good taste – he told me they were mostly by Midlands artists. His sound equipment was magnificent – he played me the latest recording of *Parsifal* at top volume, while I lay back in a reclining armchair, feeling slightly foolish and nervous. After that, he played me the love scene from Debussy's *Pelléas*. He had the windows wide open, and the smell of flowers and freshly cut grass came

came in. I asked if the volume of the music wouldn't disturb anyone. He shrugged. 'Anyone who's kept awake by it should be grateful. Now if you were kept awake by an electric drill, that'd be different . . .' He stood staring out into the night. The moon had risen over the trees. 'Yes, it's very peaceful here , . . But as usual, the peace hides a great deal of nastiness . . .' 'You mean this local farmer?' 'Oh no. He's nasty enough, but there are far worse things. A village girl was raped and murdered last week only half a mile from here. Oddly enough, she was found in almost the same spot where another girl was murdered in 1895.'

He was now on to his favourite topic – vice and scandal, preferably mixed with sadism. For the next hour, he talked of little else, telling me about the history of the area in a way that made it sound like the brothel quarter of Port Said. Vicars and choir boys, masochistic scout masters, incestuous farm labourers, even a sadistic dairy maid who was finally kicked to death by a cow . . . I listened politely, completely bored, but in a way rather pleased that I had his measure. After this, he began to tell me about his collection of pornography, which he ended by showing me. It was certainly remarkable, although in a way it struck me as harmless enough – an edition of Burns's bawdy songs with woodcuts, a French edition of *Fanny Hill* with nineteenth-century illustrations that lacked realism, De Sade in the Olympia Press editions, and so on. Before I left, he even asked me cautiously if I would be interested in visiting a certain house in Leicester. I said politely that I found science more interesting than sex. He didn't seem offended – only smiled, and said something about Joseph and Potiphar's wife.

As I lay in bed, feeling slightly soiled, as if I had been in contact with a contagious disease, I suddenly remembered his comments about Scriabin and Delius. A sudden feeling of delight rose in me like a bubble, and the bad taste vanished from my mouth. Of course he'd think my ideas nonsense! What could be more disastrous than such a person living indefinitely? Charity was all very well . . . but the sooner the earth was rid of him, the better. He might have a decent side to his nature – most people have – but his interests were entirely trivial and personal and squalid.

I realize that this thought was not exactly new to me – I had even written something close to it in my essay. Yet this was one of those occasions when it seemed to explode like a flare, becoming the centre of my attention, completely self-evident. There is a perfectly good reason that most people die fairly early. Their presence would only encumber the earth. As people are today, there is no earthly reason why they *should* live beyond three score and ten. Two score and ten would suffice for most of them.

And then I saw clearly, for the first time, the tremendous moral issue involved in this whole business of longevity. I also faced its consequence. *If*, by any chance, I should ever discover any certain method of increasing human life, it would need to be kept a secret. Because the people who would benefit would be the wrong people, the power lovers, the bosses of giant corporations, the fat rich women with a holiday home in Cannes and another in Jamaica.

This statement might seem to contradict my earlier observation that evolution favours only those who have the genuinely disinterested urge to evolve. This is true, but only of evolution *left to itself*. Marks's experiment with old people, for example, had extended the life terms of most of them, and it could do the same for an over-tired business man or a self-indulgent millionairess suffering from nerves. While I had – and still have – nothing against over-tired businessmen, an instinct told me that the correct procedure here was to begin with a small and carefully selected group, and ignore accusations of élite-ism.

I fell asleep, thinking uneasily about a world in which the gangsters and dictators and sexual degenerates could live to be a hundred or so. But I was too tired to let it worry me.

Oddly enough, it was Roger Littleway who showed us the method we had been searching for. I had been at Langton Place for three days, and Littleway and I had some fruitful discussions. We were eating a light lunch in the laboratory when Roger strolled in without knocking. He said :

'I've heard something that might interest you . . .'

Littleway obviously thought it unlikely, but told him to sit down.

'I should have remembered this at supper the other night. There's a young chap over at Houghton who got his head in a combine harvester – pierced the top of his skull and went into his brain. Oddly enough, it didn't kill him, but he lost a lot of this sort of liquid . . .' He tapped the top of his skull.

'Cerebro-spinal fluid.'

'Yes. And ever since then, he's in a perpetual state of ecstasy. Can't do any work, but he has visions or something.'

Neither of us was immediately excited. It sounded promising, but we both had a feeling that it might turn out to be less interesting than it seemed. Roger said he'd heard about it in a pub. It was now two o'clock, half an hour before closing time. So I drove Littleway over to Houghton on the Hill, a small village on the Uppingham Road. Littleway went in alone – I didn't drink at lunch time – and came out a few minutes later. Roger had been accurate for once. The case was more or less as he'd described it, and the labourer, a youth named Dick O'Sullivan, lived in a cottage in the village with his wife. We went to the address, a farm labourer's cottage attached to a farm. A rather pretty girl opened the door. Littleway introduced himself, and asked if her husband was at home. She said he wasn't, but asked us in, obviously impressed by Littleway. It was a dingy place, although tidy enough, and we sat in threadbare armchairs, and asked her to describe the accident. The topic obviously depressed her, and she started to cry almost as soon as she began to talk. We got her to make tea, after which she relaxed. Littleway had a bedside manner that would have been worth thousands a year to a doctor.

She told us that her husband had had his accident nine months earlier, a few weeks after their marriage. Before this, he had worked for the local farmer at a good wage, and was known as one of the best workers in the village. His only weakness was for rough cider. One lunch time during hay making he had taken a pint too many. The accident occurred immediately after lunch. His head was trapped between the moving belt and a metal guard, and one of the spikes penetrated the top of his skull. They had turned the machine off immediately, in time to save him from becoming completely jammed in it, but it looked as if it would be impossible to move him without killing him. Finally, with some difficulty, they sawed through the metal guard, and gently removed him. He was unconscious, of course, and his hair was soaked with a mixture of blood and cerebro-spinal fluid – the liquid that cushions the brain, and in which it might be said to float. Rushed to hospital, he was unconscious for two days, and the doctors predicted that the brain injury would result in his death within a short period. In fact, he woke up perfectly cheerful, complaining only of a headache. There was a hole in the top of his skull and a two inch crack running down to his right ear. His family were allowed in to see him, but all were warned not to tell him the extent of the injury. To everyone's surprise, he seemed to know about it, even to the length of the crack. He then looked at his father and said: 'You think I'm going to die within a week, don't you?' His father had been told this by the doctor, but none of the others knew. It was not until afterwards, when they compared notes and talked with the nurse, that it struck them that there was something odd about it all. The nurse swore that she had not mentioned the crack in the skull, and no one had mentioned dying. Who had told him? His wife went to visit him that evening, and asked him. 'Nobody told me,' he said, 'they didn't need to. I just knew.' The next day, one of the other patients stopped by the room to talk to him. As he left, O'Sullivan remarked: 'Poor old boy.' 'Why?' the nurse asked, 'he's going out this afternoon.' 'He'll be dead by tomorrow.' That night, the man died of a cerebral haemorrhage.

Examples of his 'second sight' multiplied. But it seemed to function erratically. He accurately foretold that the father of one of the nurses would break his leg, yet failed to foresee that his own mother would almost die of influenza. He told a brother that he would win a large sum of money on the football pools; in fact, the brother won a small sum at the greyhound track. At other times, he simply had a vague premonition that something was about to happen to somebody, but he had no idea of whom or what.

An X-ray photograph showed that the brain had been penetrated by the spike, but the patient showed no sign of it. His memory seemed unimpaired, and his co-ordination remained excellent. But his temperament changed completely. He had been athletic and vital, given to displays of physical strength or skill, and to practical jokes. Now he became dreamy and lethargic. He had always been good tempered and generous; now he positively radiated benevolence and affection, so that several nurses burst into tears the day he left the hospital. He had been completely uninterested in any form of relaxation except sport; now he lost all interest in sport, but would sway about in a rapturous way if there was music on the radio.

After a four-month convalescence, the doctors pronounced him well enough to work, although he was warned that any

violent exertion might damage his brain. But he had no inclination for exertion of any kind. Work obviously bored him;
he did it badly, with no attempt at thoroughness. The farmer
liked him, but finally had to give him a job watching the sheep,
and bringing the cows in to milk; he seemed incapable of anything else. And now, his wife said, they had been told that the
cottage was needed for a new labourer, and that her husband
would have to accept a large reduction in pay if he was to work
for the same farmer. She was four months pregnant, and
frightened about the future.

Littleway cheered her. He told her that he wanted to study
her husband's case, and that he would pay him a wage and
give him a cottage to live in. He could have a job helping the
gardener after we had finished our studies. She was so delighted
that she wanted to rush to her mother-in-law's house to tell
him immediately. We drove her there, and went in with her.

Her husband was sitting in the garden in a deck chair. He
rose to greet us shyly. He had obviously been strikingly good
looking in a bucolic sort of way, but his face had become thin
and lined. He walked with one shoulder slightly higher than the
other – the only observable consequence of the accident. His
smile was absolutely charming – babylike and innocent. And
as we talked to him, he kept nodding as he stared past us, over
the stream that ran at the bottom of the garden. He gave me
the feeling that he was watching or listening for something that
we could not see or hear. Later on, I realized he was simply
listening to the sound of the water, which sent him into a kind
of ecstatic trance.

He made no kind of objection to our arrangement, and we
agreed to fetch him to Langton Place the next morning, and
arrange for the removal of his furniture later in the week. They
owed money in the village, and Littleway left enough to pay
the debts.

On our way home, he said:

'This confirms a theory of mine. I always suspected that the
pressure of the cerebro-spinal fluid on the brain helps to keep
us "down to earth". I heard of a man who drilled a hole in his
head because he wanted to stay permanently "high", and apparently it worked to some extent.'

'You think this farm labourer's in a more-or-less permanent
state of poetic ecstasy, then?'

'I'm not yet sure. But I suspect something of the kind. We

don't know enough about the human brain and its states of intensity. For example, I think that drugs like mescalin and LSD have some effect on the mid-brain, the part of the brain that gives is detachment – that enables us to see things down the wrong end of a telescope, as you put it. We pay for this detachment in the usual way – with a feeling of non-involvement, as if there's a pane of glass between us and the world. LSD destroys this detachment. Suddenly you're *there*, involved in things, and things suddenly have a sensual texture instead of the clean detachment of visual experience. I suspect that's all that's happened to this young man.'

'How about the second sight? Do you think it's genuine?'

'Oh, I'm sure it is. I've seen too much of it to be sceptical about such things. I had an Irish nurse who always knew when anyone in the family was going to be ill. I've seen Richardson's [the gardener's] dog stand with his hair on end, growling at a corner of the room where Mrs Richardson used to keep a pet spaniel in its basket until it got run over.'

'You think it was the ghost of the spaniel?'

'I don't really believe in ghosts. Perhaps simply the imprint of the spaniel's personality on the corner of the room. It was a jealous little creature . . . Most animals seem to possess second sight. I'm afraid the prevalence of it among the Irish hardly argues a very high place for them on the evolutionary ladder.'

'Couldn't it mean the opposite? After all, how do we know we shan't all develop telepathy one of these days?'

'Perhaps.'

After supper, we discussed in detail how we might conduct the investigation into Dick O'Sullivan's personality changes, and we spent some hours preparing for his arrival. The next morning, early, we drove back to Houghton, and fetched the O'Sullivans. He sat in the car on the way back, staring out of the window with the same child-like excitement I had noticed the day before, occasionally singing to himself. His wife was obviously happy, and their mood communicated itself to us. When we stopped the car, I went to the back door to let them out. Mrs O'Sullivan climbed out, but her husband sat still, staring with a rapt expression at the flower beds. Finally, as if hypnotized, he obeyed us, and followed us into the house. In the hall, he shivered suddenly and said: 'Somebody died here.' 'A lot of people,' Littleway said, 'the house is very old.' 'No, here,' O'Sullivan said, pointing to the floor. Roger, who came out of the other room, said: 'There's a legend that a man was killed by two burglars over in that corner.' O'Sullivan said dreamily: 'Yes, two men did it. They hit him with sticks weighted with lead. But it was just here. His wife saw it from the stairs.'

Roger was looking with interest at Nancy O'Sullivan. At this moment, her husband seemed to notice him for the first time, and he immediately drew away. I was watching him closely, and it was an interesting gesture – far too swift and immediate to be the result of some train of thought; it was more like a man snatching his hand away from a dog that snaps at him. Roger noticed it too, but he pretended not to. He said: 'Have you had breakfast? There's still plenty left. Do come in.' Nancy O'Sullivan was obviously charmed (I could never understand why); her husband responded to the friendly tone, but obviously mistrusted Roger on sight. We all went into the breakfast room. There was a bookcase in one corner, which contained several novels and some American paperbacks with bright covers. Instantly, Dick forgot his dislike for Roger, and rushed over to stare at them. He said: 'Gor, ain't they pretty,' but his voice was almost a whisper. His wife said: ''E likes colours. 'E stands and looks at my old party dress sometimes just like that.' Littleway and I were looking at the expression on Dick's face; we both had the same thought: that we had found someone who could plunge into ecstasy at a moment's notice. Here was a Wordsworth without the power of self-expression, a Traherne who could only say 'Gor, ain't it pretty'.

Littleway's published account of our six months with Richard O'Sullivan has become a classic of parapsychology, and it would be pointless to repeat its details here. But I must admit that I would find it difficult to describe our observations at any length; I look back on it as a defeat.

What Littleway fails to mention in his book is that Roger seduced Nancy before she had been in the house a week. Her husband – whom we called Dick from the beginning, as you would call a child by its Christian name – knew about it. His attitude was strange. I don't think he minded her being unfaithful in the least.

If one spent any time with him, it was impossible to doubt that he was 'high' most of the time. This made him a little tiresome as a companion, like a drunk. Everything delighted him. It obviously cost him an effort to answer our questions and perform the small tasks we set him. If we pressed him with questions, a stubborn, petulant expression would settle on his face; then suddenly he would shout 'Look', and jump to his feet to point at a butterfly that had settled on a flower outside the window. At other times, he would sink into a kind of trance for hours, looking completely contented.

Our experiments were designed to test whether this state of contentment made any difference to his general health. Before his accident, he had suffered from asthma and winter colds, but had otherwise been exceptionally healthy. Since the accident, the asthma had disappeared completely, and he seemed almost immune from colds. We decided to begin our experiments by giving him a cold. Littleway procured cold germs from the Birmingham Research Centre, and we injected him with a fairly strong dose. Within twelve hours, his eyes and nose were streaming. We gave him ordinary treatment – aspirin, vitamin C, hot milk – and the cold disappeared in nine days. He took the cold very much in his stride; it seemed to make no difference to his appreciation of music and vivid colours. He enjoyed hearing music played very loud – we used Roger's stereo equipment for this – but would complain of a headache after a while, and become very pale.

We learned from his mother that he had always been happy at Christmas time. He loved Christmas cards with pictures of snow and robins and mail coaches. He loved the sound of bells, and his favourite 'Christmas carol' was a cheap popular tune called 'Snowy White Snow and Jingle Bells' with words as nauseatingly sentimental as its title. He was particularly fond of a toy made of a glass globe containing imitation snowflakes in water, with a small cottage and some trees; when shaken, the snow seemed to fall gently around the cottage.

Our first experiments paralleled those that Marks had done with his alcoholics and the old people. A room in the house was turned into a cinema. When Dick's second cold was at its height – so that he had to blow his nose every few minutes – we gave him a cinema show built around the idea of Christmas – scenes of gently falling snow against a dark blue sky, cottages with lighted windows, Christmas trees, cherubs in white night-dresses singing 'Holy Night', and finally; a gramophone record of 'Snowy White Snow and Jingle Bells'.

I found the whole thing more moving than I had expected – since I had arranged most of the show myself. But I was quite unprepared for the effect on Dick. It was light enough to watch his reactions closely. If his body had been made of sugar, it would have dissolved on the floor. I could almost see waves of emotion flowing over him, until he was obviously totally unaware of his surroundings. The expression on his face became so completely innocent that I felt obscurely ashamed to be manipulating his feelings in this way. It was an interesting sight – I wish we had filmed his reactions. It was like watching time flow backward, watching an adult turn into a child – as, in a film of Wilde's *Dorian Gray*, I had seen the hero shrivel and become wrinkled and old. There was an effect of magical transformation. It brought back my own childhood with such intensity that I became incapable of accurate observation for five minutes or more. It was all I could do to prevent myself from betraying my emotion by sniffing. Finally, when I could see clearly again, I found that Dick himself was crying, so that it must have been impossible for him to see the screen. I blew my nose hard before the film came to an end. Littleway switched on the lights. Dick sat completely still for perhaps five minutes. Then he seemed to become aware of us. He jumped up, grasped my hand and Littleway's in a convulsive grip that hurt, and said with great conviction: 'You're both good men. You're good men.' It cost me an effort to produce a thermometer to take his temperature. Predictably, his temperature had increased.

But in the morning, the cold had almost disappeared. It seemed incredible. It should have reached its third stage – of hoarse voice, sore throat, the thickening of nasal mucus, and so on. Instead, it was as if the clock had been put forward several days.

Twenty-four hours later, it had disappeared completely.

We restrained the impulse to congratulate one another. It could have been a fluke. Perhaps the cold germs had been weak. Perhaps he had built up a resistance from the last cold. The experiment would have to be repeated in another week or so. In the meantime, we pressed on with other experiments. I think neither of us had any doubt that it was no fluke or accident. I had seen Dick's face during the film show, and after. He had re-lived childhood innocence, perhaps with an intensity never actually achieved in childhood, and the result was a total certainty of universal goodness, complete affirmation. Any Christian Scientist would have predicted the result, the immediate recovery from the cold.

During the next three months, Dick allowed us to experiment on him with colds, nettle rash, mumps and German measles. The results of the first experiment were confirmed – up to a point. We discovered that the 'value experiences' we induced also had the effect of exhausting him; they left him emotionally drained. This meant that physical exhaustion might counteract the effect of the emotional intensity. Even so, the results were spectacular. We were constantly in touch with Marks, who was wildly excited, and wanted both of us to fly to New York to read a paper to the American Psychological Association. Littleway declined, saying the experiment was only half completed.

Towards the end of August, Dick became listless, and began to complain of headaches. We decided to suspend the experiments for a few weeks. We had been using a Black Room to hasten his recovery in between experiments; he would sleep for thirty or forty hours in the total silence and darkness, and wake up refreshed. Now the Black Room seemed to have no effect. We both wondered if some germ could be lingering in his system. On 10th September, we took him to the Leicester City General Hospital for a thorough physical check up.

An X-ray revealed that he was suffering from a brain tumour. We were both shattered, although the surgeon assured us that, from the size of the tumour, it must have been present before we began the experiments. We both had the same suspicion – that the experiments that had accelerated his recovery from colds and measles had also accelerated the development of the tumour.

Littleway has written about the next six weeks in his book, but I must confess I find the subject too painful. I find it hard to write even this brief account. I was fond of Dick, of course – we both were; but I had also been certain that he was the proof of my theory : It had all seemed perfect. Because of his accident, he was in a perpetual V.E. state. There was no need to give him mescalin or LSD. All our experiments confirmed Marks's results. Illnesses that should have taken weeks to throw off were thrown off in days. I used to find myself staring at him as he walked around the garden, wondering if we could devise some means of actually measuring his metabolism, to prove that it had been slowed down – that it was actually reversed in his 'value experiences'. And I suppose there were the usual daydreams about being the saviour of the human race and so on. Now it all dissolved. According to my theory, a brain tumour should have been impossible. I believed – as I still do – that cancers are the result of a sudden drop in vitality that allows a certain part of the human body to proliferate as a separate organism – provided some other irritant – a bruise, for example – can give it a hold. 'Value experiences' have the effect of raising the vitality – how otherwise could they hasten recovery from illness? In that case, how could value experience lead to cancer? It was absurd, totally self-contradictory – unless my whole theory was nonsense.

I stayed on at Langton Place until Dick died in late October, but we did no work. Littleway, of course, was less depressed than I was. He felt that the results of our experiments were important in spite of the brain tumour, and was inclined to accept that the tumour was the result of the original accident. He also pointed out that a cancer is of a completely different nature from a virus illness. I was unconvinced. I knew the report that recognized the connection between low vitality and cancer; it pointed out that even among young people – students, and so on – cancer tends to be associated with long-term depression or fatigue.

Roger Littleway wan't in the least surprised when he heard about the tumour. He didn't actually say 'I told you so', but one day he took the trouble to write out a list of men of genius who have died of cancer, tuberculosis, and so on. He asserted that experiences of ecstasy, far from increasing man's vitality, tend to lower it and make everyday life intolerable. Delius, the poet of ecstasy, had died blind and paralysed. Ramakrishna, the Hindu mystic, was able to induce 'samadhi' – ecstatic value-experiences – merely by repeating the name of the Divine Mother, yet he died of a cancer of the throat.

When not working, Littleway was a fairly heavy drinker; he could absorb most of a bottle of whisky in an evening without showing any effect. I also began to drink rather too much again. We visited Dick in hospital several times a week, and I always found it an ordeal. He was as gentle as ever, and obviously felt strongly attached to myself and Littleway. This was harder to bear than reproaches. In mid-October he went into a coma, and was seldom fully conscious after that. Littleway suggested that there was no point in visiting him, since he was no longer able to recognize us, and was paralysed from the waist down. By this time, I had entered the masochistic phase, and my increasing detestation of Roger Littleway increased the emotional unbalance. Under the guise of friendly concern, he gave me lectures about the importance of being a human being instead of a thinking machine, etc. Like most confused and weak people, he felt that his own messy emotional life was the human norm, and that clear thinking was a dangerous form of *hubris*. Normally, this kind of stupidity would have left me untouched; it would have been dismissed automatically as soon as I settled down to work. The active human mind was intended to flow like a river; and, like running water, it has no time to stagnate. Emotional poisons – feelings of humiliation, envy, detestation – are carried away by the flow. If this flow is dammed, sickness and stagnation follow quickly. This is what happened to me in the two months Dick took to die. Roger Littleway encouraged Nancy to believe that our experiments had caused the tumour, and she became openly hostile; her attitude increased my depression because I suspected she was right.

Writing about defeat bores me, so I shall hurry over the events of the next week or so. Dick died under drugs; I left Langton Place and went back to the cottage in Essex. During November I saw almost no one. Groceries were delivered to the cottage. It rained continuously, and one night a storm broke in the wooden shutters and flooded the downstairs rooms. I felt completely emotionally exhausted, drained of feeling, and found it hard to believe I could ever again feel interest in anything.

In late November, I hit rock bottom. I can remember staring at the sea, and wondering how long it would take to drown. I walked on the beach one grey, icy afternoon, and decided that I lacked the courage to walk into the sea. It seemed absurd that something in me obviously clung to life, and yet I felt a total lack of interest in my own existence. The damage to the cottage was repaired sooner than I had expected; but when I looked at the sitting room after the windows and shutters had been replaced, I felt only indifference. What did it matter whether it was six inches deep in sea water or dry? Its dryness gave me no pleasure.

But the day after this, I felt a renewal of interest in my essay on longevity. I read it through – in a desultory kind of way –

71

and tried to reason out where I had gone wrong. I couldn't; but the re-reading had made me feel that I was not entirely wrong.

That afternoon – it was the 2nd of December – was sunny, and the sea was fairly calm. I had turned the settee to the window, and I was half-lying on it, my back propped by a pillow, with a blanket over my leg. I remember that the oil fire made a gentle but irregular roaring noise, which had irritated me in the depth of my depression. I stared at the sea, trying to understand where I had gone wrong in my essay. Then I looked across the room at the bookcase. The sunlight shone on the backs of the books. They were mostly American paperbacks, in bright colours – classics of science, a few volumes on music, some history and archaeology, a volume of Whitehead's *Adventure of Ideas*. The sunlight on the bright paper covers produced a sense of euphoria for a moment, but it vanished almost immediately.

The sunlight hurt my eyes, so that I closed them, and lay back further on the pillow. The sight of the books caused an after-image on the inside of my eyelids. And then, in a flash, I saw with perfect clarity the solution of the problem that had almost driven me to suicide. It was as if I had seen to the inner-nature of the books, and understood that they were not books at all, but a part of the living universe. Each one of them was a window on 'other-ness', on some place or time not actually present.

An immense, soothing feeling of relief flowed over me that made my eyes moist. The sense of peace seemed infinite. I slipped into a light sleep, but it was so light that, in a sense, I continued to think; or rather, my subconscious mind repressed for so long, continued to feed thoughts and insights to my conscious levels.

I must explain this clearly, for it is the core of all I have done and thought.

First of all, I saw with perfect clarity why the 'value experience' does not guarantee long life, or even immunity of illness. *It is totally unimportant.* It is like a flash of lightning. But what is important is not the lightning, but *what you see by it.* If lightning explodes in empty space, it illuminates nothing. If it explodes over a mountain landscape, it illuminates a great deal. In the same way, if I experience a sense of total affirmation after a good dinner, or on the point of sleep, it is merely a pleasant feeling, a kind of emotional orgasm that illuminates nothing but itself. If I experience it when I am wide awake and intensely excited, I glimpse whole vistas of reality. It is this reality that is important, not the light by which I see it.

What was lacking in Dick O'Sullivan – as well as in Delius and Scriabin and Ramakrishna – could be defined in one word: will. They accepted the value-experience as good in itself.

The most difficult thing to explain is the insight about books, because they are too familiar. Every literate person has lived with books from the age of two. So it sounds a truism to say that books are man's most spectacular spiritual achievement. It is nevertheless true. Man has learned to conquer time through the written word. It explains the accelerated evolution of our civilization. After all, civilizations evolve through the agency of extraordinary men. Who can doubt that the great milestones in human history were the work of single extraordinary individuals: the discovery of fire, of the wheel, of smelting iron, of living by husbandry rather than hunting? Or the extraordinary individual might be a teacher or prophet, a Socrates, a Mohammed, a Savonarola. But before the invention of printing, the influence of such an individual was small. If, like Savonarola, he preached from a pulpit, only the people in his own city benefited much, and the few who could travel to hear him. The invention of books suddenly meant that the influence of the extraordinary individuals could be spread over the whole nation or civilization. Like radio or television, it was fundamentally a method of broadcasting. Before printing, the Master had a few disciples who benefited from his teaching; now *anyone* could benefit who was capable of grasping its essence. 'Mute inglorious Miltons' could study under Homer and Virgil. Books represented the release of immense spiritual resources in mankind just as oil derricks represented the release of physical resources in the world.

Through books, man has conquered time. The insights of poets and saints are still alive. For two million years, man ascended the evolutionary ladder slowly and painfully, changing hardly more than the ape or the horse. With the invention of books, he took a gigantic step into the realm of the gods.

This, I saw clearly, was the direction of man's evolution – from the animal towards the god. And the sign of that evolution is deeper knowledge, broader consciousness, a god-like grasp of distant horizons. The value experience is all very pleasant, but it is not a uniquely human experience. Every animal can experience ecstasy. That is not the point. But think of the difference between the ecstasy of a baby and the ecstasy of a great scientist or philosopher. The ecstasy of the scientist illuminates mountain ranges of knowledge acquired over a lifetime.

I woke up and stared at the ceiling. It was as if I had just recovered from a dangerous illness, from a delirium in which I had thought and said meaningless things. But now, at least, I could see the answer. Of course the value experience is important – just as light is important if we are to see. But I had been experimenting with value experiences for their own sake. Naturally, they had achieved nothing. In fact, they had probably ended by acting as an irritant on the organism.

I could have laughed at my own naïvety, my stupid inability to see the obvious. Dick had been an excellent worker before his accident. After the accident, he was unable to concentrate, unable to focus his mind. He had become capable of 'value experiences' at the cost of slipping back towards the animal. It had not been an evolution but a 'devolution'. But what distinguishes the greatest men is precisely that ability to focus, to concentrate the attention. So my search for longevity through the value experience was a waste of time.

There is one more point I must explain if the reader is to follow the really important steps in my search. It is necessary for me to explain something quite simple about the nature of human consciousness.

Ever since Husserl, we have realized that consciousness is 'intentional' – that you have to *focus* it or you don't see anything. Everyone is familiar with the experience of glancing at his watch while he is having a conversation, and simply not taking it in. You certainly see the face of the watch and the position of the hands; but you don't see the time. In order to grasp what time it is, you have to make that act of concentrating, of focusing. And this is true of all perception, and in fact, of all mental acts. Our language tends to cover up this obvious fact. We say 'Something *caught* my attention', as if your attention were a mouse walking into a trap; but it isn't. It is much more like a fish, that has to *bite the hook* before it can get 'caught'. It has to go halfway. We talk about 'falling in love', and the phrase is deceptively simple, like 'as easy as falling off a log'. In fact, it is extremely difficult to fall off a log; you would practically have to fling yourself off. And you have to fling yourself into love too; you don't fall.

All that is straightforward enough and most philosophers now recognize its importance (with the exception of the English, who play at philosophy as if it were cricket). But there is something else about consciousness which is even more important than its intentionality. And no one had ever recognized this.

Consider what happens if you try to read when you are drunk, or just very tired. You can focus on individual phrases and sentences, but you still don't understand what you are reading. Because the moment your eyes have roamed across a sentence, they forget it, they lose their grasp on it. So although you understand each sentence perfectly well, you can't grasp what is being said. Your mind is like a pencil-flashlight beam that travels over the page. But as it illuminates each new sentence, the rest of the page falls into total darkness.

Now think what happens when you read the page with understanding. Your mind still travels over each word like a flashlight beam, but it also continues to grasp the meaning of the sentences that have gone past. It is as if your mind *had two hands*, one of which picks up new meanings as it travels over the page, the other one of which continues to grasp the old meanings of previous sentences. And one hand keeps passing the meanings back to the other, so it can leave itself free to pick up more new meanings.

When you are drunk, your consciousness tries to work with only one hand. So it loses the meanings as fast as it picks them up.

Now a simple way of expressing all this would be to say that consciousness is *relational*. When it is working properly, it keeps relating new meanings, which it picks up with the right hand, to the old meanings, which are held in a bunch in the left hand.

Perhaps my meaning will be much clearer if I say that a healthy consciousness is like a spider's web, and you are the spider in the centre. The centre of the web is the present moment. But the *meaning* of your life depends on those fine threads which stretch away to other times, other places, and the vibrations that come to you along the web. You can imagine Wordsworth standing on Westminster Bridge, the threads of his mind stretching to distant corners of the universe and his own life.

This recognition that consciousness is not only intentional

but *relational* enables us to grasp the nature of all so-called mystical or poetic experiences. Normally, your consciousness is like a very small spider's web; its threads don't stretch very far. Other times, other places, are not very real to you. You can remember them, but they aren't realities. And our lives are turbulent, like living in a strong wind, so the web gets broken pretty frequently. But sometimes, the wind drops, and you manage to create an enormous web. And suddenly, distant times and distant places become realities, as real as the present moment, sending their vibrations down into your mind.

But such experiences are not really mystical or unusual. *All* consciousness is 'web-like', rational, but the web is usually smaller.

The consequences of this are tremendous. It means that the 'visions' and ecstasies of the mystics are perfectly normal, and that any human being is capable of experiencing them. It also means that the mystic's sense of affirmation and goodness is based upon a *real* perception, not an illusion. The pessimistic philosophers who find life meaningless are simply living in a very small web. What Sartre calls 'nausea' is living on a web that is so tiny that it can hardly be called a web at all. Nausea is meaningless because it has no threads stretching elsewhere. But even 'nausea' is a very small web. All consciousness is web-like in structure; otherwise, it would not be consciousness; it would be unconsciousness.

This insight connected up directly with what I had realized in the pub in Holborn. At this stage in his evolution, man is *naturally developing* a far larger 'web'. So poets, philosophers, scientists are always having these moments in which they grasp enormous meanings. These moments of meaning are also moments of tremendous affirmation, a clear recognition of what human evolution is all about.

This also explains, of course, why, when the romantic's 'vision' is over, and he comes down to earth again, the 'meanings' no longer seem to be there. Of course not. He can still *see* them, but they no longer seem tremendous or important. He is only seeing them, not touching them. The thread has broken. This also explains one of the oldest criticisms of mystical vision – that when the mystic can put it into words, it is perfectly commonplace, something we all know all the time. Of course it is. We 'know' it, but it isn't *real* to us.

All of this did not come to me in a sudden rush, that afternoon on 2nd December. The core of the insight came, but the rest took longer to develop. That didn't matter. What was so important was that I now *knew* that my theory was correct. Dick's death proved rather than disproved it. Evolution doesn't particularly favour 'value experiences' or ecstasies. But it *does* favour 'web-like consciousness'.

So if I could discover a way of increasing the 'relational' quality of consciousness, then I had solved my problem of human longevity.

I sat down and wrote Littleway a twenty-page letter. It was not very coherent, but it said all the important things, said them clearly.

As if to confirm my belief beyond all doubt, I began to have intense experiences of 'other-ness' over the next few days. I would suddenly recall Aubrey's place at Alexandria, or my home at Hucknall, with tremendous vividness, as if I had been transported by a time machine for a few seconds. Proust describes such a moment in *Swann's Way* when his mother gave him a 'petite madeleine', and he dipped it in his tea – sudden total remembrance of another time and place. But Proust, absorbed in his misery and hypochondria, lacked the key to such moments. I was convinced that I now had the key.

Littleway wrote back a few days later. He was as interested as I expected, although perhaps less excited. What he said was: 'In that case, it looks as if we have to start working with a different kind of subject. Ideally, we need an Einstein or a Whitehead . . . I wonder if Bertrand Russell would be interested?'

But it seemed less simple to me. I was not thinking of how my theories could be tested in the laboratory. If I was right, then man was approaching pretty close to the conquest of time. I wanted to know exactly how he could cross the threshold into the 'promised land'.

It is worth mentioning, by the way, that all signs of my suicidal depression had vanished within twelve hours of my 'dream'. Most of our assumptions about illness – particularly mental illness – are profoundly mistaken. If our physical batteries run low because of a long illness, they may take weeks to re-charge. With the mental batteries, re-charge is nearly instantaneous once the creative drives are re-established.

This was perhaps the most exciting time of my life – in spite of the remarkable experiences that I shall describe later. For I knew I was close to a break-through, and I *suspected* that it would be the most important break-through in the history of the human race.

It also seemed to me that I now had pretty clear indications of the direction my physical researches should pursue: into the human brain. For this was where the secret lay.

Consider: this brain of ours is more amazing than the largest electronic computer ever built. It is true that our largest computer today can perform a million operations per second. It can solve in a second mathematical problems that would take a great mathematician ten years. In spite of this, the human brain is a far more complex computer; you would need to build a computer the size of Westminster Abbey *and* the Houses of Parliament to rival the human brain in complexity. The largest computers at the moment have a quarter of a million transistors (and at the time I am writing about 60,000 was the maximum). The brain has billions of neurons, the basic unit of the nervous system. What is more, it seems to be able to operate on several levels, or in several dimensions at once, while a computer can only pursue one path at a time – this explains the human capacity for creativity.

However, let me emphasize: the brain is not merely a magnificent computer. It is alive. You could not build a computer, even the size of New York, that possessed freedom of choice. For man's freedom is really a misnomer; what makes him free is the evolutionary urge which drives him upward, and which therefore provides a *reason* when he is confronted by choices. To build a computer responding to an evolutionary urge (which wouldn't be too difficult – it would merely need a tendency to self-complexification built into its organization) to respond, that is, with all the subtlety and complexity of the human brain, you would probably need a computer the size of the moon.

Now different areas of the brain control different functions – sight, hearing, muscular movement, etc. There is even an area of the hypothalamus which controls sexual orgasms, and can flood the body with pleasure. (We later did some interesting experiments with it, which finally disposed of the old argument that man's highest ideal is pleasure. I found that even with the ability to stimulate overwhelming fits of pleasure in myself as often as I liked, the basic desire for knowledge remained unabated, and the pleasure finally became rather a bore.) But, in spite of our considerable knowledge of the brain, we still know very little in comparison to what we don't know. From the point of view of most of our everyday functions, from walking to writing poetry, a brain *one tenth* our present size would suffice. So why do we possess the other nine tenths?

There is also the problem of the brain waves. The brain has a basic rhythm, called the alpha wave, which runs on most of the time, like the engine of a car in neutral. When you start looking at something, this stops, as when you put the car into gear. In the black room, it also stops, but for a different reason; it is like turning off the ignition in your car. This is serious. There are also beta waves, of a higher frequency, delta waves, which are slower, and a rare wave labelled theta. These are connected with the pleasure mechanism in that they stop during pleasure, intensify in frustration.

But we know almost nothing about the actual relations of these waves to our most important mental activities. We know that delta rhythms are associated with sleep and disease; beta rhythms with tension and the activity of the will, but very little else. We know that sexual activity is associated with the hypothalamus, and that nearly all the higher human functions – self-control, imagination, and so on – are associated with the frontal lobes, which appears to be the control room of the brain.

What I now wanted to know was fairly simple, and yet incredibly difficult to investigate. The animal brain is relatively simple; it is a computer that is meant to deal mostly with present experience. 'The nearest creature to us, the chimpanzee, cannot retain an image long enough to reflect on it,' says Grey Walter in his classic on the brain. Animals have memory, of course, but it operates on a primitive, instinctive level. The human memory is on an altogether different level. For example, is there anyone who has not imagined some painful accident – trapping his fingers in a door, or something – and winced involuntarily? We have this curious ability to respond strongly to purely imaginative stimuli.

For example, I have mentioned that alpha rhythms cease when you start to look at things. They also cease if you *imagine* something vividly. Animals and small children do not possess this capacity. Like self-control, it is something developed slowly and painfully.

So what happens to the human brain as it develops this

capacity to use imagination? If the brain is a computer, what kind of circuit constitutes imagination?

I knew that if I could answer this question, then I had almost solved my problem. If the hypothalamus can be stimulated electrically to provide pleasure, then it should also be possible to 'boost' the brain's higher functions, to intensify the imagination.

Let us be clear about this problem. You may wince when you imagine trapping your fingers, but it only lasts a fraction of a second. You cannot sustain the thought for long. In the same way, you may try to recall your holiday last year, and manage to conjure up a few of its sights and smells with great vividness. But again, you can't sustain it. Imagination seems to have very limited powers.

On the other hand, there is one respect in which human imagination can reproduce some of the most important effects of a physical stimulus: I mean in the area of sex. A man can imagine getting into bed with a pretty girl, and he can carry his fantasy to the point of a sexual orgasm.

No animal can masturbate without the actual presence of a sexual stimulus. Monkeys masturbate a great deal in a zoo (although less so in their natural surroundings). Placed alone in a separate room, they eventually cease to masturbate; they need at least the visual stimulus of another monkey. A picture of another monkey, no matter how realistic, produces no effect.

And so, paradoxically enough, the ability to masturbate is one of the highest functions man has yet developed. It is the one function in which imagination can *sustain* the effects of physical reality.

The mental activity involved in imagination is the highest form known to man. You might suppose that his reasoning faculty is higher still. This is untrue. There have been many mathematical prodigies who could do incredibly complex calculations at a great speed – Vito Mangiamele calculated the cube root of 3,796,416 in a minute and a half (it is 156). Most of these prodigies have been of average or below-average intelligence, and many of them lost their powers in later life.

Now if my theory was correct, man has been struggling to develop a new level of imaginative power in the past two centuries. And he is succeeding to a remarkable degree. If we could understand the mechanism of imagination, the answer was already within our grasp. For example, suppose the answer should prove to be that imagination is associated with a power to suppress the brain's alpha rhythms. (We know that these rhythms cease in intense mental activity.) We might then concentrate upon methods of aiding the brain to suppress them – perhaps through the use of certain drugs, or certain stimulants, or even electrical methods.

I knew *this* was not the answer. Alpha rhythms are the result of inattention, of the brain 'ticking over'; they are an effect, not a cause.

No, the answer, I was certain, must be associated with 'relational consciousness'. Our normal consciousness is a thin searchlight beam. But moments of intensity, moments of crisis, break this *habit*, and give us a glimpse of broader meaning, so that the searchlight beam widens and illuminates a wider area. These are Marks's 'value experiences'.

I remembered an example that had happened to a friend of Alec Lyell's. The man had a series of minor misfortunes that made him apathetic and depressed. One day, he came home and found a note saying that his wife had left him. He was plunged into despair, and began to think of suicide. Automatically, he switched on the television set to watch the news – and learned that a small Californian town, in which he and his wife had spent part of their honeymoon, had been totally destroyed by an explosion. A dynamite truck with a trailer had skidded on an icy road and jack-knifed, so its two halves clapped together. The explosion wiped the town and its inhabitants off the face of the map. Shattered by the enormousness of the catastrophe, Lyell's friend totally forgot his own troubles. When he remembered them, ten minutes or so later, he thought: 'Oh, *that* – how trivial.'

The mechanism is obvious. The crisis – even though it did not directly concern him – acted on some cerebral hormone, snapping him into a state of wakefulness. He saw things as a whole, and saw that his personal problem was small enough compared to what goes on in the world every minute of the day.

This is the kind of over-all vision that the scientist and the poet both strive to achieve. If we could achieve control over that 'mental hormone' that breaks habit patterns, we would be on the verge of becoming supermen. For the chief human problem is our slavery to the trivial, which we can only break by rather dubious methods – alcohol, drugs, violence, and so on. Yet our need to escape the trivial is so compulsive that we prefer to commit crimes or start wars rather than remain bored.

Could I solve the problem? Even at this early stage, I had a very definite idea – a kind of premonition – that I could.

Littleway had returned to America in the January of 1969, so I had to work alone for the time being. However, he allowed me to use his library. I spent several weeks in Great Glen absorbed in books on the brain. They were mostly fairly advanced text books, and I had to rely on the Leicester Public Library for simpler works. The more I read, the more dissatisfied I became. Brain physiology has been a science ever since Hartley suggested that consciousness depends upon brain 'vibrations', in 1749. Yet our ignorance is still enormous.

The outline of my theory grew steadily clearer, but it was intensely difficult to fill in its details. I could see clearly that 'value experiences' are merely moments in which man becomes fully conscious of what he already possesses. For example, a man threatened with death suddenly becomes aware of how deeply he wants to live. But otherwise, habit patterns can be so strong that he can commit suicide without 'snapping out of' his narrow and limited state of self pity.

Now the essence of my theory was this: *there is no such thing as 'normal death'; there is only suicide*. A man does not die of 'old age'. He gets fixed in old habit patterns until his capacity for 'other-ness' is destroyed, and then he allows himself to sink into death.

If this was true, the consequence was obvious. If man could learn to 'snap out of' habits at a moment's notice, to make his brain respond as if someone were pointing a gun at his head, then he would never lose touch with the springs of life deep in the subconscious, and he would live indefinitely. The body does not die; cells reproduce themselves indefinitely. Even the brain itself responds to this will to live. It was once believed that paralysis caused by brain injuries is incurable, until someone tried encouraging paralysed soldiers to make immense efforts to move their limbs. Again and again, it was demonstrated that the motor cortex *can* recover its function, if the will to recovery is powerful and persistent enough.

Later on, Littleway invented the simple and convenient term 'newness' to describe a fully awake mind. Newness is what you experience on the first morning of a holiday, or enjoying poetry or music. The human brain, like a battery, has a capacity for 'output' or 'input'. When it is thinking, remembering, dreaming, that is 'output'. When it is passive, wide open, receiving impressions as an open flower receives sunlight, that is 'input'. Sometimes, the input channels get completely blocked – by fatigue, neurosis, triviality, and 'newness' cannot get in.

Newness is the principle of life. Deprived of it, man becomes subject to illness – physical and mental – and then dies. And this, I believed, is why all men die. Solve the problem of keeping the 'input' channels open to newness, and you have solved the problem of immortality. This was the basic idea that drove our researches.

But if I attempted to go into detail about our researches over the next two years, this Memoir would run to a thousand pages. I must try to summarize our approach to the problem.

To begin with, I should mention that Littleway arranged for me to work with him at the University of Wisconsin from September 1969 until the following May. Dr Stafford, in charge of Physical Sciences, was fascinated by Littleway's account of our experiments, and offered me a 'visiting lectureship' which involved only two hours' lecturing a week. Stafford himself has been responsible for some classic experiments concerned with the prefrontal lobes of monkeys.

From the beginning, I felt that the answer lay in the prefrontal lobes of the brain. These are the parts of the brain situated immediately behind the eyes, the fore-part of the frontal lobes. No one quite knew in those days what the prefrontal lobes were for; and experimental evidence seemed contradictory. It is known that the frontal lobes are concerned in man's 'higher faculties' – sympathy, tact, self-discipline and reflection, as well as in motor responses. It was assumed that the prefrontal cortex was probably some kind of extra storage area. Injury to this area seems to cause no damage to the nervous system – there is a famous case in which a crowbar shot through a man's skull, destroying the cortex; he lived for twelve years longer in a perfectly normal manner, except that his behaviour was in many respects coarsened. A stockbroker suffering prefrontal damage became boastful and tactless, and ceased to care for his family. On the other hand, damage to the prefrontal area has a far greater effect on children, involving general loss of intelligence. This would seem to indicate that the prefrontal lobes play some important part in child development.

Children experience more 'poetic' states than adults – 'the

glory and the freshness of a dream'. So it can be seen why I suspected that my search for the mechanism of the value experience should be concentrated in the prefrontal cortex.

Dr Stafford had performed some experiments with rats and monkeys, to test what happened when the prefrontals are damaged or removed. He discovered that, on the whole, intelligence is unimpaired, *but memory is to some extent affected.* Monkeys with prefrontal damage were shown food being placed under one of two pots, then a screen was lowered for a few seconds so the pots were hidden. When the screen was raised again, the monkey often raised the wrong pot.

I was aware of the danger of jumping to conclusions, but the more I thought about it, the more I was convinced that the prefrontal cortex is, so to speak, the centre of poetry and intelligence. After all, what is it that distinguishes the poet from the ordinary man? At a very early stage, it is obviously not 'talent'. The talent develops as a result of a certain search – the search for value experiences, the childhood moments of universal 'newness' and happiness. Most people forget them; poets cling to them – and spend their lives searching for them. It is a question of a certain kind of memory – what we might call 'feeling memory'. More mechanical forms of memory are taken over by the frontal lobes. Monkeys with prefrontal injuries can be *trained* to remember which pot the food is under – i.e. they can learn by *habit*.

Readers may also remember the obsolete operation called prefrontal leucotomy, in which a scalpel was inserted behind the eyeball to sever the prefrontal area from the rest of the brain. In violent or intensely neurotic patients, this often had a calming effect. Obviously they stopped feeling, and since their feelings had been mostly unpleasant, this was often a good thing. Unfortunately, they were also made coarser and duller by the operation, so it was eventually abandoned.

Our first six months at Wisconsin were occupied with experiments on monkeys, to try to determine whether, in fact, the prefrontal region has any function apart from 'storing' dusty memories. We experimented with baby monkeys, adult monkeys, senile monkeys. We connected electrodes to the medial hypothalamus to provoke pleasure reactions, and tested the sensitivity to such stimulation of monkeys to whom we had administered psychedelic drugs. (The results were disappointing, although later experiments with albino rats were less so.)

After six months, we changed the direction of the experiments. I was anxious to try the effects of hypnotism, and this meant that we had to find human subjects.

Hypnosis has always fascinated the student of the brain because it seems to indicate that our waking faculties are limited by the 'brain mechanisms'. A subject under hypnosis can do things that would be impossible in his waking state. What hidden powers are tapped by the hypnotist? And *how*?

Obviously, I suspected that the answer again lay in the prefrontal cortex. But first of all, we did a whole series of experiments to establish the general background. A psychiatrist friend, skilled in hypnosis, taught us the techniques. We quickly established that hypnosis makes no physical difference to the brain. If the subject's eyes were closed, and he was told that they were open, he behaved exactly as though they were open, avoiding obstacles with the uncanny skill of a sleep-walker; yet the alpha rhythms – the sign that he could *not* see anything – persisted. And when the subject's eyes were open, and he was told that they were closed, he behaved exactly as if they were closed, but the alpha rhythms ceased. When told he is asleep, the subject fails to register the typical sleep rhythms.

Since these experiments are described at length in our joint book on the subject, I shall not go into further detail here, except to say that most of our conclusions have subsequently been accepted by psychologists. Human anxiety – characterized by beta waves – prevents us from utilizing our full capacities; we cannot relax. The hypnotist soothes the waking self, the personality, out of existence, and reaches straight through to the 'robot', our deeper mechanical levels, to which the confused and tense personality often gave contradictory orders. What is involved here is the human tendency to place trust in a leader, even to submit their will completely to him, like the Germans under Hitler. The 'leader' (the hypnotist) can often evoke a response of self-sacrifice and endurance that the subject would be quite unable to evoke in himself *for his own purposes*.

These experiments led us much farther afield than we expected – for example, into the area of the pathological criminal. It was interesting to discover that crime often seems to be the revolt of the 'robot' (which, in spite of its name, is very much alive) against an inadequate personality. Criminal psychopaths are characterized by strong theta rhythms (which are produced by anger and frustration). In normal people, theta rhythms last

85

for only about ten seconds after some frustration; then a higher level of the personality suppresses them. In some psychopaths, they persist all the time. We discovered that these rhythms could often be affected by hypnosis; under the orders of his 'leader', the psychopath could achieve a degree of self-control impossible under normal circumstances, and this could often be carried over into his everyday life. Predictably, prefrontal damage tended to increase theta rhythm. I mention these results here because they were not included in our book, which only summarizes the first year's work, before the great discoveries began.

We were getting closer. I was continually aware of this. Whenever I studied the prefrontal cortex, I had a strong sensation of being in touch with the secret source of 'relational consciousness', of man's greatest powers. And yet I had found no practical method for releasing these powers. Hypnosis could often produce profound 'value experiences', after some probing into the past life of the subject. But they were exactly like Dick O'Sullivan's V.E.s. I was aware that what I was seeking was something closer to the sheer power of the sexual orgasm.

On 2 February 1971, Littleway remarked: 'The break-through will probably come by accident.' The following day, his prediction was fulfilled.

Our experiments had been concentrated for some time on the brain waves, particularly on those of the highest frequency, the gamma rhythms. This was almost routine work, since we were both convinced that these waves played no important part in the higher processes of the brain. Man achieves value experiences without the help of brain waves; they are a by-product, just as the sound of a car's engine is a by-product.

It is known that the flicker of an electric light can interfere with the brain's normal rhythms, often to the point of causing the subject to lose consciousness; this technique has been used for the control of epileptic fits. We became interested in the question of interfering with the brain rhythms, to see what results could be produced. In 1971, there was still an enormous amount of work to be done in this area. We experimented with mild currents of varying frequencies, fed into the brain directly by means of electrodes. These electrodes had to be extremely fine, of course, sometimes as little as a fiftieth of a millimetre in diameter. To begin with, we used insulated steel, until Littleway heard about the properties of 'Neumann's alloy', the metal discovered in 1931 by the Austrian brain physiologist Alois Neumann. It is an alloy of iron, copper, zinc, platinum and gallium, with a minute quantity of graphite. Neumann was interested in it mainly because of its 'delayed action effect'; with currents of less than a microvolt, it fails to conduct, but 'holds' the current for a fraction of a second, then suddenly releases it as a flash at higher voltage. Discovered accidentally by a chemist in the Krupp armament works in 1919, it has excited very little interest because it is of no particular use in science or industry. Neumann had started to use electrodes tipped with this metal in his investigation of the 'K complex' – the flashes of brain energy that occur when you are on the point of sleep, and which often jerk you awake. His researches were cut short by his death, and his son Gustav subsequently presented his papers to the University of Wisconsin. I discovered them accidentally, and we decided to try to obtain a quantity of Neumann metal. It was a long process, but we eventually succeeded. It proved to be thoroughly worthwhile, for we soon discovered that the metal had variable properties as far as 'retaining' went, and could be used to interfere not only with delta rhythms, but with theta and gamma waves as well.

Its chief trouble is that it is a great deal softer than steel, so that it cannot be brought to so fine a point. However, this didn't bother us. We stuck to steel electrodes for investigating motor areas, and used the Neumann alloy mainly for experiments with the frontal and prefrontal cortex. The results were extremely encouraging. The delayed 'flash' evidently stimulated some memory trigger process, so that subjects could recall events of childhood without the need for hypnosis. (To begin with, we used an old alcoholic patient who had figured largely in our hypnotic experiments, and whom we partly cured.)

The process of insertion of the electrodes was simple – a local anaesthetic, then two fine holes drilled into the frontal bone of the skull. The subject sat upright, his head held in a well-padded frame, to prevent brain damage in the case of sudden movement.

A week after the commencement of our experiments, Littleway noticed that the cerebro-spinal fluid seemed to have some slight effect on the Neumann alloy; it had darkened slightly in colour. Careful tests showed that it was lighter, a mere fraction of a milligram. This seemed unlikely to do any damage, and as the experiments had reached a crucial stage, we pressed on.

After the experiment, the electrodes were again weighed. This time, one of them was almost a milligram lighter. Examined under a microscope, we discovered that a very tiny piece had snapped off the point. Experiments were suspended, and the subject kept under observation for several days. There was no real cause for alarm. Obviously, if a man can survive after a crowbar has amputated most of his prefrontal lobes, the damage to be anticipated from a thousandth of a gram of soft metal is very small indeed. When, after several days, there were no ill effects, we decided to go ahead once again. (The patient was also eager for us to start; he was being well paid, and the effects of our 'electrical therapy' seemed to be entirely beneficial; he already looked several years younger, and seemed to have gained in intelligence.)

We applied the current – and the result startled us. We were both watching his face carefully, in case of ill effects. He was an oldish man – I mention his name here because of his place in the history of science – Zachariah Longstreet, formerly of Grand Rapids, Illinois. When we had first met him, he was fifty-nine, and had just served three years in the penitentiary for incest. He was a confirmed alcoholic. He was still living with his wife, and at her request had gone to Harvey Grossman – our psychiatrist friend – for treatment. Hypnosis had proved beneficial, and the attention and interest he received from the three of us seemed to improve him in every way. His eyes lost the dull, rather resentful expression, and his theta wave pattern improved. However, left to himself for more than a month or so, he tended to relapse into alcoholism, and then into sexual exhibitionism.

He was sixty-one when we conducted the test using the Neumann electrodes, and in good general health.

When the current was turned on, his face became thoughtful, as if he was trying to remember a name that had slipped his memory. We watched carefully, expecting him to say something. But the lines of his face remained composed, his eyes staring past us, still concentrated. In previous experiments, he had become drowsy, almost as if hypnotized.

The expression of concentration deepened. Suddenly, he said clearly:

'Alright. Turn it down. It's too strong.'

Littleway did as he said automatically, adjusting the rheostat – with a glance of surprise at me. He said:

'How does it feel?'

'Interesting. Extremely interesting.'

Again, we looked at one another. It was simply not the kind of phrase Longstreet would normally use. He would say, 'Pretty good', or sometimes incomprehensible slang phrases like, 'Ye're tootin'. Littleway asked:

'In what way?'

Longstreet grinned at us, and said:

'I've found your bit of alloy.'

The tape recording of this session shows that neither of us bothered to ask him what he meant immediately. We were too fascinated by the obvious change that was taking place in him. I wish we had thought to film it as well as record it. From the expression on his face, neither of us had the slightest doubt that something important was taking place.

I was the first to grasp what this was. We had induced value experiences so often that I was used to the signs – relaxation, the glow of ecstasy, self-abandonment, sometimes violent tears or convulsions of emotion. In this case, it was nothing of the sort. The face seemed to become firmer. The eyes, very pale blue, and normally slightly bloodshot, stared past us with the intensity of a man observing something that grips his interest. He reminded me of something or someone – then I remembered who it was: a certain picture of Sherlock Holmes in one of the early illustrated editions, sitting with his head against a cushion, playing a violin. The eyes had that aquiline, penetrating quality that Watson is always describing. Suddenly, I knew what had happened. I said:

'My god, Henry, we're done it.'

'Done what?'

'Induced a real value experience. Contemplative objectivity. Other-ness.'

Then he saw it too. We both stared. It was almost frightening; although for me, it was perhaps less exhilarating than the afternoon of my 'dream' in Essex. I asked Longstreet:

'Can you describe what's happening?'

'No.'

'What did you mean about finding our piece of alloy?'

He made a slight movement of his heavily gloved hands towards his face.

'It's in here. It's lodged in this front part – what do you call it? The lobe . . .'

'What is it doing?' This was Littleway.

'Can't describe it. I'm opening up.'

'In what way?'

Longstreet only smiled. It was a pitying smile, but not patronizing. He was simply condoling with us for not knowing what he meant.

His breathing became extremely calm and regular, then ceased to be noticeable, although he was obviously fully conscious. He ignored our questions. Only after Littleway had repeated several times 'What can you see?' he said briefly: 'Same as you.'

He gestured to us to push the rheostat closer to him – it was on a trolley. Littleway looked dubious, but I moved the trolley. Longstreet only wanted to turn down the current. He sat with it turned down for more than a quarter of an hour – so low that the rate of 'firings' must have been less than one every two seconds. Then he tried to turn it up again, jerked suddenly as if the effect was too violent, and turned it right down to zero. He said:

'Get these things outa my head.'

We did as he asked, sealed the holes in his skull with adhesive tape, and moved him to an armchair. His expression had relaxed; it now became very sad. We allowed him to rest for ten minutes without questioning him. Then he said:

'It's a funny thing. It didn't matter all the time.'

We could get nothing coherent out of him after that. He became sleepy. His face grew duller, and he made no objection when we suggested moving him back to bed. Before the nurse came with the stretcher, he was fast asleep, snoring gently.

Littleway said:

'But what the hell caused it?'

I said: 'I'm going to make one wild guess. That tiny piece of alloy somehow worked its way into the prefrontal cortex.'

'But what would that do?'

'Your guess is as good as mine. Maybe closed a synaptic gap.'

'That's impossible. They're only a few Angström units wide. This metal would be a hundred times too big. Anyway, it wouldn't make any difference. Nerve impulses are pretty constant. If they're strong enough to cross a synapse, they don't lose strength anyway.'

At this point, we realized we were taping ourselves, and Littleway switched it off. When I listen to the tape, I am amazed by how quickly we grasped what had happened. Perhaps Longstreet's mention of finding our metal gave us the clue.

What, then, had happened? Littleway was mistaken as we discovered later, when Longstreet's head X-rays were blown up to fifty times their size. The piece of metal that had worked its way into the outer layer of the cortex was a minute fragment of the piece that had broken off the electrode – as tiny as that had been. It *had* lodged in the dendrites of a synapse, or very close to them. And its effect was to delay the nervous stimulus, and then discharge it. In other words, it acted as an amplifier.

Then everything became clear. Poets develop by *wanting* to develop the ability for 'other-ness'. The prefrontal lobes contain vast reservoirs of memory and meaning, of a kind that is quite unnecessary for our daily survival – in fact, a nuisance, because it would distract us from the boring necessities of everyday living. But it is extremely hard for poets to divert brain energy from more practical areas of the brain to these great memory tanks; our animal caution refuses to allow it. So these strange moments of pure vision, of broad 'relational consciousness', only occur when there happens to be a lot of brain energy to spare – for example, when a crisis has led us to tense ourselves, to draw upon our reserve energy tanks, and then the crisis disappears.

The minute fragment of metal had amplified some nerve impulse, so as to produce a continual effect like the disappearance of crisis. The reason Longstreet could not describe his mental condition was that he had no way of describing it. And when he told us that he was seeing 'the same as you', he was being strictly accurate. Only he was really *seeing* it, like a wide angle camera, instead of the tiny lens through which most of us contemplate the world. He was getting a bird's eye view of his life – a god's eye view.

We had accidentally solved the problem I set out to solve – how to 'boost' the 'new faculty' that has begun to appear in man. Admittedly, we had no evidence that we could repeat the experiment. I suppose we also had no real evidence of what had happened to Longstreet – that it was not an ordinary V.E. But neither of us had the least doubt, having seen Longstreet's face.

It seemed pretty clear that the most difficult part of the experiment would be the placing of a minute fragment of Neumann alloy at the right nerve junction in the cortex. We consulted a brain surgeon about this, and he confirmed that it would be difficult without damage to brain tissue. But again the solution proved unexpectedly simple.

Longstreet was eager for us to continue to experiment on him. We were altogether less eager, because it seemed likely that we would learn as little as on the first occasion. But we were both curious about one point: whether he would be able to *learn* the ability to induce 'relational consciousness' without the need for electrical stimulation. After the first occasion, he was totally unable to recall his state of intensity. He was not even able to remember what it had been like. He seemed inclined to believe that we had caused the intensity with the electric current. When I tried to explain what had really happened, he didn't seem interested – he only wanted to know how soon we would do it again.

We were not entirely happy about it. The skin punctures on his scalp were chafing; we wanted to allow them to heal up. But he was so persistent that we performed the same experiment forty-eight hours after the first one. The results were much the same, although this time he was more talkative. One of the things he said was: 'It's better than being drunk.' Another was: 'What's wrong with most people anyway?' Littleway commented that he had re-discovered the doctrine of Original Sin for himself.

After the second occasion, we decided to allow the skin punctures to heal before we tried it again. In the meantime, we consulted brain surgeons, and looked around for another subject. Ten days later, we had Longstreet's skull X-rayed again. The piece of Neumann alloy had moved, working its way close to the outer surface of the lobe. We hurried Longstreet to the laboratory and connected up the electrodes. The movement of the metal seemed to make no difference; the effect was the same as before! It seemed to make no difference where the alloy was located in the cortex. The flow of current immediately produced the same intensity of concentration. And, oddly enough, Longstreet was aware that the piece of alloy had moved. We pressed him to explain himself. He was not very clear, but we gathered that he was aware of the metal as a source of intensity.

This was the most exciting thing that had happened since the great discovery, and the most important. It obviously meant that it didn't matter where the alloy lodged in the cortex; the effect was the same.

Three days later, the X-ray plates seemed to indicate that the metal had vanished. We assumed that it had dissolved in cerebro-spinal fluid. Nevertheless, we decided to test Longstreet again. The result puzzled us, for it was exactly the same as before. Either the metal had set up some kind of habit pattern in the cortex, that was stimulated by the current, or there were tiny quantities still in the cortex, too minute to show on X-ray plates, but powerful enough to cause the typical reaction. In due course, we discovered the latter was the case.

By this time, we had another subject for experiment – a girl of twenty-three who had been suffering from suicidal depression. Harvey Grossman had suggested that we try her when we described our results with Longstreet. She was exactly what we had been looking for – a college graduate who had published poetry in small magazines, intelligent and articulate. Her name was Honor Weiss. Her case history is unimportant, except to say that the attempts at suicide occurred after an abortion.

We took care not to say too much to her about our aims; she seemed to accept that we intended to try some new form of shock treatment. Her state of vitality seemed so low that I suspected she hoped to die in the experiment.

The same technique was used as before: a mild anaesthetic (she was afraid of pain, so we decided against novocaine), a hole an eighth of an inch wide in the flesh, made by a hot platinum wire scalpel, then an eighth inch hole drilled in the skull. This part of the operation was performed by Dr Arnold Soddy; although Littleway had a medical degree, his hands lacked the necessary steadiness. Cerebro-spinal fluid was drained off to reveal the brain surface. The fragment of Neumann metal was propelled on to the brain's surface by repulsion; a minute current was allowed to flow through the platinum wire on which it rested, and the discharge kicked the fragment off the wire on to the brain surface. Two hours later, it had been absorbed. The cerebro-spinal fluid was pumped back in, and the hole sealed. The next morning, X-rays revealed that the metal had penetrated to a depth of half an inch. Oddly enough, it was in almost exactly the same spot as the fragment in Longstreet's brain.

That afternoon, a second hole was drilled. Two hours later, when she had completely recovered from the anaesthetic, we applied the electrodes, and cautiously turned on the current.

I expected the result; nevertheless, it produced a tremendous wave of emotion. Honor Weiss was not a pretty girl; her face was small and pointed; it made me think of a mouse. The skin was grey. With the first touch on the rheostat, colour came back into her cheeks. Within half a minute, she had become an attractive and vital girl. I possess the film records of this, and they are startling. The transformation is complete, as if another girl had been substituted.

Honor Weiss showed more tendency to emotion than Longstreet had; her eyes filled with tears. But after a few seconds, she seemed to master it. Gradually, her face took on the same expression of complete calm and concentration that we knew so well. The first thing she said was: 'Thank you.' The next was: 'Why don't you try this on yourselves?' 'We intend to,' I said. 'Good. You deserve it.'

We asked her the routine questions. She answered politely, but we could tell she was bored. She asked: 'Where is it?' and when we asked what, said: 'The thing in here – you've put something in here, I can feel it.' We had not told her about the Neumann metal.

Littleway asked: 'How would you describe what is taking place?'

Subject: 'I'm more alive . . . more alive than I've ever been before.'

Littleway: 'Has it improved your memory? Can you recall your childhood, for example?'

Subject: 'If I want to. I don't really want to. I've got other things I'd rather do.'

Myself: 'What do you think about your suicide attempt of last month?'

Subject: 'I was asleep.'

Myself: 'In what sense?'

Subject (with a touch of impatience): 'Like a sleepwalker. Like one of those swimmers in an underwater ballet.'

At this point, she asked us several questions about the operation – that we answered truthfully. Then she said:

'Do you think we could skip questions for the next ten minutes or so? I've got a lot of thinking I'd like to do.'

Littleway: 'Would you mind if I ask about what?'

Subject: 'My own life. I've never been able to think much. I've always been too emotional. This is like being free on a holiday, where you can walk where you like, with no one to stop you. I want a chance to walk around.'

She added, without prompting, a moment later:

'It's like having ten minutes to tidy up a mess you've made in a lifetime.'

We asked her if she would answer more questions when she had finished thinking. She agreed. We showed her how to work the rheostat in case of discomfort, and retired a few feet away, where we talked in low voices. She became oblivious of us, as if she were completely alone.

The ten minutes went by, then twenty, then half an hour. Thirty-seven and a half minutes later, she looked at us and said:

'I'm sorry. I'm being selfish.'

We assured her it didn't matter. I asked how she felt. She said: 'Drowsy, I'm afraid.'

'You find that thinking absorbs a lot of mental energy?'

'Not really. It shouldn't. It should be a self-charging process. But I'm not used to it.'

Littleway: 'When would you like to stop?'

Subject: 'In about five minutes, if you don't mind.'

Littleway: 'I realize that it's very difficult for you to describe your present state of mind. But would you mind trying?'

Subject: 'I don't mind. But it's not really a question of describing my state of mind. That doesn't really matter much. What's important is what I'm aware of.'

Myself: 'What are you aware of?'

Subject: 'Something I always knew and wanted to believe ... I suppose the easiest way to express it is to say: The poets were always right. I've always loved music and poetry and painting – yet I never really understood what they were trying to say to me. They're trying to say: In the last analysis, the *big* remains true, not the small.' (There is a pause here for nearly a minute.) 'I suppose it's terribly simple really. Everybody – at least, all people like me – really want to know whether it's all worth while, whether poetry and music really do any good, or they're just the sugar coating on the pill. But we're always so involved in trivialities that we never really get a chance to judge. The trivialities block our vision. Great poets are like optimists who say: Better times are coming. But we don't really believe them

... So the trivialities get us down, and we want to die.'

Myself (interrupting): 'How would you feel about death if you could always see beyond the trivialities?'

Subject (pause): 'I don't know. I suppose death's inevitable. But there wouldn't be any suicide, because ... well, it would be obvious. You'd realize what the suicide's throwing away. But we lack courage, so we die.'

Her face twisted briefly with pain, and she said: 'This is beginning to hurt.' We turned off the rheostat, removed the electrodes, and helped her to the armchair. She was asleep almost as soon as she sat down. I noticed that her cheeks kept their colour.

Obviously, my main concern now was how soon I could try the operation. But Littleway was not entirely happy about the idea. To begin with, Longstreet underwent a complete change of attitude. He had been a complete nuisance, nagging us to use him in further experiments. Now he became apathetic. When I asked him about this one day, he said: 'I guess I'd be better off as I was before. After all, I didn't do anything very bad, did I?' Littleway asked: 'What about your daughter?' 'That wasn't so bad, was it? Anyway, she enjoyed it. She only said she didn't when people found out.'

Littleway took this as a sign of relapse. Before the operations, he had expressed contrition about his incest, and said he thought he had been insane when he committed it. Now he gave the impression he would do it again if he got the opportunity. His youngest daughter was a girl of twenty-three, with an extremely low IQ.

I was less alarmed. It seemed to me that perhaps Longstreet had never really been sorry, and that now he was simply being honest. Besides, I felt that Longstreet's 'relapse' was perhaps just mental exhaustion. His brain had been stretched like a spring; it was now easing back into its old position.

The other thing that bothered Littleway was that Honor Weiss showed more and more sign of strain as the number of tests increased. The spasms would occur within seconds of the beginning of the experiment. By this time, the fragment of Neumann metal had worked its way out of her brain, as with Longstreet.

Littleway and I argued about it one evening over dinner. He said that the operation could be dangerous. He reminded me about Dick O'Sullivan and his brain tumour, and asked me to account for Honor Weiss's headaches. I admitted I couldn't, but said there was only one way to find out – for one of us to try the operation. He argued that we needed more tests. I said that we already had all the material we needed; we now needed to know the 'why', not the 'how'. Finally, he agreed.

On 27 February 1971, Littleway and Soddy performed the operation on me, after shaving the front part of my skull and freezing it with novocaine. I remained fully conscious throughout, although I began to see double when the fluid was drained off. I felt nothing. I sat still in the chair for two hours following the operation, feeling curiously weak and lethargic. Then the fluid was replaced and the hole sealed. The X-ray showed that the fragment had penetrated half an inch or so, this time towards the front of the right hand lobe. (The way in which the fragment penetrates the brain is still unknown, although, of course, the brain is extremely soft. It seems certain that the brain somehow absorbs it – much larger fragments remain on the surface of a dead brain – but it is not known how it does this.)

Four hours after the operation, a second hole was bored, and the electrodes inserted. Littleway turned the rheostat gently.

The first thing I observed was the actual sensation of the current entering my brain. It was not unpleasant – a bubbling sensation, that reminded me of the water bubbling into an aquarium. A moment later, I became clearly aware of a greatly increased sensitivity which affected the *whole* of my brain. I was also aware of the location of the fragment of Neumann alloy, just as you are aware of food in your stomach after swallowing it, or waste matter in the bowels.

There was nothing very startling about the sensation of increased ability to think. It was very much like the sensation of remembering something important. There was a feeling of lightness and relief, of the kind that occurs when you have a bad cold and a stuffy nose, and then a deep breath causes the nasal passages to clear.

I had already done so much work on the phenomenology of the value experience that nothing that now happened to me seemed strange or inexplicable. Littleway said that no remarkable change seemed to take place in me, so that for a few minutes, he doubted whether the experiment had worked. I was aware that the 'powers' I felt rising in me were my own. But I could also see why Longstreet believed that his experience of intensity was entirely due to the current. For someone without the habit of introspection, this mental 'opening' must have seemed startling. It had the air of a spectacle; it reminded me of the opening of Christmas pantomimes when I was a child – the curtains sweeping back to reveal the whole cast on stage with highly coloured scenery and costumes.

Oddly enough, the insights that now arose in me did not seem to be localized in the prefrontal cortex. They involved more or less every part of the brain, particularly the hypothalamus.

After the first thirty seconds, the feeling of lassitude had completely disappeared, and a feeling of increased strength and concentration had begun to build up. At the same time, I was aware of an ability to *project* this concentration in realms of thought. It was like nothing so much as the clearing of a blanket of fog.

Littleway asked: 'What are you experiencing?'

'Ordinary consciousness.'

He looked surprised and disappointed.

'You mean there's no change?'

'Oh yes, there's a change. I didn't say it was *everyday* consciousness. I said ordinary consciousness. It's everyday consciousness that's sub-normal. This is normal.'

PART TWO

JOURNEY TO THE END OF NIGHT

It has been a year since I broke off this Memoir. The last words I wrote were not the ones on the previous page; I went considerably beyond this point, trying to describe the operation, the exact nature of my insights, my conversation with Littleway. Then I knew I could not go on, for I saw a problem that should have occurred to me earlier. What audience was I writing for? For 'ordinary people'? Or for people of the future, men who have made the 'evolutionary leap'? If for the latter, then most of my explanations were superfluous; if the former, they were inadequate.

What has happened since then has determined me to make another attempt.

The insight that came to me, on that rainy February afternoon of 1971, was that using the 'dormant areas' of the brain is simply a matter of a trick, and that the trick consists simply in 'putting it into gear', exactly as with a car. But putting the brain 'into gear' takes energy, and man seldom has this energy available. A simple parallel will make this clear. We are all aware that sexual desire is intentional. I can quite deliberately turn my thoughts towards some sexually stimulating object, and induce erotic excitement. But if I try to do this when I am tired or suffering from a hangover, I get far less result than when I am feeling healthy and wide-awake. Because when I am tired, there is simply *less energy available.*

Moods of mystical ecstasy are also intentional. In theory, they could be induced as easily as sexual excitement. Why, then, are they so rare? Because they burn up even more energy than sexual excitement does. And that is why they happen mostly to young people.

But if I have a piece of powerful electrical equipment that takes a larger current than usual, I simply install a transformer.

I put myself out to make quite sure that I shall have the electricity needed to run it.

Now the reason the Neumann alloy produces such mental intensity should be obvious. It acts as a transformer, and produces a slight 'kick' in the brain which is very similar to the relief we feel when some crisis vanishes, or when something unexpectedly pleasant happens. At least, it *reminds* the frontal cortex of this flash of pleasure. In fact, the slight electrical discharge is harmful; if continued for too long, it would destroy brain tissue. But the slight jogging of the memory is enough. The brain soon picks up the trick, of going into gear, of stepping up the will-power and 'intending' the mystical experience, as easily as we can 'intend' sexual excitement .

This is why, after my second experience with the electrodes, I no longer needed this artificial stimulus. I told Littleway to take them off, and then sustained the experience by will power alone.

All this will become clearer as I go on. For the moment, this sketchy explanation should suffice.

But what of the problem that was the beginning of these researches – the process of ageing? How can I know at this point that the problem has been solved?

I can only state that it is so. Shaw once remarked that people die of laziness and want of conviction and failure to make their lives worth living. With his poet's intuition, he came closer to solving the problem than any of the scientific gerontologists, all working upon the false assumption that life is chemical in nature. Men die for the same reason they fall asleep – because the senses close up from boredom when there is nothing to occupy them. But a man who is deeply interested in something can stay awake all night.

I have explained that the brain's alpha rhythms are a kind of 'engine noise', like a car idling in neutral. When you look at something, they cease; the car goes into gear. If you are confined in darkness for a long time, they also cease, but that is because the car engine stalls.

Now intelligent adults differ from children and animals in one important respect. If they are deeply preoccupied with some problem, using the intellect or imagination, the alpha rhythms also cease. An intelligent man's brain can go 'into gear' without needing something to look at. However, we all know that this kind of concentration cannot be sustained for long. Our mental energy flags. Why does it flag? This is the key to the whole mystery. It does *not* flag because you have used up all your available mental energy; when necessary, we can concentrate for hours. No, it flags because *the senses narrow*. Concentration is always accompanied by a certain narrowing, of course; that is what the word means. But we cannot stop this movement once it has started. We try to economize on energy, like a bad workman trying to hurry a job. Everybody is familiar with what happens if you try to read a long book in one sitting; long before the end, you are no longer reading with full attention; you are skipping, hurrying impatiently, and the result is a gradual flagging of mental energy, an exhaustion of the attention that can lead to a kind of mental dyspepsia.

To put this in terms of an image we have already used; when you are deeply interested, your consciousness is like a searchlight focused on quite a large area of the spider's web, or fishing net. You see a lot of 'relations'. As attention flags, the searchlight beam grows narrower, until it may end by focusing on only one square of the fishing net. When this happens, you feel mental fatigue.

The basic cause of ageing is the same. When we are young, the senses are wide awake; life is intensely interesting; anything might happen. So the beam of attention stays wide. As age comes on, we feel we now know what to expect out of life. And the attention gradually flags, so that a kind of life-boredom becomes an everyday condition that we take for granted.

The basic point I am making here will seem so obvious to our grandchildren that they will not be able to grasp how it could ever have been unknown. It is that *life is sustained by will*. Every living creature is a conflict between will and habit, freedom and automatism. Man has reached the highest degree of freedom so far – all other animals are mere machines compared with him – but it is automatism – gradually creeping automatism – that kills him off. The machine wins; he stops willing; slowly, the batteries run flat and the lights dim . . .

Now it should be clear why I can state with certainty that I have solved the basic problem of ageing. There are still other problems, related to mere physical ageing, destruction of bodily cells by cosmic rays and so on. These will be solved. The major problem is already solved. Control over the powers of the prefrontal cortex is the ability to widen the beam of attention at will, to see as much of the 'fishing net' as you like. The creeping automatism is defeated; there is no need for emotional poets to advise us to 'rage, rage against the dying of the light'. We have control of the light switch.

I shall not go into detail about my insight and sensations during those first days after the experiment. It would be as boring as those postcards from friends on holiday telling you how much they are enjoying it. Besides, it was not exactly a matter of pleasure. A mental balance had been tipped. All that happened was that I was confirmed in tendencies I had already had all my life. I have always loved ideas, and found the physical world relatively boring. I have never been tempted to burn out my emotional fuses, like Honor Weiss, or carry mildly perverse sexual fantasies into practice, like Zachariah Longstreet. But there had been times of despair, when I had thought the whole thing a mistake; now I knew these times would never recur. The sun was up; I could see my way.

And that, I thought, was all. A pleasant condition, but not so very different from my previous state. For I didn't want to summon up mystical ecstasies ten times a day. Health seems completely normal and natural to those who have it; so my new state seemed to me. I worked like a dynamo, and spent hours of every day writing and thinking. I became abnormally thin, as my body shed its surplus fat. I lost interest in alcohol – people drink to induce a condition that I could induce by a simple act of will – and I also became a vegetarian. I also found that four or five hours of sleep was enough for me. Shaw's suggestion that his 'long livers' would dispense completely with sleep was based on failure to understand its function : to clear the circuits of our mental computer through dreams and relaxation. But if necessary, I could have gone without sleep for days or weeks.

I suppose the most noticeable consequence, during those early months, was my constant sense of the future, stretching ahead for thousands of years. Wells once divided men up into those who live in the present, and those for whom the future is a reality. But even for someone like Wells, the future only becomes a reality at long intervals, in flashes of intensity. But I now had reason to believe that I might be the first of Shaw's 'long livers', and I could see that there was no reasonable limit to life. It is a balance between freedom and automatism; I had swung the balance decisively; theoretically, I might be immortal, unless unforeseen problems arose. This was a startling idea. We all get so used to the idea of dying, to the thought that we shall be dead when our grandchildren are middle aged, that all our speculations about the twenty-first century are in some ways irrelevant, since so few of us will live to see it. We are mildly curious about what will happen to the earth over the next few centuries, but it hardly matters much. Now I had to face that I would probably be alive to see the twenty-fifth century. And far more than this. Since my intelligence would obviously qualify me as a leader sooner or later, I would probably be a crucial factor in the history of the future. This thought gave me no particular pleasure; I have always believed, with Yeats, that 'truth flourishes where the scholar's lamp has shone', and I shrink from involvement with people. It was ordinary realism that made me face that, sooner or later, I may end as the world leader of these childish creatures called human beings.

The next obvious step was for Littleway to undergo the operation. But he was cautious. My reassurances made no difference. It was not precisely that he doubted my word. But I knew what he was thinking: that the brain is a delicate instrument, and that perhaps this crude treatment of introducing a foreign body and then discharging electrical currents into it might cause damage that was not at first apparent.

Besides, I have mentioned that neither Zachariah Longstreet nor Honor Weiss wanted to continue the treatment. I think· Honor Weiss was permanently 'cured' of her suicidal and depressive tendencies, in the ordinary sense. I know exactly why she decided not to let us continue our experiments. Under the stimulation of the Neumann alloy, she could *see* what was wrong with her messy emotional life. She could also see the answer: that she was intelligent enough to achieve an intensity that was not merely of the emotions. Longstreet wasn't, of course; his 'vision' could only show him that he would be better off dead. But Honor Weiss was not stupid, and she was young. She shrank away from the responsibility in the way that emotional people do. She has preferred to retreat into her warm damp little cocoon of emotion and 'ordinariness'.

Most human beings do. That is why there is death. Evolution has no use for those who refuse to accept its imperatives.

At all events, Littleway declined to be persuaded to try the experiment during the remainder of 1971. I could see no reason to hurry him. He could think clearly; there was no taint of intellectual defeat about him. He would come to it.

Meanwhile, I almost abandoned my scientific work. Experiment seemed a waste of time when there was so much re-thinking to be done.

My colleagues and students noticed no great change in me, except that I seemed more cheerful. This is not surprising. Think of the mood of calm and insight induced by great music – Furtwängler's Bruckner, for example; the feeling of wide horizons, of the incredible beauty and multiplicity of life. This was with me quite permanently. I now *saw* the aim of human evolution as clearly as I can see my own hand. For many hundreds of years to come, it will be to achieve increased aware-ness of the position we have already achieved. Anyone who understands cybernetics can grasp this. Cybernetics is the science of making machines think for themselves – or at least, making them behave as if they do. A train doesn't have to think for itself – it goes forward on rails, which prevent it from alter-ing its course. But a guided missile or an un-manned aeroplane needs to take constant account of its surroundings, and to con-stantly adjust itself to new conditions. Well, most human beings live like trains – they just chug forward through life, held on course by the railway lines of convention and habit. For several hundreds of years now, evolution has been aiming at creating a new type of human being, who sees the world with new eyes *all the time*, who can readjust his mind a hun-dred times a day *to see the familiar as strange*. We are fighting a war, a war against matter and automatism. So far we have fought dimly and instinctively; it is now time to drag the war into the open, and fight with all the resources of the mind.

This is what preoccupied me for day after day in that vital year 1971. But there were also practical problems. I wanted others to join me. It seemed to me that the task of immediate importance was to find a dozen other people I could trust – Alec Lyell would have been ideal – and perform the pre-frontal experiment on them. This was a seed that needed scattering as soon as possible.

And the absurd thing is that I did not even suspect the real potentialities of our discovery. I knew that my energy and vitality and sense of purpose had been multiplied by ten; that seemed enough.

Just before Christmas, 1971, Littleway decided to risk the operation. I was evidently suffering no ill effects, and my intelligence had obviously not been impaired. We hoped to return to England at Christmas, and remain there for at least two years. Admittedly, the operation could have been performed in England as conveniently as elsewhere. But the apparatus was already assembled at Wisconsin; besides, we also had the help of Harvey Grossman. He was even more sceptical than Littleway, but his tough-minded, empirical approach had often proved of value to us in the past.

Littleway was nervous. I think he had spent so much time brooding on the pros and cons of the operation that he could hardly believe it would all go smoothly. But it did. Once again, the tiny fragment of Neumann metal was absorbed without difficulty. At Littleway's insistence, we used a much smaller piece than before – he was afraid that it might set up an irritation that would lead to a brain tumour. It made no difference. As the current ran through the electrodes, a look of pleased surprise came over his face. He wanted to jerk his head round to talk to me, but luckily the padded frame held it tightly in place. But he said nothing; merely sat there, and became utterly relaxed, until he looked twenty years younger. Finally, he signalled for us to remove the electrodes, then said to me: 'Alright, you were right. I apologize.'

From then on, there was no further difficulty with him, although he experienced more difficulty than I had in learning to reproduce the intensity without the help of electrodes. This may have been due to the fact that he is twenty years my senior, and his habit patterns are more strongly established; or it may be that there is a certain physiological variation from brain to brain. It was as well that I had been through it all before, for at one point he became convinced that it could not be induced without the aid of the current. But halfway through his fourth experience, he said: 'I think I've got it. Take off the electrodes.' And he had. I left him alone for nearly twenty-four hours after that. I knew he would have a great deal of thinking – and feeling – to do.

Now oddly enough, it was the same night that I began to

suspect that we had only touched the surface of the possibilities of this discovery.

It happened in a commonplace way. I was dreaming that I had been commissioned to compose a piano concerto. (I have never composed a bar in my life.) At the climax of the dream, I sat down at the piano, waved my hand at the orchestra, and the music started. It was magnificent. I woke up with the sound of it still in my ears, and knew that it was *my* music, not some echo of my favourite composers.

I lay there in bed thinking about it. I had never thought much about the nature of dreams. I had always assumed they were nocturnal versions of daydreams, endowed with an undeserved reality by the absence of the competitive daylight. That is to say, they were a story you told yourself. But in that case, where did the music come from? I now remembered the story of Coleridge and Kubla Khan, which I had always been inclined to disbelieve, and it no longer seemed improbable.

It is true that most dreams are no more than fantasies of the sleeping mind. But certain dreams have a reality, an element of *surprise*, that implies some deeper level of the psyche. And when I came to think about this, it seemed obvious enough. The conscious mind may be inventive, but it is not creative in the real sense.

It dawned on me with a kind of shock. Here am I, Howard Lester, lying awake in bed, apparently sure of my own identity. And down below the surface of my consciousness – even below the realm of intuitions that were now accessible to me – there lay another Howard Lester, who had more right to bear my name. I was an impostor; he was the 'real me'.

It was a curious sensation: this notion of my 'real identity' lying deep down inside me, like some monstrous whale at the bottom of the sea. And at the same time, I saw with clarity that my new mastery of the prefrontal cortex had not brought me any closer to this hidden self. Admittedly, I was almost constantly aware of a sort of 'connectedness' with the universe, a feeling of belonging, of being intuitively in touch with the visible world around me and the secret world that lies beneath it. But the hidden identity lay far deeper.

I left Littleway alone most of the next day. At four in the afternoon, he rang me and asked me to go to his house. This was a pleasant clapboard structure just off campus, surrounded by lime trees. His Negro odd-job man let me in. Littleway was sitting up in bed in the west room upstairs, with the golden December sunlight falling across the counterpane. I stood and stared. The change in him was unbelievable. Working with him so closely over the past few years, I thought I knew every line of his face. Now I would have sworn that this was another man with a remarkable resemblance to Littleway – his twin brother perhaps – but with basic differences of character. I have said that he looked like a farmer – healthy, shrewd, humorous; he could have been used as a model for John Bull. It was not some kind of an 'act' he was putting on; it was the real Littleway. This had vanished, as if he was an actor who had taken off his make-up and relapsed into his real personality. This was gentle, vague, innocent and dreamy. The paleness of his face may have added to this effect.

This 'character change' has persisted to this day. It is just as well we left the University of Wisconsin that Christmas. His colleagues would have thought he was an impostor. And even now, I still get a faint shock if I hear his voice outside a door, and then he comes into the room; I expect the old Littleway, and this 'twin brother' walks in.

His first words were:

'Well, well, you've been very patient with me, haven't you? Didn't you ever want to call me a damn fool?'

I assured him I didn't. The odd-job man brought us in tea (made with tea bags, alas), and we dropped the subject. He turned to more serious matters.

'I've been thinking about your suggestion that we find a dozen more people. And I don't think we should hurry.'

'Why not?'

'This whole thing has got to be kept a secret until we've explored its possibilities. I've just been reading *Back to Methuselah* – I could never stand Shaw, you know, so it's practically the first thing of his I've read. But you remember that part where one of the politicians thinks they've invented an elixir, and warns them that people would kill one another to get it? He was right. If this ever leaks out, we'd never have another day's peace, even if we lived to be a thousand. Have you told anyone at all?'

Luckily, I hadn't. At least, I had once mentioned my obsession with ageing to Harvey Grossman, and he had dismissed it. Everyone else on the faculty thought of our work simply as an extension of Aaron Marks's experiments with value experiences.

Littleway said: 'Good. When I think of our lack of precautions so far . . . Honor Weiss might be telling everyone she meets about the experiment.'

'I don't think so. She found it all too much of a strain. I don't think she *wants* to grasp its implications.'

'Let's hope you're right. Longstreet's dying of cancer – Joel just told me.'

I said: 'But don't you see? It didn't do Honor Weiss any good because she prefers to live on an emotional level. Real intellectuality frightens her, as it does most people. It wouldn't be any good performing this operation on politicians or millionaires or gangsters. It might improve their characters, but they wouldn't know how to use it. What's more, they wouldn't want to . . .'

'You may be right. But *we* wouldn't get a minute's peace once the thing was out. So let's keep it quiet.'

We spoke of other things, and I remarked on the change in his face.

'I know. That shouldn't surprise you. I remember you once telling me that personality is only protective colouring, like a lizard's. Did you ever read that book called *The Three Faces of Eve?*'

It was strange that he should have brought this up – the psychological classic on the total personality change in a woman, a complete Jekyll and Hyde transformation, of which her 'Jekyll' half was completely unaware. I remember, when reading it, thinking that a hundred or so years ago, this would have been taken as evidence for the existence of demons or spirits that can take over a human body. It brought up the subject that I had spent half the night thinking about. I explained my idea to Littleway. He listened without interrupting, but seemed sceptical.

'You may be right, but I suspect you're not thinking clearly enough. The deeper you descend into the mind, the closer you get to our primitive animal levels and the sleep mechanisms. How could there be a "secret identity" down there? Identity's an attribute of consciousness.'

He said that, in his own opinion, total personality changes could only occur when there were severe neurotic blockages in the mind, just as extreme sexual perversions only occur when there are sexual blockages or frustrations.

I said: 'How about yourself?'

'Surely a case in point? I developed without any severe frustrations. My father's mannerisms were rather like mine – I suppose that's where they came from. I feel different now – I can see further and deeper – but I'm not radically different.'

'Perhaps you're right,' I said. But I was certain he wasn't.

We arrived back at Great Glen in the early hours of Christmas morning. It was strange to see it – like returning to another life. Roger was still there, and had moved in an Italian girl called Clareta, sultry eyed and big-hipped. She had a quick temper, and seemed to dominate him. I now no longer disliked Roger; trapped in a world of his own making, he was as pitiful as a child brought up to a life of crime in a slum.

Littleway had become unexpectedly interested in philosophy. He spent Christmas reading two enormous volumes by Jaspers called *The Great Philosophers*, apparently fascinated. He remarked to me that the most startling realization since his 'operation' was that human beings had advanced so far without the full use of the prefrontal cortex. Jasper's attempt to see the whole sweep of philosophy as a great unity is a case in point. Littleway also became interested in Whitehead and Hegel – two other philosophers who had a vision of unity.

But I wanted to pursue my insight. How could I reach down below my personality, to the hidden levels that express themselves only in dreams and intense creative activity? I was aware that it was a matter of 'relaxing'. The more we are obsessed by immediate objectives, the narrower we become, the more we take the world for granted. Poetry is relaxation, when the blood seems to flow in mental channels we had forgotten about – just as when it flows back into a numb forearm when you have been sleeping on it. Consciousness becomes web-like.

Then theoretically, web-like consciousness should gradually reveal the deepest levels of the mind, Husserl's 'transcendental ego', the hidden self. So I spent Christmas inducing intense states of web-like consciousness. On Christmas morning, I walked around the country lanes towards Houghton on the Hill. It was icy cold; the sky was grey; even at midday, there was still frost on the grass and the hedges. It struck me that the popularity of Christmas is a matter of web-like consciousness.

Childhood conditions us to relax and expand at Christmas, to forget petty worries and irritations and think in terms of universal peace. And so Christmas is the nearest to mystical experience that most human beings ever approach, with its memories of Dickens, and Irving's *Bracebridge Hall*.

Now, walking along the deserted lanes, I let myself relax and expand completely. Even the greyness of the sky seemed inexpressibly beautiful, as if it were a benediction. I saw cottages across the fields with smoke rising from their chimneys, and heard the distant hoot of a train. Then I was suddenly aware that all over England, at this moment, kitchens were full of the smell of baked potatoes and stuffing and turkey, and pubs were full of men drinking unaccustomed spirits and feeling glad that life occasionally declares a truce. Then there was the thought that this world is probably one of the most beautiful in the solar system. Mercury is all white-hot rock; Venus is all heavy cloud, and the surface is too hot to support organic life. (Oddly enough, I had a clear intuition that there *is* life on Venus, but that it somehow floats in the atmosphere.) Mars is an icy desert with almost no atmosphere, and Jupiter is little more than a strange ball of gas. All barren – metallic, meteor-pitted rocks, revolving around the blank sun. And here we have trees and grass and rivers, and frost on cold mornings and dew on hot ones. And meanwhile, we live in a dirty, narrow claustrophobic life-world, arguing about politics and sexual freedom and the race problem. Undoubtedly, the time for the Great Change is at hand.

I apologize for sounding didactic. It is impossible to say anything that is not commonplace without sounding didactc.

After half an hour of this state of intensity, my automatic mental cut-out came into operation. I was using too much energy. And I seemed to be no nearer to penetrating below my normal personality levels to the deeper-self.

A week after Christmas, I went to Hucknall to visit my family. This was an interesting experience. Although the place had changed so much since my childhood, it was still full of memories. And my ability to re-create childhood memories with Proustian intensity meant that I kept slipping back thirty or so years, and *becoming* a child again. The whole mystery of personality was underlined, for it became obvious that the being I normally accepted as 'me' was made up of layer upon geological layer of response to experience, habit patterns. To return to my childhood was to feel half-naked. But it was also to realize that the seeds of distrust-of-life are planted in us very early, and permanently stunt most human beings.

After a week at Hucknall, and a day spent at Sneinton – having ascertained that Lady Jane was in South America with her new husband – I went back to the Essex cottage. This was full of damp, with the window frames corroded and the curtains rotted from the sea. It seemed to be full of immense spiders, and it took me days to catch them all in a cardboard box and throw them into the garden. (No doubt they died there; but I was too aware of the small creatures' terror to squash them with a folded newspaper.) Large fires and a local cleaning lady soon had the place comfortable enough, and in due course, new curtains were bought and the window frames replaced with aluminium ones.

I was intensely happy there. My brain overflowed with energy, so that I had to practise a kind of yoga to get to sleep at night. If I woke up in the night, the world suddenly seemed so interesting that I had to get up and walk out on the beach. It came to me with great clarity that man is the first *objective* animal. All others live in a subjective world of instinct, from which they can never escape; only man looks at the stars or rocks and says 'How interesting . . .' instantly leaping over the wall of his mere identity. It is the first step towards becoming a god.

I decided it was time I expanded my scientific interests, which had become so narrow over the past few years. I sent for back-issues of *Nature* and *The Scientific American* for several years, and read through them systematically, searching for new directions, clues to the nature of the creative excitement I felt stirring inside me. I turned to mathematics, to see whether my new powers of relationality would improve my mathematical faculty. They did, but to a smaller degree than I had expected. I was able to see interesting relations between different disciplines – number theory, theory of functions, non-Euclidean geometries and so on. I developed remarkable powers as an algorist – a lowly branch of mathematics concerned with devising methods for solving problems – because of a completely new ability to see, for example, how certain variables could be replaced by the functions of other variables. But I was also aware that this was all a game, that to be good at mathematics is not very different from knowing the Greek dramatists by heart, or speaking fifteen languages. The real problems of human beings are so unrelated to these abstractions. The trouble with most people is an obsessive desire for security. They want domestic security and sexual security and financial security, and they waste their lives pursuing these until one day they realize that death negates all security, and they might as well have saved themselves trouble from the beginning. No wonder most philosophy and art has been so pessimistic. It is statistically true that 999,999 people out of every million waste their lives so completely that they might as well have saved themselves the effort of being born.

My great break-through occurred in the spring.

I had spent some weeks with Littleway, who was now writing an immense work to be called *Microcosmos*, that would go beyond Hegel and Whitehead. We would drive off in a great secondhand Bentley that Littleway had bought, and aim at getting to some large city before the afternoon was too far advanced. Nottingham, Derby, Birmingham, Chester, Bath, Cheltenham, Lichfield, Hereford, Gloucester, Bristol, Coventry, Exeter, were all explored. The aim was bookshops, especially secondhand ones. We would ransack these for works on philosophy, load up the car, and drive back. Littleway's collection was becoming enormous. We found works by odd, half-forgotten figures like Lotze, Deustua, Edouard von Hartmann, Eucken, Vaihinger, Schleiermacher. Then we would spend days sitting in the library in front of the fire, quietly reading, and I had to make summaries of the books I read.

One warm, showery day in April, we were driving back near Stratford on Avon when Littleway said: 'I wonder if old Miss Hinckson's still alive?' I asked who she was, and he explained she had been the governess of his wife (who had died in 1951). We turned south towards Evesham, and found the small Warwickshire village a mile off the main road, at the bottom of a steep valley. Miss Hinckson lived in a cottage on the outskirts. She proved to be a pleasant old lady in her late seventies, with an enormous amount of thick white hair. She lived with her sister, a few years her junior. The old ladies were charming. They were obviously fairly well-off, for the cottage was actually a small Tudor house, with about an acre of land, mostly smooth lawns. They gave us tea on the lawn. There was only a very slight breeze, and it smelt of lilac. Since Littleway did most of the talking, I sank into a condition of drowsy relaxation, enjoying the peace, looking at the old ladies and thinking that, like all of us, they must feel time to be a swindle. The house was of a warm grey stone, with the usual Tudor beams. Littleway was asking them if they had seen the ghost; I gathered that the ghost of a lady dressed in blue was sometimes seen in the hall, carrying a small black dog. It came to me, looking at this quiet garden, that this was why there is so much sadness in romanticism – in the thought that we can only enjoy these things for a few years. I could enjoy its beauty without any such thought, free of this feeling that there is always sorrow concealed in the heart of happiness. They came so close, the romantics . . . they saw that our capacity to enjoy beauty for its own sake indicates that we have moved into the borderland between animal and god. But it never struck them that, in that case, we might be closer to the god than we realize.

The old ladies wanted to show Littleway a new flower bed and present him with some mint; they left me sitting on the lawn.

My eye fell on a shallow ditch at the bottom of the lawn, which ran in a curve around the house. Suddenly, it came to me with complete certainty, as if someone had spoken in my ear, that this was the remains of a moat. I tried to imagine what this garden had looked like when it had a moat – idly, as one does. The result was surprising; it was as if the ditch had filled with water. I do not mean that I could *see* it full of water. This was not an hallucination. I was imagining it; but imagining *as if in a dream*, so that the imagination was a kind of inward seeing. Moreover, with the same vividness, I could see a bridge across the stream, somewhere in the direction of the garden gate, and bare ground between the trees on the other side instead of grass, although there were some bluebells.

I hardly dared to breathe, afraid this intensity would go away. I looked at the house, and tried to imagine it as it had been four centuries ago, using intelligent speculation, and my knowledge of the period. The beams would probably not be painted; they would be tarred. The roof might be thatched, but more probably, would have wooden slates instead of dull-red tiles. Again, the impression was vivid, as if I had quite suddenly dozed off to sleep and *dreamed* of the house.

Then I understood, and it was so obvious that I laughed

aloud. Human beings are completely mistaken about the function of the senses. To put it very crudely, and to over-simplify to the point of falsification: the senses are not intended to let things in, but to keep things out. We are superior to the animals because our senses let in less than theirs do. Most animals possess a degree of 'second sight', as many dog-owners will testify. Like the pet greyhound of Richardson, the gardener at Langton Place, who used to growl at the corner where his predecessor, a spaniel, had his basket. I do not believe he saw the ghost of the spaniel; his senses performed the same kind of trick that mine had just played; he was aware the spaniel had been there, and would resent him, with a reality that makes human awareness seem abstract and thin. The homing instinct is the same thing, the use of some simple, direct sense of place and time that human beings have lost. Pigeons that find their way over hundreds of miles; eels swimming from the Sargasso Sea across the Atlantic; deer mice returning unerringly to home territory. Aaron Marks had been a student of animal behaviour before he turned entirely to psychotherapy, and he had once spent an evening telling us of dozens of similar examples, all demonstrating that animals possess a kind of 'psychic radar'. Man has lost it, for the very good reason that he wanted to. Too much insight destroys efficiency. Dick O'Sullivan demonstrates this; while the accident to his skull gave him second sight and a gift of almost perpetual ecstasy, it prevented him from being able to do the most ordinary jobs, just as a drunken man loses the ability to concentrate. Man has narrowed his perceptions because narrowness is synonymous with concentration. And to compensate for the loss of this direct perception of multiplicity, he has developed art and literature and music and science.

But a point has arrived in evolution where he can afford to relax, to broaden his senses again. And this explained my 'vision' of the Tudor manor house. I have said that my 'vision' had the quality of a dream, and this explains exactly what happened. We cannot normally dream in broad daylight, because sensory impressions are so strong, and the imagination so weak in comparison. The imagination comes into its own in sleep, when there is no alternative reality to contradict it. My power to control the prefrontal cortex had amplified these powers we call imagination, so that the daylight reality was no longer strong enough to prevent its operation.

I say 'these powers we call imagination', because it is not 'imagination' in the ordinary sense – the ability to daydream. Imagination is the ability to grasp the reality of factors not actually present to the senses. These factors really exist, so the power of grasping them is closely related to sight or touch, not to daydreaming. It is a power to reach out beyond present reality just as radar can penetrate clouds. Man is slowly developing a mental power analogous to radar, to free him from this self-chosen narrowness of perception.

Now, looking at the soft grey stone of the house in the golden, late afternoon sunlight, I recalled a passage in Rilke, in which he speaks of a silence as undisturbed as the interior of a rose, and of how he was standing, leaning against the fork of a tree, when this deep calm came over him and he experienced a sense of mystical union with nature. It reminded me that man has always had clear flashes of the powers that will one day be natural to him.

I thought about the ghost of the lady in blue, carrying her black dog. I had thought of her as coming out of the front door, and walking towards the gate, and I looked in this direction; but my imagination created her coming out of a side door of the house, visible from where I was sitting, and walking towards the old bridge across the moat. The black dog was not in her arms, but running in front of her.

Littleway returned with our two hostesses. He looked at me curiously; he was sensitive to my changes of mood. We declined to go indoors for a gin and lime, and the ladies walked us towards our car. I asked casually if the 'ditch' had been a moat; Miss Hinckson said it had. I said: 'I wonder how they got across it? By drawbridge?' 'Oh no, it wasn't that kind of moat. There was a little bridge, over there, I think. The garden gate was over there in the seventeenth century – we have a print of the house indoors. You must look at it next time you come.' I wished they had suggested this earlier; I would have liked to find how close I was in my mental picture of the place. Finally, as we climbed into the car, I said:

'If the garden gate was over there, which way did your lady in blue walk?'

'Out of the side door over there. Emily saw her only a year ago, didn't you dear?' Her sister looked at me oddly and said: 'You haven't seen her, have you?' I laughed. 'No, I'm not at all psychic.' 'I am,' said Emily sadly.

I wasn't sure how much to tell Littleway. His mind was on great Hegelian syntheses; it seemed a pity to change its track. So I kept silent about it, and let him talk on about Lotze. But now I had had the basic insight, I thought about it day and night. This will.seem a little difficult to grasp for most people, who fail to recognize that all our senses are a kind of radar. You do not *see* a green tree. Your eyes record light of a certain wavelength, and a symbolic shape which you call 'tree'. If a car backfires in the next street, your ears catch waves in the air, just as a fish's sides record pressure waves in the water that warn it of the approach of an enemy. We are small spots of sensitivity, catching all kinds of vibrations from the surrounding universe. And providing the vibrations are there, there is no theoretical limit to our sensitivity. What is more, man has been developing unusual powers of appreciation of nature in the past few centuries, from Gray and Cowper onwards, these odd moments of deep communication with 'alien modes of being'. Surely this explains, for example, the odd experience of Miss Moberley and Miss Jourdain at Versailles in 1901, when they were apparently transported back in time to the days of Marie Antoinette? Why assume anything supernatural, or a 'loop in time' of the kind that J. W. Dunne suggests? All they had experienced was a presage of the powers that all men will possess one day.

One might raise an obvious logical objection at this point. Let us agree that I might somehow be capable of reaching back into the past by a kind of sensitive imaginative insight, reconstructing it, as it were, just as a palaeontologist can reconstruct the skeleton of a prehistoric mammal from a few bones; but with a far more delicate intuitive sensitivity, rather than abstract thinking. It is still a long way from this to seeing Marie Antoinette and the Comte de Vaudreuil near the Petit Trianon.

This again springs out of our preoccupation with the 'natural standpoint', the everyday life-world. Think a moment; as I look out of this open doorway at my lawn, with the trees just putting out green leaves and a thrush singing noisily, I am not really 'seeing' my garden; I am receiving light of a certain wavelength and sound of a certain pitch, and I have learned to distinguish the light green of the lime trees from the darker green of the fuchsias in the way that a good musician can immediately tell the difference between an alto and tenor saxophone, or a piccolo and a flute. What my senses receive is mere energy; *I* clothe it with colour and sound and warmth. This is a miracle; that is to say, it cannot be 'broken down' into simpler terms. Obviously, our powers of synthesizing 'reality' out of dead energy are incredible. Look at a newspaper photograph through a magnifying glass. All you will see are black and white dots. Remove the magnifying glass – you have a picture of a child laughing, and you can see the expression on the child's face. Look at it again through the magnifying glass. How can those crude dots – and so *few* of them – produce that subtle expression? If Martians were the size of fleas, and a Martian could walk over the page and look at the photograph, he would assure you that you are merely imagining that you can see the child's expression. These black and white dots cannot have an expression.

We also see the world 'close up', and we can see it is made up of mere objects, like stones and trees and houses. Staring at it, we say : 'It cannot possibly reveal any more to *anyone* than it is now revealing to me. Anyone who says so is letting his imagination run away with him.'

When I got back to Langton Place, I tried to repeat the 'trick' of letting my imagination carry me back in time. It didn't work, but I knew why. I was tired. Moreover, I had to prepare for the 'leap', as I had at the Tudor cottage; through relaxation, a sinking deep into myself, a gathering-together of my forces.

This ability to somehow reach out to the past was obviously the next stage of development beyond the ordinary use of the prefrontal cortex. And suppose there should be still further vistas beyond that?

We ate a hearty supper of a dish prepared from artichoke hearts and parmesan cheese – one of my favourites, an invention of Littleway's French chef. With it, we drank a small quantity of good wine – less for the effect than for its taste. And afterwards, we sat in front of a large fire in Littleway's library, examining our finds for the day, which included several early translations of Kant, among them the *Dreams of a Ghost Seer*. It was a pleasant room with a high ceiling, although somewhat too large for comfort on a winter evening. I found myself wondering about the portrait of the bearded man in the corner above Littleway's chair. Once again, I made the effort of projection. Again, very briefly, it worked. I saw – or imagined with dream-like clarity – the same library as it was nearly two centuries earlier, before the turn of the nineteenth century. The huge fire was of logs, not coal, and there was something odd about their arrangement: instead of being piled up in the usual manner, they were arranged neatly to form, as it were, three walls in the fireplace, with the fire burning in the middle of them. There was no grand piano in the far corner, of course. The room was lit by candles. And the bearded man sat by the fire, in a high-backed chair that looked extremely uncomfortable to me, reading a small octavo volume, with a pile of others at his elbow. All this was a glimpse, an over-all impression, without time to take anything in. I could not, of course, examine anything closely, even if I had been able to maintain the image. One cannot examine an imaginary object, no matter how vivid the imagining. To do so would be to invent what one saw. If I wanted a more detailed impression, I would have to put far more effort into the act of imagining, and get a more vivid *over-all* impression, which would include more details.

I said: 'Henry. Do you know anything about the man up there?'

'Not much. He made his money in coal – industrial revolution. Why?'

'You don't know, for example, whether he had an odd way of making his fires of logs arranged in walls around the three sides of the fireplace?'

He looked at me curiously.

'No, I don't. I believe there are letters and old diaries in chests upstairs, if you want to investigate. What's it all about?'

I told him. 'A sort of flash of intuition that came to me as I looked at his portrait.'

Littleway said drily: 'You're getting very fey in your old age.'

Neither of us spoke for half an hour. Then I said:

'Still, it would be strange if this prefrontal cortex gave us the secret of time travel.'

He looked startled.

'What on earth are you talking about? Time travel? You know that's an impossibility.'

'You thought the prefrontal business was an impossibility too.'

'I don't deny it, my dear Harry. But we're talking on a totally different level now. Time travel's all right for the people who write science fiction, but it's obviously a misunderstanding of language. Time doesn't exist as such. I mean, suppose we had a word to describe the fall of water over a waterfall, a word like "fluming", let's say. So that if you talked about the flume of water, people would know that you meant the falling of water over a waterfall. Just because there's a noun "flume", it doesn't follow there's anything definite to correspond to it. It's a lot of things – water, rock, kinetic energy, and so on. Or supposing people were born on trains, and they invented a word to describe the way that objects seem to flow past the windows of the train when it moves . . . What shall we say? – a word like zyme. When the train stands in a station, they say "There's no zyme". But if you started to talk about "zyme travel", you'd obviously be making a linguistic error.'

I quote these remarks of Littleway's to illustrate the way that his mind had begun to work in this philosophical, analytical way. It would have been completely out of character for him before his 'operation' a few months before. Power over the prefrontal regions produces a widening of perspectives that makes for brilliant, if discursive, thinking. (For example, my chief problem in writing this memoir is to stick as closely as possible to the narrative, for every sentence suggests a dozen fascinating parentheses.)

I tried to explain to Littleway the theory I have set out above, but his highly trained scientific mind rejected it. He said:

'Alright, I agree that we don't perceive the universe, we *read* it. But you can't read what's not there. And once Marie Antoinette's dead, she's not there any more. And if you think she is, that's pure imagination.'

'I agree it's imagination in a sense . . .'

'In that case, it doesn't fall within the province of science. It's pseudo science. Read Popper and Martin Gardner.'

I said: 'Look, take an example. Suppose these papers up-stairs revealed that your great great grandfather *did* make the fire in the way I've described. Wouldn't that be a sort of proof?'

He smiled in a way that indicated that he was humouring me.

'I suppose it would be. You go ahead and prove it if you can.'

That ended the discussion.

One of the best things about this new consciousness was the experience of waking up in the morning. Its nearest equivalent in ordinary consciousness is the feeling on the first morning of a holiday, with its sense of excitement and expectation – of the enormous *potentialities* of the day ahead. Most people are already in mental harness when they wake up. Their eyes are fixed straight ahead, on the next job to be done; they don't look to left or right. They behave as if they had no choice – which indeed, they probably haven't, as far as work goes. On a holiday, there *is* choice; the mind withdraws and contemplates the world with pleasure, surveys it before moving into activity. And this bird's eye view of one's life brings a surge of affirmation, of energy. And one suddenly realizes that the choice was always there, even on the busiest day. For it is not a choice of activity, but a choice of consciousness. You can start *any* day with the sense of multiplicity and excitement that a holiday induces.

Now I woke up every morning to the feeling of life as an immense holiday, a holiday from death and darkness. And on the morning after my experience at the Tudor cottage, it was much stronger than usual. I drew my curtains, and looked down on the gardener weeding the flower beds, and on the smooth lawns. Littleway had had a fountain placed in the centre of the main lawn. Before the operation, he had been indifferent to nature; now he loved to sit on the lawn and watch the play of water, and the movement of the goldfish under the floating leaves.

Again, the surge of insight came, as on the lawn of the cottage. But this time it was not related to Langton Place, but to the cottage we had been in yesterday. It came as a 'realization', that is, a feeling that it was something I already knew – like searching for a key and then finding you had it in your hand all the time. It was the feeling that Miss Hinckson's cottage had in some way been connected with Ben Jonson and Sir Francis Bacon. For a few minutes, I wondered if I had read about it somewhere and then forgotten it, but finally decided that this could not be so.

At breakfast, I asked Littleway if he knew anything about the cottage. He said no. Miss Hinckson had bought it out of a legacy at the end of the war. His wife had spent some time there, but he was too busy at the time to take any interest in the place.

I said: 'I think I'll drive down there this morning. I'd like to ask them more about the place.'

There was no need for him to ask what I had in mind. He only smiled and nodded.

Driving down towards Evesham in my open-topped car, it came to me that there was nothing very strange in this faculty I seemed to be developing. When I look at an object, I assume that my senses are giving me its 'reality'; but this is untrue. For example, looking at the Tudor cottage, I see its shape and colour and dimensions with great clarity, and I feel that my senses are telling me the 'whole truth' about this cottage. I forget that it possesses a dimension that is not apparent to my ordinary senses: a time dimension. It has a history; other people have lived here and died here. Now if I sink into a condition of meditation, the 'silence like the interior of a rose', this historical dimension becomes real to me. As I look at it, I *realize* (and the word is important) that it has a history. In other words, my senses give me more of its reality than when I am stuck in the present. This is not imagination. It really *has* a history, and I can realize this, as clearly as if I could see long-dead tenants walking around the lawns. So why should there be a limit to how much one can 'realize' about a place? It should be possible to look at a rock in the Grand Canyon, and intuitively grasp its history over millions of years . . .

It took me about an hour and a half to get to the cottage. The old ladies were sitting under the trees, one of them sewing, the other reading. They seemed glad to see me and offered me coffee. I accepted and came to my point immediately, explaining that I was interested in Tudor architecture, and wondered if they knew anything about the history of their house.

Miss Hinckson said: 'You could have saved yourself a journey. Diana Littleway was fascinated by the place, and she looked up all kinds of old records. I thought I had them in my room, but I can't find them. So they must be at Langton Place.'

I asked: 'Did she find anything interesting?'

'That depends what you mean by interesting. It was built in 1567 by a relative of Lord Burghley's. There are the usual documents – account books and so on.'

'Has it any literary connections, as far as you know – with the Elizabethans, for example?'

'I don't think so. Certainly none with Shakespeare.'

They were polite and charming, but they obviously knew nothing. I drove back to Langton Place and arrived at mid-afternoon. The day had become almost uncomfortably hot, and Littleway sat in the library, with all the windows open, surrounded by books, and making notes on a tape recorder.

'Any luck?'

'The materials should be here somewhere. Miss Hinckson said your wife became interested in the place and made a lot of notes.'

'Yes, I told you that. Damned if I know where they are. There's a couple of chests of her things still in the attic. It'll be too hot up there at the moment. Why don't we look early in the morning?'

But I was too interested to be put off. I borrowed the attic key, got Roger's permission to go through his part of the house (for the stairs to the attic were in his half) and went up immediately. Once in the attic, I saw why Littleway had never taken the trouble to look through his wife's effects. The place was very hot and very dusty, and piled to the roof with cases and trunks, broken chairs, spare mattresses, old magazines and newspapers, items of disused garden equipment, rolls of wire netting. The large bundle of keys Littleway had given me seemed to fit none of the trunks or cases, so I started by investigating a chest of drawers jammed in a corner. It contained bundles of letters, neatly tied with ribbon and labelled: 'Letters from Henry, 1937–1939', 'Letters from mama, 1929–1941', and so on. Lady Diana had been an obsessively tidy woman. It took me only ten minutes to track down a stiff covered notebook with a typed label 'Notes for history of Bryanston House'. Although I did not know the name of the cottage, I knew intuitively that I had found what I wanted. She had written inside: 'Notes based on books and documents found at Bryanston House, near Bidford on Avon, and at Gorhambury House, the home of Sir Francis Bacon, June 1947'. I took my find down to Littleway, and showed him the inscription. 'What the devil would the documents be doing at Gorhambury House if the cottage had no connection with Bacon?' Littleway said 'I dunno,' and leafed through the volume. Then he smiled, and pointed. 'Bryanston House (so named by its fourth owner, Major Thomas Bryanston, in 1711) was built by Lord Burghley, the uncle of Sir Francis Bacon'.

I spent the rest of the afternoon reading Lady Diana's neat and pedantic notes, fifty-two pages of them. Littleway had been in America that year – at M.I.T. – and his wife had become fascinated by Bryanston House, and slightly exasperated at the Misses Hinckson, who saw it simply as a pretty cottage, and were totally uninterested in its history. She had decided to devote a few months to finding out about it. She found documents in a priest's hole in one of the upstairs rooms, and took them to the British Museum, to be looked at by the Elizabethan expert, Yorke Cranton. She found the Elizabethan writing impossible to decipher. Cranton was able to tell her that the cottage had been built to the order of one Simon D'Ewes, of Stamford, a cousin of Lord Burghley. But from 1567 until 1587, it was occupied by two ladies, Jennifer Cook, of Hillborough, in the Parish of Temple Grafton, and her cousin, Annette Whateley, or Watley. In 1587, both ladies married, and the account books found in the cottage ended in this year. In 1622, the cottage was sold by Thomas Burghley, the son of Queen Elizabeth's great minister. The new owner was William Hoare, a landowner of Bidford on Avon.

Yorke Cranton was apparently sufficiently intrigued by the Burghley connection to check at Hatfield, the home of Burghley's son, where most of the Burghley papers are preserved. A clue there led him to Gorhambury House, near St Albans, where, apparently, there was definite evidence that Lord Burghley was the owner of the cottage.

To judge from Lady Diana's account – less explicit than it might have been – Yorke Cranton had become rather excited about these documents, indicating that Burghley, known for his caution and virtue, had been involved in a sexual intrigue with the daughter of a Charlecote gamekeeper – for the evidence indicated that Jennifer Cook, born in 1549 (and therefore only sixteen when she became mistress of Bryanston House) had been some kind of a servant maid at the home of Sir Thomas Lucy when Burghley met her. If the intrigue could be proved, then it threw a new and interesting light on Burghley. And then, for no discernible reason, Cranton's interest seems to have evaporated. Perhaps his researches led into a blind alley. Lady Diana refused to be put off, and spent some time at Gorhambury House, examining documents that showed that the cottage was given a new roof in 1588 – the year after the two ladies left, indicating that it was still in use – and that a local farmer was allowed to plant wheat in the field adjoining its orchard. From this, Lady Diana made two deductions: that Burghley ceased to use the cottage after 1587 (for otherwise, he would have wanted to preserve his privacy, and would not have allowed the farmer to use his field), and that it *was* used by some other person, probably a member of the family, since the account books were found at Gorhambury House. Who paid for the repair of the roof? Not Burghley, who was reputed to be mean. Then it was probably either Francis Bacon or his brother Anthony. The indication would therefore seem to be that one of the Bacons used the cottage after 1587. (Their father had died in 1579.)

Although the notebook was full of details copied from accounts and documents, this was the sum of its information. So my intuition had been correct. The place *had* been connected with Sir Francis Bacon after 1587. There was only one minor puzzle – why was there no definite evidence of this? Surely a village the size of Bidford would be full of gossip about the visits of a man as important as Bacon, particularly after the trial of the Earl of Essex in 1601. Some local historian would almost certainly have preserved the memory. The only mention of a name in connection with the cottage was of a Mr John Melcombe, who paid twenty-seven shillings and eight pence in 1590 for 'three hogsheads for the storing of cyder' to Nicholas Cottam, a cooper of Stratford upon Avon.

I had never before done any literary research, and this fascinated me. I found a life of Sir Francis Bacon in Littleway's library, and read right through it. That Bacon used the house was soon verified when I discovered that he became a member of parliament for Melcombe in 1584; 'John Melcombe' and Francis Bacon were almost certainly the same person. A life of Lord Burghley gave no indication whatever of an intrigue with Jennifer Cook of Charlecote. But the story of his run-away first marriage to Mary Cheke, sister of the great teacher, indicates that he was of a romantic disposition, while his second marriage, close on the death of his first wife, indicates that he was a man who did not enjoy celibacy. And why a priest's hole in the house of a man who was a staunch Protestant and persecutor of Catholics, unless as a hiding place for someone who could not afford to be caught having a love affair with a gamekeeper's daughter?

Littleway was interested enough in the puzzle to lay aside his philosophy, and help me in my search. He wrote to Yorke Cranton to ask if he had made any new discoveries about Bacon's tenancy of the cottage, and received a curiously evasive reply, whose main point seemed to be that Cranton thought the cottage may have been used by Bacon's invalid brother Anthony rather than by Bacon himself. He made no comment at all on the question of Burghley's affair with the game-keeper's daughter, and ended by excusing his handwriting in grounds of ill-health, and mentioning that he expected to be leaving soon for the south of France. This seemed a pretty clear hint that he would not welcome further correspondence; in fact, he did not reply to a second letter from Littleway.

The more we looked into the affair, the stranger it became. In Bidford on Avon, we discovered that there is a tradition that Shakespeare and some friends held a drinking contest there, and that Shakespeare caught a bad cold – from which he died – after a drinking bout with Ben Jonson and Michael Drayton (in the course of which he fell asleep under a tree in the rain). Jonson is known to have been a friend of Bacon's. Both were at court; both wrote masques (although none of Bacon's have survived). The whole thing was beginning to fit together into a pattern. Where was Jonson staying when he and Shakespeare had their drinking bout at Bidford? Obviously at Bryanston House.

We were both complete amateurs at this kind of thing; otherwise, our next discovery would have been made earlier. Every student of Shakespeare's life knows that shortly before the poet's marriage to Anne Hathaway in 1852, the clerk of the Bishop of Worcester issued a special licence for 'Willelmum Shaxpere and Annam Whateley de Temple Grafton'. No more is heard of Ann Whateley, for Shakespeare married the pregnant Anne Hathaway, eight years his senior. Could there possibly be two Ann Whateleys of Temple Grafton? If not, then the woman whom Shakespeare first intended to marry lived as the companion of Jennifer Cook from 1567 until 1587. Assuming that she was about the same age as Jennifer Cook, she must have been thirty-two or three at the time of the issue of the marriage licence.

By now, I had discovered that my powers of insight were strongest early in the morning, although there were sometimes vivid flashes during the evenings too. During the time when I was reading the biographies and other documents, I made no attempt to use my 'intuition'. I was interested only in collecting the facts. But in the morning we received the reply from Yorke Cranton. I induced the state of calm intensity that I had induced on the lawn at Bryanston House, and then concentrated on the mass of facts. Immediately, without any possibility of doubt, I saw the general outline of the solution to the first part of the problem. In 1566, Queen Elizabeth had visited the Earl of Leicester at Kenilworth, then gone on to see Sir Thomas Lucy at Charlecote. Burghley had seen Jennifer Cook there, and probably seduced her during the days they spent at Charlecote. The forty-six-year-old minister must have found the fifteen-year-old girl an important emotional experience. In the sixteenth century, forty-six was more than middle age; it was the threshold of old age. Burghley experienced one of those total infatuations, to which virile old men are prone; (Goethe and Ibsen had much the same experience). He could easily have bought a house in Bidford or Stratford, but isolation was important; using his relative at Stamford as a cover (Stamford was the Burghley family borough), he built the house half a mile from the village, and moved in Jennifer Cook, together with her cousin, Ann Whateley. It was a rash action, but men who are cautious in business or political life are often prone to rashness in love; besides, Burghley's first marriage showed him as capable of recklessness. The parish register at Bidford on Avon shows the baptism of a girl 'Judith Whateley' on 4 June 1569. The names of the parents are not noted – an unsual omission. Had Ann Whateley also become the mistress of the insatiable minister, or was this designed to protect the real mother, Jennifer Cook? I suspect the latter.

There is a persistent tradition that Shakespeare was caught poaching deer on Sir Thomas Lucy's estate at Charlecote. I place the date for this in 1852, when Shakespeare was eighteen.

It is certain that Sir Thomas Lucy knew of the intrigue between Burghley and Jennifer Cook, since she was his gamekeeper's daughter. (It may have been her father who caught Shakespeare.) Sir Thomas would have every reason for being helpful to the powerful minister. He was aware that Burghley was getting tired of his affair with Jennifer, and wanted to break it off. A useful first step would be to find a husband for Ann Whateley, now well past the usual marrying age for Elizabethan girls. Shakespeare was either bullied or bribed – or perhaps both – into agreeing to marry Ann. Then, at the last moment, plans were changed, and he married the other Anne, Anne Hathaway. Why? Was she already pregnant by Shakespeare, as most biographers believe, and insisted on her prior claim? This is hard to believe for two reasons, (1) that Burghley was not a man to be trifled with; (2) that the connection between Shakespeare and the Bidford household continued; it would almost certainly have ceased if Shakespeare had simply married his own mistress. The alternative view is that Shakespeare married to serve Burghley, but simply accepted another choice. Burghley's taste for young girls was unabated by his sixty-two years; Anne Hathaway was pregnant, and Ann Whateley was not. So Anne Hathaway got the husband. Ann Whateley had to wait another five years.

All of this came to me as self-evident when I surveyed all the materials. It was no speculation but insight. Our discovery of the entry in the Bidford parish register, and the letter from Thomas Burghley to his brother Robert in which he speaks of 'our father's friendship unto Sir J (*sic*) Lucy of Charlecote' came later.

The next question was an obvious one: what did Shakespeare get out of his marriage to Anne Hathaway? Probably money, for there is no record of his following any occupation between his marriage and his flight to London five years later, although he was living with his family in Stratford, and his father was in serious financial difficultes. But almost certainly, to some extent, the friendship of Queen Elizabeth's most powerful minister. For it is significant that in 1587, the year Burghley finally gives up the Bidford cottage, Shakespeare also abandons his wife and goes to London. I am inclined to believe that Duke Angelo in *Measure for Measure*, the upright statesman who is secretly a lecher, is a portrait of Burghley.

It was at this point in our researches that Littleway came across a description of the Northumberland manuscript in Spedding's biography of Bacon, and we suddenly understood the whole plot. In 1867, the Duke of Northumberland commissioned a Mr James Bruce to examine his manuscripts. In Northumberland House in the Strand, Bruce found a box containing various documents, including the twenty-two sheets which are the remains of a notebook kept by Francis Bacon. This notebook has since become known as the Northumberland manuscript, and it contains copies of a number of his works – speeches, essays and letters. But the cover, which contains a list of the contents, also contains the words: 'Richard the Second, Richard the Third', and 'By Mr Ffrauncis William Shakespeare'. The word 'Shakespeare' is written in several other places on this cover – someone obviously doodling: 'Wlm, Wlm, Shakspe, Will William Shakespe, Sh, Sh, Shak, Shak' and so on. Significantly, the sheet is headed: 'Mr ffrauncis

Bacon of Tribute or giving what is dew'. The 'of' is so faint that it could easily be 'a'.

This discovery, of which I had never heard, has always been cited by believers in the Baconian theory as their major piece of evidence. It was immediately clear to me that, in association with the facts about Shakespeare's marriage, it is precisely this.

Since anyone can borrow the various books on the Baconian theory from the library, I shall not go into detail here. Very briefly, the chief arguments are as follows. There is no evidence to connect Shakespeare of Stratford with the plays that bear his name. No plays are mentioned in his will, and he was not known in Stratford as a writer but as a successful businessman who had made his money in the theatre. The original bust in Stratford church, as portrayed in Dugdale's *Warwickshire*, does not show Shakespeare holding a quill pen and a sheet of paper resting on a cushion, but with both hands resting on a sack – a symbol of trade. Shakespeare's father, like Shakespeare's children, was illiterate, and Shakespeare's own signature is a curious scrawl that is illegible even by Elizabethan standards. The only traditions concerning Shakespeare when he returned to Stratford as a successful businessman contain no mention of literature; on the contrary, he seems to have been known as a highly unpleasant man, who enclosed land that actually belonged to the townspeople, and engaged in several law suits over petty sums of money – on one occasion, as little as two shillings.

The evidence that Bacon was the author of Shakespeare's plays has never convinced many people, for it is purely circumstantial. There is legal jargon in the plays, and Bacon was a lawyer; there are phrases that are echoed in Bacon's own essays. The explanations as to why Bacon should have concealed his authorship are not entirely convincing; certainly, the theatre was regarded as a lowly occupation, no place for a nobleman and a servant of the Queen; but why should Bacon have written the plays at all, unless driven by some demonic literary urge?

Our discovery made everything clear. Shakespeare went to London under the protection of Burghley. Bacon was asked to do the young man a favour. He began by doing something he thoroughly enjoyed – making absurd pastiches of Elizabethan melodrama, out-ranting *Tamburlaine* and *The Spanish Tragedy*. Significantly Shakespeare had found employment with the

Queen's company of players. To Bacon's surprise and amusement, these bombastic absurdities – *Titus Andronicus, Timon of Athens, Henry the Sixth*, were extremely successful. To begin with, Bacon took his task so lightly that he shared out the work among friends and acquaintances, including his brother – hence the variations of style in these early plays. But as Bacon became more successful at court, this became inadvisable. To be known as the author of such popular stuff would not improve his position at court. It would be rather as if a present-day Prime Minister or President of the United States became successful as the writer of Mickey Spillane-type novels, written under a pseudonym. So the atmosphere of secrecy increased, and the early plays are published without anyone's name on the title page, as a measure of caution. Finally, after about twenty years in London, Shakespeare is prevailed upon to return to Stratford, and Bacon heaves a sigh of relief. He still produces the occasional play, but is forced to give up in 1613, when he becomes Attorney General. Seven years after Shakespeare's death, the plays are re-published in the first folio, with many alterations, Bacon having had time to revise thoroughly. Bacon's authorship was never a close secret; Jonson and a great many others knew of it, and Jonson referred to Shakespeare as a 'Poet-ape' in *The Return from Parnassus*. Nearly all the works that now actually bear Bacon's own name were written in the last five years of his life, after his downfall in 1621; he evidently decided to make up for lost time and try to establish his name in literature with some serious work.

About a fortnight after our visit to Bryanston House, I lost interest in the whole question. One evening, Littleway suddenly uttered an exclamation of disgust, and threw his book on the floor. I asked him what was the matter, and he showed me the passage he had been reading. It was from George Gilfillan's *Gallery of Literary Portraits* (1845), and ran 'That Shakespeare is the greatest genius the world ever saw is acknowledged now by all sane men; for even France has, at last, after many a reluctant struggle, fallen into the procession of his admirers. But that Shakespeare is out of all sight and measure the finest artist that ever constructed a poem or drama, is a less general, and yet a growing belief . . .' And so on in this vein for several pages. I understood the cause of Littleway's disgust; this kind of gushing platitude is an insult to human intelligence. I had read a great many isolated passages of Shakespeare, quoted in books on the Bacon controversy, but never a complete Shakespeare play. I now took down his collected works, and started to read at *Antony and Cleopatra*, which T. S. Eliot had described as his masterpiece. After half an hour of this, I decided that I had made a bad choice, and passed on to *Macbeth*. By skipping, I managed to get through to the end of this, and then began to read scenes at random throughout the volume. I looked up and found Littleway watching me. I said:

'I didn't realize he was so bad.'

'I wondered how long it would take you to find out.'

Littleway had a one-volume edition of Bacon's works. I now opened this, and started to read *The Advancement of Learning*, then switched, after a few pages, to the *Novum Organum*, and finally to the essays. I said:

'They have something in common. They're both second rate minds.'

As a scientist, I had got used to thinking clearly and logically about important issues, ignoring the trivial, steering clear of negative emotions. In reading about Shakespeare and Bacon, it had never struck me that their 'life world' is made up almost entirely of the trivial and negative. Judged by any modern standard, they are both as outdated as the phlogiston theory of combusion, or the Edison phonograph. Reading their works, I found myself in a petty, stifling atmosphere, such as I once noticed at a party when two homosexuals began quarrelling. It was impossible to get involved in the action of *Macbeth* or *Antony and Cleopatra* because I felt from the beginning that these people are fools, and that consequently nothing that happens to them can possibly matter. In spite of magnificent literary flashes, I had no more desire to remain in the company of Shakespeare's characters than in the company of the two queers at the party. They simply didn't matter, any more than the quarrels of children matter. As to the Bacon of the later works and essays, I found his mind altogether more congenial, but lacking a centre of gravity. They do not spring from any intuitive view of the universe; they are clever bits and pieces on any subject he chooses to turn his mind to. They are the work of an industrious lawyer, not an inspired thinker.

Later, I read Tolstoy's essay on Shakespeare, in which he says all that I have just said, and a great deal more. I found it surprising that his clear analyses should not have completely destroyed Shakespeare's reputation. And then, on reflection, I saw that it was not surprising. Most people live on a level of emotional triviality which means that when they read Shakespeare, they experience the pleasure of hearing their own feelings echoed. And since the language is impressive, and requires a certain intellectual effort to follow, they can have no doubt that this is really Great Literature. This combination – of fine language with totally trivial content – has kept Shakespeare's stock high for three hundred years, and will continue to do so until the movement of evolution consigns him to the dustbin of quaint but meaningless antiquities.

It is amusing to find myself in accord with those critics who, when asked whether Shakespeare or Bacon wrote the plays, reply that it makes no difference. For indeed, it makes no difference.

Very slowly, I was beginning to grasp what was happening to me, and I was able to explain it clearly to Littleway, so that he could no longer accuse me of unscientific thinking. It seemed fairly obvious that this ability to obliterate time was the second stage of development after control over the cortex. The first stage was of 'contemplative objectivity', the simple ability to pass beyond the gates of my own personality and to really *see* things, to realise they exist. This is the basic human trouble; *not* the body. Great scientists and great poets, in their moments of intensity, *see the same thing*: the objective multiplicity of the world. Einstein once said that his chief aim was to see the world by thought alone, without anything subjective. This expresses it. This is the great 'outward urge', experienced by all explorers. It is an attitude of mind, nothing to do with the body.

Both Littleway and I achieved this as soon as we realized what the prefrontal cortex is supposed to be for. Its purpose is to rescue us from the present, to allow us to approach the world from many different angles and points of view instead of stagnating in a subjective life-world. *To escape the subjective.*

Once this was achieved, the next stage followed. The completely steady contemplation of the real world – no longer eclipsed every few moments by the personal – now began to broaden and develop, as objectiveness became a habit. Just as a good conductor can hear a single false note when fifty instruments are playing, just as a good motor mechanic can diagnose a fault from the sound of the engine, so I began to develop this ability to sense 'meanings'.

It first came to me about a week after the Shakespeare business. Littleway and I were back to philosophy. We drove down to Salisbury one day, to explore the excellent book shop close to the cathedral, then decided to go on to look at Stonehenge which Littleway, surprisingly enough, had never seen. I was curious to see how my 'historical intuition' would work on the monument, but I certainly expected no remarkable results. As we drove out of Amesbury, and saw the great stones against the skyline, I felt a tingling of all my nerves, and a prickling of the scalp. This did not surprise me; Stonehenge had always had this effect on me. But as we approached closer, the sensation continued, and grew stronger. I shivered, and Littleway glanced sideways at me and said: 'Impressive, isn't it?' I knew then that he was feeling it too.

The sensations were so strong when we pulled up opposite Stonehenge that I let Littleway buy the tickets, while I crossed the road towards the stones. It was a quite indescribable sensation. If I were trying to represent it in a film, I should use a curious, menacing vibration. But that would be to simplify it. In a sense, it was more like a smell, picked up by some inner sense, a smell of time. Suddenly, I was looking down a corridor of time, and it was perhaps the most extraordinary moment of my life. When a person who has stayed at home all his life travels for the first time, there is a negative, painful sense about the things he sees. He would like the whole world to be at his elbow, witnessing what he is now seeing, verifying that he is really looking at a mountain range or sunset over Hong Kong. There is a kind of pain in being alone in the face of these things.

I was now seeing something that no human being had ever seen; I was looking over an enormous vista, like the Grand Canyon or the Victoria Falls, but it was a vista of time. But I was undoubtedly *seeing* it, grasping it as a reality. It was a vertiginous sensation, like looking over some immense cliff, down thousands of feet of sheer rock, and still being unable to see the bottom.

I had to pull myself together, as a man would have to look away from such a drop. The sense of loneliness was freezing. My identity was negated by the vista of time.

As we passed through the wooden gate, and walked across the turf, I had an unreal sensation, like a diver wading through water. Another party of people passed us, and I had to restrain a desire to laugh at their comfortable cockney voices. To be here in the twentieth century was somehow *quaint*, like a traveller returning from Mars to revisit his home village, to discover everyone still happily preoccupied with local gossip and church bazaars.

Although I had averted my mind from the sheer drop down through time, the 'vibration' persisted as we drew closer to the stones. I asked Littleway: 'How do you feel?' His lips were pursed, as if he was tasting something sour. He said: 'Odd.'

I opened the pamphlet Littleway had bought, and read: 'Stonehenge was built in three stages, the first between 2000 and 1900 B.C. . . . The Aubrey holes seem to have been used as cremation pits, and a piece of carbon from hole 32 was dated by the radiocarbon method at 1850 B.C. . . .' My mind blurred, for a picture had presented itself to it, a picture that I could either look at or avoid. I decided to look at it. The contours of the plain were somehow different, less flat; the grass underfoot was longer and coarser. Enormous, ape-like men, well over ten feet high, seemed to be engaged in dragging a flat slab of stone. Around Stonehenge there appeared to be a moat. Bones of dead animals lay on the ground.

But as soon as I allowed myself to become aware of this picture, I was overwhelmed by other impressions. It was a thoroughly unpleasant experience, like being hit by a large wave as you walk by the sea, a cold, choking sensation. Dozens of impressions of Stonehenge were superimposed on one another. I happened to be staring at one of the upright stones from a distance of a few feet, and all the marks on its surface were somehow quite plain, as if they were writing, an overwhelming feeling of rain and air and time, as well as the adzes and heavy chunks of stone used to chip and pound this surface into smoothness.

There was no point in trying to grasp anything in this confusion of vibrations and impressions. It was a kind of tower of Babel. I began to walk back to the car, and Littleway followed me. And he was now sufficiently in tune with me to remain silent for most of the drive back to Great Glen. I felt completely exhausted, as if I had been through some great danger.

But as my mind calmed, certain things seemed fairly clear. And one was this: that I could see distant epochs of time much more easily than recent ones. It is difficult to explain why this should be so, except to say that 'close-upness deprives us of meaning.' It *is* possible to survey more recent periods of history, by a technique which I shall describe in a moment; but since what is perceived in history is meaning, distant periods are easier to 'see' than close ones.

But the thing that puzzled me most about my Stonehenge experience was this: that there was an odd sense of evil, of menace. This was something I had almost come to discount since my 'operation'. The only time I had experienced impressions so wholly unpleasant was when Lyell and I had looked down into the horrible well of Chichen Itza, with its slimy green surface, and thought of the children thrown into it as a sacrifice to the god.

Why should looking back over long periods of time produce a feeling of terror? Admittedly, there is the sense of one's own unimportance; but all science produces this, to some extent. Besides, thinking closely about this, it came to me that my problem was still one of immaturity. I had not yet learnt to stop seeing myself as Harry Lester, aged thirty-six, one of fortune's favoured children. Once I managed to lose this personal equivalent of provincialism, time would cease to negate me. But why the feeling of menace?

I was so preoccupied with this problem that we were passing through Honeybourne before I asked Littleway: 'Have you ever heard of Stone Age men over ten feet tall?'

'Yes, but not in England.'

'Where?'

'In Java, if I remember rightly. Von Koenigswald dug up some immense skulls and jaw bones – it was some time during the war. He called it *meganthropus* or something. Why?'

I told him of my curious vision of giants. After the Shakespeare business, he was less inclined to be sceptical. He said:

'Your giant theory would be marvellously convenient for explaining how Stone Age men handled stones of that size and weight. But it doesn't sound too likely, does it? I mean, if they *were* giants, they'd have found bones, as in Java.'

Oddly enough, neither of us raised the question of what he had felt at Stonehenge. It was several weeks later that he told me he had also experienced the same 'vibrations'. He said he thought they might be emanating telepathically from me.

Back at Langton Place, Littleway looked up the Javanese 'giant' in Wendt's *Ich Suchte Adam*. From this, we discovered that 'giants' had first been discovered in China, in the same beds as Peking Man, *homo erectus*, the first 'true man', who is approximately half a million years old. Wendt writes: 'As

134

soon as Weidenreich had made a thorough examination of the bones of Chou-kou-tien, he declared that these Peking men had been slaughtered in a body, dragged into the caves of the Dragon's Mountain, and there roasted and devoured. Exhaustive examination seemed to prove him right . . .'

As Littleway read this passage, I experienced again the unpleasant vibration, the sense of evil and violence. '. . . all the Chou-kou-tien skulls had an artificially opened occipital gap into which the hand could be inserted to extract the brain.' *This* caught something of what I felt on Stonehenge. Wendt goes on to describe the finding of the enormous skull fragments near Sangiran in Java, and asks 'had there actually been three forms of early primitive man in Java, one of normal size, one above the average, and one of gigantic type?'

'There were giants in the earth in those days,' Littleway quoted from Genesis. 'But there have been surprisingly few fossil remains. So I think we can assume they weren't all that numerous.'

During the next week, my interest in early man was side tracked. Roger Littleway invited Professor Norman Glazebrook from Leicester University to supper. Glazebrook is the author of a popular illustrated life of Shakespeare, and he told us he was producing a book on Mary Queen of Scots, with excursions into various other aspects of Elizabethan life. He wanted to see Diana Littleway's notebook on Bryanston House. There seemed to be no harm in telling him about my discovery in the parish register at Bidford on Avon. It was not a matter that interested me any longer, and as far as I was concerned, Glazebrook was welcome to the credit for my discovery.

I asked him whether he had seen the Northumberland manuscript. He said he intended to; he had written to ask the present Duke's permission, but was told that it had been loaned to the British Museum for an exhibition of Elizabethan manuscripts and books. I asked him whether he didn't think it demonstrated that Bacon and Shakespeare were known to be closely associated by some of their contemporaries. He shrugged:

'The manuscript also mentions Thomas Nashe. Do you think he was another of Bacon's pseudonyms?'

'But only once, if I remember rightly. Shakespeare's name is written over and over again. So is Bacon's.'

He was not exactly evasive. But it was perfectly clear that it was a subject he preferred not to pursue. In spite of this, we found him a likeable and pleasant man. Littleway said afterwards:

'It's curious the way these scholars seem to get upset about Bacon and Shakespeare. For heaven's sake, they don't have to behave like a virgin who's been importuned. Why not admit that Bacon *could* be Shakespeare and leave it at that? It doesn't make any difference to the plays.'

He mentioned it twice more the following day, and I could see it was bothering him. He said:

'It would be amusing if we could find some absolutely solid piece of evidence that Bacon was Shakespeare. Would they still try to ignore it?'

A few days later, we received a card from Littleway's London bookseller, who said that he had purchased a library with a large number of eighteenth- and nineteenth-century philosophical works. We set out after breakfast, arriving in Piccadilly about three hours later. By two o'clock, Littleway had examined the books and arranged to have some of them sent back to Langton Place. Neither of us was hungry – we seldom ate between breakfast and supper – so we decided to go straight to the Museum to look at the Elizabethan exhibition. I knew what Littleway had in mind. But he didn't broach it until we had spent nearly an hour peering into the glass cases in the King's Library. We were looking at a first edition of the sonnets, open at the dedication page, 'To the onlie begetter of these insuing sonnets Mr W. H. . . .' and so on. Littleway said:

'How is your intuition working?'

I laughed. 'Not too well at this hour of the day. I'm a little tired.'

'No clue as to whom W.H. might be?'

I stared hard at it, and tried to allow my mind to become passive, receptive. I said:

'It might be better if I could touch it.'

'That might be possible. Have you got your ticket to the manuscript room with you?'

I had. It was only three fifteen – nearly two hours to closing time. We went to the manuscript room, and I filled in a ticket asking to see the Shakespeare Sonnets. Littleway asked to examine the Northumberland manuscript. We were both known to the librarian; it took only ten minutes for the book and the manuscript to arrive.

London had fatigued me; my feet had that curious ache that seems to come from London pavements. But I felt pleasantly relaxed. I have always loved the Museum, but now the whole place, with all its rooms, seemed to be present all at once in my mind, the Egyptian mummies and Babylonian sarcophagi and Buddhist deities and Greek statuary. As I sat there, waiting for the book to arrive, my brain began to work with beautiful clarity, and I saw that man's only final salvation lies in the mind. For most animals, life is a slum. For the definition of a slum is a precarious, harsh, hand-to-mouth existence. Life has inserted itself into matter, but its beach-head is small. Matter leaves it only a narrow, cramped space in which it can operate. So life is, almost by definition, narrow, difficult, trivial, Laocoön wrestling with the serpents. Now, through civilization, man has come close to solving the subsistence problem. The *lebensraum* he now needs is purely mental : to survey the world from a distance, to see life as a whole. And he has always known this instinctively, and built libraries and churches and museums, all to aid the mind in its struggle to escape the narrow present . . .

The book arrived. I was physically tired – the room was warm – but felt totally at peace. Now, as I stared at the dedication page of the sonnets, I tried to envisage the publisher who had written it – Thomas Thorpe (who signed the dedication T.T.), and immediately got a clear mental picture of a nondescript little man, well under five feet tall, with a cast in one eye. But it was somehow unconvincing; it had none of the 'vibrations' of reality I had experienced on Stonehenge; it could have been simply a kind of waking dream. I concentrated on the question of 'W.H.', and this was altogether more satisfying. The name seemed to actually be written on the page : Wylmotte Heywood, and was accompanied by a mental image of a coarse-faced man in his mid-thirties, an alcoholic with red veins standing out on his nose. I wrote on a sheet of paper; 'Wylmotte Heywood, elder brother of dramatist Thomas Heywood, who like Shakespeare, was a member of the Queen's Players'. There was undoubtedly a connection with Shakespeare, but it was certainly not one of close friendship. I tried to concentrate again, and this time experienced a clear insight that the dedication, to Mr W. H., had nothing to do with Shakespeare. After this, I had to relax for five minutes before trying again; my insights were dim and unreliable. I tried again; this time, I had a distinct image of some conspiracy. Heywood had carried the sonnets to Thomas Thorpe, who acknowledged him as the 'onlie begetter'. And Shakespeare protested to Bacon that they had been printed without his permission. In fact, it was Shakespeare who had handed the sonnets to Heywood . . . Here, the insight faded.

Littleway, sitting beside me, glanced at the sheet of paper, and nodded slowly. Then he removed the book from in front of me, and replaced it with the Northumberland manuscript. The manuscript consisted of a number of folded sheets, which had obviously been stitched together at some date. It could never have been very bulky, since folded sheets of this size would quickly have become unwieldly. It had obviously been in a fire; the bottom left-hand corner was charred. The sheets themselves were badly worn at the edges.

By now, I felt tired, and my interest in the manuscript was limited. I turned the pages casually, and then stifled a yawn. Pretending to bend over the manuscript, I supported my forehead on my hand, and closed my eyes. My mind immediately drifted into a blank, pleasant void. But at the same time, I became aware of 'vibrations', of smells and sounds. I opened my eyes quickly, for long enough to confirm that the smells and sounds were not actually present in the manuscript room, then closed them again. What was happening was of great interest to me. Free of my conscious personality, my awareness of my identity, my mind was drifting gently, like a boat on a calm sea. Then the stinks and sounds were back again. The stench was overwhelming. It was like a combination of an uncleaned urinal and an equally unhygienic butcher's shop on a hot day. The sounds were the sounds of a market place: cries, the creak and thump of carts, dogs barking, children squalling, and a high, whining buzz of flies.

I was in a narrow, winding street, with timbered houses that almost met overhead. The stink came from the cobbles underfoot, which were slippery with excrement, urine and fragments of food. A broad open sewer ran down the middle of the street. But the people walking along the street did not seem to be bothered by the smell. A small boy progressed by leaping from side to side of the sewer, in which I could see a dead cat. Enormous blow flies buzzed over the sewer, and clouds of them rose in alarm as the boy jumped over them. A coach with two horses was actually clattering along this street, its wheels on either side of the sewer. It had no springs, and jarred and bumped on the cobbles. Most of the people looked extremely poor. A fairly well dressed man who came out of a yard between the houses was wearing metal objects strapped to his feet, which lifted him three or four inches above the sewage; he walked clumsily, with a clanking noise. He held a handkerchief against his face, and its smell – a cheap and very strong perfume – was wafted to me with the other smells of the street.

I was not asleep. I was fully aware of being awake, and even of being in the British Museum (although I hardly noticed this). Littleway asked me later whether I could walk along the street, as one can walk along streets in dreams. The answer is no. Although I felt the physical presence of the street, I was not actually aware of my own body; I was purely an observing mind, and I could change my viewpoint simply by thinking of something else. The odd thing about it was my sense of familiarity with the things I was looking at, as if this were simply an exceptionally vivid memory of childhood.

I changed my vantage point to the end of the street. On all four corners of the street, there were vendors selling food from carts. The one nearest to me was selling cooked fish from a large earthenware bowl. On a wooden slab beside this there was cabbage – the leaves cooked as they lay on top of one another, so they formed a kind of block; the vendor simply sliced parts off this block as though it were cheese. The lumps of fish and mussels floating in the earthenware bowl looked completely unappetizing.

The curious thing about this London of the late sixteenth century – for I had no doubt at all that this was what I was looking at – was its alternation of tightly packed houses with open spaces. I was looking across at a square, whose houses were larger than in the street behind me. The windows had regular leaded panes, although upper windows seemed to have glass in the top half, and shutters on the lower half, which could be opened to let in air. (In the street behind me, there were few glass windows; only open spaces that could be covered by shutters.) In the centre of the square there was an enormous bonfire, whose flames were as high as the tops of the houses, and a troop of mountebanks, with fifes, drums and fiddles were making a remarkably tuneless racket. I observed especially the narrowness of the roofs, some of which looked like pointed witches' hats. Few of these had gutters, so that the rain must have poured off them direct on to pedestrians below. At the far side of the square, there was an open green space with trees. I observed the number of slim church spires against the skyline, and also the number of flags and streamers and weathercocks on the roof tops – conveying the impression that Londoners enjoyed giving their town a festive appearance. And yet the overall effect was not at all festive. It was somehow shabby and depressing. Most of the wood of which the houses were built was unpainted. There was an odd and very distinctive smell in the air, which in this open square triumphed over the smell of stale urine. I cannot describe this. It was musty, rather tarry, and also spicy with a touch of cinnamon or cloves. (I observed that an enormous number of the better dressed people carried pomanders, oranges covered over completely with cloves, and held these to their noses as they walked along. Defoe mentions that these were regarded as being a protection from plague.)

There was no 'unreality' about all this. I could see it as clearly as I could see the actual faces in Piccadilly a few hours before. A large number of the men wore beards, and the Henry the Eighth beard seemed popular. An unusual number of the faces I saw seemed disfigured in various ways. A girl of about sixteen was standing with her back to me, and looked trim and pretty. When she turned, I saw that her left nostril was missing, as if it had been cut off with a knife. Many faces were pock-marked. A large percentage of the women – even the young ones – had hair streaked with grey, which may well have been due to some vitamin deficiency in their diet. I also noticed several rats strolling across the street as casually as if they had been dogs, and this made me speculate whether some of the disfigurements might not be due to rats attacking sleeping babies.

Perhaps one of the oddest features, to my eyes, was the juxta-position of poverty and wealth. Some houses were magnificent in a tall, Rembrandt-ish way, and these might be next door to hovels whose floors were made of stamped earth. Elaborately painted coaches and crude farm carts drove across the square, often at a pace that seemed highly dangerous for pedestrians. Beggars and well dressed men with swords pushed against one another. I noted that the clothes seemed extremely coarse by our modern standards. Most people, rich and poor, wore stock-ings of lumpy wool, and the cloth of their garments struck me as little better than sacking. In spite of this, people looked healthy enough, and there were a great many more obese men and women – grossly, wobbingly fat – than could be seen in any modern city.

I came back to the manuscript room with immense relief. It was like returning from a long – and rather unpleasant – journey. I looked at the clock; it was only four fifteen. It seemed to me that I had been away for hours. I touched Littleway's arm and whispered 'Come on'. We handed in the manuscript and edition of the sonnets, and left. As we came into the court-yard of the museum, with its noise of pigeons and the sunlight on trees, I felt a great wave of satisfaction, and found myself looking with delight at the unlittered ground, the neat house fronts opposite, the light summer dresses of girls.

As we climbed into the car, I told Littleway briefly what I had experienced. He was more excited about it than I was – I was now feeling oddly tired and flat. He asked me at least half a dozen times: 'Are you sure it wasn't a *dream*?' I said I was quite certain it wasn't, because I had opened my eyes and looked around me before sinking back to this 'visionary' level. Then he wanted to know if I could be sure I hadn't dreamed I had looked round the room. But this was not his usual cautious scepticism; he didn't really doubt that something strange had taken place. What he now wanted to know was what had happened – how it had worked.

We discussed it all the way back to Great Glen, driving at forty-five miles an hour on the inner lane of the M.I, and ignoring cars that hooted irritably. The discussion was too long to set out here, but I can try to summarize it.

First of all, what is the nature of time? It is a *function of consciousness*, nothing else. What goes on in the external world is 'process' – metabolism. There is no time out there. This is why the traditional stories of time travel are so absurd, and why it gives so many paradoxes – a sure sign of absurdity; i.e. that if I could go backwards in time, I would confront a whole series of 'me's' – myself of a minute ago, myself of two minutes ago, etc. No, there is no 'time' out there; it is an artificial abstraction from the idea of process. And obviously, it is ridiculous to talk about 'travelling in process' or in metabolism.

I had not, therefore, really travelled in time. But neither had I dreamed. So what had I done?

My own view, at first, was this: that I had used my 'imagination', much as on the lawn at Bryanston House, and that my fatigue had removed some obstruction – my sense of identity, my interest in the external world – so that my imagination had reached a peculiar concentration and continuity.

Littleway said: 'But if it was imagination, why was it so detailed?'

He was right. My earlier argument – about the vision of Bryanston House – no longer applies here. I was wide awake then, and my senses had expanded into a wide net, 'reading' things into reality that I am not normally aware of. In the Museum, my eyes were closed and my senses were narrow – I was half asleep.

We toyed with the hypothesis that this was quite ordinary imagination – that memories from books I had read or pictures I had seen had somehow combined to produce this vision of Elizabethan London. But when I really thought about it, I had to agree that this was not so. To begin with, I knew almost nothing about the Elizabethans; history is not my subject. I said: 'It was like an exceptionally vivid memory.' We both brooded on that. Littleway said: 'You mean a memory of some previous existence?' 'Something of the sort.' 'You think you lived in London in the time of Shakespeare? That's a bit too much of a coincidence.' He was right, of course.

The alternative seemed so wildly speculative that neither of us was very happy with it. It was this: that I had simply tapped resources of *racial* memory – that I had simply descended below the level of my conscious identity, and become identified with some broader human identity. This bothered us, because it implied such an odd theory of identity. I had never been convinced by Jung's talk about the racial subconscious. And if I *had* been tapping the racial subconscious, then why was I still aware of the room around me? I had never lost consciousness, in the sense of falling asleep.

We were both feeling exhausted with talk by the time we drove through Great Glen. By way of terminating the discussion, I said: 'Anyway, I've got a feeling we're still making some childish error about the mind itself. Human beings have always been trapped in a kind of dream-state, like being under the influence of some drug. We've only been free of this dream-state for a few months. Its ways of thought still cling to us.'

What puzzled me about all this can be easily explained. I am perfectly willing to believe that many people possess gifts of second sight, telepathy and so on, and I am even willing to concede that certain of the psychedelic drugs may induce these states of insight. But people with second sight cannot control their gift. They see 'ghosts', or get a glimpse of the future, whether they like it or not. If my vision of Elizabethan London was really a kind of second sight – or 'sixth sense', or whatever – then surely it would operate all the time? For example, I would have a clear 'vision' of the history of this ancient Bentley, the factory where it was made, its previous owners, and so on? Why not? And even supposing that, for some strange reason, it was easier to see the *distant* past than the immediate past, then I should certainly experience 'vibrations' looking at every old chunk of granite used as a mile stone, for it was all millions of years old.

I was too tired that night to try any fresh experiments with my mind. I went to bed shortly after supper, and slept late the next morning, waking well after eleven. I thought that my Elizabethan experience might induce some interesting dreams, but as far as I know, it made no difference.

I stood by the window as usual, enjoying the smell of the hot sunlight and mown grass and flower beds, and also wondering what new experiences the day might have in store for me. For I had a very strong sense of being in the middle of a period of discovery. The door opened quietly and Littleway peered in.

'Oh, you're awake. I decided not to disturb you.'

'What's that?' I noticed the statue-like object he was carrying in his hand.

'I thought you might try your insight on this. Roger brought it back from Turkey years ago. It's a basalt figurine, probably made by the Hittites.'

'Thanks,' I said, extending my hand for it. Then I touched it, and my body froze. Littleway was watching me seriously.

'Are you alright?'

'Yes. I'll be alright.' I sat down on the bed, and took it from him. Again, I was looking down the well of the past, and the sensation was just as real and distinct as if I had taken the top off a real well, and peered into its depths. There was almost a musty, decaying smell, and a hollow echo, although I realize this was superimposed on the experience by my way of grasping it. (Anyone who has read Husserl will understand this.)

It was a disturbing sensation. How can I describe it? Although I was still in the room, with the smells of a hot morning in late spring, this was so much realler that I became another person. My mind had been ready to encounter another pleasant and interesting day, already fixed in its expectations and responses, and now, in a moment, everything was changed; as if someone should switch on the television in the middle of a happy cocktail party, and hear the announcement of war.

There was always a smell of violence about the past, the feeling of men and animals killing without a second thought. But there was something quite special about this figurine that went beyond this ordinary animal disregard for life. It would be over-dramatic to call it a smell of evil, but that comes closer to it than any other phrase I can think of.

I said: 'What was the approximate date of the Hittites?'

'Very roughly, between 1800 and 1200 B.C.'

'Then this thing isn't of Hittite origin. It's a great deal older than 2000 B.C.'

'How can you be sure of that?'

'Don't you feel anything as you hold it?'

'No.'

'Make the effort.'

I took hold of his hand at the wrist, and tried to make him feel it. For a moment, he resisted, flinching; then I felt him make an effort to become receptive to the blur of feeling flowing from me. His resistance was natural. For a few seconds – perhaps half a minute – it *was* merely a blur of feeling, as when someone looks through one of those children's stereoscopes and for a moment, sees merely two pictures, side by side; then, with a mental effort, the two pictures are forced to move together into one, and it is very clear and three dimensional. This is what Littleway had to do, and he made the effort. And slowly, the blur of feeling focused – I could feel it – and he saw what I could see. He said:

'My god, you're right . . . But you can't be right.'

I knew what he meant. The basalt figurine we held was half a million years old – the age of *homo erectus*, the first true man. And that was impossible. The first art was created by Cro-Magnon man – the Venuses of Willendorf, Savignano, Vestonice and the rest. And that was a mere 35,000 years ago. This thing was about *fifteen times* as old.

I think we both suddenly knew that we were on to a problem that went beyond anything we had expected. This was something of which none of the students of early man had any suspicion. We were dealing with something new and profoundly alien.

It was almost immediately after this episode that Littleway began to develop powers of 'time vision'. I believe this was because I had somehow showed him the way. According to my diary, it was on 3 June of that year that he spent two days in his room, having his food sent up to him. On the second day, at eleven in the evening, he tapped on the door of my room. I said: 'Where have you been?' by way of a greeting. He said: 'Wandering around in the past.'

I said nothing. He sat down in the armchair by my window. It was a clear, soft night, unusually warm. The changes in him were more marked than they had been since Christmas; the inward, contemplative look. He told me what had happened. His contact with the basalt figurine had convinced him that 'time vision' was an ordinary potentiality of the human brain. This was all that was necessary – for I must keep emphasizing: all men *already* possess these powers, as they possess, let us say, the power to ride a bicycle. But before the invention of the bicycle, it must have seemed self-evidently impossible that anybody could balance on two wheels. Littleway had spent the day trying to sense the age of various objects in the house – at first, with a frustrating lack of success; and then, at about two in the morning, when he felt completely exhausted and discouraged, success came as he stared at the basalt figure. (Significantly, he had been practising on more recent objects; making again the point that it is easier to 'see' distant epochs of time.) He was so anxious not to lose the faculty that he stayed awake until dawn, practising on everything he could find, including stones from the garden wall. He slept through most of the following day; and when he woke up, found the power had 'consolidated', and that with an effort, he could 'see' the building of the house in the thirteenth century. Then, like a bird that has just learned to fly, he had spent the whole night focusing upon various periods of past history. Since he had become as fascinated by the Bacon problem as I had, he concentrated on the Elizabethan period, with immediate success. He is writing his own notes on it and I was interested to hear that he thought he had actually seen Shakespeare in some kind of tavern. He described the place as having an earthen floor, with a tree actually growing in the centre of the room. He said there was sand scattered on the floor – he was even able to supply the detail that it was brought by cart from a place near the present Southend – and that the lavatory in the back yard was simply a trench dug in the ground and covered with a plank. I asked him his physical impressions of Shakespeare; he said he was physically much smaller than he had expected – little more than five feet tall – and that he had a very lively and aggressive manner. He also mentioned that Shakespeare spat a great deal into the sand, and kept sniffing a bunch of dried flowers in a little wooden box, which seems to suggest that he was afraid of the plague, and thought that spitting might rid him of its 'humours'. Littleway added that most people in the tavern were drinking red wine, drawn from barrels into uncorked glass bottles, and that Shakespeare had a two pint pot of it in front of him, and drank it as if it was beer. If this is really an accurate picture of Elizabethan drinking habits, it may help to explain why the expectation of life was so much less in those days.

But, strangely enough, my own powers advanced to a new stage at the same time that Littleway developed 'time vision'. But there is very little to say about it, except that the sheer 'engine power' of my brain suddenly increased. I woke up in the morning – two days after the basalt figurine incident – with a strangely increased feeling of mental power. My eyes felt as if they had turned into two searchlights. At first I assumed this was simply the ordinary wellbeing due to a good night's sleep until, as the morning progressed, I realized that it was not wearing off, but becoming stronger. And then I knew that I had been mistaken to think that the 'operation' with Neumann's alloy had caused a deep and crucial change. It had only started a new process of development. The brain was just beginning to operate properly. And then I suddenly understood fully, and it seemed self-evident. Lord Leicester once remarked that man is the satellite of a double star; he is permanently torn between two worlds : the external world of matter, and his inner world of intensity. Sometimes, his life becomes so difficult and depressing that the 'inner world' seems an illusion, and he feels that matter always gets the last word. But a great scientist or philosopher, absorbed in his work, knows that the material world is not all that important. He has almost escaped the gravitational force of the 'outer' star. Yet he takes it for granted that this is only a temporary victory; he can never escape the material world.

This is careless thinking. It is not a question of 'escaping' the material world (which would mean death), but of ceasing to be bullied and negated by it; to possess such intensity of vision that man becomes the satellite of the inner-star, never again subject to strong perturbations from the other star. Surely every sensitive person can recognize the truth of this image? In that case, why has it never struck anyone that a time *must* come when the satellite would have passed the midway point between the two stars and become the satellite of the inner star? It was T. E. Hulme who said that life has invaded the realm of matter, but has paid the price of *automatism* for its foothold. Automatism dogs us. A tree is almost entirely a victim of automatism; a dog or cat is much less so; a man is the least automatic creature on earth. And again, it is self-evident that a time *must* come when the balance of power gradually tips, when life gradually outweighs the automatism of the matter it has invaded; it ceases to be a beleaguered garrison and becomes an army intent upon conquest.

And what would such a change in the balance of power entail? Could anything be more obvious when the question is stated clearly? – for the seat of power in human beings is the brain. This brain which, at its best, can generate an intensity of consciousness that lifts it away from material limitations as a hovercraft lifts off the ground. And quite evidently, this increased power will simply be a more powerful engine for the hovercraft. When I had my 'operation', the evolutionary balance was finally tilted; but, like an ordinary balance, it took a long time to swing definitely in the opposite direction. And I had assumed that my new freedom, my new sense of no longer being a slave of material consciousness, was the end of the process. It was only the beginning. At first it was almost a frightening sensation, like driving a car with an enormous engine. I got an uncomfortable feeling that I had gone too far, that I was upsetting the 'balance of nature' by this development of 'head power'. Then I realized that I was the victim of muddled thinking. There is no balance of nature. Nature is a tug of war, and I was winning it.

I also realized – with a certain self-mockery – that the solution has always been within the reach of human beings – to deliberately increase the brain's capacity for concentration by a sustained effort of will. Shaw understood, when he made Shot-over talk about struggling to attain 'the seventh degree of concentration'.

Changes were taking place inside my head, and I did not yet understand them, except to realize that I had developed some strange muscle of the will. I was completely unaware of its potentialities, and had to discover them one by one, accidentally. One day, for example, I was typing some of the earlier pages of this memoir, and I was struck by an interesting insight. I looked across the room at the bookcase opposite, and stared with concentration, as I thought about it. Then, still staring, I moved my eyes to the other side of my typewriter. As my gaze ran across the page in the typewriter, the paper quivered. I did it again, turning the opposite way; it quivered again. And I realized that I was focusing the beam of 'intentionality' to such an extent that it had become an actual force, exerting pressure on things I looked at. Stories of the 'evil eye' have a solid basis in fact; a concentrated beam of malevolence could cause actual damage to its object, just as an acid can erode metal. And human beings have always possessed this power.

The following day, crossing the lawn with bare feet, I stepped on a stone hidden in the grass, and bruised the sole of my foot. I sat down, held the foot in my hand, and stared at the bruised area. The pain immediately vanished. No bruise subsequently appeared; I had somehow instantly rectified the ruptured cells. The following day, I caught the skin of my index finger on a sharp staple sticking out of a sheaf of papers. The scratch began to bleed. I stared at it, and the sting vanished immediately. Then it ceased to bleed. As I continued to stare – it took about a quarter of an hour – the scratch gradually dried; then a thin film formed over it; then it healed up.

When I told Littleway about this sudden increase in the 'engine power' of my brain, he asked me: 'What are you going to do?' What I was going to do was quite obvious. My consciousness now had a far wider grasp. It could suddenly *see* great ranges of fact, like a view from a hilltop. And I was aware that I didn't *know* enough. I felt like a man in a foreign country who has neglected to learn a single word of the language: the sudden regret for wasted time, and the desire to make up for it quickly. I had thought my knowledge of science fairly broad; now it seemed careless and amateur, little more than a dilettantish dabbling. When I considered the material that was actually available for my study, I couldn't help feeling amazed that human beings have come so far under such difficult conditions. Considering how much man is still a slave of his everyday life, it is incredible that he has gone so far in the search for pure knowledge. To contemplate this was to realize the enormous strength of the impulse that drives him to reject the everyday world and try to breathe a purer atmosphere of ideas and poetry.

So instead of bothering to investigate my new powers systematically, I hurled myself into a course of studies that occupied me fourteen hours every day. First of all, it was necessary to learn a dozen foreign languages, for much of the material I wanted – on science, on the earth's natural resources – was available only in foreign publications. I discovered that a week of intense study was enough to give me complete fluency in a language, and that even three days was enough to enable me to pick my way through books or articles.

In order to read these publications, I had to spend a great deal of time in London, much of it in foreign embassies. And I found this an unexpected strain. I had to learn to ignore people; but before I succeeded, I felt like a doctor in a madhouse. To look at a crowd in the Charing Cross Road was depressing, like being in an under-developed country where the harshness of life has made everyone stolid and brutish. What seemed amazing to me was that more of them did not commit suicide; for their consciousness was little more than a prison. I felt twinges of loneliness, the wish that there were a dozen or so others like me with whom I could talk and eat and drink. There was also the upsetting fact that women no longer struck me as even minimally attractive. My sexual impulses were perfectly normal, but the women around me might have been female apes for all the attraction they possessed.

It must be understood that I was not thinking of myself as a kind of superman. I was hardly aware of myself at all; I was too aware of the enormous amount of ground I had to cover. This was the result of a lifelong training in mental activity. And this obsession with forward motion made me fail to grasp certain fundamental issues, as will be seen later.

Let me give an example. The problem of psychical research struck me as an important one, and I spent a week in the library at the Society for Psychical Research, reading up on the whole subject, from Tyrrell's *Apparitions* and Myers's *Human Survival* to the latest and most sceptical material. It was plain to me that I could now account for a great deal of psychical phenomena in terms of the intentionality of consciousness. The human capacity for self-hypnosis is greater than is generally realized, and the deeper regions of the mind are capable of throwing up all kinds of alien bogies. Ghosts can also exist in a more objective sense. I have tried to explain how I came to realize that a 'racial subconscious' really exists. And if this is so, then our notion of our individuality is in some sense an illusion, fostered by the 'separateness' of our bodies. The disappearance of an individual body does not affect the great racial ocean of which it is a part. Life has not only established a foothold in physical bodies; it has a second line of defence 'behind' matter, in which it has more freedom of movement but less actual power. This second line of defence would vanish completely if all living creatures were destroyed, for it might be thought of as a sort of magnetic field emanating from living creatures. This is the 'realm of ghosts'.

While studying in the library of the S.P.R. I met Sir Arnold Dingwall, whose book on poltergeists has long been a classic. It was he who invited me to go with him to investigate a case of poltergeist haunting at the Old Rectory, Croxley Green, north of London. This was an extremely active poltergeist, that threw things, groaned, and made loud noises – one of which was described as sounding like a grand piano dropped from an aeroplane. The house was occupied by a Mr Mudd, an accountant, his second wife, and three teenage children – a boy, age nineteen, and two girls of thirteen and fifteen. There was also a baby by the second wife, a mongoloid, and a Welsh nurse.

The Old Rectory stood more or less alone, but close to an area of modern flats. There was also a children's playground on the other side of its garden fence. We arrived there at six o'clock on a Saturday evening. The nurse let us in: a grey haired woman in her mid-forties, with a sweet and rather pretty face. She looked at me and said immediately: 'Ah, I can see you're psychic.' Surprisingly enough I knew immediately what she meant. She possessed a sort of animal power of 'relational consciousness', which came from inner harmony and a complete lack of ability to use her brain.

I met the lady of the house, a tall, good-looking woman with a cultured voice and a stylish manner of dressing. Obviously, she had been a career woman before her marriage – in fact, I discovered, the editor of a business magazine. Her husband was plump, bald, and not particularly intelligent; it was fairly clear that she had married him for security, and felt superior to him.

The three children came in later. The fifteen year old was plump, and still very much a schoolgirl. Her thirteen year old sister was already much more sophisticated; she was also prettier. The youth of nineteen was gangly, pimply, and apparently bored. I gathered that the major interest of his life was a motor bike, which he had in pieces in the basement.

The family knew the well-known theory about poltergeists: that they are caused by teenagers passing through a difficult puberty, and they talked about this openly over the evening meal. I could see that all of them were glad to have us in the house, although none of them professed to be worried by the poltergeist. The nurse explained that it had started nearly three months before, by knocking a lamp out of her hands when she went to get coal from outside, and then pelting her with lumps of coal. She assumed that it was a child from the playground, and ran into the coal-house, trying to find him. There was no one there. Later that evening, the door of the coal-house was opened – the latch was not difficult to open – and coal scattered around on the snow outside. This went on almost every evening for ten days, while the snow lasted. When the thaw came, the poltergeist apparently lost interest in throwing coal, and now began to make various noises – bangs from the cellar and the area under the roof, tremendous vibrating crashes with a twanging noise – the 'grand piano falling from an aeroplane' effect. There was never any disturbance of furniture after these crashes; even the dust in the room was untouched.

The poltergeist also specialized in shrieks, groans, creaking noises, and a rather interesting effect as if a bag of money was being scattered all over a stone floor. (The floors were of wood.)

They had tried sending the children away one by one for brief periods, but it had made no difference. Several people from the S.P.R. had investigated, but reached no conclusion, except that the 'haunting' was genuine. The poltergeist was noisy but non-destructive, and the Mudd family was assured that it would eventually go away.

Sitting eating supper with them, I was aware of the naivety of their whole approach. All of them were trapped in a very ordinary, dull existence in a rather uninspiring neighbour of Rickmansworth. Their lives were lived on a largely automatic level – a plodding, habitual round. And the house burned with a dull, aching frustration. I found, looking around at them, that I could grasp their problems intuitively, as clearly as if they had all talked to me about them. The thirteen year old, Susan, had already lost her virginity to an older boy, who had now left the district. She wanted to leave home and follow him. Her sister Elfreda knew about this and resented it; she was still a virgin, and had no boyfriend. The stepmother was bored with her family and running a house, and was also upset by her lack of feeling for the mongoloid child; she had always believed she would make an affectionate mother. She was thinking actively about taking a lover, or rather, taking back a lover she had thrown over to marry Mudd. Mudd himself was a dull man, reasonably contented, but aware that nobody else was, and worried about it. The nurse had been in the family since the birth of Susan, and she had hoped that Mudd might marry her. The son was potentially the most intelligent of the family, with an extremely active and questioning intelligence, which he deliberately suppressed at home. He was thinking of leaving home and going to Liverpool to join a motor cycling club who called themselves the Warlocks.

These discoveries were not entirely 'intuitive'. I spoke to the family at length before and after the meal, and they told me enough to give me a clear picture. The wife in particular was frank, and the nature of her interest in me came over pretty clearly.

I still found it hard to understand the poltergeist disturbances. I was far more aware of the depths of my own mind – of my whole subliminal apparatus of will and perception – than anyone in this family could ever be, and I simply could not imagine 'forces' from my subconscious causing things to move around. I was convinced that the disturbances were, in some sense, 'willed'.

The family insisted on watching television after the meal – some song contest involving all Europe. I amused myself by trying to 'see' the age of the house. It had been some weeks since I had tried to practise 'time vision'; it struck me as so much less important and interesting than the work I was doing. But now I had nothing else to do, so my conscience was clear. I let myself sink into a condition of inner peace, cutting out the disturbing vibrations of the family and tried to see the whole house from outside. (I had been shown over every room.) Then, quite suddenly, I became aware of a new factor working in my mind, which is almost impossible to describe. It was a kind of amplifier, picking up my impressions, feeding them through the prefrontal regions of the brain and checking them against everything that had ever happened to me. It is an extremely obvious and simple process, but would take several pages to describe adequately. All I can say is that all one's experience becomes suddenly available for comparison with the present moment, and one's knowledge of the present moment becomes theoretically limitless, for new facets can be illuminated at will.

And suddenly, I knew this place as if I had lived in it and studied its history. And I became immediately aware that there was something in its history . . . Then it came. Of course, the Stanton murder case! The famous 'murder at the Vicarage', one of the most famous cases of the 1860s. Major Arthur Stanton was poisoned with arsenic, and his wife, Valerie, was put on trial. She was acquitted, although it was proved that she had access to arsenic, because there seemed to be no motive for the crime. She gained nothing from it, and never remarried. Now, by focusing upon it, I could grasp the whole drama that had been played out in this house, and understand all its hidden motives. Valerie Stanton was the daughter of an officer who had been killed in the great Indian mutiny of 1857. She had seen her father's body, and those of others who had died with him, and sustained a severe mental shock. This affected her sexual feelings, making her feel that sex was frivolous and sinful. Nevertheless, she married Stanton three years later, and managed to suppress her feelings to the extent of making him a satisfactory wife. Stanton retired from the army after breaking his foot, and they came back to the vicarage. He had been a sportsman before the accident; now, frustrated and bored, his sexual demands became excessive, and there were also certain unusual demands which were never mentioned publicly until the time of Havelock Ellis. Her neurosis returned in full strength. She confided in the maid, for whom she felt some obscure lesbian attraction. The maid, without being explicit, encouraged her to take violent action, and left the weed killer where her mistress would see it. Valerie Stanton poured a quantity of it into her husband's port on 21 April 1866, and he died in agony early the next morning. The case has been written about many times. I have not been interested enough to check whether any of the writers grasped Valerie Stanton's real motives.

After the ten o'clock news, the television was switched off. I said casually:

'By the way, wasn't the famous Stanton murder case somewhere in this area?'

Mudd answered immediately:

'Yes, the old vicarage used to be next door. It was pulled down years ago after a fire.'

I could see he thought he was telling the truth. It was reasonable enough. A house in which a murder has been committed is hardly an estate agent's delight. Dingwall's researches later revealed that there had been a far more sinister and appropriate-looking house several doors down the road (not next door), which became known to local children as 'the murder house'. After this was burnt down in 1910, the estate agent managed to convince a purchaser of the vicarage that it was the 'murder house' that had been destroyed, and one of the books on the subject has stated this as a fact.

But my question led the family to begin talking of the murder. And I immediately became aware that Gwyneth, the Welsh nurse, was far more interested than she would show. She remained bent over her knitting. In fact, I could tell that she *sensed* this was the murder house, using much the same kind of intuition that had come to me about the Bacon cottage near Bidford. The two girls also showed a morbid interest in the story, although it is not particularly horrific, as murders go – and the younger one said 'I shan't want to switch out my light tonight'. I was immediately aware that they also knew something – that the nurse had told them stories that embodied her own intuitions.

Towards midnight, the two girls went to bed. The nurse fell asleep in her chair. We had agreed to sit up until the early hours of the morning, for the disturbances usually took place between midnight and two a.m. Mrs Mudd went upstairs to change the baby. At about ten minutes after midnight, the noises began. First of all, there was a perfectly ordinary-sounding crash from the basement, which none of us noticed for several moments. Then there was a thud that made the windows shake, as if a bomb had fallen a few streets away. This was followed by a moaning sound, not loud, as if a hysterical tennager was crying herself to sleep. This seemed to be coming from a passageway on the other side of the door. Mudd tiptoed to this and opened it. The sounds continued, but now no longer sounded as if they were coming from the passageway.

I now allowed myself to sink into a state of relaxed perceptivity, trying to sense what was happening around me. It was like entering a nightmare. There was a tension of panic in the house, an unpleasant, cold terror, somehow associated with the smell of damp whitewash on a lavatory wall. And I could see that it was not emanating from any individual in the house. It was like a net stretched between them – or rather, between the two girls, the nurse and the mother. The two males played no part in it. I was able to understand quite clearly what it was. The strongest element in it was the nurse's feeling about the house, her knowledge that it was the murder house, or some similar frightening intuition. The second strongest element was the mother's feeling of repulsion towards her husband, and guilt and disgust towards the baby. It was somehow these two feelings that entered into combination, into phase, as it were, with each other. The two daughters played a relatively minor part, but were aware of the vibration in their sleep. It should be observed that the nurse and both daughters were by this time asleep.

The problem here was the complete *negativeness* of everyone in the house. Basically, this was the father's fault. He was self-absorbed, thought about nothing but his job, and completely failed to introduce any element of vitality or creativity into the atmosphere of his home. This meant that everyone was free to develop their own neuroses, with no counter-force, no breath of some interest beyond their personal obsessions.

What surprised me most was the clear, undivided *force* of these negative obsessions. Freed by the sleeping brain, they were as dangerous as a strong wind. .

Still I found it hard to understand how they managed to express themselves physically. I tried to concentrate more deeply; my brain responded with a surge of power and insight. Suddenly I understood. My mistake was in thinking of this house as a more-or-less quiet, still place shaken by forces from the subconscious. But it wasn't. The earth spins through space at a speed greater than an express train, and we ourselves and the chairs we sat in and the walls around us were masses of buzzing atoms. The air was full of every kind of wave and energy. And human beings are deep wells of energy, immense reservoirs of force, the force of life determined to subdue matter. A little of this force was utilizing and controlling some of the great waves of energy that beat against the house like the sea against a cliff. It was a frightening picture; suddenly, the whole universe became a roaring inferno of energies. But the core of the poltergeist activity was the *negativeness* of the human energies in this house. This conflicted with other energies, like pouring water on a hot fire.

I was aware that some of my own mental energies were joining in the uproar, which had increased to a startling extent. There were noises like braking cars, falling money, someone choking and gurgling. Mudd, who was sweating, said: 'My God, it's never been like this before.' Dingwall was looking rather pleased and making notes on a minute pad in the palm of his hand.

I tried withdrawing my mind from the 'rhythm', and succeeded. As I did so, I realized that I could control it. What was going on was a sort of collective nightmare of negative people. It had no purpose or direction; it was rather like the pointless violence of boys who slash the seats on buses, or tear out public telephones. But I had a purpose, and could impose my own rhythms. At first, I tried increasing the noises. The effects went beyond my expectations, amplified by the other minds in the house: banging doors, whistles blowing, breaking glass, and unidentifiable animal noises. Then I concentrated on producing a rhythmical sound, like wind. After a moment, I succeeded; the other minds did not oppose me, but made it louder, so that it was a tremendous uproar, like sitting underneath Niagara Falls in a typhoon. Articles began to blow around the room, although, of course, there was no real wind. Then I caused it to rise and fall regularly. The sheer energy and power of the movement began to destroy the negative vibrations, as someone might start to tap their foot to music. I saw Mudd was listening with an odd, half-delighted expression, and Dingwall looked astounded. (He described it afterwards as the most remarkable poltergeist experience of his whole career.)

Once I had created a rhythm, the rest was easy. It was like spinning a top, making it go faster and faster. I projected a sound like breaking waves into it, then regular thunderous volleys of wind, then a high pitched humming, as of something spinning at a great speed. I was thinking of those lines from *Faust*:

> 'And cliffs and sea are whirled along
> With circling orbs in ceaseless motion.'

The result felt as if the whole house was dancing to some tremendous music. I noticed out of the corner of my eye that Gwyneth had awakened, and was staring around her in amazement. I allowed the sounds to grow less violent, to relax into long, smooth sweeps, like a rolling sea without breakers. Gradually, it lessened, until the sounds died away completely. Gwyneth was staring at me; *she* knew I was responsible. No one else did. Mudd said, 'Well well well . . .' Dingwall had stopped writing, and looked dazed.

No one else spoke for several minutes. Then I said:
'I think that's probably all for tonight.'

I wanted no more of these negative people; they irritated me. Ten minutes later, Dingwall and I drove back towards central London. We had intended to stay the night, but there was no point. Dingwall talked excitedly all the way, and I must admit that some of his conjectures came very close to the truth. He was instinctively aware that the poltergeist was the expression of negative psychic energy. Naturally, he was baffled by the rhythmic quality of the sounds. I took care to drop no hint to enlighten him, but I suggested that he investigate the possibility that the vicarage was the murder house. I should add that the murder had no direct connection with the poltergeist disturbances. This was not a ghost from the past, but negative forces from the present.

The 'haunting' of the vicarage ceased after that night. I expected it to. The disturbances were, as I have said, of a negatively criminal nature, like juvenile delinquency, the result of a sense of pointless freedom, of total lack of disciplinary forces. My intervention revealed the existence of other forces; moreover, positive forces. The poltergeist went back into its shell.

I mention all this, not because I think it of real interest, but because I failed to follow up the clues that it offered me. I should have grappled with the question: In what *level* of the mind did the poltergeist energies originate? But things were developing at such a pace that I had other things to think about.

Besides, I was certain that the question would answer itself sooner or later.

At all events, the poltergeist episode switched my energies back to the question of time-vision. And the following day, in the Victoria and Albert Museum, I realized that these powers were also developing. I happened to be looking at a print that showed Goethe and Wieland being introduced to Napoleon. I stared hard at Goethe, for of all great writers, I had always found him the hardest to visualize physically. Quite suddenly and spontaneously, without any conscious effort, the lines of the picture became reality. Napoleon's chair had its back to a huge pillar, and beyond this pillar there seemed to be vague shapes. Without looking directly at these, I had vaguely assumed it to be a picture hanging on the wall. Now there was a burst of music, and I realized that it was an enormous ballroom behind the pillar. A man called Kraus was standing in a corner of the room, making a sketch. Goethe was a great deal taller than I expected; for some reason, I had always assumed he would be short. I saw why it had always been so difficult for me to form a physical impression of him. If it had belonged to a duller person, his face would have been ugly, or at least, plain. The nose was slightly too large; the cheeks were rather flabby; the face gave the impression of a large blancmange, bulging at the bottom under its own weight. But the mouth was the mouth of a man of impressive self-discipline. It was this discipline that gave the face power to support its own plainness. If I had passed him in the street, I would have assumed him to be the managing director of a big corporation; the face had the kind of strength that one often sees in big businessmen; seldom in poets. Wieland, by comparison, struck me as an academic and aesthetic kind of person, very much the man of letters; the bald head and beaky nose reminded me of a portrait of Wordsworth in old age. Goethe's voice was somehow like his appearance; deep, pleasant, speaking French with a clipped German accent. It struck me clearly that, in a sense, he was as much a man of action as Napoleon, and that there was a deep frustration in him; he would have made a good President of the United States. This is the reason that portraits of him are so unsatisfactory. The painters are trying to see him as a poet, to squeeze him into a mould as a 'poetic' kind of person, missing the curious element of frustrated dynamism.

I must repeat: this was not 'imagination', any more than it is imagination that enables one to see a line drawing as a representation of reality. It requires a certain training to see lines on a sheet of paper as three people having a conversation. For a dog, it would be a sheet of paper with lines on it; not a picture. I was simply able to *see* deeper than an ordinary person. How did I know that the name of the man who made the sketch was Kraus, and that he was the director of the Weimar art academy? Because I was involved *in* the situation, as I might be involved in listening to a familiar piece of music, knowing what is to come. I was tapping a form of memory that went beyond my individuality. The consequence was that I had to make a conscious effort to retain the knowledge when my attention came back to myself and the room I was in. It was, in a sense, like waking from a dream. Yet at no point did I cease to be aware of the room.

It would be tiresome if I went on to describe all the other experiences of a similar nature that now occurred several times a day. I found that I simply had to stare at certain objects for my mind to pass into them, as it were, to reach out and grasp them almost physically, so that the object seemed to suddenly absorb my own nervous system. It happened, for example, looking at a fine Queen Anne dress in the Victoria and Albert, and again, at some early American glassware. It was an almost vertiginous sensation, like falling. Normally, we look at something, and we remain behind our eyes, surveying it as an alien. Now I would seem to *swing* beyond my own eyes, like an ape swinging from branch to branch, out of myself and into the object, *becoming* the object for a moment, but retaining my own mind and nervous system. Bergson rightly called this mode of apprehension 'intuition'.

I should add, in parenthesis, that Goethe came closer than anyone I had ever seen to being a man on the brink of the 'evolutionary leap'. He understood completely the primacy of the will. But he did not understand how to use it. It remained static in him.

I tried to describe to Littleway what was happening to me, and I could see he thought he undersood. But he would have to wait for the experience before he would really understand. Now I suddenly saw the real meaning of the change that had taken place in me, and understood what human evolution has always been aiming towards. The world became a *living* entity, all the time. This is easy enough to understand by analogy. If the ordinary man walks down a crowded street, the street is alien to him; he shrinks into himself, as if wanting to avoid contact with it. But if he returns to his home town on a summer evening after long absence, he allows his being to expand, to open wide, to take the street into himself as if it were someone he loved. In the same way, the historian, reading some favourite page of Gibbon or Froude, opens his being to the past, dissolving into it for a moment. Man's normal attitude to the universe is a shrinking; the thought of the emptiness of space, the eternity of time, causes an involuntary tension, a rejection. Yet his whole evolution has been an attempt to embrace the alien, to expand instead of contracting. The immature and the insecure reject; evolution *means* an expansion and acceptance. Man has so far used art as his chief medium of 'acceptance', for once something is reflected in a work of art, it becomes digestible, acceptable. The human mind can control it. This was the significance of the romantic movement; the human mind was suddenly learning to swallow mountains and forests, ceasing to shrink from their alienness.

The sort of acceptance that a historian feels towards history, that a poet feels towards mountains, I was now feeling all the time, as a matter of course. One effect, incidentally, was to make things appear *more coloured* than usual. The effect was not unlike that described by men who have taken psychedelic drugs : a tremendous three dimensional warmth and richness in everything. But psychedelic drugs suspend the sense of time, absorb man in the flux of his senses, anaesthetize the will. My will was as vital and healthy as ever; it felt all the time like an athlete waiting for the crack of the starter's pistol to hurl itself into motion.

My feeling of dislike of people vanished completely two weeks after I came to London. London crowds ceased to bother me; I no longer felt them alien. A man of the late-twentieth century might feel a nostalgic affection for the London of Sherlock Holmes, with its cobbles and gas lights and horse cabs, and if he could be transported backwards in time to watch the crowds in Baker Street on a foggy evening in the 1880s, he would feel an expansive affection, intense interest. This was exactly what I felt, standing in a bus queue in South Kensington at half past five on a rainy afternoon. For I was no longer in the present. I could look at this scene from a hundred years in the future, as if it were a late nineteenth-century print.

More than this. Everything I looked at struck me as a kind of echo; it seemed to lead on to something else. Looking around me, I was clearly aware of Surrey and Berkshire and the Chiltern Hills beyond High Wycombe and the North Downs beyond Rochester. The meaning and nature of poetry was clear to me; it creates *other* places, *other* times, produces this sense of affirmation. I should add that I was aware of a level of my mind controlling all this intuition. Uncontrolled, it would have been mind-wrecking, for my awareness would have gone on expanding outwards until my mind exploded like a bubble.

My attitude to the people around me had changed from intolerance to pity. Civilization had expanded too fast for them, and their vitality could not keep pace. They are all like gangling teenagers who have grown too fast, and who are consequently pimply and sallow cheeked. But this is slowly ceasing to be true. The pessimism of the twentieth century has been a massive burp of indigestion; but the stomach ache is passing.

And from this position of security, of affirmation, my mind wanted to pierce barriers of space and time. There was a tremendous hunger to look back to the dawn of our world, and to the stars beyond the solar system. And I was aware that these were powers that were embryonic. I had taken the leap to the next stage in human evolution, to become aware of the immense distances man still has to travel.

There was a minor inconvenience involved in all this. I have always been a fairly friendly and sociable character, but obviously, people were now rather irrelevant; they could only distract me. I tried to keep quietly to myself, attracting as little attention as possible. And I found, to my embarrassment, that people seemed to be drawn to me, and that it was difficult to get rid of them without being rude. Ramakrishna once remarked that when a man becomes a sage, people are drawn to him like wasps to a honey pot. In my own case, I am strongly disposed to believe that it *was* some telepathic or psychic force that operated. I could be standing quietly in the Museum Reading Room, looking through the catalogue, totally self-absorbed. Someone would whisper: 'I wonder if I could look at that after you?' and I could tell instantly that this was an attempt to establish contact rather than an ordinary request. If I delayed for more than a few seconds, I would find myself involved in a conversation and then very quickly in an acquaintanceship. The new acquaintance would come and sit beside me on a bench outside when I was relaxing in the sun, and offer his – or her – name, and ask my own. I seemed to have a particular attraction for charming and garrulous old gentlemen, who would invite me out for dinner. Life became so complicated that I was forced to stop using the Reading Room. And then, one day, I was looking through the stacks of the London Library when an elderly gentleman, who had been sitting opposite me in the reading room and trying to catch my eye, advanced towards me. There was no escape, and I experienced a flash of impatient annoyance, a feeling of 'Oh *no*, not again,' and I tensed myself and scowled at the book, willing him to go away. He was about to speak; then, to my surprise, his voice stopped, as if someone had gripped his windpipe; I glanced at him, in time to catch a look of astonishment as he turned and hurried away, his face suddenly red. And I understood something that should have been obvious to me; the power of attraction was accompanied by a power to repel. I subsequently tried this on Littleway and asked him what he felt. He said there was an almost physical sensation of detachment and coldness emanating from me. It had taken me so long to discover this – over a month – because I never felt irritable or frustrated nowadays; I could avoid negative emotions as easily as a good driver avoids other cars. But having learned the trick, I used it to good effect. I was even able to return to the Reading Room again, and break gently with previous acquaintances by emanating an air of self-absorption and slight anxiety.

One morning in mid-July, a book arrived for Littleway, wrapped in an old copy of *Look* magazine, and I saw a photograph of the well of Chichen Itza. The article described the excavations of the previous year, when the well had finally been drained by a pump that could remove two thousand gallons a minute. But what caught my attention was the great double page colour photograph of objects removed from the mud at the bottom of the well. Among the skulls of children, beads, earthenware pots and so on, there was a small black statuette. And as I stared at it, I knew that it was related to the basalt figurine Littleway had shown me.

It may seem strange that I had not returned to this matter in several months; but this was because I was absorbed in so many other things. I had become fascinated by modern history, from 1750 onwards, observing the way in which the great evolutionary current, so easy to recognize in literature and music, becomes distorted when it tries to express itself in politics; the way in which it is driven to compromise, and even to oppose itself. Above all, there was no feeling of *hurry*; I could return to the problem of the basalt figure next year or the year after.

The characteristic of the basalt figure at Langton Place was a certain flatness, an air of abstraction; it might have been by Gaudier-Brzeska. The one retrieved from Chichen Itza had the same quality. I stared hard at the photograph; for a moment, it became a reality, and again I had that sense of looking down an immense cliff of time. Then I realized that my historical intuition had sharpened in three months. I had a sudden and very distinct sense of something hidden, deliberately concealed. I knew with certainty that there is something in the world's prehistory that cannot be found in any of the books on the past. And it was obscurely connected with the sense of evil at Stonehenge.

Littleway was eating his breakfast on the other side of the table. I pushed the colour photograph over to him. He said mildly 'Good heavens,' and went on eating; but he understood. After breakfast, without either of us saying a word, we went up to his room. The figurine was in a cupboard. Littleway took it out, held it across his two palms, and concentrated. He gave a slight start, and quickly put it down. I picked it up, and stared at it.

For a moment, the shape of the object seemed enriched, intensified; I was seeing it as it was when it had first been carved. And, strangely, there was no impression of primitiveness, and certainly none of the 'evil' I had sensed on Stonehenge. The thing somehow spoke of a complex and highly evolved civilization. Now at this point, it should have been a matter of ease for me to direct my mind at the maker of the figurine. I tried to do so, and captured a sense of a more headlong and dangerous world than the one we live in; it reminded me of my feelings looking down the Victoria Falls. But at the point where the insight should have continued, it vanished. It was hard to say why it vanished. It could have been a failure of concentration on my part, a momentary distraction. But I knew there had been no distraction. I tried again, concentrating harder. This time, there could be no doubt; in some odd way, the thing was *resisting* my mind.

Littleway said: 'What do you make of it?' and I shrugged.

We had the same suspicion – we were so closely in sympathy with one another that there was no need even to verbalize it – but we could not be right. This was a piece of dead stone – no, not even dead, since it had never been alive. So there must be some other explanation. I felt what a reader of these notes might feel if the print suddenly began to swim under his eyes and move sideways. It must be *me*. So I concentrated again, and opened my mind, simply trying to apprehend what was there, to 'read' the thing, as one might try to 'read' a person's character from his handwriting. Here it was, in my hand. Someone had made it. Who? And again, just as it seemed about to answer my question, there was the odd feeling of the thing blurring, as if it was some odd optical illusion. The only thing of which I could be certain was the immense age of the thing.

Littleway and I tried for the next hour to break this 'barrier' about the figurine's origins. And when it was obvious that we were not going to succeed, we decided to attack the matter from the intellectual standpoint. Where *could* it have originated?

Littleway said: 'Robin Jackley's the man. I'll phone him now.' Sir Robin Jackley is, of course, one of the world's foremost authorities on ancient man; his name became famous in 1953 for his part in exposing the Piltdown forgery.

Littleway rang the Museum, and was put through immediately.

'Hello, Robby. This is Henry Littleway. Have you ever seen that picture of the basalt figure they found in the mud at the bottom of the well at Chichen Itza? You have? What do you make of it? . . .' He listened for five minutes, then said: 'I've got a similar thing here I'd like you to look at. Will you be there in the morning? . . . Good. I'll be down around eleven. Perhaps we can have lunch together.' He hung up.

'Sounds promising, anyway. He says the basalt figure's rather a puzzle. They recovered a number of statues and figures made of obsidian and rhyolite, but not basalt. There's not all that much basalt to be found in the Yucatan peninsula, and it's mostly greenish stuff. The nearest place where the black basalt's found in quantity is the Parana basin in Argentina – several thousands of miles away. They're still investigating the basalt statue from Chichen Itza, but it looks as if it may have orginated in Parana.'

I looked at the figurine again and tried to probe it with my mind. I said:

164

'This thing's not from South America. It's from the Middle or Near East.'

He shrugged.

'In that case, it can't be from the same culture as the Yucatan statue. Let's see what Jackley's got to say.'

We drove to London together, but I had work to do at the V and A; Littleway dropped me there towards midday, then went on to the Museum. At three o'clock I took a taxi to the Museum; we had agreed to meet in the room with the Elgin Marbles.

For the past hour or so, my mind had been entirely pre-occupied with the Elizabethan period; so the change in historical perspective came to me as a kind of pleasant shock, a sense of coolness and simplicity. I realized immediately that my powers of time-vision had developed considerably since the last time I was in this room. I stood in front of the central tableau, and gave myself up to the inner-flow of time that seemed to wash around my mind like a stream around a projecting rock.

What now happened gave me a sense of being a victim of a practical joke. The Elgin Marbles suddenly glowed with bright, almost garish colours. The flowing draperies were suddenly red and purple and green, and the eye sockets actually had eyeballs painted on them. At the same moment, I perceived that my notion of classical Greece – the feeling of coolness, simplicity, blue skies and white marble columns – was an invention of western historians. Greece had never been like this. The Greeks were a semi-Asiatic race, closer to the Turks or Arabs than to northern Europeans. They were violent and often cruel; they were superstitious, bigoted, and often brilliant. It was a brilliance derived from the passion and sensuality of the Asiatic character – the same brilliance that had made the Arabs the greatest mathematicians of the Middle Ages. They loved bright colours, and all their statues were painted. Compared to them it was the Romans who seemed classical and northern. The classical Greeks never existed, except in the imaginations of Grote and Winckelman.

I wandered from room to room, so absorbed in this new vision of Greece that I started violently when Littleway laid his hand on my shoulder. He was carrying the figurine, wrapped in brown paper. For a moment, I failed to understand him when he said:

'He agrees with you. It's from the Middle East. Probably Mesopotamia.'

'Did he recognize it?'

'He thinks it's a Sumerian bull god – he says it probably had horns sprouting from the side of its head. He dates it about 3,800 B.C. He showed me a similar thing – he called it Halafian – that's a related culture – and it looked very similar to this.'

I said : 'He's wrong.'

'I'm not so sure. I agree I get a strong feeling that it's much older, but that may be to do with the stone itself. Basalt's an igneous rock.'

'In which case, it's a damn sight older than half a million years. Half a billion would be closer.'

'Not necessarily. It could be more recent volcanic activity. I'd like a chance to see the thing from Yucatan.'

'Where is it?'

'In Mexico City. But Jackley has a friend who lives at Calne who has a piece of jadestone from Chichen Itza. He says it's carved with some symbolic figures.'

'Where's Calne?'

'Near Reading. I thought we might call there on the way back and see this man – his name's Evans – Professor Marcus Evans.'

In the car, as we drove out of London, I asked Littleway :

'By the way, did you know the Greeks used to paint their statues in bright colours?'

'Yes, I believe they did. I've read it somewhere – can't think where though.'

We phoned Professor Evans from Reading; he told us to come over immediately. We arrived at about half past five, after a traffic jam in Marlborough. The professor was a middle aged, chinless man, who talked in a humming drawl that reminded me of an insect. He gave us tea, and produced the jade stone from Chichen Itza.

This was a small, irregular piece, about the size of a hand, and extremely heavy. Carefully carved and scratched into its surface was a drawing of a hideous god, seated on crossed thigh bones, his mouth open, his head tilted back, a distinctly gloating expression on his face as he stares at a human head which he holds on his raised palms. I touched the stone, and instantly received an insight into its history that was as alien and power-

166

ful as some bitter incense. I was aware of hot, blinding sunlight, of a wide space cut into the jungle, and of half a dozen or so immense step pyramids. This was a land of green rain forests, alternating with deserts of limestone rubble, of swamps and bayous and tall, coarse grass. But its hot blue skies were somehow associated with terror, suffering and death. Strangely enough, the name that came into my head was Tezcatlipoca, whom I discovered later to be an Aztec god, 'Lord of the Smoking Mirror' and god of the curved obsidian knife. Under the Spaniards, he degenerated into a bogey man who walked the roads and killed and dismembered travellers – a kind of Aztec Jack the Ripper. (The Aztecs, of course, came much later than the Maya; they bear roughly the same relation to the Maya that the Romans bear to the ancient Greeks.) It was this god of the knife who seemed to me somehow the symbol of the Maya religion.

The block of jade stone was not old, by the standards of the basalt figurine – it had been carved roughly five hundred years B.C. And holding it in my hand, sensing all its history – and the history of the Mayas over three thousand years – I experienced a feeling of disgust, of rejection, very similar to my feeling about the Elizabethan era. Sentimentalists dream about the simplicity of the past, but the truth of the past is a truth of stupidity and coarseness and brutality and inconvenience, and of human beings stuck in the present like flies on fly-paper.

I was also clearly aware of the green waters of the cenote of Chichen Itza; but, strangely enough, there was no horror associated with this. Those who were sacrificed were frightened, but not terrified; they went as messengers from their people to the gods below. They were thrown in at dawn; those who could tread water long enough were pulled out at midday. They told stories of conversing with the gods, and of seeing great multitudes of people in the water below them. So the well evoked no horror; only wonder and fear. Later, I read the book by Edward Thompson describing his exploration of the well; it confirmed what I had grasped while holding the stone. He believed that the 'voices' of the gods were echoes of voices from above, and that the crowds of people were reflections of the faces looking down the well.

The professor offered us tea, and talked about the Yucatan peninsula. He had spent six months there with the Franklin expedition. He was inclined to be dismissive about the mystery of the basalt figurine. 'The Mayas were a great people. They might well have penetrated as far as Argentina. They built their cities in the midst of the jungle when they might just as easily have chosen more convenient places. They thrived on adversity during their great period. They preferred the jungle earth because it was more fertile. People like that are capable of anything . . .'

Littleway, eating a slice of fruit cake, asked:

'Are you sure that explains why they chose the jungle?'

I knew what he meant. Professor Evans's theory was a good theory; but we could *see* the truth about the Mayas. It was not some Nietzschean 'fascination for what's difficult' that made them prefer the jungle. It was the primitiveness of their agriculture and the rigidity of their caste system that left them no alternative.

Evans said: 'Of course, I'm not sure of anything. No one really knows anything about this people. Why did they abandon their cities around 610 A.D. and migrate to the north? We know they weren't driven out by enemies. We know it wasn't some epidemic like the Black Death. We know it wasn't earthquake or floods. So what was it? It's as strange as if all the people of southern England abandoned their homes and migrated to Scotland.'

Littleway was casually examining the stone as he listened: I knew that he was staring into the past and seeing the answer to the mysteries. It suddenly struck me that it should not be necessary to actually *hold* the stone to receive its vibrations. I was only about six feet away from Littleway. I stared at the stone in his hand, and made my mind empty, opening it to the past. For a few moments, nothing happened; then, as I kept my mind passive, the impressions began to form. And, to my surprise, they were much *clearer* than when I held the stone in my hand; altogether sharper and flatter. Actually holding the stone, I experienced intuitions and feelings, like walking into a large kitchen where many things are cooking at the same time. Now all these 'smells' had vanished. I was simply seeing, with a cold clarity, like looking down the long end of a telescope.

What I saw was too complicated to explain briefly to Evans – or to explain at length here. Littleway was right. The Mayas achieved their impressive civilization through rigid discipline and caste structure. It was the opposite of a democracy; the nobles remained nobles; the farmers remained farmers; the shopkeepers remained shopkeepers. The nobles and the priests were completely supported by farmers and workers, so they became lazy and decadent. But the workers never rose to become nobles, no matter how talented. It was a civilization designed to crush genius in the people and encourage decadence in the nobles and priesthood. So it had no power of adaptation. They stayed in their cities until the land that fed them was exhausted; then there was no alternative to a mass migration.

This was not the whole explanation. There was something more sinister here. *Why* was the social structure so rigid? Why was the priesthood so dominant? Behind Maya civilization lay the conception of the Great Secret, a mystery symbolized by the enormous heads of serpents in their temples. The priests held a secret that was so terrifying that the world might be destroyed if it was ever revealed. It was the priests who had ordered the mass migration. And they believed they were under orders from Someone Else, some appalling ambassador of the Great Secret.

I should add that I saw all this simultaneously, as it were, all in a flash; there was no slow process of taking it in. So that when I tried to look more closely into the Great Secret, it was impossible to see further. No one understood it fully. Only one thing was certain : it was far older than the Mayas.

I sat and drank my tea, saying nothing, while Littleway threw out casual hypotheses about the Mayas. Under different circumstances, I would have been amused by the professor's attitude. At first he was kindly and slightly patronizing; then, as Littleway advanced some of his 'hypotheses', he became impatient and rather acid; finally, at some point, it dawned on him that Littleway had some unknown source of information, and he became avidly curious. I think he was convinced that Jackley had stumbled upon some important discoveries and was keeping them secret for the time being. So he became attentive and receptive, and began asking questions about the Maya religion and social structure. Littleway, thoroughly enjoying himself, answered these fully. At six o'clock, I coughed and said we had to be leaving. At the front gate, Evans looked into his eyes and said seriously : 'I'm grateful to you for these hints, and I appreciate that you can't speak more fully. But I don't quite understand why Jackley should treat me as an outsider. After all, we've been friends for years . . .' I interrupted again, before further confusion could develop, and got Littleway into the car. I glanced back as we drove away; Evans was standing by his gate, his hands behind his back, staring thoughtfully after us.

I said: 'Really Henry, you ought to be more careful. You've probably started a feud between Evans and Jackley now.'

'Why?' He was genuinely puzzled. When I explained he shrugged it off. 'I don't see why I should hold back scientific information, just because I can't tell them where it came from.' But I had an intuition that a great deal of trouble could come of all this.

We had decided to stay the night in London at Littleway's club, and so were returning towards Marlborough. I started to talk to Littleway about the 'Great Secret'. He gestured towards the huge mound that towered up close to the road on the right hand side.

'Talking of mysteries, that thing's one of the classics.'

For a moment, I suspected him of trying to change the subject. It had been a great many years now since I had taken an active interest in the archaeology of Britain – so much so that I had completely failed to notice Silbury Hill when we had passed it on our way to Calne. I reached for the gazetteer that we kept in the glove compartment, and read: 'Silbury Hill, large barrow, Wilts, in the valley of the Kennet, seven miles west of Marlborough. Is 1,680 feet in circuit at the base, 315 at top, and 135 feet high. Rising from the landscape like a huge inverted boiled pudding, Silbury Hill has all the appearances of a burial mound. Traditionally it is the grave of King Sil or Zel, who was buried on horseback; Stukely declares that King Sil's grave was dug up in 1723, but there is no evidence to support this statement. A shaft sunk from the top in 1777, and a tunnel dug from the side in 1849, failed to reveal the purpose of the mound. It was once surrounded by sarsens similar to those at Stonehenge.'

It was not until I read the word Stonehenge that I had an intuition that this was something important. Littleway had parked the car beside the road; we found a gate, and walked across the field to the great mound. I had forgotten to mention to Littleway my discovery that I could 'intuit' things from a distance. I now tried this with the mound ahead of me. The result was elusive, like a blurred picture seen through a pair of unfocused binoculars. I tried harder, and realized that I was sweating from the effort. At this moment, my eye fell upon a small boulder, almost buried in the turf – obviously one of the sarsens mentioned in the gazetteer. It was like an electric shock. Again, I experienced the current of menace that I had felt at Stonehenge. I walked over to the stone and stared down at it. The vibration was unmistakable. I looked up again towards the mound. This time, I received no impression at all. It was as if a thick fog had descended. I could see the mound clearly enough; but it was somehow 'innocent'; it told me nothing.

Littleway was looking at his watch.

'If we want to get to the club in time for dinner, we hadn't better waste much time.'

Obviously, he felt nothing whatever. I could virtually read his mind by now.

'Let's walk to the top of the mound first.'

We followed the small path to the top. Everything looked harmless and normal : cars passing on the Bath road, a tractor cutting hay in the next field. But my powers of 'insight' seemed to have dwindled to a minimum, as if I was too tired to make any effort.

Standing on top of the mound, I looked around – at Avebury to the north, the Long Barrow a mile to the south, the pleasant hazy warmth of an English June on the horizon. And I experienced suddenly the desire to relax, to sit in a cool corner in a small pub and drink a long, cool pint of beer. The grass looked golden in the sunlight; England and its history seemed all pleasant and green and secure.

At the same time, I felt a flickering of suspicion about this relaxation. Two years ago, it would have struck me as wholly pleasant, one of those 'breathing spaces' that seem a gift of the gods. But in the meantime, I had learned to induce value experiences at will, and to understand the inner-pressures that cause them. There was something wrong with this one, a whiff of the confidence trick. And I was vaguely disturbed by the fading of my insight, my sense of being merely 'here, now'. As we walked back down the mound, I made a sudden effort to throw off this fatigue of the will, to grasp what lay in the earth under my feet. And for a moment, I was successful. And what I glimpsed made me cold, as if I had fallen into icy water. *There was something down there*, down deep under my feet. For a second it was obvious; *that* was why excavations had never uncovered the purpose of Silbury Hill. It was far deeper than any archaeologist would dream of digging.

And then, immediately, the insight vanished. It was as if my will was pinioned, in the grip of a powerful wrestler who prevented me from moving my arms or legs. The odd thing is that it felt somehow *impersonal*, as if I had simply stepped into a magnetic field that held me trapped. And in fact, as we walked across the field to the road, the pressure relaxed; once again my mind could turn to the past, become aware of myself standing at a certain point in the vast galleries of history.

Littleway had obviously noticed nothing at all. I said to him: 'How do you feel?' 'Fine. Thirsty though. How about stopping at that pub outside Marlborough for a quick pint?'

I have mentioned that we had almost stopped drinking alcohol, because it no longer seemed worth while; it dulled the mind and body. But we both drank occasionally, especially in old country pubs. So there was nothing unusual in Littleway's suggestion. Still, we had both drunk a large quantity of tea less than an hour before. I recalled my own desire for a drink on top of the mound. As we got into the car, I said:

'Well, what do you think of the mystery now?'

Littleway glanced back at the hill with mild speculation.

''S matter of fact, I didn't really bother. Did you?'

'*Why* didn't you bother, since that's why we stopped here?'

'I don't know – laziness, I suppose. And all this stuff about the Mayas.' He started the car. 'Why do you ask?'

'Because I'm pretty certain there's something up there that doesn't intend us to be curious.'

He was suddenly alert.

'What makes you think so?'

I described my sensations from the moment I had seen the sarsen. He said slowly:

'You could be right. But I noticed nothing . . .'

'Why did you say we had to get back to the club? We'll be back before nine in any case.'

'I . . . don't know. Tiredness, I suppose.'

We drove in silence for ten minutes. Then he said:

'Do you think it's anything active? Or is it just some odd limitation of our minds?'

I tried to focus the question, but it evaded me.

'I don't know. It could be either. But look at the facts. This basalt statue. Neither of us think Jackley's right about it being only five thousand years old. And suppose the statue from Chichen Itza *is* of the same period? How did it get there?

172

What's the connection between Mesopotamia at the time of Sumer and Yucatan three thousand years later?'

'Perhaps there's none at all. One piece of primitive art looks very like another.'

'Alright. But supposing this thing *is* half a million years old. Do you realize what human beings were like as long ago as that?'

'I think so. It's about the date of Heidelberg man.'

'Quite. And if you've ever seen the skull of Heidelberg man, you'll see my point. He may have been the first true man, but by our standards, he was still an ape. Can you imagine an ape carving that thing?'

'If he didn't, who did?'

I sat there, groping my way into the problem, trying to fit together the pieces of the jigsaw puzzle, wondering whether I wasn't making some simple and obvious mistake out of inexperience. But then, there have always been certain facts that archaeologists have failed to fit into their schemes. Sabre tooth tigers were extinct long before man became an artist. How, then, do we account for cave drawings of the sabre tooth tiger? Racial memory? The age of great reptiles ended seventy million years ago. Man may be two million years old. What about legends of dragons, that look so much like the tyrannosaurus and stegosaurus?

I also found myself reflecting on my vision of giants building Stonehenge. The sarsen stone at Silbury had produced in me feelings that closely resembled those I experienced at Stonehenge. Avebury is less than a mile to the north of Silbury Hill, and is generally reckoned to be the oldest neolithic monument in Britain. Some historians believe that the centre of neolithic religion moved from Avebury to Stonehenge for unknown reasons. Was Avebury also built by giants? I began to wish that we had looked at Avebury as well as the Silbury mound.

I spoke about these speculations to Littleway. He interrupted me with: 'Incidentally, did you ever read Hoerbiger?' I said I hadn't. 'It's a long time since I read him, but if I remember rightly, he believed there were once giants on the earth – or rather, that human beings were once giants. He believed the earth has had several moons, and that they all came closer and closer until they crashed. And of course, as the moon approaches the earth, the earth's gravitational pull is diminished.

So people grew bigger. I was rather impressed by the theory when I was a kid.'

'Have you any books on it?'

'No, but I think Roger has.'

Later that evening, as we were eating dinner in the club, he said:

'I've just remembered one of the things that impressed me about the Hoerbiger theory. He points out that Darwinian evolution can't account for certain facts about certain insects. There's an insect that strikes at the nerve centre of a caterpillar to paralyse it, so the caterpillar can provide food for the insect eggs as they hatch out. I seem to remember that Fabre pointed out to Darwin that there couldn't be any trial and error here. If the insect doesn't succeed at his first attempt, then its children die and the species comes to an end.'

'What has that to do with the giant theory?'

'Not much. He brings it up as evidence that the earth hasn't always had seasons. I think Hoerbiger believes that the sun was once much hotter, and that the earth's axis was upright instead of tilted, so that it was summer all the year round. In that case, the insects probably lived much longer, and they had time to learn about paralysing caterpillars and so on. So when the axis finally tilted, certain of them had turned the trick into an instinct, so they could do it every time.'

'That's assuming the babies *had* to be fed on live caterpillars. But there could have been alternatives before they learnt that trick.'

'Oh, I'm not seriously defending the idea. It's just a thought.'

I lay in bed thinking about it that night. A reader may be inclined to ask: What was to stop me 'looking backward' into the past and finding the answer? The answer becomes clear if I compare 'time visions' with astronomy. The sky is full of millions of stars, planets, comets and the rest. The earliest astronomers must have thought it completely impossible to map them all. Yet they *were* mapped, and Mars, Mercury, Venus, Saturn and Jupiter quickly understood to be planets. I was like these early astronomers – the past was simply a magnificent, starry confusion. But I had no way of focusing on the event I was looking for; unless, that is, I possessed actual clues, like the Bacon manuscript or the jade stone fragment. All I could hope was that long practice in the use of time-vision would introduce some order into the chaos, and teach me to distinguish stars from planets.

This was clear enough to me as I lay there. Obviously, the real problem was the question of 'clues'. For some strange reason, the obvious clues failed to provide an answer; somehow, my vision was blocked by forces whose nature was a mystery to me. Very well; then I had to think of some other approach.

I was convinced that the basalt statue found in the pool of Chichen Itza would be a starting point. It would be an excellent beginning if I could locate this. Robin Jackley was the obvious person to ask about it. I decided to ring him up before we left London in the morning. Another possibility was to search the museums and collections for Mayan religious objects, dating back as far as possible. The Sumerian and Halafian cultures would also be worth investigating. The search would have to be exhaustive and systematic.

I should mention that my attitude towards all this was not deeply serious. It was a fascinating business – but there were a thousand other problems, just as fascinating, for me to investigate. And the most important of these was the question of the ultimate possibilities of human consciousness. For it was now clear to me that it was not limited by the body. In that case, what *were* its limitations? Could it spread throughout the universe and answer the question of where space ends? Or actually penetrate beyond the wall of matter, to grasp what lies beyond the birth and death of the body? Compared with all this, the problem of why certain objects refused to yield up their secret was of minor importance.

We ate breakfast at nine o'clock the next morning, and then I rang the Museum. I asked the girl on the switchboard for Sir Robin Jackley.

'He's on the phone at the moment, sir. Would you like to hang on?' I said I would and she asked my name. A few minutes later, Jackley's voice barked at me: 'Ah, it's you. I've been trying to get on to Littleway at his home. What the devil's he up to?' I asked him what he meant. 'I've just had Evans on the phone accusing me of being in some conspiracy against him. Damned annoying and embarrassing. If what he tells me is true, Littleway's gone off his head . . .' I said I thought there must be some misunderstanding, and that I would get Littleway to ring him back. I found Littleway downstairs paying

our bill, and told him what had happened. He said: 'Oh damn
. . . I suppose I'd better talk to him,' and went off to phone.
Meanwhile, I had the car brought round to the front of the
building, and moved our bags into the boot. When Littleway
came back, he was looking worried.

'I don't understand the chap at all.'

'What happened?'

'He was damned unpleasant. As good as accused me of being
insane. Wanted to know if I was playing a practical joke . . .
Of course, I told him I was only advancing my theories about
the Mayas, but he said: "That's not what Evans told me," and
then proceeded to misquote me.'

'Did you finally convince him?'

'Well, no. That's what I don't understand. I've known Jackley
for years. We've always got on well together. I'm inclined to
wonder if he's not ill. My mother once had a cook who got like
this when she had diabetes.'

'But he must have given you some clue as to *why* he was so
upset?'

'Not really. Except that I gather that Evans was pretty bloody
to him, and ended by threatening to report him to the British
Archaeological Association. It's just some stupid academic
storm in a teacup. But I thought Jackley was above that sort of
thing. I'll ring him again when we get home.'

Littleway was driving. It was another fine, warm day, and we
drove out along the Edgware Road, then down the M.1. Littleway kept talking about Jackley, and I found it hard to understand why he was so upset. I was feeling exceptionally cheerful,
allowing the countryside to induce memories of the past, aware
of England spreading around me as if I was looking down from
an aeroplane. The M.1 was fairly crowded, and we drove in the
middle lane. Littleway had stopped talking, and we were coming
up close to an enormous lorry loaded with timber, which indicated that it intended to pull into our lane. I expected him to
either accelerate to pass it, or to slow down to allow it to go
first. I realized suddenly that he intended to do neither, and that
the driver was assuming that he intended to slow down, and
was pulling out in front of us. What happened next took only
a few fractions of a second. I glanced at Littleway, and realized
that he seemed oblivious to the lorry. Without thinking, I
grabbed for the handbrake between us, pulling on it with all
my force, and shouting his name. The brake cable snapped, but

not before the car had slowed enough for Littleway to brake, so the lorry could go ahead. We were within seconds of impaling ourselves on the baulks of timber sticking out of the back of the lorry. Littleway was obviously shaken. He pulled into the inner lane and slowed down to forty miles an hour. I said: 'What on earth happened?' He said: 'I'm sorry, I don't know. I suppose I was just inattentive.'

'Hadn't you better let me drive?'

'Yes, perhaps I'd better.'

He pulled on to the side of the road, and we changed places. I was puzzled. Littleway was always a careful driver; it was simply not like him to become inattentive.

As we drove on, my feeling of intensity vanished; I experienced a sort of foreboding, or rather, a slight oppression. Littleway now began to talk again – about Evans and Jackley, and the pettiness of academics in general. I found this irritating, and was tempted to point out that he was being equally trivial. The heat was making me sleepy, and I opened the window to its limit. Then suddenly, it struck me clearly that there was no reason for this feeling of oppression. Ten minutes before, I had been full of vitality; now an increasing dullness was pressing down on me, a sort of hypnotic tiredness. I concentrated on on it, to try to discover its source – and almost scraped a Jaguar that was overtaking us at seventy miles an hour. His indignant hoot brought me back to consciousness of the road. Littleway glanced at me oddly. But now I knew what had happened to him, and I concentrated on the road, ignoring the feeling of oppression. As it became heavier, I moved into the inside lane, and slowed down to forty. Littleway said: 'Are you alright?' 'Tired.' 'I wonder if some of the exhaust fumes are getting into the car?' But that was obviously impossible, for *he* now felt lively enough. It was then that I realized that the 'forces' I had been treating so lightly were active and dangerous; that they were prepared to destroy us both.

I said nothing to Littleway; it was costing me an immense effort to keep my attention on driving, but I felt my will power was equal to the task. I was glad when we turned off the M.1 near Northampton and cut across country. The lanes were quiet, and I slowed down to less than thirty miles an hour. By the time we reached Great Glen, the tiredness had vanished but I experienced an odd mental 'ache', a kind of throbbing exhaustion of the will.

As soon as we got into the house, Littleway said:

'I think I'll ring Jackley.'

'I shouldn't.'

'Why not?'

'Because you won't get any sense out of him. He doesn't know why he feels so furious with you, but he thinks it's quite reasonable. His mind is being manipulated.'

He stared at me. 'By what?'

'By whatever tried to make you drive into the back of a lorry. And I'm pretty sure it's to do with Silbury Hill.'

He listened to what I had to say without interrupting, although I think he began by suspecting my sanity. And this was natural enough. Ever since the 'operation', we had lived in a new world, a world without superstition and ingrained defeat. What I was saying must have sounded like some strange reversion to an earlier stage – the kind of thing that had happened to Zachariah Longstreet. But before I'd finished, his disbelief had vanished. He said: 'But what the hell *is it*?' And this was a question to which I had no answer.

We sat in the sunlit room, drinking tea, listening to the bees in the flower beds, and feeling that the sunlight was a confidence trick.

The problem, of course, was that we had absolutely nothing to go on. If I was right about these 'forces' from the past, then there should be some way of investigating them, some *starting* point. And this was precisely what we lacked. It seemed almost certain that they had some way of interfering with the mind; but neither of us had any feeling of interference. Littleway expressed what we felt when he said: 'It's like being in the middle of a flat, open desert, and suddenly being shot at.'

As we sat, staring out of the open window, I found myself thinking about his comparison. I said:

'What would you think if someone fired a shot at you in the open desert?'

'That it was somebody hiding in a hole in the sand . . .'

'Or that they were perfectly *camouflaged*. Couldn't that be the answer? That we're unaware of these things because we're so used to them. Because they're like the air we breathe . . .'

I think he grasped what I meant intuitively, for we both had the same idea at the back of our minds. For all the evidence pointed in the same direction. It seemed to indicate that there had been intelligent life on earth a long time before the earliest men. And if this could be accepted, then certain conclusions followed inevitably. I shall not try to detail the processes by which we reached our conclusions, but only state the conclusions themselves. First: was this intelligent life 'human'? Almost certainly not, for it would have left geological traces. Then what *was* it? The likeliest guess was that it originated elsewhere in the solar system, or perhaps even beyond this. Evolution on this planet has followed a simple and well-defined course, recognized by Haeckel soon after Darwin published this theory: from primitive sea organisms to worm-like and fish-like creatures, then through reptiles to mammals, and eventually to pre-hominids and human beings. And there seemed to be no evidence of creatures outside this scheme.

But if these 'creatures' (or, for all we knew, it might be one *single* creature) had left no traces, did this not suggest that they were not physical organisms as we are? This would also explain why they still possessed certain powers, capable of operating after several millions of years.

And what exactly were the powers of these creatures? When we thought about this, it seemed less frightening than at first. They could 'block' time-vision. But since time-vision is, as I have explained, merely an extension of our normal senses, this only meant that they possessed some power of blunting the senses. This seemed to be verified by our experience in the car; we had simply become sleepy. Their effect on Robin Jackley and Professor Evans could be explained in the same way. When the brain is dull, trivialities assume larger proportions – for example, one is more inclined to worry when one wakes up in the middle of the night, because the vitality is low. If Evans and Jackley had simply been thoroughly 'depressed', it could account for their violent, almost paranoiac behaviour.

If this was so, then we had no reason to fear. 'Their' powers were limited. It was merely a question of keeping our wits about us, and driving the car as little as possible.

After two hours of discussion, in which we reached the conclusions I have stated, we both felt more cheerful. We observed that we felt less 'alive' than usual; obviously, then, these forces were at work on us, interfering with the operation of the brain. On the other hand, both of us could throw this off with a slight effort. The brain is an engine, and our engines were producing far more horse power than the ordinary human brain. If necessary, we could call on more still. So there could be no immediate danger.

I reminded Littleway of the Hoerbiger book he had mentioned, and he went next door to look for it. He returned an hour later, carrying half a dozen big volumes.

'I've been talking to Roger. He tells me there's a writer of weird stories called Lovecraft who has legends about the earth being inhabited by some 'elder race' that still possesses some powers. That might be worth looking into. I've also found some volumes by Gabriel Guénon. He's a French follower of Hoerbiger. I seem to remember he has some similar legend.'

We both settled down to searching through the books. After half an hour, Littleway found the key passage in a book by Guénon, deceptively entitled *The Ages of the Earth*, published by the Planetary Society in Paris, 1928. It ran:

'The scientist is inclined to scoff at superstition. But it would be more truly scientific to ask how a superstition arose. Scientists dismiss the story of the Curse of Tutankhamen, explaining that the deaths of twenty or so people associated with the expedition were all "from natural causes". They do not comment on the statistical improbability of so many deaths within five years of the opening of the tomb.

'According to Steinach, the German warlock, certain men in the ancient past possessed the power to awaken the Great Old Ones, who have been sleeping for seven million years. The Great Old Ones are without bodies of their own; they are glad to use human beings as servants; in exchange, they will grant certain favours. They possess, for example, the power to change a man into a serpent or a wolf. The Great Old Ones also control the power to curse material objects, so that they become infected with a kind of psychic poison that can destroy anyone who disturbs the object. This, in Steinach's view, explains the nature of the curse of the Pharoahs.'

Guénon's 'Great Old Ones' certainly accorded with our own theory about the 'forces' that were obstructing us. Then what if he were right about the 'curse'? Could it be that these forces were not still alive, but had simply covered their traces with 'psychic poison'?

I must admit that neither of us was inclined to place much reliance on Guénon. Even in the passage I have quoted above, his tendency to indulge in *non sequiturs* can be seen. On the other hand, he had obviously read just about every book on magic and occultism that had ever been published, so he was a valuable guide.

Guénon had died in 1941 in German-occupied Paris. His last book, *The Secrets of Atlantis*, published posthumously, has a great deal about Lovecraft, the American writer of horror stories (who had died four years earlier). According to Lovecraft, the Ancient Old Ones had come from the stars, and once dominated the earth, building immense cities of gigantic stone blocks. They had destroyed themselves through the practice of black magic, and were now 'sleeping' under the earth. Lovecraft, in turn, seems to have derived some of his ideas from the Welsh writer Arthur Machen, who also has stories of strange people who live under the earth, the remains of an 'elder race', and who are capable of turning themselves into reptiles and of causing objects to fly through the air. Guénon does not explain how the Great Old Ones could have destroyed themselves through black magic, if 'magic' is simply another name for what happens when human beings invoke them.

It was fairly clear that there were no profound insights to be derived from Guénon. On the other hand, he seemed to have access to all kinds of ideas that struck me as important. For example, I was particularly intrigued by his insistence that the *Necronomicon*, a fictional work on magic invented by Lovecraft, really existed, and that he had seen a copy. Guénon was obviously a gullible crank, but I did not get the impression that he was a liar. If he said he had seen a copy, then he certainly believed he had.

A further comment by Guénon intrigued us: 'Biologists and anthropologists hold the view that civilized men evolved slowly from his primitive ancestors . . . But occult traditions are singularly in accord in stating that the first men reached a remarkable degree of civilization in a relatively brief period, and that it was after this that a series of catastrophes caused a regression to earlier stages. Earthquakes, floods, the complete destruction of whole continents.' And he goes on to explain his view of 'moon catastrophes', each one of which caused a degeneration to a more primitive condition. It had to be admitted that Guénon had a certain genius for collecting odd facts about primitive tribes and correlating them to support his theory. For example, he speaks of a dying tribe called the Urus on the shores of Lake Titicaca and the River Desaguero in Peru, and says: 'The Urus and the Aymaras (a neighbouring tribe) support the view that the Urus are not human. They are the degenerate descendants of gods who once ruled on the shores of the great lake.' Lyell had been intrigued by the Urus, and we had once paid a visit to their reservation on the shore of Titicaca – which is, of course, the highest fresh water lake in the world, and the largest in South America. And in Callao, we had stayed in the house of a Peruvian geologist, Herando Capac, who spoke to us about the strange line of maritime deposits that runs for nearly four hundred miles *up mountains* between Lake Coipasa and Lake Umayo, indicating that the sea may once have formed a kind of belt around the centre of the earth. Lyell, I remember, argued that this was due to the displacement of geological strata, and neither convinced the other. Guénon mentions the same maritime deposits, and argues that the moon was once close enough to the earth to gather all the seas in a bulge around the equator, until it came too close and exploded, causing the seas to rush back, destroying the great civilizations that existed on what is now the bottom of the Atlantic and Pacific oceans.

All the time, as I read this, I had a feeling of instinctive certainty that there was much truth in it. But what was perfectly clear was that I would have to embark upon a careful and systematic study of all the evidence about this remote past – biological, geological, archaeological – and try to gain an overall picture. The 'direct' method was obviously not going to work.

The answer lay somewhere in the early history of the creature called man: that was plain enough. But since the history covered some millions of years, it was clearly going to be a long search. Nevertheless, the thought of it exhilarated us both. This may seem strange considering the object of our search – invisible and apparently malignant forces that might still be active. But it must be remembered that our minds responded instantaneously to challenges, and gained strength from them. The whole past of the human race seemed a fascinating and intensely beautiful prospect, like the night sky in the tropics. That it contained a certain amount of darkness did not worry us. Evil is a form of stupidity, and science is the enemy of stupidity. We were confident of our strength.

Both Littleway and I had, I suppose, a fairly good amateur working knowledge of primitive man and the evolution of civilization. It was not until we began our systematic search for the creator of the basalt figurines that we realized how sketchy and inadequate this was.

Our first idea was to study as many of the primitive remains as possible. The obvious starting point seemed to be the British Museum. But this would depend on whether Jackley was still hostile. And a phone call to the Museum the next morning made it clear that he was; he refused to speak to Littleway. We were not particularly worried; Littleway wrote a letter to Albrecht Kircher, head of the Berlin Ethnological Museum, and an acquaintance from M.I.T. days, saying that we wanted to come to Berlin for a few weeks to study the remains of primitive man, particularly the Neanderthal and Aurignacian remains discovered by Otto Hauser at Le Moustier and the Combe-Capelle cave. The Berlin collection is in many ways superior even to that of the British Museum, and contains older specimens. While we waited for a reply, we settled down to study at home. Littleway concentrated upon the development of ancient man; I decided to concentrate on mythology and legend. The myths quoted by Guénon had thoroughly aroused my curiosity.

A week later, a reply came from Albrecht Kircher. It was a strange, incoherent letter, that seemed to accuse us both of all kinds of malevolent plotting, although it never specified what this was. Jackley had communicated with Kircher; that much was clear. It was also clear that Kircher could not, in the ordinary sense of the term, be regarded as sane. He seemed to believe that Littleway had some plan for destroying all the pre-historic human remains in the Berlin Ethnological Museum, and that the British and American governments were behind it. Kircher had once been a devoted Nazi, although after the war he denied this. Obviously, some latent neurosis had erupted.

We were aware this was no coincidence. Some power was deliberately checkmating our moves, and we knew how it operated. It had not tried to attack us directly – except in the car on the M.1 – and we took this to be a good sign. Our control over our minds meant that we could not be driven to paranoia by mental blockages. What *was* disquieting was that apparently decent and clear-headed scientists like Jackley and Kircher were susceptible to its attacks. And this surely meant that almost anyone must be. Anyone with the slightest cause for irritation with us could be driven into a state of insane resentment.

I must admit that my first thought was of Roger Littleway.

He had never basically liked me, and he resented his brother's success. Over the past few days, I had noticed that he was becoming moody and brusque. I said nothing to Littleway himself, but I think he divined my thoughts. I noticed that he started locking the door between Roger's part of the house and ours.

But by the time the letter came from Kircher, we were both thoroughly absorbed in our studies, and it made little difference to either of us. I was discovering traces of the giant myth in the most unexpected places. Montaigne, surprisingly enough, comments on the Mayas in his essay on coaches, and writes: 'They believed that the world was divided into five ages and into the life of five consecutive suns, four of which had already run their time . . . The first age perished by a general inundation of water; the second by the heavens falling upon us . . . to which age they assigned the giants, whose bones they showed to the Spaniards . . . The third by fire, which ended and consumed all. The fourth by a wind storm which levelled even many mountains; the human beings did not die therein, but were changed into monkeys . . .' And so, according to Lopez de Gamara, Montaigne's source, the fifth age of the earth began. Guénon insists that by 'suns', the Mayas actually meant moons. Obviously, the earth has only had one sun; but a moon circling closer and closer to the earth would finally appear so vast and bright that it might well have been called the sun by savages who felt they were dealing with jealous and powerful gods.

In G. C. Vaillant's *The Aztecs of Mexico*, these beliefs are ascribed to the Toltecs of Mexico.

What struck me as interesting about this tradition was the statement that monkeys, or monkey-men, followed the early age of giants. The earliest ape, pliopithecus, dates back some twenty million years. Proconsul, the ancestor of the chimpanzee and the gorilla, dates from fifteen million years ago. Of pliopethecus, only a few teeth and skull fragments have ever been found. A single ape skull, Aegyptopithecus, found at Fayum in 1967, may predate this by some eight million years, and there is even speculation that a jaw fragment of Oligopithecus may be more than thirty million years old. If the 'age of giants' predated these, it is hardly surprising that no fossils have yet been found.

This whole question of apes raises another curious speculation. Compared to the apes, man is a relatively *primitive* creature. Evolution develops the qualities needed for survival, and in this sense, the ape is more evolved than man. It developed a bracing bone inside the V of the jaw which man does not possess; it developed powerful fangs and long arms, and the thumb – relatively useless for life in trees – has become unimportant. The earliest apes resembled man in all these respects – it possessed no bracing bone, a highly developed thumb, underdeveloped fangs, shorter arms . . .

All this was pointed out in 1926 by the Dutch anatomist Ludwig Bolk, who declared that, from the anatomical point of view, the apes are more advanced than man. Bolk's view could be summarized by saying that man is a retarded ape. Mongoloid children are caused by some defect in the genes that produces mental retardation. The Mexican axolotl lizard is physically retarded in the same way; it has remained stuck in the halfway stage between prehistoric water salamanders and modern land salamanders : that is to say, it retains all its life certain characteristics which it possessed as an embryo, and which it ought to lose as it gets older. This process of remaining stuck in an early stage of development is known as neoteny. And Bolk pointed out that man is, in fact, an ape suffering from neoteny, from arrested development. If the development of an ape's embryo could be artificially arrested, it would produce something very like a man.

It was Littleway who pointed this out to me; so it will be seen that our researches complemented one another to a surprising degree. Here was scientific support for the Mayan belief that man preceded the ape.

It was also Littleway who pointed out to me a passage in Plato that bears close resemblance to the Mayan view. In the *Timaeus*, Plato states : 'There have been, and will be again, many destructions of mankind arising out of many causes; the greatest have been brought about by fire and water.' He goes on to speak of the myth of Phaeton, the son of Helios, who burned the earth with his father's chariot, and said : 'Now this has the form of a myth, but really signifies . . . the bodies moving in the heavens around the earth [i.e. Helios and Phaeton are really the sun and the moon – Plato believed the sun moves around the earth], and a great conflagration of things upon the earth that recurs at long intervals; at such times, those who live upon the mountains and in dry, lofty places are more liable to destruction than those who dwell by rivers or on the sea shore . . . When, on the other hand, the gods purge the earth with a deluge of water, the survivors . . . are herdsmen and shepherds who dwell in the mountains.' (I found myself thinking of the Urus.) And later in the same dialogue, and in the *Critias*, Plato describes the destruction of Atlantis by an immense tidal wave. Certainly, all this agreed closely with Guénon's view that the earth has had a number of moons, each one of which has plunged on to the earth, causing catastrophes.

What impressed me most about the Kabbalah – to which I also devoted much study – was its insistence that the universe was not created by God, but by a number of demiurges or powers. A. E. Waite declares that this is because the Jewish mystics believed that God must be remote, boundless, completely beyond our material universe. This struck me as a reasonable explanation until I began to actually study the Kabbalah. Then I immediately sensed another reason behind the legends of demiurges – some remote ancestral memory of immense, god-like powers operating on the earth. The tenth century Karaite historian Joseph ben Jacob al-Kirkisani has an interesting passage about the eighth-century Persian sect, 'Men of the Caves': 'For their secret tradition has it that the demiurges who created the universe subsequently came to dwell on the earth and under the sea. They possessed the power to cause mountains to rise up *by means of the moon* [my italics] or to cause the sea to swallow up fertile places. These demiurges were destroyed in one of their own calamities, although Philo's history declares they are only asleep.' The action of the moon in creating the tides has, of course, always been known. Hoerbiger asserts that mountain ranges have been created – in Abyssinia, for example – by the action of the moon, which remained stationary over Abyssinia when it was revolving at the same speed as the earth's rotation. But the Persians of the eighth century can have known nothing of the theory that the inside of the earth is made of molten rock.

My vitality and sense of purpose remained at a high level. And yet I was aware that my powers of time-vision had diminished. I was still capable of exercising them if I made an effort; but spontaneous insights – like my recognition that the cottage at Bidford on Avon was connected with Bacon – had ceased. There was no actual sense of oppression; on the contrary, there was an unusual sense of happiness and wellbeing. But it was no longer possible to settle down to long periods of uninterrupted work. Minor distractions arose with unbelievably frequency. First of all, Roger Littleway suddenly took it into his head that he wanted to move to Italy and sell or lease his half of the house. Henry was naturally unwilling, but finally agreed, on condition that he approved the tenant. A succession of completely unsuitable people then came to visit us, including a drunken Scotsman who smashed several windows one night, and a homosexual Indian rajah who obviously wanted to use the place to house a harem of young boys.

Then my own elder brother Arnold came to see me to ask me to finance a farming venture. I reluctantly agreed to this – for he has never been very practical – and the troubles were endless. Arnold began to drive over from Longeaton twice a week to drink Littleway's whisky and explain his problems. Since he was my brother, I could hardly ask him to stay away.

Colleagues of Littleway began to write to him by the dozen, and many of them came to stay. It seemed that every American he had ever known had decided to come to England that summer, and take him up on his invitation to look him up. In late August, our former department chairman came to see us, bringing his wife and two daughters, whom I knew slightly. To my embarrassment, both girls conceived a violent attachment to me, and entered into open rivalry. The younger of the two decided to steal a march on her sister by climbing into bed with me one night; I found her passably attractive, but knew that if I made love to her, the complications would be endless. I finally persuaded her to return to her own bed; but the elder sister found out somehow, and the atmosphere became so highly charged that I finally made some excuse, and went off to the Essex cottage.

In early September, Littleway decided to join me there until the visiting season was over. And then the most unpleasant distraction of all erupted. Roger Littleway was charged with the rape and attempted murder of a teenage girl. The evidence against him was perfectly clear. He had been driving back from Leicester late on a Saturday night, and had offered the girl a lift to Oadby, halfway to Great Glen. He had turned off in some remote lane, and threatened to kill the girl if she resisted him. The girl sensibly decided not to resist, but this made things worse. He ended by leaving her naked and apparently dead in a wood beside the road. A car passed half an hour later, and saw her trying to crawl down the middle of the road. She was unconscious in hospital for nearly a week, then recovered enough to describe her assailant and his car. In an identity parade forty-eight hours later, she identified Roger as her assailant.

I rushed back to Langton Place when Littleway phoned me. He believed that we were responsible; that the 'powers' that had made Jackley and Kircher turn against us had induced temporary insanity in Roger Littleway. I had no doubt that he was right. The Italian girl, Clareta, told us that Roger had been strange for many weeks. He became moody, and spent hours in a room at the top of the house in which he kept some of his prize gems of pornography. He was reading a great deal of de Sade and talking about writing a book proving him to be the most revolutionary thinker in western history. He made excuses to go out in the late afternoon, and sometimes stayed out all night. And he developed a taste for being whipped by Clareta.

Littleway was allowed to see his brother after his arrest. He said Roger seemed to be in a state of shock, and that he admitted to being the girl's assailant.

Littleway asked him if he had mentioned this to anyone else. Roger said he hadn't. Littleway advised him to keep quiet about it until he had seen his lawyer. It struck him that the best possible defence was one of insanity. But the lawyer who usually dealt with the family business was old and very conventional; Littleway decided to hire the best lawyer he could find. He heard of Trevor Johnson-Hicks, who specialized in defences of insanity, and sent him to see Roger in gaol. The result was unexpected and unwelcome. Johnson-Hicks listened to Roger's story and decided that the evidence against him was weak. Roger had denied everything so far. He had had no scratches or marks on him (since the girl had decided not to resist). But the girl claimed she had fought back and scratched him – perhaps out of shame at giving way so easily. She had been mistaken about the make and colour of his car, and in her original description, had said that her assailant was a 'very tall man'. (Roger was about five feet nine inches.) All this made Johnson-Hicks decide that Roger could risk a plea of not guilty. And Roger, suddenly elated at the prospect of an acquittal, agreed completely.

There would be no point in describing the chaos in the Langton Place household for the next seven weeks. Littleway told

Johnson-Hicks that he knew Roger was guilty, and that any other plea was immoral. Johnson-Hicks said that he was inclined to believe Roger innocent. If he had 'confessed' to his brother, this was because he was an emotionally unstable personality who wanted to suffer. Clareta's evidence proved that he was a masochist, not a sadist . . . And so on.

The case never came to trial. The girl withdrew her deposition, stating that she believed her identification to be mistaken. I am fairly certain that Clareta had a hand in this, probably offering the girl a large sum of money. I am also fairly certain that Johnson-Hicks's line of defence was that the girl was little better than a prostitute, and that she had climbed into the car with every intention of selling her favours to the driver. Probably Clareta pointed this out to the girl – and also pointed out that Roger's conviction would not benefit her, while it would be greatly to her advantage to drop the charges.

At all events, Roger was back at Langton Place by mid-October. And life became completely unbearable. Everyone in the area believed him guilty – which was true; but everyone also believed that it was Littleway's money and influence that had led to the case being dropped, and resented it accordingly. There were threatening phone calls by the dozen until Littleway had all calls intercepted. The gardener and the housemaid both left. Broken bottles and large stones were flung into the lawn every night, and on two occasions, whole dustbins of garbage were emptied in the middle of the drive. Our windows were broken so often that Littleway finally had traps set in the grounds to warn when anyone was approaching the house; he also bought two fully grown wolf hounds. One of these immediately attacked the laundry man, causing still more trouble. The worst of it was that Roger was obviously uncured. He was sullen, bad-tempered, and inclined to spend hours alone in his attic room.

All this confusion had not prevented us from continuing to pursue the problem. We both had the capacity to forget it completely for hours together. But it slowed us down greatly. We lived with a sense of constant danger. If 'they' were capable of turning Roger Littleway into a sex maniac, what might they not do if we came too close to their secret? Roger already resented Henry to the point of hatred – Johnson-Hicks had told him that Littleway wanted him to plead guilty. What if he suddenly decided to burn down the house?

Littleway and I were sitting in the library one evening in early November; I was reading a book on the Mayas and Littleway was staring into the fire. He said suddenly:

'You know, everything would be alright if we simply stopped trying to find out about them.'

There was no need for me to ask whom he was referring to. But something in his tone made me look at him oddly.

'How do you know?'

'I just do.'

But I persisted.

'How?'

He then told me that he had been staring into the fire, thinking of the possibility of leaving Langton Place for six months or so, and then rejecting the idea because it would have amounted to desertion. Then quite suddenly, there came into his head the thought: 'If you stop concerning yourself about "them", your problems will be over. If you don't, they'll get worse.' He said it was not a verbalized thought, but a sudden insight that carried a feeling of total conviction, of unquestionable truth.

I asked: 'Do you think it was a communication from "them"?' After a long silence, he said: 'I think so.'

So there it was: an offer. It was certainly enormously tempting. Complications were becoming a nuisance; we were both beginning to develop something like a persecution complex. And after all, what did it really matter? We had the whole future ahead of us, so why should we make a fuss about some remote epoch of the earth's past?

On the other hand, we were both scientists. To accept this prohibition would be the equivalent of a doctor breaking the Hippocratic oath. And *why* were 'they' so anxious for secrecy? What did it matter?

All the same, we toyed with the idea. What finally led us to reject it was something that happened the following day. Roger was set on by three youths and beaten so badly that he was taken into hospital with a fractured skull. The postman found him unconscious by the side of the road. He later claimed that he had simply been taking a walk when the three youths recognized him and started to call him names. He told them to shut up, and they attacked him, knocked him down, and kicked him into unconsciousness. I suspect they found him trying to look in through a window – the village doctor told us that Roger had a reputation as a peeping Tom.

To have Roger in hospital was an immense relief – particullarly when the doctor told us he might have to stay in for several months. Luckily, there was no brain damage. And it suddenly struck us that 'they' had made a mistake. They seemed adept at stirring up emotions of hatred, and in this case, it had given us a breathing space. The results were immediately apparent. The hostility of the villagers ceased; they were pleased Roger had been 'punished'. There were no more broken windows or dumped garbage or filthy language scrawled on the gate posts. Clearly, 'they' were not infallible. And the effect of this realization was to make us more determined than ever to try to find out more about them.

The break-through came a week later, when we heard of the discovery of the Vatican Codex by the papal librarian. The report in the *Catholic Herald* that mentioned this stated that it was believed to be an account of Mayan history and tradition.

Until this discovery, only three Mayan texts were known to have survived the destructive zeal of the Spanish priest Diego de Landa, who also wrote *Relación de las Cosas de Yucatán* some time before 1566; they were the Dresden Codex, an astronomical treatise, the Tro-Cortesianus Codex, which is astrological, and the Peresianus Codex, which deals with religious rituals. The Maya had many books; Bernal Diaz reports seeing a whole library in a Maya temple. Diego de Landa gave a 'dictionary' of the Mayan language, but it proved to be largely inaccurate, so that large parts of the Mayan texts are indecipherable.

As soon as we saw the news item about the discovery of the new text in the Vatican library, Littleway rang through to Fr Benedetto Corradini of Rome University, whose connections with the Vatican were close. Corradini had not heard about the discovery – his field was astrophysics – but he promised to find out about it, and ask permission for us to see the text. Neither of us entertained any great hopes for this long-distance negotiation, being fairly certain that 'they' would frustrate it. Ordinarily, we would have taken the first plane to Rome; but after the incident on the M.1, we were aware of the dangers of travel.

There was no need to go to Rome. Corradini rang us back

later in the day to say that we could certainly get permission to examine the codex without too much difficulty, but that in the meantime, he was sending it to us on microfilm. His department had just purchased some expensive microfilm equipment, and he was eager to make use of it.

It seemed too good to be true; again, we decided not to hope too much; instead, we made enquiries about trains from Dieppe to Rome. But four days later, the microfilm arrived. By this time, we had both concluded that the Vatican Codex would contain nothing of interest; otherwise, there would have been interference. Littleway drove down to Leicester University that afternoon; the librarian there had explained that it would be fairly easy to produce 'blow-ups' from the microfilm. These were ready the following morning, they were in colour, and were obviously excellent reproductions of the original manuscript.

The Vatican Codex consists of one long piece of bark paper, just over seven feet long and eight inches high, folded like a screen. There are several ferocious pictures of Maya deities, which might easily be mistaken for Japanese pictures of demons. The glyphs themselves are all in neat squares, and look like decorations from some Red Indian totem pole.

In the week since we heard of the existence of the Vatican Codex, I had studied all the available material on the decipherment of Maya inscriptions; J. E. S. Thompson's *Rise and Fall of Maya Civilization*, Morley's *Ancient Maya*, and articles on the Maya language by Whorf, Knorozov and Gelb. Most of the Maya inscriptions are ideographic – that is to say, the signs are pictures which represent things. But Whorf and Knorozov argue that it is also partly phonetic – most ancient languages undergo this transition from one stage to the other.

Now, as we drove back to Langton Place, I studied the photographs, and found myself recognizing many of the symbols. But many were completely strange to me. Less than a third of the Maya symbols have been translated, although the language is still spoken by a quarter of a million people in Yucatan. From this, Gelb argues that the symbols represent ideas that have now been forgotten, not letters or syllables. An additional complication is the fact that the Maya books were only intended to be read by the initiates of the temple. When Landa stamped out the Maya religion, he also stamped out knowledge of how to read the inscriptions.

Back at home, I took the photographs into the library, where all the available books were spread out on the large round table that stood near the fire. And then I settled down to a careful, slow, painstaking study, examining every glyph minutely through a magnifying glass, trying to feel my way into its 'essence'.

Within a short time, I had become aware of one major difference between this codex and the other three; it was a great deal older. The glyphs themselves showed this; they were far more obviously pictorial, representational.

I had read Landa's descriptions of the Maya religious festivals: drums, to induce a hypnotic feeling of unity, a kind of mead, 'into which a certain root was added by which the wine became strong and stinky', and finally, a great deal of fornication. But these were of the later period, when the religious essence had been diluted — in the way, for example, that our Christmas season is a diluted version of the original festival. The religion of the 'great period', nine centuries earlier, was altogether darker and more forbidding. Only a few initiates in the priesthood understood its essence, but it carried with it an atmosphere of violence and fear. And here, at the head of the seventh sheet of the Vatican Codex, was the Maya glyph for 'gods' combined with the glyph representing night or death; the 'gods of night'? or the dark gods?

Before the day was over, I had made one discovery that none of the Maya experts had stumbled upon, unimportant in itself, but very indicative. This early Maya religion of 'dark gods' was paradoxically associated with humour. There is a fine Mixtec turquoise mask in the British Museum, a kind of mosaic skull with a few very white teeth. As one stares at it, one becomes suddenly aware that it conveys a ferocious humour, and that this has nothing to do with the traditional 'grin' of the skull. This humour is terrifying and supernatural, the humour of pitiless gods who find man's suffering amusing. And yet somehow, it can be accepted by men themselves, who acknowledge their mortality and misery.

When I made this discovery, I knew that I was getting closer to the secrets of the Mayas. For it was now clear to me that the Vatican Codex is a kind of Maya Pentateuch, their account of creation and the early history of the tribe. And since, in many respects, their mythology resembles that of their neighbours, the Quiché Indians (whose 'Old Testament', the *Popol*

Vuh, was committed to paper by some anonymous Quiché scholar in the sixteenth century), I found myself in possession of many clues to the meaning of the 'unknown two thirds' of the Maya symbols.

I must admit that what baffled me was why the 'interference' had ceased – or at least, ceased to be persistent and noticeable. 'My 'time vision' was still relatively feeble if I tried to apply it to the distant past, although it still seemed clear enough when applied to less remote epochs. As to the basalt figurine, its history no longer seemed completely opaque. When I stared at it now, I could sense that it was connected with some strange religion of appalling humour. There was something oddly refreshing about this insight. Man tends to make his gods in his own image, to humanize them. But these gods were savage and totally alien.

Why had 'they' ceased to be actively obstructive? Was it because I was following a false trail? This seemed the only reasonable explanation.

Late that afternoon, I was staring at a photograph of the face of Chac, the long nosed rain god, on a façade in Sayil in Yucatan. And sudden insight crystallized. Suppose *all* primitive gods spring from the same source? What if all the barbarous myths – from the Hindu goddess Bhowani eating her victims to Cronos devouring his children – can be traced back to 'them'? Historians of religion explain man's gods in terms of ancient fears – the thunder is Thor beating on his anvil, and so on. But how do we explain the transition to the *barbarity* of human sacrifices? Natural forces are awe-inspiring, but not cruel. And as often as not, they are wholly beneficent: the rain makes the crops grow, the sun ripens them, the wind blows away pestilence. Yet with a singular accord, primitive religions are full of cruelty and fear.

The more I thought of it, the more obvious it seemed. Primitive man was a hunter and trapper; he was as much at home in the dark as in the daylight; so why the fear of the dark? It has always seemed natural enough to explain man's superstitions in terms of ignorance? But does ignorance really explain it?

It may seem that these speculations were not really so revolutionary, since we already knew – or suspected – that remote ages of the earth had been dominated by the powers we called 'them'. But indeed, it had never struck me that they might be in some sense the *source* of all human history.

And when I followed up this line of thought, the consequences were frightening. For example, my speculation that
man might be a kind of 'retarded ape' took on new meaning.
Littleway had said: 'If the development of an ape's embryo
could be arrested, it would produce something like a man'.
Which immediately raises the question : *Who* arrested it?

Expressed in this way, my train of thought sounds arbitrary;
but it must be remembered that I was guided by intuitions
about 'them'. The total darkness of the pre-human epoch was
turning into a thick twilight.

Nothing very exciting happened during the next four days. I
plodded on, using Garsia's textbook of the Mayathan language,
and every available source on Maya symbology. But there was
a satisfying sense of achievement, of moving forward a fraction
of an inch at a time. In the evenings, Littleway and I discussed
our findings. He was still immersed in his study of ancient man,
and much impressed by the theory put forward by Ivar Lissner
that the very earliest man possessed a high degree of intelligence and was monotheistic, and that man degenerated through
the practice of magic.

After the fifth day of studying the Vatican Codex, light began
to break. I was now able to translate whole sentences at a time,
and to guess the meanings of unknown symbols. The opening
sentences run :

'Izamna ruled the sky, but because he was stretched throughout all space, was unable to see his own body. Therefore he
filled the sky with blood in the form of a raincloud. [The Mayan
word for raincloud is the same as the word for steam, so this
passage could be translated "blood in the form of a gas".] Then
the drops of rain condensed, and became the stars. Then Ahau,
the sun, was appointed king of the stars. He gathered the fragments of cloud that were left, and moulded the earth. But
before he was done, his wife Alaghom Naum, called to him,
and he left the work half finished. Now the spirits who inhabited the cloud [the earth] had no bodies, and they lived in
this state for many ages [the text gives the precise length of the
period], until the cloud became the earth, and their bodies were
of earth.'

The first remarkable thing about this passage is their apparent
knowledge that *the sun is a star*. Ancient astronomers believed

the sun to be a unique body at the centre of the universe, quite unlike anything else.

Next, there is the statement that the 'spirits' who inhabited the cloud of blood were 'bodiless'. Most primitive people believe that stones, trees and so on, possess 'spirits'. Before the earth had solidified (again, a remarkable idea for an ancient Maya), these spirits had not stones or trees to inhabit. But when the earth finally solidified, they were trapped inside it, still bodiless.

The Vatican Codex goes on to describe the creation of mountains, groves of cypresses and pines, and how the Mother Goddess separated the waters into rivulets with a comb. In many respects, the text here resembles that of the *Popol Vuh*, which is probably based on it.

Then, following the symbol of the dark god on the fifth sheet, there is a curious episode, Ghatanothoa, the dark god, also known as Father Yig, descends to earth from the stars, and attempts to rape the dawn goddess, who is bathing in the sea. She manages to escape, and his sperm rushes out over the earth, creating all living things. To judge by the Dresden Codex, the star from which Yig descends is to be identified with Arcturus. The 'lords of the earth' rise up in fury, and imprison Yig under the earth; his attempts to escape produce great cataclysms. Meanwhile, the seas are full of the tiny creatures from Yig's sperm. (Again, this is either imaginative guesswork, or the sign of a highly developed science, capable of examining sperm under a microscope.) Soon, these creatures emerge on to the land, and become reptiles and animals. They are too many to be controlled by the Ancient Old Ones. And at this point, the Ancient Old Ones *create man to be their servant*. The account is quite unambiguous: 'They caused the earth to open, so the monkeys were imprisoned below the mountain of Kukulcan. They kept them there for a period of a katun [twenty years], and when they came out, they had lost their hairs, and their skin was white from the darkness.' Men now became the servants of the Ancient Old Ones, hunting animals, catching fishes, building temples. The world endured for a period of 1716 tun (or years), when the imprisoned Yig destroyed it by drawing a passing star down on to the earth, causing floods and lightning. The account that then follows – of the subsequent four periods in the history of the earth – is close to the account given by Montaigne, which I have already quoted.

This is the substance of the Vatican Codex, which I translated into English. Littleway read my translation as I made it, night by night; and when I had finished, he read the whole thing aloud. Our feelings were mixed. Certainly, it was full of fascinating details; but in another sense, it told us nothing. How seriously could it be taken? It offered us an account of the Ancient Old Ones and of the creation of man that was consistent with the theory of Neoteny. Yet on the whole, they appeared as benevolent deities. Yig, the demon from the stars, seemed to be the principle of evil in the world. It should also be noted that men are the creation of Yig – since they developed from his sperm – although it was the Ancient Old Ones who redeemed them from beasthood and turned them into human beings.

The morning after I had finished my translation, I woke up feeling curiously happy and expectant. The grass and the bare branches of the trees were covered with frost. The cool smell of the air brought back childhood memories of winter. For three weeks, I had been totally concentrated on the translation. I had worked at a rate that would have given me a nervous breakdown before my 'operation'. Now I could again forget these obscure, confused stories of the remote past, and look out at the infinite complexity and beauty of the universe. What did it really matter how man was created? We still didn't know who created the Ancient Old Ones or Tloque Nahuaque (Izamna), the creator himself. And surely, existence itself is bound to remain the final, unanswerable riddle? But there are all kinds of questions that *are* answerable, and that could take me closer to the basic nature of the life force; for example, the question of colour, and of the origin of the sexual impulse.

Once again, I experienced that overwhelming joy in the universe that I had felt in London outside the V and A. But this time, my consciousness of the world seemed larger, more complex. It was the mystic's sensation of oneness, of everything blending into everything else. Everything I looked at reminded me of something else, which also became present to my consciousness, as if I were simultaneously seeing a million worlds and smelling a million scents and hearing a million sounds – not mixed up, but each separate and clear. I was overwhelmed with a sense of my smallness in the face of this vast, beautiful, *objective* universe, this universe whose chief miracle is that it exists as well as myself. It is no dream, but a great garden in which life is trying to obtain a foothold. I experienced a desire to burst into tears of gratitude; then I controlled it, and the feeling subsided into a calm sense of immense, infinite beauty. When my eyes fell on the photographs of the Vatican Codex, lying on the bedside table; it seemed rather absurd.

Littleway was already eating breakfast – an unusually large breakfast of fried eggs, cheese, watercress, chicories, onions and buttered toast. He said: 'Ah, morning, Howard. Come and eat.'

'You're looking very cheerful.'

'I'm feeling very cheerful.'

I noticed the book beside his plate, and glanced down at it. He said:

'Ah yes, it's an anthology of Elizabethan poetry. My wife used to be very fond of the Elizabethans. We used to read it aloud to each other. I'd forgotten how fond I used to be of poetry . . .'

I read a few lines from Marston:

> 'Thou mightly gulf, insatiate cormorant,
> Deride me not, though I seem petulant
> To fall into thy chops . . .'

I was suddenly reminded of Lyell and his first wife, with a feeling of immense nostalgia, for the Lyells had been fond of Elizabethan madrigals and songs. I sat turning over the pages of the book as I ate my breakfast. I observed that the food and drink tasted better than I could ever remember; the coffee had a fragrance that reminded me of a shop in the Nottingham market place that ground its own coffee and filled the air with its smell. I said to Littleway:

'I wonder how far one would be capable of experiencing an intensification of sensual pleasure? Psychedelic drugs increase visual awareness. Supposing all the senses were deepened . . .'

He nodded. 'I was thinking something of the sort myself this morning. I happened to be shaving with a hand razor – I've let my battery get flat – and using the old stick of shaving soap with a brush. I haven't used it in years. The smell of the soap was suddenly quite intense – it almost made me dizzy, like walking into a perfumer's shop. My mother once had a burglar who broke every bottle of perfume in her bedroom . . . I can still remember the smell. I thought it was delicious.'

And indeed, it came to me that our senses are usually quite flat. Unless we are really hungry, we don't taste food with any

198

intensity. But there are moments when you taste food with the delight a drowning man feels as he gulps down a lungful of air. Or when a spring morning seems to soak into the senses with a delight that borders on pain. What would happen if the senses were fully awake, so that every taste or sight or sound produced deep echoes throughout one's being?

Suddenly, it seemed to me that I had found a subject really worth the fullest investigation – to find what man is capable of becoming when he is fully awake. The body's dullness cuts us off from the outside world. But supposing one became totally aware of the world, so that every perception became a symphony played with full orchestra?

I ate a much larger breakfast than usual, and I felt sleepy afterwards. The sun had come out, so I put on my overcoat, and went for a walk – for the first time for months. A girl came running past me – a schoolgirl of about ten, carrying a school satchel, with a small mongrel running beside her. Her cheeks were pink from the cold, and her hair bounced up and down as she ran. Again, I was overtaken by the tremendous nostalgia. I have remarked that I found most women unattractive since my 'operation' because they seemed too earth-bound, trapped in the heaviness of the flesh. But the girl running past me was like a vision of the 'eternal feminine'. No doubt she was a very ordinary schoolgirl who would marry a local farm labourer; but she was also far more than that, more than she could possibly understand; she contained the whole history of woman-kind with its craving for motherhood and domestic security.

A young farm labourer passed me. I suddenly understood what Traherne meant when he said that men looked to him like angels. Again, it was a matter of seeing through to the inward vitality, the essence – what Boehme called the 'signature'. I smiled at the farm labourer, and he smiled back and said: 'Mornin' sur.' I felt suddenly very happy.

My senses kept registering quite ordinary things with a pleasant shock. And I also found myself thinking with nostalgia about women I had known: about Lady Jane and her pretty French maid Juliette, about Dick's wife Nancy. I was suddenly aware of the world as a huge sexual roundabout, and for a moment, I ceased to be either male or female, but became both, so that I could feel simultaneously the delight of a man as he enters the softness of a girl and the delight of the girl as she feels his maleness inside her. I spent the remainder of the walk trying to grasp the essence of the sexual mystery. It struck me that it has much in common with the mystery of music. Enjoyment of music is intentional; that is to say, you can cultivate a love of music, learn to enjoy things you didn't enjoy before, and so on. But there is also some strange element in music, something in the shape of a melody or the sounds of a harmony, that is *already there*, quite apart from what we put into it. (This is why Schoenberg's twelve tone system contains a hidden fallacy that invalidates the whole idea.) And the same goes for sex . . .

I was still thinking about this when I got back to Langton Place. To my surprise, there were sounds of music coming from the sitting room in Roger's half. Clareta had been away for the past few weeks, on a visit to her parents in Italy. Yet here was the music of Handel's *Samson* thundering over the lawns. I knocked cautiously, and peeped in through the door; Clareta was sitting in front of the fire, her eyes closed, letting the sound flow over her like water. She looked sunburned, and much prettier than I remembered her. I sat down quietly, and listened to the music. When it was finished, she opened her eyes and looked surprised and pleased to see me. We talked about Roger and other subjects, and I found myself thinking: 'How very pleasant to be a human being, quite apart from this obsessive drive for knowledge and power . . .' I was perfectly aware that she was attracted to me, and I felt a distinct sexual interest in her – an interest that seemed to go beyond the physical; that seemed to be an awareness of her feminine essence. After a while, she herself suggested playing more music, and as I sat listening to it – it was the Handel *Brockes Passion* – I had a sensation of the music binding us together, as if there were no clear distinction between her inner nature and mine. I was also surprised that I had ever found her unsympathetic. It was suddenly clear that all human beings can enter into a close, deep communion if they will make the effort to break through the normal barriers of pettiness and self-absorption. This was an interesting idea that had never really struck me before – the idea that the whole human race might eventually enter into such deep sympathy that everyone will care as much for other people's welfare as his own, so that everyone treats every other member of the human race as a mother treats her baby : with a deep, open sympathy. The idea seemed to me so beautiful that I felt close to tears. It was so clear that this would solve every problem : that there is enough of everything to go round;

that all misery could be eliminated; that the problem of the population explosion would cease to be insoluble when everyone felt this deep mutual understanding. All the human race needs to move to an entirely new stage of its evolution is this vital recognition that, spiritually speaking, it is a single organism. It came to me that Jesus had been a visionary of the most incredible order: that he had seen something that will one day seem self-evident.

Before the music came to an end, I stood up and tip-toed out of the room. She was still lying with her eyes closed, her legs resting on a leathern hassock, the broad peasant dress she was wearing falling loosely around the upper part of her thighs. For a moment I was tempted to lean over and kiss her forehead; then I had a clear insight that she would take this as an advance. So I went up to my room, and sat by the window, fascinated by this great richness of feeling that was welling up in me, tingeing everything with a curious radiance, Traherne's 'strange glory'.

I continued to study the Mayas, but in a rather half-hearted way. Since I had now worked out the meaning of most of the glyphs, I was in a position to translate the 'unknown two thirds' of the remaining three codices. They revealed nothing new, but at least there was a certain intellectual pleasure in the manipulation of these strange symbols. What now gave me far more pleasure was to spend hours every day playing music, recalling the long, pleasant days at Sneinton. Everyone has experienced this feeling: to suddenly recall clearly a part of one's own past, and to realize that one's life has been far richer and more interesting than one normally allows. Even the less pleasant times in the past can bring this same feeling of affirmation, of how delightful life is if one didn't have to live it with one's nose to the grindstone. I felt a deep, very powerful desire simply to contemplate the beautiful complexity of the universe. I wasn't worried about 'lotus eating', for I was sure it would pass off in its own good time, and leave me ready for action.

My translations made it clear that Littleway's 'guesses' about the Mayas had been correct. I wrote to Jackley and Evans, enclosing parts of my translation, explaining how I had arrived at my results. The following day, Jackley rang me:

'My dear boy, this is simply unbelievable. I don't know how

you've done it, but you've certainly done it. I really can't apologize enough . . .'

He went on to explain how his annoyance with Littleway had been based on his feeling that Littleway had become a crank, a faddist, rather than a serious investigator. 'If I'd only known how seriously you were both working . . .'And so on. The apology was handsome and complete. He was also, of course, tremendously excited about my decipherment of the remaining two thirds of the Maya symbology, and asked when he could see my complete results. It was only eleven thirty in the morning; I had a number of things I wanted to do in London. I offered to drive down immediately. Jackley said he would put me up in his flat overnight if I would like to spend the evening with him. Littleway was also pressed to come, but he had promised to visit Roger that afternoon. So at one o'clock, I drove off to London in my own car, with the translation and the photographs in the boot.

I drove carefully, although I no longer felt that 'they' were hostile to me. It was as well that I did; I came close to having three accidents. In one case, a car I was overtaking swerved out into my lane without warning, causing me to lose control for a moment; the other two occasions were too involved to describe, but seemed to indicate that the drivers were not paying attention. I found myself wondering whether 'they' had really declared a truce. Then decided that all three near-accidents could be coincidence.

I was also pondering another question that had been occupying my mind a great deal of late: whether we should not publish the results of the brain operation; or at least, persuade a few intelligent people to undergo it. What would happen if Littleway and I met with an 'accident'? Would it not be better to risk the consequences of making it public?

It was one of those clear, cool afternoons in late November, with that grey, autumnal smell in the air. I parked the car in the courtyard of the British Museum, and walked down to Piccadilly, then to St James's Square. It was strange how completely my feelings about London had changed since the last time I had been here. At the time I had seen it as an enormous zoo; now I realized this was because I had been too involved. Now I felt soaked in its atmosphere and its history. It seemed tragic that so many great writers had lived and worked in this city, and all had lived 'too close' to it. 'Close-upness deprives us of meaning.' Yet they had lived and worked bravely, and died in the usual frustration and exhaustion: Blake, Carlyle, Ruskin, Wells, Shaw, all visionaries. And I was getting the reward they should have had: able to hold the world at arm's length, to see its meaning, to grasp something of the complex pattern. Whitehead said 'Life implies a certain absoluteness of self-enjoyment', and human beings have developed the mind, the imagination, to this end. And *all* these people around me should be capable of this contemplative detachment that made life seem so wholly good to me.

I had a cup of tea in the Strand Lyons, for the pleasure of recalling old times, then walked up St Martin's Lane and back to the Museum, experiencing all the time this cool, flowing delight. The sight of two pretty students walking up the steps of the Museum ahead of me brought another idea: supposing I looked for an intelligent girl as a candidate for the brain operation? Might we not produce children who were born with this faculty of 'contemplative objectivity'?

Jackley was in his office; a short, dynamic man who looks much younger than his fifty-seven years. There was also a girl, and two small children aged about five and three. Jackley said: 'Ah, my dear chap, I'm so glad to see you. This is my niece Barbara. Like a cup of tea? I'll be ready to leave in ten minutes, if you could just excuse me . . .'

The small girl – who introduced herself as Bridget – asked me whether it was time for Captain Marvo yet. I gathered that he was a TV character who came on at five o'clock. Her mother assured her there was still time to get home for Captain Marvo. The five year old boy asked me if I owned an aeroplane; when I said no, he looked disappointed. 'Uncle Robby says you're a Trasslater.' Evidently he thought this was something like a navigator.

Their mother was tall and slim, although obviously about six months pregnant. I liked her calm, intelligent face, and the large grey eyes. She said she had read my letter to Jackley, and wanted to know how long I'd been studying the Maya language. I said evasively: 'Oh, quite a long time.' She said: 'Uncle Robin's really a bit embarrassed. He feels he's made an utter fool of himself. I must say, I can't imagine him getting furious with anybody – it's just not like him.' In order to steer the subject away from these topics, I took out the photographs of the Vatican Codex, and showed her the pictures of the Maya deities

and demons. The small girl looked at a grimacing picture of
the god of destruction plunging a double-headed spear into a
dog-like creature, and asked : 'Why does he look so frightened?'
For a moment, I thought she meant the dog, then realized she
was pointing to the demon. It suddenly struck me that she was
right, and that she had seen more deeply than I had. Why this
dreadful, menacing grimace? It was the reverse of the terrible
mirth of the turquoise skull; this was basically fear, not
strength.

When Jackley came back, and I had finished the tea that his
secretary brought me, we left the museum. When Matthew, the
boy, saw my red touring car, he declared his intention of riding
in it. So the mother and children drove with me, and she
directed me to Jackley's flat off the Kings Road. I felt intensely
curious about this quiet, obviously intelligent girl (although
there was nothing strange about this; I had felt the same immense curiosity about the waitress who served me in Lyons).
She mentioned that she lived in Dorset, and was staying in her
uncle's flat. I asked her what her husband did, and she said he
was a painter. Then she added : 'But we're separated now. I'm
divorcing him.' 'Didn't you get on together?' 'It wasn't that.
He's terribly unstable.' She added in a lower voice : 'Apart from
which, he's gone off with somebody else.'

'And what do you intend to do?'

'I'm doing some secretarial work for Uncle Robin. I'd like
time to think things out . . .'

I said on impulse : 'If you're interested, you could do some
work for us – myself and Littleway.' This was true; Littleway
had been saying only that morning that he needed a part-time
secretary to deal with his correspondence.

'What about the children?'

'He wouldn't mind them. They seem quiet enough.'

She smiled. 'You don't know them.'

When we got out of the car, half an hour later, it seemed we
had known one another for years. It was very like the feeling
I had had with Clareta – of a deep, telepathic sympathy.

The children watched television while Barbara prepared a
meal, and Jackley and I sat in his study and talked about the
Vatican Codex. I didn't like lying about it, but there was no
alternative. I had to give him the impression that I had been
studying Maya symbology for years, and that many of my conclusions had been reached by long and complicated reflection,

for it was impossible to explain to him the mental processes by which I had reached my conclusions. They would have struck him as guesswork. Luckily, Jackley regarded himself as a complete amateur in the field – although his knowledge was very considerable – and he assumed my knowledge was much wider than his own. So when I attributed some piece of reasoning to William Gates or Whorf or Knorozov, he didn't press me for exact references. As we talked, I was struck by his painstaking honesty and decency. It was hard to imagine how he could have become so enraged with Littleway – and disquieting to think that 'they' possessed such power.

We went back into the sitting room to watch the news and have a drink. The small boy made much of me, asking questions about the car – and the girl followed his example. Later, I told them a story in bed, with their mother sitting on the side of the bed beside me. I told them a variant of Beauty and the Beast. And when it was finished, an event occurred that struck me as odd. The small boy said suddenly: 'There aren't really such things as monsters, are there?' In fact, I had been thinking of the children thrown into the well at Chichen Itza, and of the dark gods who demanded such propitiation; the question took me unawares, and I flinched – although not physically. Barbara was smoothing the hair of the small girl, her arm lightly touching me as she reached past me. She suddenly flinched – physically – and looked at me for a moment with fright in her eyes. I said: 'What is it?' She said: 'Nothing. Somebody walked over my grave.'

But when I left the bedroom a few minutes later, I knew that, in some curious way, she was in direct mental communication with me, as if we were two telephone subscribers whose lines had accidentally crossed. But why? It is true that I had been consciously toying with the possibility that she might be the girl I was looking for: someone to share our secret, to undergo the operation. It was not simply her beauty that attracted me – although her soft, oval face was extremely attractive. I suppose it was seeing her with her children, recognizing that she was a mother as well as an intelligent girl. I liked Clareta; but she stood for herself; she wanted a man for personal reasons, as a lover. This girl wanted a husband in a perfectly disinterested way; because she loved her children and wanted to bring them up with as many advantages as possible. It gave her an advantage over a single girl; made her maturer.

But that did not explain the definite telepathic contact. And it was now, for the first time, that I began to suspect. What interest could 'they' have in bringing us together? And the answer was appallingly obvious. Because I would be more vulnerable with a wife and children.

The thoughts that followed were deeply disturbing. Had all these mystical insights during this whole period of 'truce' been nothing more than an attempt to lull me into false security? For the plain and obvious fact was that I had lost interest in 'them' since I had completed the translation. I was strongly inclined to accept the view that the Ancient Old Ones were fundamentally benevolent. And was this not the whole point of the Vatican Codex? That 'they' had been constantly on the side of the human race?

During the course of the evening, I suppressed my misgivings, knowing that they would communicate themselves to her. I was not too worried. 'They' seemed to have no direct power over me. And I could easily be mistaken about their hostility. I would wait until returning to Langton Place before really examining the matter.

Now I was aware there was a kind of telepathic contact between us, it was interesting to observe how it operated. By an act of intentionality, I could become aware of her consciousness. It reminded me of an occasion when I visited the Marine Laboratory in Florida, and listened to the voices of fishes through earphones; the same odd underwater sensations. I could become aware of its forward flow, of its intentions and pre-occupations. When the girl woke up and cried, I became aware immediately of her attention in my own consciousness, as if it were the ringing of an electric bell.

She had no conscious suspicion that we were in telepathic communication, but she was instinctively aware of it. Jackley gave us one or two odd looks during the course of the evening; I think he suspected that we had known one another before. He was also surprised, when we studied the photographs, with Barbara looking on, at the speed at which she seemed to catch the meaning of the glyphs.

Towards midnight, when Jackley was out of the room for a moment, she asked: 'Does that offer still hold?' I said casually: 'Of course.' 'Hadn't you better ask Sir Henry first?' 'I don't think so. I'll ring him in the morning before we set out.'

I knew, without having to ask, that she wanted to come back with me.

In a way, it was a relief when we retired to bed; the constant communication was broken, and I could think without danger of her 'overhearing' me. I was sleeping on a bed-settee in the sitting room, and she was sleeping in a single bed in the study. The children occupied a double bed in the spare bedroom. There was a great deal to think about. I could not, as far as I knew, establish this telepathic communication by an act of will. It had happened occasionally with Littleway, but only when there was a conscious effort by both of us. What, then, had happened in this case? I assumed 'they' were in some way responsible. How had they achieved it?

The most obvious and sensible step would be to somehow break communication with her. If I had suspected at an earlier stage what was happening, this would have been easy; it would merely be a matter of maintaining normal social relations. If I did it at this stage, she would be hurt and bewildered; and although I knew in theory that this might be the best course, I couldn't bring myself to do it. I had an odd feeling of well-being, and although I couldn't determine whether this was another trick, it seemed pointless to reject it. So I fell peacefully asleep.

I was awakened at about three o'clock when the girl woke up and cried. Barbara came out of her room holding a torch, and went in the children's bedroom. She was there for about ten minutes, and I could hear her talking in whispers. Then she came out again, hesitated for a moment, then leaned over the back of the settee where she could see me. I glanced up at her, and made only the slightest movement, pushing back the bedclothes. She understood, and a moment later, was lying beside me. We lay without speaking, and a deep feeling of satisfaction came over me. Now our bodies were in contact, I was aware of the actual flavour of her consciousness, as if it was a unique taste; I was even aware of the baby inside her. There was no sexual excitement; making love is an attempt to bring about a closer intimacy, and we had already established this. She slept beside me until six in the morning, then went back to her own bed. I lay there, trying to analyse the satisfaction that comes from marriage, and wondering how far Plato's myth about divided souls seeking their other half is correct.

I was aware that, in taking this step, I had placed both of us in danger – not to mention her children. But I also knew it had brought things to a head. There would be no more fighting in the dark.

Jackley left us shortly after eight thirty, to go to the Museum; I left the photographs of the Codex and my translation with him. At about nine thirty, just as Barbara was finishing her packing, he rang us from the Museum. 'I've been showing your translation to a colleague here – Otto Carolyi. He'd very much like to meet you. Do you have time to call in here before you set out?' I said I had. I wasn't anxious to meet Carolyi – I knew nothing about him – but it wasn't too inconvenient.

Carolyi proved to be a short, broad shouldered man with a long head and hatchet-like nose, who spoke with a strong Hungarian accent. Jackley introduced him as the author of the monumental *Creation Myths.** He had the great charm that so many cultured mid-Europeans possess. The three of us (Barbara had taken the children for a walk) went down to the staff restaurant for coffee.

Carolyi, I discovered, was a Jungian. He saw myths as pure poetry, the earliest creation of the human spirit. He considered the Vatican Codex so important that it should have had a prominent place in his immense work, and compared himself wryly to Bertrand Russell, who had just finished the *Principia Mathematica* when a letter from Frege proved the whole thing redundant. In any case, he would have to write a long appendix to the English translation on the Maya myth of creation.

We continued to talk long after Jackley had had to return to his office, discussing Jung, Fromm and the whole 'mythopaeic' movement in psychology. I was impressed by the depth of his insight; it demonstrated to me that a man does not need to possess 'time vision' to grasp the realities of history. I was tempted to set him right on a number of points, but realized that he would want to know *how* I knew; so I contented myself by disguising some of my insights as hypotheses. And then, just as we were leaving, he startled me by saying: 'You know a great deal more than you are willing to tell me.' I decided not to deny it; I said: 'Perhaps. But I'm afraid I can't discuss that for the time being.' He said: 'I understand. But when you can discuss it, I would be happy if you would remember me.' I said: 'I promise I will.' As we stood on the steps of the

* Budapest, 1940–1953, 10 volumes.

Museum, I said: 'By the way, have you ever come across any other creation myths that involve strange forces that inhabit the earth?' He thought for a moment, then shook his head. 'Not in the sense of your Maya scripture. There are plenty of myths of monsters. And the Wahungwe Makoni tribe in what was Southern Rhodesia has a myth of a dark god from the stars. But nothing like your Ancient Old Ones.'

As I was reversing the car, he came up and leaned in at the window. He was smiling.

'I have just thought of an absurd parallel to your Maya legend. Have you ever heard of the Evangelista case?'

'No.'

'It was a murder case in Detroit in the late twenties. I won't go into the details . . .' (his eyes gestured towards the children) 'but the victim was the leader of a religious cult. He wrote an enormous bible about the ancient history of the world, and I seem to remember strange beings like your Ancient Old Ones. I may be able to send you an account of the case if you're interested.' I said: 'Thank you. I'd be very interested indeed.' I was being polite.

The drive back was uneventful; we drove across country instead of up the M.1, arriving back at mid-afternoon. I had phoned Littleway before we left London; he was obviously pleased at the idea of having a woman around the house. The children took to him immediately. It was clear that our arrangement was going to be a success.

I told Littleway about Carolyi, although I forgot to mention the murder case. It struck me that we might risk taking Carolyi into our confidence and persuading him to undergo the operation; he struck me as the kind of person we needed as an ally.

After supper, when Barbara had gone to bed, he said:

'Charming girl. Are you thinking of marrying her?'

'I think so. It's time I got married.'

'Oh, quite so. But don't you think it could be dangerous?'

'In what way?' I knew what he meant, but wanted to hear him say it.

'I've been wondering if all this couldn't be a trap? I was looking at Roger in hospital this afternoon. That poor devil's been through hell – I don't think he'll ever be really sane again. I can't believe that these things *can* be all that benevolent.'

'I know. I thought of that.'

'I had an unpleasant experience while you were away. I decided to have another go at reading the basalt statue.' (We used the word 'reading' for the attempt to exercise time-vision on objects.) 'I made quite an effort – kept at it for the best part of an hour. Then I suddenly got the feeling that the damned things were somehow around this place – looking in the windows. It really felt unpleasant. In fact, Clareta felt it too. She insisted on sleeping in the spare bedroom in this part of the house.'

'Did you get the feeling they could have done any harm?'

'I don't know. It's hard to say. It was just a prickly, nasty feeling – as if you knew a man-eating tiger was watching you through the window.'

'Not in the house itself, then?'

'No, not in the house.'

The next morning, a book parcel arrived from London. It contained two books: an American paperback called *Murder by Persons Unknown*, and a battered, blue volume without lettering on the spine, whose title page read: *The Oldest History of the World, Discovered by Occult Science in Detroit, Mich.*

The story of the Evangelista murder case was contained in the paperback. On the morning of 3 July 1929, a man went into a house in St Aubin Avenue, Detroit, and found the owner, Benjamino Evangelista, decapitated in his office. The police discovered that Evangelista's wife and four daughters – whose ages ranged between eighteen months and eight years – had also been murdered, and there had been an attempt to amputate the arm of Evangelista's wife and one of the children. The police came to believe that the murder weapon was a machete. It was subsequently discovered that Evangelista was the leader of a religious cult, and claimed to possess supernatural powers. He also claimed that he received supernatural revelation every morning, between midnight and 3 a.m. and that this had enabled him to write his 'Oldest History of the World' in three volumes, between 1906 and 1926.

No clue to the murders was ever found; none of Evangelista's followers were ever located. A man called Tecchio, whom the police suspected, died five years later, when a certain amount of evidence against him had accumulated. The case is still unsolved.

I turned to the *Oldest History*. It was written in a curious, foreign English. 'By the Willingness of God, my respect to this Nation, I shall do my best to tell you about the world before God was created up to this last generation.' The book was full of allusions to a 'prophet Meil', who may have been Evangelista himself, in some previous incarnation. Meil travelled over the world, with two assistants, aiding the righteous and bringing the evil to justice. The book was full of violence and fantastic events. At a casual glance, it seemed a typical piece of ordinary crank literature, badly written and frequently mis-spelled.

And then a passage on page eleven arrested my attention: 'In the *Necremicon* it is told how the Dark Ones came to the earth from the stars, and created men to be their servants.' I caught my breath, as if I had suddenly plunged into cold water. This had been written around 1906, long before Lovecraft 'invented' the *Necronomicon* 'by the mad Arab, Abdul Alhaz-red'; even in 1926, when the *Oldest History* was finished, Love-craft was still an apprentice writer.

There could be no doubt that 'Necremicon' was a misprint or mis-spelling of *Necronomicon*, for it occurs again on page twenty-eight as 'Necronemicon'. And again, on page 214, it describes how the Prophet Meil brings about the destruction of Prince Trampol because he is 'a dabbler in the magical mysteries of the *Necromicon*'.

Suddenly, without possibility of doubt, I knew one thing. Evangelista had been destroyed by 'them' – that is, by someone deliberately driven half-mad by 'them', and imbued with an insane grudge against the whole Evangelista family.

I showed Littleway the book. And he immediately asked the question that had already occurred to me. If the *Oldest History* contained matters that 'they' wanted kept secret, why had they allowed the book to fall into our hands? It would have been easy enough to influence Carolyi's mind against me and make him decide not to post it.

And then, as I read through the *Oldest History*, I thought I understood the reason. The book was an incredible farrago of nonsense. Parts of it may have been 'inspired', but for the most part, it was the attempt of a semi-literate – with a touch of the rogue about him – to imitate the Bible; I could also discern the influence of the Book of Mormon. Apart from the sentence about the Dark Ones creating men, there was nothing very profound or interesting about the *Oldest History*. And yet certain things emerged quite clearly. For some reason, Evangelista *had* developed some strange faculty of visionary second-sight. There was probably some truth in his assertion that he received his revelations between midnight and 3 a.m. every day. He had no power to distinguish between the turbid fantasies of his own subconscious mind and genuine moments of 'time vision'. But his endless attempts to peer into distant epochs of time, combined perhaps with some brain abnormality (second sight is often associated with head injuries), had given him glimpses into the pre-Pleistocene period of the Ancient Old Ones (I have said that it is easier to see remote epochs than more recent ones.) He may have started as a slightly unbalanced charlatan; but his awareness that many of his 'visions' were genuine glimpses of the past – for they bear a stamp of reality that makes them unmistakable – may well have convinced him that he was a reincarnation of the Prophet Meil, destined, like Joseph Smith, to found a great religion. And if all three volumes of his *Oldest History* had appeared, he might well have succeeded. At the time he was murdered, he had converted the basement of his house into a kind of chapel, draped with green cloth, with 'bestial, malformed figures' made of papier mâché suspended from wires above the altar, and a great eye, made to glow with an electric bulb, as a centre-piece. (Was this a symbol of the Ancient Old Ones, of whose constant surveillance he was aware?) The second two volumes of his work were still in manuscript at the time of his death. Were there more revelations of the 'Ancient Old Ones' in them? It seems likely, for the faculty of time-vision grows with practice.

And suddenly it was clear why 'they' had allowed the *Oldest History* to reach me. *It was a warning.* I now had a 'family'. And Littleway's brother had already attempted one murder. The inference was clear. It could be war or peace, as I chose.

I must admit that it would have taken a great deal to make me endanger my 'family'. Shaw asks: 'Is there a father's heart as well as a mother's?' and to me, the answer is self-evidently yes. That Bridget and Matthew were not my own children made no difference. They kept me in a perpetual state of amusement. It was obvious that they needed a father's attention. Matthew approached me after they had been in the house for two days and asked me: 'Are you going to marry Mummy?'

I said: 'I expect so.' 'Oh good. I'll go and tell her.' Everything in the house fascinated them; they had lived in a small farm cottage, and had never been inside a large house. During the first week or so, they would disappear completely, and we would find them in the attic, covered with dust and draped in old curtains, or building a house out of tea chests in the cellar. Their father had never been able to buy them toys, so they were easily satisfied, having learnt to invent their own amusements. It gave me pleasure to take them around the big shops in Leicester and let them make a list of the things they wanted Father Christmas to bring them. I think that perhaps the immediate strength of my feeling for them was due to the telepathic link with their mother, so that her feelings communicated themselves to me. It was an unpleasant thought that I owed so much pleasure to 'them'.

Shortly after Christmas, Barbara left on a visit to her parents in Cartmel. And once again, I found my thoughts turning to the 'Dark Ones'. Since reading the *Oldest History*, I had been working on other matters, questions of philosophy and astrophysics. Bennett's immense work on radio-astronomy was just out, and both Littleway and I found it absorbing – so much so that we bought two copies, so we could read it at the same time. But periodically, my mind returned to the problem of 'them', toying with the unanswered questions. How did they interfere with our minds? What was their purpose? How powerful were they?

The day after Barbara left, Roger came out of hospital. He looked old and very thin; but his eyes still had the same intense glow.

On the first evening, Littleway invited Roger and Clareta for dinner. Roger was slightly drunk when he came in at half past seven. I was immediately aware that he felt a contemptuous hostility towards Littleway and myself. Clareta had told him about Barbara. He said: 'I hear you've become a family man,' and his meaning was very clear. He saw me as a comfortable, dull stick-in-the-mud, completely devoted to abstractions, completely ignorant of reality.

He proved to be a tiresome guest. He drank a great deal of wine with his meal – on top of whisky – and then went back to whisky afterwards. And he seemed to become more preoccupied, as if listening for something. Then he picked up a volume of Carolyi's *Myths of Creation*, and began talking about savage tribes and human sacrifice. His talk was incoherent, but this central point was fairly clear: that the savage, with his dark myths and nightmarish rituals, understands something that civilized man – particularly such poor specimens as myself and Littleway – had forgotten. Periodically he would pause and seem to listen, then gabble on again – the words at times coming so fast that they were indistinguishable.

Suddenly, he looked at me with an odd smile and said: 'No, my name's not Renfield,' then went on talking about the head hunters of Borneo. Littleway and Clareta missed the significance of the remark, but I was electrified. For it had come into my head that Roger was like Renfield, the maniac in *Dracula* who eats flies and spiders, and listens for the voice of his master. Perhaps he reminded me of the actor who played Renfield in the old Lugosi version of *Dracula*. At all events, the notion had stuck in my mind, and had kept recurring to me as I listened to the flow of his voice.

It meant that Roger was somehow able to read my thoughts – that his mind and mine were on the same wave-length. And this was incredible. For I had absolutely no feeling of mental contact with him, none of the instinctive sympathy that I felt for Barbara or Littleway.

And now I was reminded of something I had half forgotten – that evening with the Mudd family in the Old Rectory in Croxley Green. So many things had happened since, and my interest in psychical phenomena was so slight, that I had never really thought about that evening. Now I remembered how I had been able to 'listen in' on the vibrations that emanated from the various minds in the house, and finally to control them. I had done this by withdrawing from them, by sinking into a semi-trance state in which I felt suspended outside time. I certainly had no telepathic sympathy with any of the people concerned. It was simply a matter of detachment. And because I was familiar with this house, and with Roger and Henry and Clareta, it had not occurred to me to perform the same act of detachment.

I turned and stared into the fire, so that my abstraction would not be apparent, and I toyed with the glass of wine on the arm of my chair, to give the impression that I was listening with mild impatience. Then I launched myself into a sea of serenity, ignoring my personality, my interest in the people in the room, as if observing the earth from some distant point in space. I ceased to hear Roger's voice, ceased to be aware of the room.

Then I became aware of the 'vibrations'. They came from Roger, and they were very similar to the disturbances in the Old Rectory; they were basically negative. I could also sense Clareta's feelings – her attachment to Roger, her failure to feel any sympathy for this violent stranger. Littleway's vibrations were disturbed, but controlled.

To a large extent, Roger's troubles were the result of his own attitude. Mentally, he was static; he had ceased to develop many years before. So he was an easy victim. All he needed to keep him violently neurotic was a certain isolation, and a few obsessions. His own frustrated vitality did the rest.

I focused my time-vision on Roger, completing the epoch, the act of detachment, trying to intuit him purely as an object. And as I did so, I became aware of an interesting fact about 'them'. Their power was low. Roger had been an easy victim. They had no power over Littleway and myself because we were moving too quickly.

With a sudden surge of cheerfulness, I allowed my own mind to 'interfere' with Roger's vibrations, using the same technique that I had used at the Old Rectory – that is, re-directing the alien vibrations with a minimum of effort. This is the same principle as getting a car into motion by rocking it. To begin with, I simply allowed my own 'vibrations' to coin-cide with Roger's. Then I began to increase their force, so that Roger's flow of words – which had slowed down for a moment – became a torrent. I began trying to influence his mind by projecting images. I imagined an immense spider, with a man trapped in its web. Immediately, Roger said : 'The Phoenicians had a spider god called Atlach-Nacha who came from the planet Saturn with Tsathoggua. He was imprisoned beneath a mountain in northern Siberia. He spends eternity spinning webs across a tremendous gulf. Do you know how often giant spiders turn up in savage mythology? Of course you don't, but I do, and I bet you friend Carolyi does too . . .' And so on.

What amazed me was the depth of the level from which his images were emerging. In effect, Roger was creating a dream made of words, a sort of mad free-association of images which meant that he could go on talking without a pause for breath. There was very little logic in his talk, and that little was accidental.

I remembered something else. I had seen Atlach-Nacha, the spider god, mentioned in one of the occult texts I had been studying. Had Roger read the same text? Or . . the idea seemed barely thinkable . . . could he be drawing direct from the Ancient Old Ones? I tried projecting another image from the same occult text, this time of Azathoth, the blind idiot god who rules from outside space and time, and whose gibbering is the sound of Chaos. Roger said immediately: 'And then there's Azathoth who led the Old Ones in their rebellion against the Elder gods and was thrown out of the universe of dimensional space into a blind hyperspace . . .' I said casually, hardly interrupting the flow of his conversation: 'But what is he afraid of?' 'What do you think?' Roger said, without pausing for a moment, 'How would you like to be tied hand and foot? He's in a wilderness and he doesn't know the way out because he's asleep and dreaming. It's a damn good thing for us they're all asleep because they'd make short work of us otherwise. They've got to hurry or we might beat them to it. Because we're asleep too. It's like putting a snake's egg in the same nest with an eagle's egg. Which one hatches first and destroys the other?' I said: 'But how did they fall asleep if they were once awake?' This time Roger stopped. I turned and looked at him. He started to say something then stopped, as if a hand had seized his throat. I was seeing him from a position of total detachment, as if examining him through a microscope. A look of horror came into his eyes. Then his lips parted, and a strange, croaking sound came out, which changed into a wailing scream. His head jerked back suddenly, and he fell sideways out of his chair, his head striking the carpet. His body was rigid, his tongue tightly clenched between his teeth, so that a sort of bloody foam ran down the side of his mouth. He jerked several times, his whole body like a steel spring, then became unconscious. Clareta screamed and jumped up. Littleway said: 'It's alright – it's a mild epileptic fit. He used to have them as a child.'

We picked Roger up and carried him to the settee. Littleway's eyes met mine briefly, and I knew that he guessed what had happened.

Ten minutes later, the congestion disappeared from Roger's face, and it became grey. The rhythm of his breathing changed; it became soft and regular. Littleway said: 'I think he'd better sleep here. I'll get a blanket.'

It took another half hour to comfort and soothe Clareta;

then she went to bed. Littleway and I sat by the fire, talking;
I explained what had happened. As we talked, Roger muttered
in his sleep, then opened his eyes and sat up. He said: 'What
the hell happened?' I said: 'You fell asleep, that's all.' He
groaned. 'I've got a filthy headache. Where's Clareta? Gone to
bed? Lazy devil.' I said that she had been worried about him.
'Yes, I know. She's a good girl really. I'm very fond of her. I'll
probably follow your example and marry her. If she'll have me.'
He stood up and yawned. 'Think I'll get to bed. Nice supper.
Thank you both for being so decent. I really appreciate it.' He
went out. Littleway and I looked at one another. There was
no need to express the thought aloud. Roger was obviously
'cured'. 'They' had realized the danger of a permanent psychic
link with him. He could give away their secrets. So they had
left him. But for how long?

Roger's image – of an eagle and a snake in the same nest –
struck us both as ominous. So it was a race against time? But
why? What was at stake? And how could 'they' be asleep when
their activities showed them to be conscious and calculating?

I woke up the next day feeling oddly tired and depressed,
and realized that I had overslept by two hours. The period of
truce was over. 'They' were attacking again.

It took me about half an hour of mental effort to restore my
brain to clarity. Then I went to Littleway's room. He was taking
a shower. I called into the bathroom to ask him how he felt.
He shouted: 'Pretty awful. Got a headache.'

I found Clareta sitting by the window, staring out at the
falling rain. She was obviously depressed. She told me Roger
was still asleep. I went up to his room. He was covered only
by a sheet; the bedclothes were all over the floor. The pillow
itself was damp with sweat, Roger looked awful, with his hair
plastered across his forehead with perspiration, and his skin a
yellowy-grey. He was sleeping with his mouth open, and his
eyes looked sunken. I sat on the windowsill, looking out into
the garden, and induced the mood of quiet. It was difficult;
'they' were resisting, trying to distract me. But after a few
seconds, I accomplished it. It was immediately clear that 'they'
were back; the room vibrated with the peculiar, morbid violence
that I had first experienced on Stonehenge. I did exactly as I had
done the night before: entered into the rhythm of Roger's dis-
ordered imaginings, and began to exert a very slight pressure

in the same direction. He seemed to be dreaming of a city terrorized by two embodiments of evil, Toveyo the Doomster and Yaotzin the Enemy, who were waylaying travellers and burying their bodies in a swamp. Periodically, half decomposed corpses were dug up and left in the town square . . . I could tell that his dream was a variant of the legends of Tezcatlipoca, Lord of the Night Wind.

I was fairly certain that Roger would wake up before I could achieve any results; my chief hope was that he would not have another attack of epilepsy. So I exerted pressure very slowly and cautiously. He began to mutter in his sleep. The muttering would have sounded incoherent to any other person; but since I was already 'inside' his dream, I could understand what he was trying to say. He was speaking about a creature called the Head Hunter who only walked abroad in the moonlight. He was now jerking and sweating; I knew it could only be a matter of minutes before he woke up. I stood by the side of the bed, and whispered: 'Where can I find the *Necronomicon*?' I remembered that Evangelista also spoke of it as *Al Azif* in the *Oldest History*, so I asked him: 'Where is *Al Azif*?' I repeated the question several times in a whisper. His mind was becoming a confusion of opposed forces, and I saw he was about to wake up. Then he said something that sounded like 'The ladder . . .' The image that accompanied it in his mind vanished too quickly for me to be able to grasp it. Then his eyes were staring up at me with an expression of shock. I smiled at him. 'You were having nightmares.' He said: 'Give me a cigarette for Christ's sake.' From the tone of his voice, I knew that 'they' had gone.

Clareta brought him coffee and bacon. I stayed talking with him for ten minutes – long enough to verify that he was back to normal – then went to report to Littleway. He was eating kippers, and buttering toast with an appetite that showed he was feeling better. I told him what had happened. He said 'What a pity we didn't know all this earlier – while Roger was really sick. We might have tried hypnotizing him.' I said: 'They might come back.' But I was not hopeful.

Thinking about it later that morning, it struck me that Roger's delay in waking up afforded a certain clue. If 'they' were fully conscious, they would have made sure he woke up as soon as I entered the bedroom; or at least, have severed contact with him. As it was, I had almost caught them unawares. And yet they had resisted my effort to establish 'contemplative objectivity' as I sat on the windowsill. Obviously they failed to connect this with Roger, even though I had done the same thing the night before. They were either very stupid – or their defence system was somehow *automatic* and slow to react. This was confirmed by Roger's assertion that 'they' were asleep.

In that case, we had the advantage. Littleway and I were awake. But how could this advantage be pressed?

Littleway came in an hour later. He said: 'I've been thinking about what Roger said. The ladder. I've been looking through the index of the world atlas to find a place that sounds like 'the ladder'. There are several in India and Burma. But it just struck me. Are you sure he said "*the* ladder"? Could it have been "Philadder"?' 'Philadder? Where's that?' 'There's Philadelphia. If you started to say "Philadelphia" and then broke off: "Philadel..."'

I slapped him on the shoulder. 'My god, Henry, what genius! You're probably right.'

'Well, it's possible... The only trouble is, how do we find out whether there's some kind of occult collection in Philadelphia? It might be a private collector. Or it might belong to some crank group. I seem to recall that Evangelista was in Philadelphia at one time...'

I said: 'I know Edgar Freeman, the head of the English Department at the University of Pennsylvania. He's lived there most of his life, I think.'

'Ring him. What's the time now – half past one. That's eight thirty in Pennsylvania. Give him until ten o'clock.'

It seemed a very long shot, but we were determined to explore every possibility, no matter how remote. I placed a call with the trans-Atlantic telephone operator, and said I wanted a call to the University of Pennsylvania at ten o'clock. The call came through a few minutes after ten. Luckily, Freeman was in his office.

When I'd identified myself and exchanged greetings, I said:

'I've got rather an odd problem. I'm trying to locate a book – a mediaeval book on magic and the supernatural. Are there any libraries in Philadelphia that specialize in such things?'

'Not as far as I know. I could make enquiries for you. I believe the Rosicrucians have a branch here, but I don't think they have much of a library. We have a pretty good section here at the university, of course. Any idea of the book's title?'

I explained that it was sometimes known as the *Necronimi-*

con, but that I couldn't say definitely. He pointed out that the *Necronomicon* was a fictional work invented by Lovecraft, and I explained that I had reason to believe it really existed – or was based on a real book. He said:

'Gosh, I just don't know what to say. I have to admit I don't have the first idea . . . I suppose it's in Latin?'

'Not necessarily. It could be in Arabic.'

'Well that shouldn't be too hard to check. I could find out whether we've got any volumes in Arabic on magic. Frankly, I doubt it. Would you like me to check the Library of Congress catalogue?'

'No. I think it's in Philadelphia somewhere.'

'Well, alright. I'll go down to the library right now. Can I call you back?'

'Let me call you back. In say an hour.'

The possibility seemed absurdly remote. It was only my determination to follow every possible lead that made me pursue it.

An hour later, the operator rang me with my call. Freeman was in the library. He read me out a list of books on which Lovecraft might have based the idea of the *Necronomicon* – Paracelsus, Cornelius Agrippa, John Dee, Alkindi, Costa Ben Luca, Albumasar, Khalid Ibn Jazid, Rasis, and the anonymous author of the article on Hermetics in the *Kitab-Fihrist*, the tenth-century Arab encyclopedia. The opinion of the librarian was that Lovecraft may have based his 'mad Arab, Abdul Alhazred' on Morienus, a legendary sorcerer who wrote a number of books on magic – all of which have vanished. The only Arabic book on magic in the library was John of Spain's twelfth-century translation of Costa ben Luca's *Difference of Soul and Spirit* into Latin.

I spoke to the librarian, who was an admirer of Lovecraft, and had taken some trouble to look up every possible source for the *Necronomicon*. I didn't like to mention Evangelista's *Oldest History* in case he thought me a total crank. We talked for twenty minutes, and covered every possibility. Then he said:

'There's also, of course, the Voynich manuscript, although we know very little about it, of course . . .'

'What's that?'

'Don't you know about it? It's been arousing some interest

recently. Professor Lang became very interested, but of course, he disappeared...'

'He *what?*'

'He was involved in a plane crash, I believe. His nephew works in the English department here.'

'Could you give me details?'

'Wouldn't it be better if I wrote to you? You must be running up an enormous phone bill.'

'It's all chargeable against tax.'

Goodwin's – the librarian's – story was, briefly, that Professor Lang of the University of Virginia had become interested in the Voynich manuscript seven years before. He had had it photographed in colour and enlarged, and subsequently told a few close friends that he had succeeded in translating it. But he had disappeared on a plane trip to Washington in 1968 – the plane, a private one, was never found.

I asked: 'But what is this Voynich manuscript?'

This story was longer and more complicated. The manuscript had been found in an Italian castle and brought to America in 1912 by a rare book dealer named Voynich. It was believed to be the work of Roger Bacon, the thirteenth-century alchemist. But it seemed to be written in code, or in some strange symbols. A Professor Newbold of the University of Pennsylvania had devoted several years to breaking the code, and announced at a meeting of the American Philosophical Society in 1921 that the manuscript proved that Bacon was about five centuries ahead of his time as a scientist and philosopher. Newbold died in 1928, and his translation of the cipher was published. Another cipher expert, Professor Manly of Chicago, now examined it thoroughly, and realized that Newbold had deceived himself. The cipher was 'uncrackable', simply because too much ink had peeled off the vellum for the symbols to be read. Newbold's 'translation' was wishful thinking. And that, in effect, ended the story of 'the most mysterious manuscript in the world', until Lang's attempt at translation in 1966.

As Goodwin told me this story, I felt the stirrings of an immense excitement. Even without the significant touch of Lang's disappearance, I would have felt this inner-certainty that I had found what I was looking for.

I asked Goodwin: 'Would it be possible for me to examine the manuscript if I came there?'

'Of course. But wouldn't you prefer me to send you a microfilm?'

'No. I think I'd like to see it for myself.'

'Very well, you're very welcome . . .' His voice showed his bewilderment. When I hung up, I could imagine him saying to Freeman: 'Another crank. I can't understand it . . .'

When Littleway came in, I said: 'Have you ever heard of the Voynich manuscript?' 'No, what is it?' 'With a little luck, it may be what we're looking for.' I told him about Lang. I picked up the phone. 'Do you want to come?' 'Well yes, of course.' I got through to Cooks and said I wanted to get the first plane to New York. Littleway placed his hand on my arm. 'Book me on another flight. We can't risk both of us on the same plane.'

I did as he asked, booking myself on a flight that night, and Littleway at 11.15 the next morning.

He said: 'You realize we're risking a great deal by flying?'

I said: 'No. There's no risk. Because I know in advance we shall win.'

And this is perhaps the most difficult thing of all to explain in the language of everyday consciousness; it was a realization that had been growing in me over the past few days. Everyone knows what it is to feel 'accident prone' – to feel tired and depressed, and to somehow *know* that things will go wrong. And everyone has experienced – at some time – the reverse of this: the feeling of inner-pressure and *rightness*. You could be driving at ninety miles an hour, and somehow *know* that you wouldn't have an accident. This feeling is not an illusion, born of over-confidence. Our subconscious roots spread farther into the soil of reality than we realize, and in times of unity-of-mind, they control things. This is not as strange as it sounds. I control my body, although it is basically a piece of alien matter. What is more, I control it without knowing how; all I know is that I can make it run and jump and walk. And in moments of intensity, the same will that controls my body extends beyond it, to material things. We apprehend something of the reality of the outer universe, and draw strength from that reality.

Well, my mind was travelling at ninety miles an hour most of the time. And I had that driving sense of confidence that comes from speed – and perhaps also a dim apprehension that there were 'other' powers working for me. I had no idea of their nature, but no doubt whatever about their reality. This is how I knew that there would be no plane crash.

I landed in New York at midnight – 5 a.m. London time – and was able to catch a plane to Philadelphia forty minutes later. I spent the rest of the night in the airport Hilton, and was up at eight the next morning. I had only coffee and toast for breakfast, for I was full of that feeling of excitement that comes when 'the game is afoot'. I took the airport limousine into Philadelphia, and was at the University shortly before ten. Edgar Freeman looked amazed to see me walk into his office.

'What's all the urgency? I didn't expect you for at least a week.'

'I can't spare a week. The library might burn to the ground.'

'Oh, you heard about that did you?'

'About what?'

'Your joke nearly came true last night. One of the watchmen smelt gasoline, and he found some crazy student making a trail of it across the lawn outside the library. He pulled a gun when the watchman tried to grab him. Luckily, he fell backwards over a roller somebody had left out. They found later that he'd emptied the best part of two gallons of gasoline in the library building.'

'What happened?'

'Oh, nothing much. We're not making too much of it. We found a suicide note in his room – he intended to shoot himself after he set fire to the library. Afraid we get a lot of that, as you know – we had five suicides last semester. Overwork and worry about grades. This is the first time anyone's tried to take the library with him.'

'It might be better not to publicize it. You might give somebody else the idea.'

'That's our feeling too. Anyway, come on down to meet Julian Lang. That's the nephew of John Lang. He's convinced his uncle was mad . . .'

Julian Lang shared an office with two other assistant professors; it was also jammed with students. He suggested we go down to the faculty lounge for coffee. He was a tall, serious young man with a clean profile and close-cropped hair. Freeman, who had a class, left us.

'Where did you get this idea that the Voynich manuscript

might be the *Necronomicon*? Have you come across my uncle before?'

'No. It's pure coincidence.' I told him about finding references to the *Necronomicon* in Evangelista's book, and I threw in a few more invented references for good measure. He listened very seriously, obviously troubled.

'You've got me worried.'

'Why?'

He told me the full story of his uncle, James Dunbar Lang – one of Ameica's foremost experts on Poe – and his 'translation' of the Voynich manuscript. Lang had reasoned that even if a great deal of ink had peeled off the vellum, it should have left some faint signs. He had huge blow-up photographs made, and claimed that this enabled him to 'complete' the damaged characters. He then discovered, according to his nephew, that the manuscript was written in mediaeval arabic characters, in a mixture of Greek and Latin. He translated the manuscript, and discovered it to be the famous *Necronomicon*, or at least, a part of it. He now became convinced that the remainder of the manuscript was to be found in England, for he believed that the stories of the Welsh writer, Arthur Machen, prove that Machen had examined the complete *Necronomicon* at some time. In Machen's home town, Lang became acquainted with another occultist, a mad colonel, named Urquart, who, according to Lang's nephew, was the villain of the piece. For the mad colonel somehow convinced Lang that Machen's legend of a strange, ancient people, living underground in the Black Hills, was literally true. And from this point onward, Julian Lang explained, his uncle became the victim of an obsession – the belief that these strange people – or forces, for he believed them to be bodiless – were planning to take over the earth. He wrote letters to famous people, urging them to wake up to the danger. And finally, he became convinced that the President of the United States could save the world by ordering underground atomic explosions. Lang's family had warned everybody – including the President's secretary – that the old man was harmlessly mad. And when a privately chartered plane, carrying Lang and Colonel Urquart disappeared between Charlottesville and Washington, the family was secretly relieved. Lang had apparently written a pamphlet about these 'things' that intended to take over the world, and at the time of his death, the manuscript was in the hands of a Charlottesville printer. The family was not entirely in favour of suppressing it – Charles apparently wanted it issued in a limited edition, with an explanatory note about his uncle's final illness – but a fire at the printers removed the cause of the dispute.

'How did the printers catch fire?' I asked.

'Oh, some madman with a grievance. He used to work for the printer and got dismissed for dishonesty . . .'

There was no need for Lang to finish the story. I knew the rest.

Lang – the nephew – told me that he had examined the blow-ups of the manuscript, and had become convinced that his uncle's 'completion' of the symbols was self-deception. He had never actually seen the translation, so he had no idea of whether it could be considered a serious piece of scholarship. Now my arrival made him wonder whether the whole affair should not be reconsidered. He laughed in an embarrassed way. 'Of course, I'm not suggesting there was anything in his ideas about bug eyed monsters. I saw a great deal of this colonel, and I can tell you that he was sane enough. He was just a damn swindler. He invented the whole damn thing about underground monsters. Still, if the Voynich manuscript *is* the *Necronomicon*, it proves my uncle was sane enough before he went to Wales.'

'What happened to the translation?'

'I'm pretty sure my mother destroyed it.' *

'And the blow-ups?'

'They were destroyed too. But if you're interested, I have some of his notes. I've never studied them. You're welcome to examine them.'

'I'd love to. But what I really want to see is the Voynich manuscript itself.'

'Sure. Well come on downstairs. I'll introduce you to the librarian.'

And half an hour later, I sat alone in the librarian's room with the manuscript in front of me. It consisted of 116 folio pages written in a sort of black ink that had turned purple and brown.

What was, of course, totally predictable, was that the manu-

---

* When the present book was in its proof stage, Julian Lang succeeded in locating an early draft of his uncle's manuscript. It was in the possession of Fr Anthony Newbold, the editor of the *Carmelite Review*, to whom Lang had sent it. It will be published by Therdel and Sauk of Wisconsin.

script had no 'vibrations' whatever. I could put myself into a condition of total detachment, and still nothing came over – not even the faint vibrations that came from the basalt figurine. This was total, 100 per cent interference.

Again, I was puzzled that I was not aware of their presence in the room. This led me to suspect that the 'interference' was not *active*. It was simply that the manuscript itself had been 'deadened', so as to betray no hint of its origin.

But there was something they could not prevent. My heightened awareness made it easy to 'complete' the symbols. If I examined one of the ink squiggles under a magnifying glass, and concentrated on it, I could suddenly grasp what it had been like before the ink had peeled. This was not at all a matter of 'time vision' or intuition, but of the ordinary critical faculty sharpened to an extraordinary degree. I also had an Arabic language primer on the table beside me, and I only had to stare at a page for a few seconds to imprint every symbol on my mind. It is a technique very similar to ordinary 'speed reading'. Then it was not difficult to grasp resemblances in the Voynich manuscript.

Julian Lang went back to his house at mid-morning and returned with his uncle's notes. These were in two red spring-backed folders. They were very much apprentice notes. Lang knew Latin and Greek, but he had no knowledge of Arabic, so pages were devoted to the laborious copying out of an Arabic alphabet and vocabulary.

Placing myself in a condition of contemplative objectivity, I was able to discover a great deal about Lang from the two folders. As a person, he was rather bad tempered and impatient, but basically gentle and self-effacing. The first notebook and half of the second had been written on a boat on the Atlantic; the remainder of the second book was written in a London hotel room, and later, in a hotel room at Caerleon on Usk. It was all written before Lang had any suspicion about the real existence of 'them'. The detailed translation itself was apparently made in a third notebook – presumably the one destroyed by Julian Lang's mother – but the present notebooks were full of interesting fragments. And halfway through the first notebook, there was an actual transcription, in Arabic characters, of the first page of the Voynich manuscript, which enabled me to check my own results. I had made a great many mistakes –

many of them due to the difference between mediaeval and modern Arabic – but had been 80 per cent accurate.

What became immediately clear was that this book was not the *Necronomicon* itself, but a commentary on it by some monk of the thirteenth century whom Lang calls Martin the Gardener. But it contained so many long quotations from the *Necronomicon* that it undoubtedly gave a very full and accurate picture of that work.

The opening page of Lang's translation ran as follows : 'The book of the black name, containing the history of that which came before men. The great old ones were both one and many. They were not separate souls like men, yet they were separate wills. Some say they came from the stars; some say that they were the soul of the earth when it was formed from a cloud. For all life comes from the beyond, where there is no consciousness. Life needed a mirror, therefore it invaded the world of matter. There it became its own enemy, because they [bodies?] possess form. The great old ones wanted to avoid form; therefore they rejected the heavy material of the body. But then they lost the power to act. Therefore they needed servants.'

As I read this, I felt slow waves of delight, of anticipation, of a kind of certainty, pouring over me. There was no ambiguity here. It put into words what I already suspected. Fundamentally, it is a statement of the Shavian-Bergsonian philosophy. This can be expressed briefly as follows : Running parallel to the universe of matter there is another universe, of pure life. And life has invaded matter – at first by sheer force (as in the plant and the amoeba), later with the use of insight and cunning, through the creation of the brain.

Now individual consciousness, as typified in human beings, has great advantages and great disadvantages. Individuality means a narrowing, and narrowness can be useful. It is good for close-up work. We have invented the magnifying glass and the microscope to narrow our vision, because narrowness makes for precision. But narrowness also makes for failure of purpose, for exhaustion of the will; for purpose depends upon a broad vision, a clear sight of one's objective.

According, then, to the Voynich manuscript, life's earliest attempt to 'invade' matter' was non-individualistic. Gaseous star-matter was chosen as the point of invasion. And the 'beings' who came into existence in the interstellar spaces were little more than aggressive clouds of vital energy. (Lovecraft has an interesting story about one of these beings, *The Colour Out of Space*.) As the star-clouds condensed into planets, these beings found their activity restricted. Hence the words of the Vatican codex: 'they lived in this state for seven hundred and eighty thousand katuns, until the cloud became the earth, and their bodies were of earth.'

All this must be supposed to have taken place before the origins of 'life' as we know it in the pre-Cambrian era, before the seas had formed and cooled enough to sustain the simplest micro-organism. And when these first tiny, deathless organisms formed, life had taken another course, the course of individuality. And for millions, perhaps billions of years, it must have seemed to the 'watchers' that individuality was not going to pay off. Life remained static – until some chance mutation introduced death. And with death came the possibility of reproduction; and with reproduction came new mutations. Evolution was launched. But five hundred million years had to pass before there were creatures sufficiently evolved to be useful as servants. Perhaps Bolk was right, and they created man by somehow arresting the development of an ape's embryo.

But what then? Did the Voynich manuscript contain the rest of the story? I searched through Lang's notebooks, tantalized by fragmentary sentences. Lang had been less interested in the legendary than in the scientific parts of the manuscript. It is full of sketches, some of them obviously astronomical and astrological, others far more mysterious. There is a drawing that Newbold assumed, correctly, to be of a human spermatozoon. It proved that the unknown genius who wrote the Voynich manuscript had invented the microscope four hundred years before Leeuwenhoeck. And according to Lang, some of the astronomical speculations anticipate the latest theories of the twentieth century.

Using his notes as a guide, I set about the transcription of the manuscript into Greek. Long before I had completed the second page, it was time for the library to close.

Littleway joined me at the hotel in time for dinner. He shared my excitement when I showed him Lang's notebook, and checked my rough translation of half the second page. It was disappointing. The monkish chronicler obviously felt that the idea of men being created by the Ancient Old Ones conflicted with the Book of Genesis, so he proceeds to argue that the creatures created by the Old Ones were not men, but demons, 'brown in colour, their skins made leathery by the fires of hell'.

We had dinner sent up to our room – we were sharing one – and spent the evening going through Lang's notebooks. Littleway had already been involved in a drunken brawl at Kennedy airport with an American sailor who said he didn't like Littleway's accent; 'they' were quite capable of inciting one of the hotel's guests to pick a quarrel with us : so we locked ourselves in. At nine sharp the next morning, we were both back at the library. Littleway had brought his own camera for filming documents – of the type used by spies during the war – and we spent the morning filming every page of the manuscript, in case the original was destroyed. Then we worked together on transcription and translation, each taking a different page.

We ate no lunch – food tended to disturb the clarity of the brain – but we stopped at about one o'clock for coffee.

Littleway commented that the account given in the Voynich manuscript differed from the Vatican Codex in that it said nothing about the dark god from the stars, who came to earth and set up a rivalry with the Ancient Old Ones. He had translated another half page, and it contained the familiar statement that the Old Ones had taken up the practice of black magic. I suggested that the Mayas probably wanted to flatter their gods because they were afraid of them – in the way that contemporary historians always describe tyrants as 'good'. So they invented an enemy, responsible for all the world's ills.

But even so, the black magic explanation of their downfall made no sense. For surely black magic is a human invention, meaning the attempt by human beings to ally themselves with the Great Old Ones?

We were both relaxed, drinking our coffee, our minds temporarily 'idling'. We both sat thinking, staring at the manuscript. We had the same thought: if only the interference would stop, so that we could gain some insight into its history . . . Littleway said : 'I think you're probably right about the interference. It's purely automatic.' We both made an effort to 'see' the history of the manuscript, but it was like trying to push down a stone wall.

Littleway said : 'You know, if it *is* automatic, we ought to be able to do something about it.'

'What?'

'Well, supposing we both tried to grasp it together? Two minds ought to be twice as strong as one.'

This had not struck me, for I had not seen it as a question of force.

'Let's try.'

We both concentrated on the manuscript, drifting into a state of detachment, trying to see it from a 'distance', as it were. At first it seemed to make no difference. Then, after about a minute, I had a distinct sensation of meaning. Littleway had it too; he glanced at me in triumph. We returned to our concentration. The sweat rolled down my forehead, and every muscle in my body was tense. Then a curious thing happened. I became aware of Littleway's concentration too. I can only explain it in this way. Supposing two men stand shoulder to shoulder and try to move an enormous rock that is embedded in the ground. It remains absolutely solid, and neither of them is aware of the other's effort, for each is concentrating wholly on pushing. Then the rock moves very slightly, and both increase their efforts. It moves more, and now each of them is aware of the help of the other, for the rock is now returning their pressure, and each can feel the effect of the other's effort.

This is what happened with us. We became aware of one another's minds pushing at the barrier. And like the two men pushing the rock, we ceased to move independently, and locked our minds so that our efforts were concerted.

And now, very slowly, the rock-like barrier began to give. More and more meaning became visible. It ceased to be merely a heap of yellowed parchment; its history began to form around it. It was an exciting sensation, as if someone had opened a window and let in a breeze smelling of melting snow and spring flowers. Our minds could move, and I realized that the 'barrier' had been some kind of a lock on the mind. It was quite simple. The manuscript possessed emanations that acted upon the sleep centre of the brain. But it would be a mistake to think of these emanations as a kind of odour issuing from the manuscript, for an odour would be constant, and these emanations were dormant until there was an attempt to 'see' the manuscript's history. They could be compared to a kind of burglar alarm, that would not operate unless there was an attempt to 'break in'. Littleway and I had simply forced the thing to a limit – for one must imagine a burglar alarm that rings louder and louder, the harder the burglar tries to break in.

Quite suddenly, all resistance disappeared; the history of the manuscript lay open to us.

And at the same moment, we both became aware of something else – something that temporarily destroyed all interest in the manuscript. The 'alarm' had wakened something up. We both knew this instantly. And then we also realized that so far, neither of us had dealt directly with the Great Old Ones, but only with their robot servants.

It was completely impossible to describe what happened, for this was a direct intuition or feeling – like sitting on a log and discovering it is a crocodile. It might convey something of the terror of that moment if I say that it was just as if a giant black face had suddenly appeared in the sky over Philadelphia, a great face with yellow eyes and a beast's fangs. We had awakened some vast, sleeping force, and its movement was like a psychic explosion, some great spiritual earthquake.

We were both petrified. We felt like someone who walks into a cave, and stumbles upon some sleeping monster, that growls and stirs. Suddenly, I understood the meaning of Lovecraft's line: 'In his house at R'lyeh dead Cthulhu waits dreaming.' No wonder Lovecraft had nightmares that destroyed his health; through some strange gift of second sight, he understood the sheer size and power of the Old Ones.

Neither of us dared to breathe; we wanted to efface ourselves completely. For this 'thing' seemed to shake the earth; it was a power that could have wiped out Philadelphia like a man stamping on an ant hill.

We sat there for more than an hour. I am glad that no one came into the room; it would have disturbed our stillness, and perhaps warned 'It' of our presence. And yet I had no idea that we had been there for an hour; I would have guessed five minutes. Our concentration was so intense that all physical processes seemed to stop.

We had no idea of whether the 'Thing' was aware of us. I am inclined to believe it was not. It stirred in its sleep, looked around for a moment, saw nothing of interest, and gradually drifted back to sleep.

And as we sat there, we both had the same vision: of the horror that would ensue if the 'Thing' woke up. We had visions of mountains ripped apart, of the ocean bed opening into an immense gulf into which the whole Pacific Ocean would vanish, of continents folded and crumpled like sheets of paper. The whole earth could be crushed out of shape, as easily as a power-ful man could crush a ripe orange in his fist.

Gradually, the sense of earthquake died away. It was terrify-ing while it lasted, for we were both so clearly aware that this was not *calculated* movement, but only uneasy stirrings. If the 'Thing' woke up any more, there was no telling what might happen; even its stirrings were like the eruption of Krakatoa.

When everything was quiet again, we both became aware that the Voynich manuscript had 'closed' again. It was com-pletely impenetrable. But I had glimpsed enough, in the few seconds before 'It' had stirred, to know most of the answers to the problems that troubled me.

Yes, 'they' had created human beings as their servants. 'They' had power, but no precision. And for long ages, human beings served them faithfully, and were allowed insights into many secrets. And then their Masters had brought the great disaster upon themselves, something so cataclysmic that it had de-stroyed most of the human race. But before they succumbed, they saw their danger: that their servants would themselves become the masters of the earth, and learn the ancient secrets.

All this I had *seen* very clearly, in the few seconds before I lost all interest in the Voynich manuscript. I had not seen the nature of the disaster that had almost destroyed the earth – and the Old Ones; neither had Littleway. But he had seen other things. He had seen that the Old Ones created robot forces to guard their interests during their great sleep. And they had also taken certain steps to try to prevent their ex-servants from be-coming too powerful. The most important of these was a re-ligion of torture and sacrifice. It was their aim to turn men back into beasts. And this was not too difficult since the char-acteristic of men is a certain narrowness of vision that makes them easy to deceive. The age immediately after the destruction of the Great Old Ones was the age of the Religions of Terror. Men believed that the gods could only be propitiated by torture and death, and they went to war solely to capture enemies who could be tortured to death, and then eaten. When no enemies were available, then virgins of the tribe were sacrificed to the gods. The age of the Religions of Terror lasted for thousands of years, and its mark is still upon the human race. The Great Old Ones came close to their aim of turning their former ser-vants into a race of killer apes. I had caught a glimpse of this horror when I visited Stonehenge with Littleway. The barbarities of which human beings have been capable have left a permanent mark on the human race. As recently as the 1830s, a sect of the Religions of Terror still existed in India under the name of Thuggee, and the Thugs devoted a month of every year to murdering travellers and burying their bodies. Similar sects flourished among the Incas, the Aztecs and the Mayas. Strange subconscious memories of these sects influenced the Nazis in their attempt to exterminate the Jews.

Our experience of the afternoon had shaken us both. It would not be true to say that our curiosity had vanished; but it was dwarfed by the fear that possessed us. Something had stirred in its sleep; when would it wake up? Today, tomorrow, a hundred years hence? What did human evolution matter in that case? When they woke up, they would destroy us all.

There seemed no point in staying in Philadelphia. We had learned all the manuscript had to tell us. Before we retired for the night, we booked our flights back to New York. We decided to sail from there. There was no point in rushing home.

That night, for the first time since my operation, I slept badly. I woke up long before dawn, and sat by the window, listening to the rain, and fighting off the depression. Everything seemed pointless; I could not stop thinking of that terrifying force that had stirred in its sleep. Less than twenty-four hours before, I had believed that the road of human evolution lies wide open. Now I knew it was closed. I found myself wondering whether there might be some future for the human race on another planet of the solar system – perhaps Venus.

Littleway's voice startled me, speaking out of the darkness, and I realized that he had also been lying awake.

'What do you suppose caused the disaster?'

I said : 'Do you think it makes any difference?'

But I saw his line of thought. And although it seemed a pointless preoccupation, I devoted the next hour to thinking about it. On the surface, it seemed unanswerable. These 'creatures' possessed no individuality, in the sense that we do. Now most of our human problems are due to the self-division that arises from individuality, for all our problems can be summarized in one word : triviality. We are victims of the 'demon of the trivial'. All human evils can eventually be traced to the narrowness of human consciousness. But these 'powers' could never be entrapped in the trivial. They were elementals.

Or was this entirely true? They could calculate. They were intelligent enough to create human beings by some interference with the normal biological processes. And how can intelligence exist without self-criticism, self-discipline? For example, a stupid man is confronted by an obstacle and loses his temper — which may leave the obstacle unaffected. The intelligent man controls his frustration, examines the obstacle, and calculates how it can best be removed. It is not that he is naturally patient. Impatience is a sign of high vitality, and intelligence should be more vital than stupidity, not less. He *directs* his impatience as the barrel of a gun directs a bullet.

And so I had to suppose that the Old Ones possessed some degree of self-control, self-criticism. And this implies self-division, for one half of the being is set up against the other. And self-division immediately creates the possibility of bad mistakes. All neurosis and insanity is due to self-division, to self-criticism out-weighing vitality. Self-criticism is a brake, and brakes sometimes jam.

And where did all this lead? I had to admit: nowhere. For what could be more absurd than to suppose that all the Old Ones succumbed to some kind of collective neurosis? In fact, what could be less likely? I remembered that terrifying impression of power that I had experienced in the library, and knew that this could not be the answer. A creature that could create such a psychic earthquake, even in its sleep, could never suffer from 'locked brakes'.

On the plane from Philadelphia to New York, I stared out of the window at the grey rain clouds below us. It had been raining heavily before we boarded, and the air had that distinctive smell of wet clothes. It struck me that I had not noticed such things before my operation; it meant that my subconsciousness was dull and narrow; non-relational. I made a half-hearted effort to throw off the dullness, and realized that 'they' were sitting heavily upon me.

At least I now understood why I couldn't sense their presence; they were machines, robots. But what brilliant, ingenious machines, that could respond so intimately to my own mental states!

I found myself forgetting the terror of 'that hideous strength', touched suddenly by admiration. What kind of civilization was it they built? I already knew, from the Voynich manuscript, that they had been responsible for the building of the legendary civilization of Mu, which may have been destroyed as long ago as six million years, in the mid-Pliocene. Mu was, of course, a civilization of men, built according to the instructions of the Ancient Old Ones: 'the servants' quarters', as Littleway called it. And what about their own 'civilization'? It was true that they were almost bodiless, judged by human standards; but then, they were also immortal; they had whole geological epochs in which to exercise their ingenuity.

What a relief it must have been to them to finally have 'servants', after waiting five hundred million years for them! For servants are all-important. The pyramids and the megaliths of Europe were planned by rulers of genius; but without the man-power to move the stones, all the genius would have been wasted.

It may seem that I am contradicting myself, for I have said that their power was that of a spiritual earthquake. But all the energy of Niagara Falls would be useless for repairing a Swiss watch, just as the powers of the hydrogen bomb would be useless for building a pyramid. In creating man, the Old Ones developed a *tool*, a precision tool.

Thinking about it in this way, I ceased to feel fear and horror. This was no melodrama with a hero and a villain, but a universal tragedy. 'They' had made the wrong choice; so had we. They had power and immortality; we have precision and patience. Given time, man will escape the consequences of his narrow consciousness. And given time, 'they' might have escaped the consequences of their power. But something had gone wrong . . .

I thought of those great underground cities, described by Lovecraft, cities with 'cyclopean blocks' of masonry and huge inclined planes. And I remembered my insight on Silbury Hill. Was there such a city below Silbury? And might it afford some clue to the cause of that catastrophe that had almost destroyed the world?

My thoughts passed to the civilization of Mu. It must have been altogether incredible. Man's chief problem has always been his belligerence; civilization after civilization has collapsed through war. For as a species, men seem incapable of working for the common good. Wells pointed out long ago that we could create a super-civilization if men could experience a 'change of heart', and cease to feel separate from one another. The men of Mu were servants of a Master whom they regarded as a god. They worked together to do his bidding, without rivalry, without self-interest. It must have been an almost perfect civilization while it lasted – undoubtedly the origin of all legends of the 'golden age'.

Then *what had happened*?

The deep feeling of oppression had lifted when we landed at La Guardia. Littleway and I had not been sitting together on the plane, and now I started to tell him some of the thoughts that had come to me during the past twenty minutes. We were standing in the terminal, waiting for our baggage to arrive. As we talked, I was vaguely aware of someone saying something in a loud voice, and after a few minutes, we both looked across at the cause of the commotion, an obviously drunk man wearing a huge stetson hat, who was arguing with a Negro porter. Suddenly, it became clear that the man was about to hit the porter. An air hostess who was walking past tried to intervene, and the porter seized the opportunity to slip away. A few moments later, the man in the stetson come and stood close to us, obviously still in a rage and looking for somebody to listen sympathetically to his side of the story. Littleway caught his eye for a moment, then quickly turned away and began to talk to me. The man stood there, swearing in a fairly audible voice. The baggage began to arrive on a moving belt; Littleway stepped forward to take his own case, and collided with a lady who tried to lean across him. He said: 'Oh, I'm so sorry,' and stood back. The man in the stetson caught the English accent, and repeated in a mocking voice: 'I'm so sorry.' Now Littleway, as I have said, had never been a man of any great patience, although his character had altered so much since the 'operation'; he could have pretended not to hear, but the voice was so loud that it would have been obvious that this was not so. He turned and glared irritably at the man in the stetson. And before I could intervene, the man had grabbed Littleway by the shoulders, and was shouting: 'You trying to pick a quarrel, buster?' Littleway said, with quiet anger: 'My name is not buster, and if you don't take your hands away . . .' 'You'll what?' said the man, obviously delighted to have a real quarrel on his hands.

What happened next happened in far less time than it takes to tell. I was in a rage; hectoring and bullying make me feel like committing murder. So was Littleway. As we stood there, both glaring at the man, I became aware of Littleway's mind, just as I had been aware of it when we were trying to 'break' the interference around the Voynich manuscript. I have mentioned my discovery of my ability to 'repel' unwanted acquaintances in the Victoria and Albert Museum; it was this, rather than my ordinary power of 'focusing', that I suddenly found myself exercising. It all happened too quickly for calculation; it was simply that Littleway and I directed our instinctive fury against the man as we might have shouted at him. There was a feeling like an explosion – although not a physical one – and the man simply dropped sideways on to the moving belt. All this had happened within a few seconds of his grabbing Littleway, so for a moment, no one took it in. Then a woman screamed, and I tried to support the man as he fell off the moving belt and hit the floor. His eyes were open, but completely blank, and there was blood running from the corner of his mouth. A moment later, three men and a woman came running up – evidently of the party of the aggressive Texan. It was a pity they hadn't found him a few minutes earlier. The woman asked: 'What happened?' and Littleway said. 'I think he's had a heart attack.' I was feeling the man's pulse, and was glad to find it had not stopped. Other people came up, including an American Airlines pilot who had seen the whole thing, and who verified that Littleway had not touched the man. My case arrived at this moment; and since the crowd was now enormous, we both slipped away. Littleway asked: 'Was he dead?' 'No.' 'Thank God for that.' But both of us knew that, in a sense, the man might as well have been dead. It was not a physical power we had exerted against him, but a mental power, and the damage would be mental, not physical. As soon as it happened, we both felt thoroughly guilty about it. To begin with, we were perfectly aware that it had been engineered by 'them'; it was not the fault of the aggressive Texan. And even if it *had* been, we would have taken care not to cause real damage. Moreover, if either of us had acted alone, there would have been no severe damage. It was because our wills had acted in concert that the man was so badly hurt.

There was no point in worrying about it. It could not be undone. We simply had to be more careful next time. I had to made a deliberate effort to forget the blankness in the man's eyes as he collapsed on the belt.

But as we travelled in to the East Side Terminal on the

airport bus, I found myself trying to recollect the experience in detail, in slow motion, as it were. For there was something about it that struck me as interesting. Then it came to me. My explosion of anger had been *directed* with an accuracy that was new to me. It had been like firing a high powered rifle with a telescopic sight; whereas my previous experiences of this same power – in the London Library and the V and A – had been more like firing an old blunderbuss. It would have been better for the Texan if I had not been so accurate.

What did it mean? Obviously, my powers were slowly maturing, increasing. But in what way?

Then I understood. What had increased was my actual power of *concentration*. Captain Shotover in *Heartbreak House* talks about trying to achieve the seventh degree of concentration. And what could be more to the point? Moments of ecstasy, of increased vitality, are accompanied by a feeling of concentration, as if consciousness could clench itself like a fist. But this moment of intensity is usually followed by an involuntary relaxation, which we cannot control. One could imagine a concentration so intense that there was no question of loss of control. What was happening to me was simply that my ability to concentrate was increasing.

I said to Littleway: 'Would you mind very much if we returned by air after all?' He looked surprised. 'Of course not. Why?' I said: 'I've got a feeling things are moving. I don't want to be stuck in the middle of the Atlantic if anything comes up.'

It sounds absurd, but it is nevertheless true that one of the most important parts of this story is untellable. For all I can say is that I spent the five hours between New York and Heath Row airport investigating the possibilities of this power of concentration. I did nothing that can be described; I merely stared out of the window and concentrated. And each time I did so, my mind felt like a lead weight that I was swinging through the air; that is, it felt concentrated and *controlled*.

And suddenly, in a flash, I understood. *I knew what had almost destroyed the Great Old Ones.* I knew what had plunged them into a death-like sleep for six million years.

The way it came about was simply this. I was revelling in the feeling of controlled power, and I contrasted it with what had happened at La Guardia, when my rage had taken me unawares. I had not wanted to permanently wreck the man's mind; it had happened because my *instinctive* rage had suddenly been concentrated and directed by this conscious power of my mind.

What do we mean by 'man'? We mean his *conscious* being, the part of him that distinguishes him from the beasts. When we speak of 'the humanities', for example, we mean art and music and poetry and classical languages, although war and competitive sports are equally human and perhaps deserve to be included.

Man has developed a conscious mind that marches in the opposite direction from his instinctive drives. Every young man who becomes obsessed by literature or music or science is aware that he is *creating* a personality that has nothing to do with his more violent emotions: rage, lust, jealousy.

All this is plain enough; I have already spoken about man's self-division.

But what I suddenly realized on the plane was that in these past months, I had been steadily developing my 'human', controlled part, my powers of thought and concentration, until my conscious mind had become a deadly weapon. So that when, for a moment, my instinctive rage took possession of my will, the result was the almost complete destruction of a fellow human being.

I could put it very crudely like this. While my conscious mind developed the accuracy of a high powered rifle, my subconscious mind had been developing the power of a piece of heavy artillery. Therefore, the greater my powers of 'focusing', the more deadly my potential power of destruction.

For example, one of the hostesses on the plane reminded me of Barbara. After looking at her for a moment, I stared at the seat in front of me, and conjured up her image in my mind. The power of my concentration was so great that I projected an image of the girl on the seat-back, just as if my eyes were a cinema projector. It was, of course, a purely mental image, not a real one; but its intensity was so great that a person with any degree of 'second sight' would have been aware of it. I found myself wondering how the girl's figure compared with Barbara's before Barbara was pregnant. My projected image of the girl immediately proceeded to remove her clothes, and continued until she was naked. This was not a matter of imagination, any more than my time vision was a matter of imagination. It was 'relational consciousness'. For example, I observed that the girl was wearing an underslip of a pale green colour as she removed her clothes. Later, when the 'real' girl was reaching up to take down some pillows from the overhead rack, her blouse parted company with the top of her skirt, revealing the green underslip.

Now the sight of the girl undressing produced little or no sexual excitement. But if I had possessed this same power in my late teens, I would undoubtedly have spent most of the day 'undressing' every girl of my acquaintance. But then, although my sexual appetites have always been normal enough my intellectual enthusiasms have meant that I could never, at any point, have been described as 'highly sexed'. I remember reading a biography of Theodore Dreiser that mentioned that he simply wanted to possess every woman he saw in the street, and that he could not be in the same room with an attractive girl for more than a few minutes before experiencing a compulsion to touch her. What would have happened to Dreiser if he had possessed this power of focusing his imagination? The overwhelming power of his sexual impulse would have taken over his conscious powers of focusing; his life would have been an endless orgy of mental rape.

I think my central point should be clear. Conscious powers of focusing are dangerous according to one's degree of control of the subconscious levels of the mind.

The Old Ones created man, apparently by arresting the development of an ape's embryo. But in order to create anything, we have to harness the powers of the unconscious. Try threading a needle when you are in a hurry. It is difficult, because you have summoned up energy to drive you at top speed, and you have to repress it in order to concentrate on the eye of the needle. No precise act of creation is possible without repression of our energies.

The Old Ones were creatures of incredible power; elementals. And yet they became man's collaborator in building the world's first great civilization. They observed these humanoids they had created, and they realized the power of the human imagination fuelled by optimism and purpose. And they suddenly knew that, no matter how great the risk, they also had to develop a conscious 'filter', the ability to *focus* their incredible powers. They used men for the most delicate and precise jobs; but they themselves also strove to develop delicacy and precision. They went through the phase that every intelligent teenager experiences: of developing a new, individualized consciousness, and leaving the instincts to fend for themselves. And to begin with, it was successful. Until one day, the suppressed instincts exploded, destroying all they had created, destroying the civilization of Mu and their human servants. And only a remnant remained . . .

That, I was certain, was the answer to the mystery of how the Great Old Ones became sleepers. They were, in effect, stunned by the catastrophe they had brought on themselves. And six million years had passed like a single night, and the remnants of the human race had organized themselves and learned to build their own civilization. But how long would the Old Ones go on sleeping?

As we waited in the customs queue at Heath Row Airport, I explained my discovery to Littleway. He was fascinated by my description of my new power of imaginative 'focusing'. But with his usual scientific caution, he asked: 'Can you be sure it isn't ordinary imagination? I mean, it could have been coincidence that the girl was wearing a green underslip . . .'

'I don't know. There must be some way of testing it.' On the other side of the customs barrier, a smartly dressed woman was greeting her husband. A large alsatian dog was also licking his hand. I remember Littleway remarking once that he thought thoroughbred dogs possessed a larger degree of 'second sight' than mongrels. I focused on the ground close to the dog, and conjured up the image of Lady Jane's siamese cat – an extremely bad tempered animal that detested dogs. The alsatian reacted immediately, turning its head sharply and staring intently at the imaginary cat. Meanwhile, its master and mistress had linked arms and were walking away, without noticing that the dog was preoccupied. I now ceased to 'focus' the cat, and instead projected an image of the man and woman walking away *in the opposite direction*. At this moment, the man looked round, noticed the dog was staring into space, and whistled. The dog started, and ran after my imaginative projection. It did not even turn its head when its master called 'Dinah!' I relaxed and allowed the projection to vanish. The dog stopped, bewildered, then heard its master's shout, and ran back in the opposite direction. Littleway was watching all this; he was following the direction of my stare. 'What on earth did you do?'

I explained. He said: 'I wonder if it works with people? Try it.' The customs officer had just dismissed the woman standing beside us; he now glanced into our cases, and showed us the usual declaration. We both shook our heads, and the officer looked down into our open cases. At this moment, I concentrated all my powers into projecting an image of a pretty girl opening her case in the spot the woman had just vacated. Nothing seemed to happen; the customs man nodded to us to close our cases. I made an additional effort. The man turned to the empty space next to us, his hand already reaching out to show the 'girl' the customs declaration. Seeing the blank space, he blinked with surprise, but recovered himself immediately, and turned to the middle aged lady on the other side of us. Littleway asked: 'Well?' I nodded and smiled. The effort had not been as spectacular as with the dog; but I was certain that my image *had* conveyed itself to the customs officer; his surprise had been unmistakable.

On the airport bus into London, Littleway commented: 'I'm beginning to wish I hadn't waited six months before my operation.' I said: 'As far as I know, you won't have to wait that long for the power of focusing to develop. It should be possible right away.' In fact, the 'operation' is unnecessary to develop this particular ability; any human being can do it. Consider: if you try to crack a walnut with a hammer, and the walnut is resting on a cushion, you need to use all your strength. Put the walnut on a concrete floor, and the slightest tap breaks it. While the nut is on the cushion, the energy of your blow is *diffused*. And this explains the apparent feebleness of the human imagination. We try to conjure up an image in a half-hearted way, and we make no real effort to sustain it. We don't *expect* anything to happen, so the act is aimless, vague, and its energy is diffused.

On the drive back to Langton Place, I tried to explain the technique to Littleway. The only difference between his powers and mine lay in my slightly superior ability to focus; you could say that my 'focusing muscle' was stronger. But a muscle can be strengthened by exercise. And this was all Littleway needed to do. To sit in a chair staring at a blank wall, to conjure up an image – preferably something familiar – and then to 'look at' the image as if it was real, to project the intention you would project if it *were* real. The success of the operation depends solely on the will-power with which the image is focused. Most human beings would not dream of exerting will-power on a focused image, because they wouldn't expect it to have the slightest effect. In fact, the amount of will-power needed to 'realize' an image is well within the range of any intelligent person.

The consequence was that Littleway, with very little help from me, was 'focusing' within a couple of hours. I knew he had succeeded when I was leaning over the fountain, fishing out a spider that had got itself marooned on a floating leaf. Suddenly I had a clear impression of a huge figure standing behind me, about to hit me on the back of the head with an iron pipe; I almost fell into the fountain as I turned, raising my arm to defend my head. There was no one there, but I saw Littleway standing in the window of the library, grinning at me.

We spent the rest of the day playing this fascinating game. It was one of the strangest sensations I had ever known – to see, for example, a small man in green, the size of Tom Thumb, walking across the table top, clearly visible in every detail, and bowing to me with a flourish of his green hat. It was horrifying to look at the window, and see a monstrous, hairy face, rather like King Kong, glaring in at me. Littleway even tried to project an image of his wife for my benefit, but it lacked detail – obviously because his attitude towards her was self-divided.

We were both so interested in the possibilities of this new power that I totally forgot about the basalt figurine. I was reminded of it by Barbara, who rang me up at nine in the evening to say she intended to return the following day. She said: 'By the way, there was another article about Chichen Itza in one of the Sunday colour supplements. There's a photograph of a basalt statue that looks rather like the one you've got.'

The Sunday newspapers were in Roger's part of the house, and I saw that the cover of the colour supplement carried an excellent photograph of the figurine that was taken from the well. Inside, there was another full page photograph, taken from another angle. This statuette was covered with fine carvings, which explained why they had photographed it twice.

I stared at the photograph on the cover. It was, as its finder had remarked, quite unlike the usual Maya carvings: less fantastic, plainer. The face was angular, hard and strong. A photograph is normally altogether less satisfying than a real object for the exercise of 'time vision'. But in this case, the photographs were so detailed, and the resemblance to our own figurine so remarkable, that I was able to 'take a hold' of it with my mind and explore it almost as thoroughly as if it had been real. It was altogether easier to grasp than our own figurine, for the carvings on it gave it more character, and the Mayan language was now familiar to me.

And then, with a shock of amazement and delight, I realized that *there was no interference*. For a moment, I assumed that 'they' had decided to stop trying to block my time-vision. Then I understood. It was a photograph, and the interference was made to operate only from the real object. Of course! In spite of the incredibly advanced level of their civilization, the people of Mu knew nothing about photography, which depends upon the chance discovery that silver salts are darkened by light. A drawing of the figurine, no matter how accurate, would convey almost nothing of its life history. And so 'they' had made an incredible mistake. The interference was connected with the object itself, like a burglar alarm; but it did not apply to photographs! With a tremendous rush of triumph and delight, I realized we had our solution! I hurried upstairs to tell Littleway. He was in the bath and I went in without knocking. He said: 'My god, are you sure?' 'Look.' I held out the colour supplement. 'Better wait until I get out or I'll get water on it.' I left him to get dry. Ten minutes later, I went back. He was sitting naked on the edge of the bath, staring at the colour photograph of the figurine and murmuring: 'Well, well, well.' He was so absorbed that he was startled when I said: 'What do you think?' He looked up. 'Have you looked at it?' (He meant had I 'looked' into its past.) I said no – I'd rushed straight to tell him. Without speaking, he handed me the magazine. I took it into his bedroom, sat in the armchair, and allowed myself to sink into contemplative objectivity. This took rather longer than usual, since I was so excited. But when my mind was free, hovering over the photograph, I was instantly overwhelmed by the same feeling of grisly horror that I had felt on Stonehenge, and the same frightening sensation of looking down a ravine many miles deep. There was the same hallucinatory effect of vast distances and endless horizons. Then, as I stared, the horror passed away; I was seeing through it and beyond it, at prospects far more distant. And what I then saw produced a sensation of beauty and vitality that dazzled me and seemed to shake all my senses.

I was looking into a fresher, more primitive world, a world that seemed far more alive and green than our own. It reminded me of how I had sat with Alec Lyell beside a deep, fast flowing mountain torrent in Scotland, looking down into green water that flowed like molten glass, but that seemed almost still, except for slight swirls on its surface. Something about the vision produced a tremendous surge of pure gladness. It was a spring-like sensation, and yet this was a lush, tropical spring of endless benevolence, like the romantic dream of a south sea paradise. I knew that I was not seeing the 'real thing', of course; this figurine was scarcely half a million years old, and I was looking back seven million years. What I was seeing was a legend, a tradition, but these words completely fail to describe its vitality. This was a tradition nurtured and believed with such intensity that it was as real as everyday life. The nearest parallel I can think of is the Christian story of the crucifixion and the absolute power it has exerted over so many minds.

What I realized immediately was that the Mayas were direct descendants of the people of Mu. But I also saw something else that came as a surprise, even as a shock. The great tradition of the Ancient Old Ones had been continued for many thousands of years *by men*, by a caste of priest-magicians who had been the absolute rulers of the civilization. For the first half million years after the 'disaster', the Old Ones were so deeply asleep that they ceased to be an influence in any way. Their priests remained loyal, waiting patiently for the day when They would rise again. And the greatest of these magician priests, a man whose powers were so astounding that he was worshipped as a god, was called K'tholo of Souchis – clearly the origin of Lovecraft's Cthulhu. And according to the traditions, this man lived for half a million years, escaped to the continent of South America after the destruction of Mu, and was killed by an eruption in the Yucatan peninsula. But even after the catastrophe that almost destroyed the Old Ones, Mu had remained a united and healthy civilization, under the leadership of K'tholo. Mu was the Garden of Eden of biblical legend, a great, green, grassy country twice as big as Canada. It had no mountains; only green, rolling hills, and one immense chasm that ran for over five hundred miles across its eastern side. There was often volcanic activity in the depths of this chasm, and it was worshipped as the home of the Old Ones. It was a land of giants – birds and animals as well as men. Great coloured butterflies with a wing span of four feet fluttered among the vast trees. Enormous birds as large as modern air liners were worshipped as symbols of the Old Ones. In coastal regions, an immense killer whale was also worshipped, and in later years, human sacrifices were offered. Elephants and mastodons grew to a size that rivalled that of the dinosaurs of an earlier age. And in the sky hung an enormous moon, bluey-white in colour, that counteracted the earth's gravity and caused the tremendous growth of all the living creatures of Mu. But because they grew so large, the bones of these creatures were lighter than those of modern man, so that few fossils have survived. Those few lie beneath the Pacific.

I saw all this, almost instantaneously, and was staring fascinated, when Littleway touched me on the shoulder and startled me as I had startled him ten minutes earlier.

Neither of us spoke. There was too much to say. But Littleway went to the cupboard, and took out the basalt figure. He placed it on the table between us, then took his polaroid camera out of its case and fitted the flash attachment. As he did this, I tried 'seeing' the history of the figurine. It was no use; it was like trying to listen to music on the radio during a thunderstorm that creates constant crackling and whining.

Littleway turned off all the lights except a dim one at his bedside, and then photographed the figurine. One minute later, we had the colour photograph in front of us. We placed it on the table and stared at it. There was strong interference. Littleway said: 'Perhaps it's coming from the figure itself.' We locked the figurine back in its cupboard, and took the photograph downstairs. This time, there was no interference, and the figure revealed its history immediately. And I discovered why our figurine had no inscriptions on it. It was a sacred figure from the inner temple, the holy of holies, and it was regarded as a portrait of K'tholo of Souchis. Once again, there was the sense of losing my bearings in the present, like falling asleep with my eyes open, and then the feeling of horror and cruelty. As before, this seemed to pass by, as when an aeroplane emerges from low cloud, and I was again touched with the feeling of pure joy in contemplating the 'Garden of Eden', the first home of man. But there was a difference; I was now seeing it from the point of view of a kind of god-man whose business was to rule a gigantic and complex civilization, a man who regarded his

246

subjects with a kindly contempt, recognizing that they were inexperienced children.

Under K'tholo, Mu reached an unparalleled prosperity – wide, smooth roads running for hundreds of miles, reaching to every corner of the land, and cities were built on huge level areas of ground covered with stone slabs, engineered with such precision that there was no room for grass to grow up between them. K'tholo instituted worship of the sun, to counterbalance the worship of the dark gods, who were already haunting men like a nightmare.

One of the most interesting and characteristic touches about Mu is that it was a land of crickets. Because the climate was mild, and the giant birds were more interested in small rodents than insects, crickets increased in number until Mu became known as' the land of greeting' – the Mu word for 'hello' resembling a chirp. The people of Mu were born and lived and died to the chirping of crickets. When it ceased in the depth of winter, they felt it was an evil omen, and became silent and depressed. One of the chief qualifications for a candidate of the priesthood was the ability to imitate the sound of crickets, although crickets were not worshipped in Mu.

But what of the question that interested us most – the cause of the catastrophe that plunged the Old Ones into sleep? Unfortunately, the photograph was simply not good enough to see that far. It was clear enough to give us the outline of the period; but it lacked detail. Obviously, we would have to get immense photographs of the figurine from every possible angle.

And then a thought struck me. It seemed absurd, but it seemed worth investigating. Supposing I focused an imagined picture of the figurine? I could hold and sustain such an image for as long as I could stare at a photograph. Time-vision, as I have explained, is a complex way of intuiting the inner-reality of an object, in the way that a handwriting expert can 'read' the writer's character in his formation of letters. Now a photograph of handwriting will tell the graphologist as much as the original; it makes no difference if it is a good photograph.

Imaginative re-focusing of images may be regarded as a branch of photography. But it is combined with the complex intuitions of time-vision. It seemed possible that one could practise 'time-vision' on a focused image. It was worth trying anyway. So without saying anything to Littleway, I stared at a spot in the middle of the table, and 'focused' the basalt figurine – which I had examined for hours at a time. Then, as it suddenly appeared – rather smaller than life-size – I attempted to move into contemplative objectivity. It was impossible; as soon as I stopped focusing, the image vanished, overlapping with the objectivity for only a fraction of a second enough to give me a very brief and very swift glimpse of long corridors of time. I focused the image again. Littleway saw it in the middle of the table, and started. Then he understood what I was doing, and joined in, also focusing the image. And now, we made one of our most important and far reaching discoveries. For we discovered that when our minds focused the figurine in concert, it instantly assumed a reality so tangible that it looked totally real. I cannot explain this except to say that we never really believe in our own imaginings; deep down inside us, we know they are unreal; so a focused image is never more than a game. But if you join in the focusing of another person's image, you are aware before you start that the image has an objective reality, as a part of the world out there. This affects some subconscious spring of energy, and the image suddenly solidifies. The images we had been playing with earlier in the day – the green elf and King Kong peering through the window – were like visual illusions, convincing only for a moment. But when our minds combined, the figurine ceased to be a focused image, and seemed to appear out of the air, as if it had an objective existence apart from our minds. (Anyone who has read Eisenbud's remarkable book on Ted Serios, the man who can make photographs appear on a photographic plate by concentrating on it, will understand the basic principle of what I am saying.)

But there was another, and even more important stage. Once the image had taken on this air of total reality, it could be sustained at this level by either of the minds that originated it. *The other mind could withdraw.* For when I said to Littleway: 'Hold it while I let go,' and then ceased to focus the image, it did not slip back to its earlier level of semi-reality, but remained quite solid. Obviously, whatever unconscious spring in Littleway was providing the energy to sustain it remained convinced of its reality, and continued to provide the necessary 'conviction'.

And so I was able to withdraw, and induce a state of contemplative objectivity. And as soon as I did so, I knew we had succeeded. For the prospects that now opened themselves to my time-vision were completely real and sharp. It was as if I had been looking at something through a pair of binoculars, seeing it as slightly blurred; then a touch on the wheel suddenly brings everything into clear focus, bringing out details I had not even suspected, and seeming to present a completely new picture because of its freshness.

Everything was realler, bigger. Above all, I was now aware of the detailed history of Mu, from its beginnings as a continent sucked from under the sea by a moon that hovered over it, (revolving at the same speed as the earth's rotation, so that it appeared stationary), to the appalling end in a lake of fire. Now I saw not only the endless calm sea of grass, but the terrible catastrophes that had periodically destroyed whole cities. They now stood out very clearly. An immense tidal wave, nearly half a mile high, struck the southern shore when a comet caused a perturbation in the moon's orbit. It swept over cities, bringing the vast roofless temples crashing down on the sun worshippers, sweeping away human beings, cattle, elephants and great bears, and finally depositing its rubble, mixed with sea weed and the carcasses of giant sharks, nearly two hundred miles inland. Then there were volcanic explosions that raised up the ground like great mole hills and shaking the whole continent. The lava from these eruptions could not flow far in this flat land, so it often formed a kind of great boil that cooled quickly, leaving a strange cone with terraced sides. There were many of these cones in Mu, and they were regarded as sacred to the Old Ones.

When the Great Valley opened up like a deep scar along the eastern sea coast, Mu's largest city, La-ho, spilled into the gulf, and all its inhabitants died within minutes from the suffocating sulphur fumes. Then a river poured into the gulf, turned to steam, and covered the whole of Mu with a pall of grey cloud that remained unbroken for nearly a hundred years.

And in spite of these catastrophes, Mu remained prosperous. Her ships sailed all over the world – a world in which few of the continents we know today existed. Colonies settled on islands in the Pacific and in part of the land that is now South America. The disasters were forgotten. Prosperity seemed so constant that the people deteriorated; they became happy and mediocre. K'tholo found it increasingly difficult to find youths with the necessary vitality or intelligence to aid him in the task of ruling the land. He decided that his people needed fear and self-discipline if they were not to become decadent. So he announced that the Old Ones were angry, and intended to visit the people with great disasters. Then his helpers infected great areas of the country with a plant disease that killed the crops and the grass, so there were many famines. One of the priests, Korubin, was ordered to create a sect of assassins whose task was to terrorize the people of Mu. These assassins were devotees of Uriqué, the god of violence and sudden death, who later became known as Tezcatlipoca. They would kidnap people from their homes, torture them to death in ways that are too horrible to describe, and leave the mutilated bodies in the main squares of the towns to horrify the citizens. They would often deliberately choose people who were popular and much admired, so that the impact of the crime seemed more terrible. They created such an atmosphere of horror that the character of the Muvians – the people of Mu – changed within a generation, and K'tholo soon had plenty of brilliant young candidates for the priesthood. The sect of assassins continued to flourish, and still existed fifty thousand years later under a name that could be translated 'the drowners'. Members of this sect trained themselves to hold their breath for several minutes at a time. They swam in rivers – and swimming was always a favourite sport of the Muvians, since their continent was full of rivers and lakes – and seized swimmers by the right foot (never the left), drowning them, and later weighting the body with a stone so that it never came to the surface. It was regarded as a mortal offence to seize a swimmer by the left foot, or to weight the body so badly that it eventually reappeared. The punishment for this was to be skinned alive and then burned.

Most interesting of all was K'tholo himself. He had been high priest when the Old Ones were still awake, and they had given him immortality by causing his body cells to reproduce at a rate that made ageing impossible. I wondered what sort of a man K'tholo was, and immediately had a clear vision of him. This man, who engineered the horrible death of millions in the name of discipline, had a thin, boney face and shrunken eyes, but looked basically kindly. He was immensely tall, and walked in a stiff, automatic way, like a robot. And although it was one of the most remarkable faces I have ever seen, it was curiously impersonal, abstracted. When he was a thousand years old, and knew he was condemned to be immortal, he strove to project his spirit into outer space, and learned to wander around the solar system as easily as around Mu. He spent only a few minutes of every week on earth, receiving the reports of his lieutenants. His name inspired such awe that it was often enough to tell an offender that K'tholo was angry with him to cause him to die of fright, or go mad.

If I continued to describe the history of Mu, this Memoir would become an encyclopedia. I have merely tried to indicate the points that interested me most on that first 'trip'. (Littleway sustained the image for over two hours, and I later did the same for him.)

But obviously, the thing that impressed me most was my vision of the final destruction of Mu. There had already been one catastrophe so enormous that it had killed all but a few of the inhabitants and destroyed all the cities – this was the explosion of the 'stationary' moon. But the final destruction of Mu, sixty thousand years later, was almost the end of the world. It happened when the earth captured another moon, an erratic fragment of an exploded planet that became the asteroids. The fragment was enormous, and caused an immense tidal wave in the Northern hemisphere, which never reached Mu. But the earth's crust beneath Mu had been thin ever since the previous moon had caused so many volcanic outbursts. Now the new moon caused another surge of molten rock from the earth's core. The result was a tremendous gas explosion in the centre of the continent – Mu was situated over an enormous 'gas fault' – which was like the explosion of a thousand hydrogen bombs. A huge column of blazing gas *fourteen miles wide* erupted into the sky, hurling up molten lava and rocks larger than cathedrals. Almost everyone in Mu died that night. K'tholo, who expected the catastrophe, was safely in South America by then. By morning, the great eruption was over, and the centre of Mu sagged into the gulf below. A tidal wave now rushed in from the south and the west, sweeping down the slope towards the great hole that still threw up sulphur fumes and black smoke. And then the sea swept into the hole. The result was the greatest explosion the earth has ever known. The seas foamed and boiled, and Mu disappeared, torn and blown apart by the explosion. The cloud of black dust became a pall that eventually filled the atmosphere of the world, cutting off all sunlight for many months. A few inhabitants of Mu who lived on mountainous islands in the Pacific managed to survive the explosion and the subsequent tidal wave, but died horribly of starvation and burns from the hail of fire that came down from the sky. One island was completely obliterated by a single block of stone. The great dust clouds from the explosion remained in the atmosphere for millions of years. In the Pleistocene era, drawn together by the gravitational force of the falling moon, they caused sudden tremendous changes of climate, abrupt switches from an ice age to an age of tropical heat, and back again.

And all of this was known to priests of the cult of K'tholo, who carefully preserved full records of their homeland. The Great History of Mu was among the works destroyed by Diego de Landa.

The basalt figurine was an enormous treasure house of the history of Mu. Subsequently, we learned enough from it to fill many volumes. Even now, at the time of writing, its possibilities have not been fully explored.

The only matter upon which we continued ignorant was the disaster that overtook the Old Ones. The tradition was very clear about K'tholo's relation with the Old Ones. He had been their instrument, their confidant. But the history of Mu seemed to begin with the period when K'tholo became the high priest and ruler. Of what happened before that, we had only a hint. That hint lay in the curious phrase 'the night of the monsters', preserved in Muvian mythology. It was a phrase that had occurred, in a slightly different form, in the Vatican codex ('the night of the great fear'), and again in the Voynich manuscript.

I should add that we rushed to our photostat of the Voynich manuscript as soon as I made the discovery about the figurine – only to discover that in this case, interference was as strong as ever. And the reason for this is plain enough. Writing *can* be reproduced with great accuracy by a scribe – even traced from the original. And although it is true that a copy – no matter how accurate – would not carry the full history of the original, it would, in fact, carry a great deal of it. The Old Ones – or rather, the priests of K'tholo – had taken care that the interference should also apply to copies of written records. (I later discovered the method by which they did this, but it would occupy a disproportionate space at this point.)

But this was a matter of indifference; the written records were unimportant. We now knew that nothing could hinder us from solving the problem, since there must be objects in which we could trace the history of the pre-K'tholo period. It was merely a question of finding them.

And find them we did – with such ease that my description of it must sound anti-climactic. We found them the following day in the British Museum, with the help of Robin Jackley. We travelled down by train, leaving orders that Barbara and the children were to be met at the station in the evening. We decided against the car, because it would be absurd to risk everything at this point. But the precaution was unnecessary; there was no interference. We explained to Jackley that we were looking for the Celaeno Shards, referred to in the Voynich manuscript. He was so excited by our news about the trans-lation of the manuscript that he accepted our story unquestion-ingly, and took us along to David Holzer who, in the absence of Dr Chalmers, was in charge of the cataloguing of South American antiquities. Holzer, a barrel-chested young man with the face of a bulldog and the eye of a fanatic, threw himself into the quest with enthusiasm. Carolyi, who was also present, had some excellent suggestions to offer. He was able to point out, for example, that the Celaeno Shards are also mentioned in Ludwig Prinn's *De Vermis Mysteriis* (a book I had always thought to be an invention of Lovecraft's), secretly printed in 1611, the year after Prinn's execution for sorcery.

Much of the most promising material was stored in the base-ment of a building in Malet Place, behind the Museum. Housed in a mews that was actually a part of London University, this department was a laboratory for the restoration of antiquities, and its ground floor and basement were used as store-rooms. And it was in the basement of this building that we found the two enormous crates of Maya material, all of it uncatalogued, and one still unopened (although it had been there since 1938). Holzer, Carolyi, Littleway and myself spent two hours, from 11 a.m. until one, exploring this incredible wealth of material. Carolyi and Holzer must have wondered at our curious method of examination. If either of us found an item that seemed likely to belong to the pre-K'tholo period, we would stand side by side and examine it carefully. And then, putting down the piece and moving away from it (to avoid 'interference'), we would appear to converse together in low voices: in fact, we were focusing an image of the object. Then, while one of us held the image, the other would explore it, allow his mind to intuit its essence.

We could spare little time for this activity, with the other two watching us curiously, and so we had to arrive at a judgment fairly quickly. But in every case, we found ourselves facing the same problems as with the figurine; it had been created and used by priests who had no definite idea of what had happened during the 'night of the monsters'.

At one o'clock, Holzer looked at his watch and intimated that it was time to eat. Littleway immediately said that we had eaten a huge breakfast and would prefer to continue our search. Holzer was dubious; after all, we might accidentally break some priceless relic. But Carolyi removed his doubts by saying in a tone of mild reproof: 'You realize these two are probably the greatest Mayan scholars in the world?' And so we were left alone, surrounded by straw, broken potsherds and corroded arrow-heads. And then, towards the bottom of the case, I found what we had been looking for. The label attached to it said: 'Ceremonial basin?' The doubt was understandable. It was a cylinder made of atacamite, a copper mineral of extraordinary beauty, with feathery, dark green and blue crystals. It was about a foot wide, and nine inches high. The sides were smooth, polished like ice, but with deep rings scored round the circumference of the cylinder. The top was hollowed out into a shallow saucer, about five inches in diameter. Looking down into this saucer was a strange sensation, for the mineral shimmered and glowed. Although I had never seen anything like it before, I knew its purpose. It was the equivalent of the clairvoyant's crystal ball. The saucer was filled with spring water, and placed in a room where there was not the slightest stirring of the air, but where it caught the sunlight from above. (The temples of Mu were roofless.) And then the luminous, feathery crystal became hypnotic, and visions appeared in its depths.

I knew something else that produced a stifling sensation, a mixture of awe and horror. This crystal had belonged to Great K'tholo himself. Even now, after four million years, its vibrations were unmistakable. In spite of interference, its personality came over very clearly. I should say *his* personality came over very clearly.

Littleway had been standing with his back to me, but some psychic link told him I had found what we were looking for. He turned round and looked down at the blue cylinder. Until one examined it closely, it looked commonplace enough. But it carried a vibration of tremendous power. And this is hardly surprising. K'tholo was the greatest man who has ever existed; he came closer to being a god than any other human being. He was the great archetypal magician. All other legends of great magicians are dim memories of K'tholo.

We were both immediately struck by the same realization. This man was no demoniacal figure of cruelty. Even through the interference, we could sense deep humanity, and a sort of ironical humour. It was amazing to experience this over such a gulf of time. It was as if the thin, hawk-like face with the sunken eyes were regarding us from the depths of his crystal cylinder, smiling at some hidden joke.

We suddenly became conscious of time. We both handled the cylinder. We stared into it, fascinated by the mountain ranges and cloud patterns in its depths. We turned it over, and caressed its smooth surface. Then we placed it back in its straw, and turned away from it. We both tried to focus its image. It was hopeless; interference was more powerful than we could ever remember. We went outside into the mews, closing the door behind us, and walked down towards the museum. And finally, the interference ceased. We sat on the low stone wall at the back of the museum, and focused the cylinder between us. It appeared there, apparently quite solid. It was evidently also visible to other people, for a passing pedestrian glanced at it curiously. Then I slowly withdrew from it, leaving Littleway to 'hold' it. I felt no excitement; only a deep calm and deliberation. I felt as if I were present at the last act of some great drama, playing a predestined part.

I noticed immediately that there was a slightly different quality about my 'time-vision' as I stared at the crystal. It may have been due partly to the unusual definition of the crysal. Our earlier experiments in imaginative focusing had produced objects with a very slight lack of clarity. A photograph may be extremely accurate as far as it goes, and yet lack certain details. But in the case of the K'tholo crystal, it was as if my subconscious mind had absorbed every facet of the object, and then reproduced it with an incredible accuracy.

Secondly, the crystal itself had been made for exactly this purpose – for aiding K'tholo's subconscious mind to liberate its visionary powers. (And incidentally, it was clear that K'tholo did *not* possess time-vision to the extent that we did; he never stumbled upon the great secret of the prefrontal cortex. Or possibly at that point in evolution, the cortex had simply not developed to its present extent.) The result was that it acted as a kind of magnifying glass to my own powers of time-vision.

There was a dizzying sensation of being sucked into it, of falling down a lift-shaft of time. For a moment, I felt physically sick. Then the sheer interest of what I was observing overcame the sickness. For K'tholo's mind had left its stamp upon the crystal, and to plunge into it was like becoming K'tholo – a total loss of my own identity, and an immense feeling of liberation.

And then another feeling came upon me – a total, deep, ecstatic loyalty to the Great Old Ones. It was simply self-evident that they were the most powerful beings in the solar system, and that they therefore deserved the greatest devotion, the deepest love. It was the Blakeian principle: 'Everything that lives is Holy, life delights in life.' And since they were more alive than any other creature that had ever inhabited this earth, their claim was absolute.

But it must also be remembered that, in my identity as K'tholo, I was completely aware of the nature and history of the Old Ones. I knew they had waited for millions of years to launch themselves into the terrestrial evolutionary process. And so great was their sense of purpose that a million years seemed no more than a million days. And finally, they had created man.

There was no 'first man'. A whole tribe of apes was chosen – as told in the Vatican Codex. The development of their embryos was arrested, so that the females gave birth to wizened, hairless, undeveloped creatures. At first, the other apes killed these freaks. They continued to kill them for a long time, until one day, a crippled, ugly female refused to destroy her child, and hung around on the edge of the tribe, an outcast, defending the hairless monstrosity against all attacks.

All this part of the history was not physically present to me, for obviously, K'tholo knew it only at second hand. Nevertheless, this account of the beginning of the human race fascinated me more than anything I had discovered since I developed the power of time-vision. I groped hungrily for every detail stored in K'tholo's memory.

As the hairless, maladroit babies continued to be born, the tribe ceased to regard them as abnormal; finally, they ceased to feel revulsion. The first man-creature had matured into a slobbering, cowardly adult with a highly developed sense of self-preservation, and the cunning that springs from it. The tribe disliked and mistrusted it; but they came to respect the cunning. And as more and more of the creatures grew up, and the older apes died, the man-creatures became increasingly valuable to the tribe, for their cowardice made them excellent watch-dogs, and their intelligence made them devise interesting methods of overcoming their enemies.

The first 'true man' appeared a long time later – perhaps thousands of years. For the aim of the Old Ones was to produce a man-creature with intelligence enough to fear and respect them. The apes were too stupid to be driven by fear; their fear was an instinctive shrinking that was forgotten as soon as its cause was removed. The Old Ones set out to create a man who would be intelligent enough to remember. And one day they succeeded in creating a man who was intelligent and neurotic as well as cowardly. He became their first true servant, the first of all priests. Through the favour of the Old Ones, he became the leader of the tribe, and instilled his terrors into the other man-creatures. Gradually, a tribe of apes became a tribe of men. They were crueller and more savage than apes, but also more inventive. And they were murderously superstitious; they sacrificed the healthiest members of the tribe to appease the Old Ones. Until finally, it became clear to the Old Ones that their servants would destroy themselves unless something was done. They tried the experiment of direct communication with these creatures, at first through the medium of dreams. And even the Old Ones were amazed by the results. It worked beyond their most sanguine expectations. These vile, savage, moronic dawn-men became civilized overnight. The Ancient Old Ones had made an interesting discovery : that Man was basically a religious animal, at his best when he feels himself to be doing the will of One above, or striving for some purpose beyond himself. This creature who was intended to be a crude tool suddenly turned out to be the finest of precision instruments.

The first of these priests of the Old Ones was called Ulgum (Adam?), and he died in a 'magnetic cataclysm', the exact nature of which was not clear. The second was P'atla, and he failed the Old Ones in some unspecified way, and was destroyed by them (Hubris?). The third, Paa, was an experiment in longevity; the Old Ones had discovered how to cause his own subconscious mind to renew the cells of his body. Something went wrong, and he died of cancer. The fourth, Kub, was an unqualified failure, for his sexual urges were so strong that he took advantage of his position to possess all the women in the tribe (which now numbered over a thousand). He was also destroyed. The fifth was K'tholo.

One day, I shall write a biogaphy of K'tholo, and it will run to many volumes. But here I can only summarize the most important points. This man became the greatest of all the instruments of the Old Ones. As a child, he was shy and permanently ill. At the age of twelve, he was bitten by a poisonous spider, and paralysed in both legs. It was assumed that he would die. By this time, these first men had learned to build houses, make fire and cultivate certain crops. Instead of being left to die, K'tholo was cared for by his three brothers and a sister. He went into long trances, and in these trances, the Old Ones spoke to him. His paralysis disappeared; he began to grow at an astounding rate, until he was nearly twice as tall as the other men of his tribe. (These early men were seldom more than three feet tall.) By this, they knew he was favoured by the gods and destined to be their king. He was able to tell the hunters where to find herds of bison and mammoth, and how to trap them without endangering themselves. One day, he told his people to abandon their city and move to a place twenty miles away. Many of the Elders refused; they all died when a volcanic eruption destroyed the city and buried it in lava. After this, K'tholo was made king, and the earth's first great age of civilization began.

What I have related so far was little more than a dim memory in K'tholo's mind; even his own early years had faded away, as one's memories of babyhood disappear. But from this point onward, I was able to *see* the history of the Muvian civilization. And what I saw was so absurd as to be almost beyond belief. For in their greatest period, the Muvians were very like the men of modern Europe. Their cities were immense and well designed, rather on the lines of Stockholm or Copenhagen. They used glass in the windows, and the windowframes were made of metal. The streets had sidewalks and shallow gutters, and a system of underground drainage. They knew the principles of hydraulics, and used steam for raising heavy loads, although their engineering skill was not great enough to make internal combustion engines possible. They were expert gardeners, and their cities contained immense parks and public gardens full of flowers and shrubs. They had a high degree of medical skill – a doctor was automatically raised to the nobility – and education was a public responsibility. The temple of K'tholo stood on an artificial mount outside the capital city, Haidan Kolas ('Deep Green Place'). Standing on the highest point of this temple, K'tholo could look down on a scene that might have been an illustration of H. G. Wells's *Modern Utopia*. The city stretched for nearly ten miles, with immense broad avenues. In its centre was a large and deep lake, into which ran a river as broad as the Thames or the Hudson, and several canals, which ran as far as the eye could see into the countryside. The city was built of a golden coloured sandstone. Unlike our modern cities, it had no slums, and no outskirts. The great streets and squares simply stopped where the countryside began. In the centre of most of the public squares, there were huge piles of cut logs, sometimes fifty feet high. These were there for the citizens to help themselves to; in Mu, fuel was free. (The climate of the mid-Pliocene tended to coolness, rather as in modern Europe.) All these neatly cut logs had been peeled of their bark; the Old Ones had decreed that it was unlawful to burn wood with the bark still on it.

With the aid of crystals similar to the one I was now looking at, the priests of K'tholo could see what was going on in any part of Mu. The consequence was that there was no crime in Mu; no dishonesty of any sort. The degree of self-discipline among the citizens was high, for the simple reason that the Old Ones promptly destroyed anyone who lacked it. A man who lost his temper was likely to disappear into thin air before he had finished swearing.

It may sound as if the civilization of Mu was a super-tyranny. In fact, the harmony between the people and the Old Ones was so great that there was no sense of strain. Discipline was high, so boredom was unknown. Since discipline was high, the whole civilization had a constant sense of forward drive that in turn led to an exceptionally high level of vitality. Disease was almost unknown, and men frequently lived to be more than two hundred.

K'tholo himself was the linch-pin of this civilization. He was the one man who knew exactly what the Old Ones were aiming at. He understood their purposes; he understood why they had created men. He understood their need to establish some kind of solid foundation for their power. You cannot jump without solid ground under your feet. The Old Ones were all power; they could uproot forests and rend mountains; but they had no real control over their power. Through men, they began to achieve control. And when Mu was at the height of its power, the Old Ones and their servants were so completely in harmony that there seemed to be no distinction between them. Men had ceased to be the tools of the Old Ones, and become their limbs.

This concept is almost impossible to grasp, since human beings are so used to their sense of identity and of alone-ness. Each man is an island. But it must be remembered that in a basic sense, the Old Ones were not 'plural'; they were more like a single being. And as they learned to express themselves through human beings, it was exactly like acquiring hands and feet. And they were acquiring more than hands and feet. They were acquiring self-consciousness. Man was a mirror in which the Old Ones could see their faces – or rather, their Face.

But here was where the trouble began. Man was the perfect servant; but he was fundamentally *separate*. Each individual stood alone, even though he felt identified with the Old Ones. As the Old Ones used him, man evolved at a tremendous rate. He never wasted his time on boredom, on lack of direction, on self-division. Imagine the strength and purity of purpose of the greatest saints; and then imagine a civilization in which every human being possessed such drive and purpose.

The speed of man's evolution troubled the Old Ones. Their own rate of evolution was slower – although even so, they had evolved more since the creation of Man than in the past fifty million years. And they came to an incredible decision. Instead of using man as a tool, they would attempt to make a tool of matter itself, making use of the knowledge they had gained since the creation of Man. *The Old Ones made themselves bodies.* They were crude compared to the bodies of human beings, but they served well enough. Their inner structure was simple; they were little more than heaps of grey protoplasm.

K'tholo was one of the few men who ever saw their underground cities – the Old Ones built underground, because they knew that man would eventually penetrate to every corner of the earth. And what impressed me most when I 'saw' these cities was the accuracy of Lovecraft's time-vision. For he had described them very much as they were – and as they still exist, miles below the surface of the earth. These cities were built of immense stone blocks – Lovecraft speaks of them as

260

'cyclopean'. It was easier for the Old Ones to handle huge blocks than small ones, so their buildings were sometimes a mile high. They themselves assumed a roughly conical shape, so that they looked like great cones of wet grey leather. They moved on the base of these cones, which expanded and contracted in the manner of a slug or a limpet. Consequently, there were no stairs in their cities, only huge inclined planes. The top of the cone was fringed with tentacles, and above the tentacles there was a sensitive area that served as an eye. It could be said that the whole top of the cone was one enormous eye, looking perpetually in all directions. The Old Ones themselves were usually more than a hundred feet tall when they first assumed these 'bodies', for they preferred to handle huge bodies just as they preferred to handle huge building blocks. Later on, it became a sign of evolution to reduce the size of the body, and they competed in becoming smaller and smaller.

They were amazed by the success of their experiment. It was a constant effort to control the tight mass of molecules that formed their bodies; but the greater their concentration, the greater the degree of self-consciousness they were able to achieve. And with self-consciousness came the ability to focus their powers. They possessed an ability to focus that went far beyond the degree achieved by Littleway and myself. One of these creatures could move a million ton building block by a single effort of will, or project an idea as complex as a modern city, so that it became *visible* to the other cones. There was no problem about creating the immense underground spaces required for their cities. A few seconds of fierce concentration could direct a beam of will that dissolved earth as a flame turns water into steam. These tremendous underground explosions occasionally caused some of the earthquakes that destroyed parts of Mu.

Their chief city was some two miles below the desert in what is now Australia (whose northern coast was less than three hundred miles from the southern coast of Mu). It was nameless, and larger than London and greater Los Angeles combined. It was also – as far as human eyes went – in complete darkness, for the Old Ones projected energies like a bat's radar, and had no need of light. It differed from the cities of Mu in being more chaotic. Because of their tremendous latent powers, the Old Ones lacked patience for the niceties of architectural symmetry. But the lack of symmetry made the city all the more impressive – hundreds of square miles of giant eyeless blocks, rectangular, cubical, hexagonal, triangular – the Old Ones borrowed many of the natural forms of crystals.

K'tholo saw this city, by means of a phosphorescent light projected by the Old Ones for his benefit. Its image remained as clear and sharp as a photograph – I could create it now in all its detail. And perhaps the most impressive thing about that monstrous underground city was the walls that surrounded it, great walls of rock that towered a thousand feet above the city. (The place had been chosen because it was virtually a giant slab of igneous rock, over a hundred miles long and more than six miles thick in its centre.) For the Old Ones had decided to learn to write – they grasped the tremendous evolutionary value of writing long before men did – and they needed large pages on which to practise. These great walls were their writing tablets, and they were covered with immense symbols, forty feet high, and blasted out of the rock by a beam of pure energy that atomized the solid granite. When one of them made a mistake, he simply wiped his slate clean by blasting another ten feet off the whole rock face. And so immense were their energies that it was easier for them to do this than to use the beam of energy as a 'pen'.

In spite of their crudity, their underground cities were the greatest achievement that has ever appeared on the earth. It is impossible for a human being to grasp the discipline that went into creating them; the task of engraving the Lord's Prayer on a pinhead is nothing compared to it. The Old Ones had no reason to be jealous of the civilization of human beings, for their own efforts were god-like. They deserved to become lords of the solar system.

And then what happened? I already knew the answer to this question, even before I turned my attention to the 'night of the monsters'. They advanced too quickly – even though the building of their city took them ten thousand years. They actually learned to record their knowledge in books – great stone tablets held together by indestructible metal bands: iron compressed so tight that a cubic inch weighed a ton. They explored the mechanical secrets of this world of dead matter, and learned to use its laws for their own benefit. They made the amazing discovery that matter does not need to be coerced by brute force, that once its laws are understood, it becomes compliant and obedient.

And so the next step was obvious: to learn all the laws of the universe, to become super-scientists.

And there came their downfall. They had overlooked one absurd point. As the conscious mind learned to project its visions of reason and order, the vast energies of the subconscious writhed in their prison, and projected visions of chaos.

At first, no one understood what was happening. One day, a tremendous explosion rocked the city. The building housing the central library was completely destroyed. At first they were inclined to believe that some strange hostile agency – perhaps beings from another planet – was at work. Gradually, it dawned on them that one of their own number had done this. And everyone was gripped with a tremendous sense of shock. For they suddenly realized the consequences of their evolution into separateness. In their early days of 'unity', this would have been impossible.

What was worse, twenty of the Old Ones had been destroyed in the explosion of the library, hurled back into non-existence. In their earlier days they had been indestructible. Now they could be killed.

A deep and terrible doubt possessed them. Had it all been a mistake? The road of evolution had seemed long and straight. Suddenly, it looked like a trap.

And who had destroyed the library? Every one of them opened his mind to the examination of the others. And every one was innocent. And then they began to understand. Whoever had done it was totally unaware that he had done it. Some monster from the subconscious mind had taken advantage of his sleep – for the Old Ones now slept after long periods of concentration – to strike this blow for chaos.

As I watched all this, I saw the solution. They were simply trying to evolve too fast. It was like trying to train a wolf to become a sheep dog. It was not an impossible task, but it needed to be done with great deliberation. They were rushing it. All they needed to do was to slow down, perhaps even to retreat a step or two. Even K'tholo could have told them this, if they had explained the situation to him. But they were terrified; it seemed that an abyss had opened underneath them, and they shrank back. And the Night of the Monsters began.

It was not an ordinary night of twelve hours or so. It went on for several weeks, and it spread to all of their cities. When

K'tholo spoke later of the Night of the Monsters, he meant the blackness of their underground cities.

The outrages became more frequent – the great walls defaced, whole areas destroyed. As the fear increased, so did the sense of claustrophobia; and the unconscious desire to destroy everything and start afresh increased. A few of them even understood this, and killed themselves rather than endanger all they had created. But it made no difference.

And then, like a dam bursting, it happened. Monstrous forces ripped the cities apart. Sometimes they had forms – the form of nightmares – monstrous red things, hundreds of feet high, with faces like human beings, great white worms, a vortex in the shape of an octopus into which things vanished without leaving a trace. Total madness reigned. The surface of the earth was convulsed. All Mu would have been destroyed if it had not been for K'tholo, who used all his powers to set up immense counter-forces to protect the continent. During the Night of the Monsters, K'tholo remained the only sane man on the surface of the earth, observing the fall of his Masters, determined that human beings should not share in that fall. He watched the Old Ones disintegrate under the terror and slip into non-existence. He saw some of them become insane from the effort of trying to break down the barriers between the conscious mind and the forces that were destroying them. He saw the destruction of Haidan Kolas, struck by a shock wave that crumpled the ground like a sheet of paper, and then spilled its fragments into a great void. (This was the immense chasm that opened up down the western side of Mu.) He expected his own destruction from minute to minute – for he was surely a symbol of the subconscious fears of the Old Ones?

And then, quite abruptly, there was silence. At first, he thought they had all been destroyed. Then he understood. They had taken the only possible course to preserve some fragment of their achievement. Just as a great fire may be prevented from spreading by destroying everything that lies in its path, so this madness had been prevented from spreading by a form of self-destruction. What the Old Ones had done was the equivalent of knocking themselves out. They did this simply by allowing an uncontrolled explosion of the psychic energy they had learned to control – an explosion *within the mind*. They were hurled back into unconsciousness – but not into death.

264

The convulsions of the earth gradually ceased. The winds dropped; the sea became a great mirror reflecting the sunlight. And K'tholo looked at the broken ruins of the civilization of Mu, and the few thousand survivors, still half insane with fear, and knew that he had won.

The Old Ones would awaken one day. Meanwhile, he would keep the faith. He kept it for half a million years...

I came out of my trance abruptly. Littleway had allowed the crystal to dissolve, since all his effort to attract my attention had failed. For a moment, I failed to recognize him, or to understand where I was. I was K'tholo, waking from a sleep of four million years. I opened my eyes, and looked around at this civilization of great buildings – the British Museum and London University – so like the civilization of Mu, and I felt a sense of enormous loss. What had these human beings achieved in five million years? Almost nothing. A few technical triumphs, a certain mastery over nature. But they were still pygmies.

And then I knew, with complete certainty, what we had to do. All misgivings had disappeared. Ever since Littleway and I had taken the great step and become the first truly human creatures on the face of the earth, we had experienced complete freedom from the human fear of mortality. And this sense of having hundreds of years in which to develop made us feel that there were no immediate problems: time was on our side. Perhaps we would initiate a few carefully chosen colleagues into our secret, perhaps not.

The truth is: time is not on our side. They have slept for five million years. They cannot sleep for much longer. One day they will wake up – either tomorrow, or in twenty years, or in five hundred years. But it will happen.

But *we* are awake. And we can choose what they find when they wake up. In five million years, man has changed very little from the servant the Old Ones created. He has invented his gods and built his civilizations; but he has remained essentially a servant. He is not comfortable without a master. That is why he has had so many gods – and so many tyrants. In my teens, I remember being impressed by a history of Ivan the Terrible. It described how Ivan, after committing the most appalling atrocities throughout a long reign, decided to abdicate, and left his court one morning. One might have expected his people to heave a sigh of relief and bolt the door of the palace. On the contrary, they presented themselves at his retreat in sack-cloth and ashes and begged him to return on any terms.

I had never quite understood that story. But now I understood. Man is incorrigibly a slave. And if he waits for long enough, he will have a Master again. And the choice is entirely in his hands. He can become a slave again. Or he can confront the Old Ones as a Master.

But there is one thing I must point out. The Old Ones will not make the same mistake twice. This time, there will be no Night of the Monsters. They will evolve slowly, and they will become the dominant species in the solar system. When that happens, they will feel grateful towards man, of course – as man is grateful towards the horses and dogs that have enabled him to build civilization, and towards the cattle that have provided the labour for tilling the ground. But this has not stopped him from eating the cattle and allowing the dray horses to drift towards extinction. Why should an evolving species feel sympathy for its less successful competitors? The Old Ones will not destroy man. They will simply allow him to stagnate until he suffers the price of stagnation : death.

The alternative is clear enough. The Old Ones must awaken to find a society of Masters, with whom they can collaborate on equal terms. What is more, *they must be awakened by these Masters.* For nothing is more clear to me than that man will soon need the Old Ones as much as they once needed him. While the new stage in evolution is restricted to people like myself and Littleway, there will be no difficulty; we shall deal with problems as they arise. But we shall be a very small proportion of the human race. The greater portion of the human race consists of people like Zachariah Longstreet and Honor Weiss – people who will shrink from the great step to inner freedom. There will be far too many of these people to be helped by the minority who are ready to make the leap. Only the Old Ones can solve the problem. They can provide the vast majority of Longstreets with the kind of subtle guidance that they provided for the people of Mu.

When I explained all this to Littleway, as we travelled back to Langton Place, he asked me the obvious question : why bother with the majority of the human race? If they are not ready for the next step in evolution, then why not concentrate on those who are?

Because there is a law that says that evolving species cannot be destroyed. If the whole human race is directed towards the same objective, it can be in no danger. I have no illusions about my own indestructibility; my memory of what happened in the library in Philadelphia is too clear. The power that we almost awakened might snuff me out as casually – and accidentally – as an earthquake kills a flea. And it might snuff out another thousand like me. But it would not destroy two billion creatures, spread over the whole surface of the earth.

There was no need to argue this point with Littleway. Before we were back in Leicester, he had also experienced the Night of the Monsters. We re-created the crystal cylinder of K'tholo on the train, and I focused it while he explored. I watched his face become grey and still, and his eyes ceased to focus as they turned inward. When we left the train at Leicester, he was dazed and silent. I knew he understood.

When I started this memoir, over two years ago, I had no idea of how it would end. And yet I now believe that, in some obscure sense, I knew all the time. There are strange forces at work here, and they are unconnected with man as well as with the Old Ones. I can sense their nature, although I could not express it in language. If the Old Ones were once an impalpable force that learned to manipulate man as an instrument, is it not possible that there are other forces for whom the Old Ones were also tools?

It is man's destiny to be immortal. For five million years, he has managed to side-step the issue. Now the choice has to be made. And to me, it seems absurd. Who could possibly prefer being asleep to being awake, especially on a spring morning? And yet there are many men who open one eye, scowl at the sunlight, and pull the blankets over their heads. Sleep seems infinitely desirable to the sleeper.

Let me put this in the clearest way possible. Man should possess an infinite appetite for life. It should be self-evident to him, all the time, that life is superb, glorious, endlessly rich, infinitely desirable. At present, because he is in a midway position between the brute and the truly human, he is always getting bored, depressed, weary of life. He has become so top-heavy with civilization that he cannot contact his springs of pure vitality.

Control of the prefrontal cortex will change all this. He will cease to cast nostalgic glances towards the womb, for he will realize that death is no escape. Man is a creature of life and the daylight; his destiny lies in total objectivity.

By the time this memoir is published, there will be more of us – a dozen at least. And we shall take care to provide proof of all my assertions. Neumann alloy is not difficult to manufacture; before the end of this century, there could be a million of us.

My wife Barbara has been typing this memoir from my tape transcription, and we have observed an interesting thing. Her prefrontal cortex is beginning to work of itself. The knowledge that this thing *is* possible, and the constant encouragement of myself and Littleway, has apparently awakened in her the hidden evolutionary drives. And I suspect they may be transmitted directly to the child that is due to arrive in a few weeks. If I am right, the whole problem may be immensely simplified. Power over the prefrontal cortex would be transmitted by heredity, and it would only be a matter of time before the whole human race had developed that power.

That word 'time' causes a momentary contraction of the heart. For what if They wake up too soon . . . ?